(Athena)

Praise for *I (Athena)*

"Ruth DyckFehderau is a master in that beautiful art of the slow reveal. She has created in Athena a character I will not soon forget. Athena's story is fascinating and piercing, sometimes funny and sometimes utterly heart-rending; it is thoroughly researched and so well told. I read with wonder from the opening pages to the delightful final scene."
ASTRID BLODGETT, author of *You Haven't Changed a Bit*

"As Athena breaks free from her stolen years, she's plunged into a world she must make sense of. By turns funny and heart shattering, rich with mesmerising detail and unsentimental prose, her journey is a profound exploration of what it means to be human."
FRAN KIMMEL, author of *The Shore Girl* and *No Good Asking*

"In this harrowing, heartbreaking, and ultimately triumphant novel, Ruth DyckFehderau peels back the complex layers of identity and shows us, in moving, clear-eyed prose, how swiftly human rights can be stolen and how urgent is the fight to win them back."
FRANCES PECK, author of *The Broken Places*

"A catastrophic misdiagnosis shunts a young life off the rails, leaving young Verity Blessure to waken, again and again, to worlds that profoundly mistake her. In *I (Athena)*, Ruth DyckFehderau leads us on a memorable quest for human recognition and dignity through the eyes of the irrepressible Verity (Athena). A journey full of surprises, both wrenching and joyous, *I (Athena)* also uncovers along the way the endlessly resourceful bonds of longing and belonging among the socially discarded and historically spurned, immersing us in a community that remains too often unseen, unheard, unwritten, to this day. A debut novel that on multiple levels reflects a triumph of informed empathy and imagination."
CHRISTINE WIESENTHAL, author of *Instruments of Surrender* and editor of *The Collected Works of Pat Lowther*

I

(Athena)

Ruth
DyckFehderau

NeWest Press

Library and Archives Canada Cataloguing in Publication
Title: I (Athena) / Ruth DyckFehderau.
Names: DyckFehderau, Ruth, author.
Series: Nunatak first fiction series ; 59.
Description: Series statement: Nunatak first fiction series ; 59
Identifiers: Canadiana (print) 20220407231 | Canadiana (ebook) 2022040724X | ISBN 9781774390672 (softcover) | ISBN 9781774390689 (EPUB)
Classification: LCC PS8607.Y35 I23 2023 | DDC C813/.6—dc23

NeWest Press wishes to acknowledge that the land on which we operate is Treaty 6 territory and a traditional meeting ground and home for many Indigenous Peoples, including Cree, Saulteaux, Niitsitapi (Blackfoot), Métis, and Nakota Sioux.

Editor for the Press: Paul Hjartarson
Cover and interior design: Natalie Olsen, Kisscut Design
Cover photo: colaimages / Alamy Stock Photo
Author photo: Manikarnika Kanjilal

This book has been designed with readability in mind.

Canada Council for the Arts   Conseil des Arts du Canada   Funded by the Government of Canada / Financé par le gouvernement du Canada   Canadä

accessCOPYRIGHT FOUNDATION   Alberta Government   Alberta Foundation for the Arts   Edmonton   edmonton arts council

NeWest Press acknowledges the support of the Canada Council for the Arts, the Alberta Foundation for the Arts, and the Edmonton Arts Council for support of our publishing program. We acknowledge the financial support of the Government of Canada through the Canada Book Fund for our publishing activities.

NeWest Press   #201, 8540-109 Street
Edmonton, Alberta   T6G 1E6
www.newestpress.com

No bison were harmed in the making of this book.
Printed and bound in Canada   22 23 24 25   5 4 3 2 1

In every koan there's only

the desire to put you back in the

world where you always were   anyway

DOUGLAS BARBOUR, *Listen. If*

Prologue

NOVEMBER 04, 1963
THE TOWN OF STENSON

A man carries his daughter, she is four years old, to the car. Her curls are unruly and her cheeks still flushed from chasing her brother around the house. He sets her into the front passenger seat, tucks a red blanket around her. She smiles up at him, a little bewildered, but trusting him all the same.

He shuts her door, checks the oil, washes his hands under the tap at the side of the house where the stone veneer is chipping, and wipes them on a cloth which he fastens to the clothesline. He slides behind the wheel and honks the horn. His other three children, left with a neighbour girl, pause in their play and wave. He starts the car and they are off.

They drive past the dime store and the library, past the Laundromat and the new A&W, past the feed mill, there from Stenson's earliest days, past the quarry where he has worked for nearly twenty years, past the new residential communities expanding like yeast dough at the edge of town, past the town dump and McLaughlin's field (these days a ball diamond), and then Stenson is behind them. They drive through town after town, each with its own dime store and library and Laundromat and feed mill and ball field and dump. They drive through rolling farmland with red-roofed barns and fields now at rest, tan pinstripes of grainstalks on dark clay. They drive through orange and purple woods, once home to deer and foxes and timber wolves who tired of human crowding and moved elsewhere. The roads widen, become broad highways that bypass Toronto, cars cars everywhere. They drive past new automobile factories belching promises, past road crews frantically laying asphalt, steam from tar vats bitter on the tongue, past the runways and long terminals of Toronto International Airport (newly renamed and under construction again). Opportunity everywhere, if only you take it. They drive further still, past the reaches of commerce and industry and smog. They drive by rivers and cliffs, through more rolling countryside, more small towns. They drive for hours.

The father talks to the girl as he drives. He tells her about his childhood at the end of the Great Depression, how he sorted trash for things his mother could turn into something useful, how he was going to be a geologist, how close he came. He talks about his sister whom he loves dearly and his brothers who moved away. He talks about his remarkable wife, her mother, who is bedridden in hospital, waiting for their fifth child to be born.

And then he explains this astonishing decision he has made. Not justifying it exactly, just explaining. She hears nothing, but he says it anyway. She watches his face as he speaks. Once, he reaches over, strokes her cheek, and a tear falls from his eye. Silently, she looks at him. He has never cried in front of her before.

He stops the car at a sunny part of the riverbank for lunch. They are almost at their destination, but he wants to spend time with her, only her, before they arrive. The November day is warm and neither of them needs a jacket. He spreads the red blanket on the ground and opens the hamper he packed that morning. He reaches into a paper bag of grapes and pops the best unbruised ones right into her mouth. The juices squirt out from between her teeth. Then they eat tuna sandwiches that have been cut into quarters followed by brownies with frosting. He lets her eat as many brownies as she wants. When she turns a streaked and contented face to him, he wipes it with a wet cloth and finishes the last one himself.

After lunch, the last meal, he focuses his attention on her again. He gives her piggyback rides, throws her into the air and catches her, gets on hands and knees, and chases her around the trees in the soft grass until she laughs silently, face lit by a huge open-mouthed grin. And then he folds the blanket into a cushion for his back, leans against a tree, and holds his arms out to her. She climbs into his lap and he cradles her tightly to his chest for the longest time, until she falls asleep. With the blanket, he makes a bed for her in the back seat, then begins again to drive.

When she wakens, they have arrived and are parked in front of a large building. He has been watching her sleep. He gets out of the car, walks around to her door, and lifts her out. He holds her closely, there beside the car, not moving, for a long time. Still waking, she nestles into his neck.

Finally, resolutely, he turns around and carries her past the huge sign into the building and to the reception desk. "Hello Mr. Blessure, we've been expecting you. The paperwork has been prepared." A receptionist in a navy suit smiles and marks an X on a paper of fine print, while a nurse in a pink uniform stretches out her arms. He passes the girl to the nurse and signs the paper.

He hands the receptionist one pillowcase stuffed with toys and another with clothes and asks her to make a note of what foods the girl likes. And when that long list is done, he tells her what colours she likes, what games she likes, what frightens her, and how to make her laugh.

The girl must sense something amiss; she wiggles 'til the nurse sets her down and she promptly runs to her father where she wraps herself, legs and arms and body, around his leg. His eyes fill with tears and he wipes them on his sleeve.

"Mr. Blessure, are you sure about this?" The nurse asks because this man does not behave like someone about to do this final, definite thing.

He nods. He cannot speak for the crying. He leans down and picks the girl up. He kisses her hands, her head, he kisses away her tears in a gentle farewell.

And then he hands her back to the nurse. (This is not easily done; the girl clings with the aggressive strength of a four-year-old.) And turns on his heel and walks out the door, past the large sign that says *Elora Home for the Feeble-Minded*.

He makes it to the car where he collapses behind the wheel. He sits, weeping, for hours. Only after sunset, when the light flicks on in the Children's Ward window and the nurse's silhouette tucks her charges into bed, only then does he start the car and pull away.

That is how it happened. That is what it was like, the last day Verity Blessure had a father.

One

Writer's Note: Still I flinch, after all these years, every time I smell carbolic acid or see a nurse pull back the plunger on a syringe. Some things you never get used to.

I have found some records of Esau Blessure's early years. It seems he was an ordinary boy who lived in an ordinary small town and grew into an ordinary man. But ordinary people have children and raise them and love them and keep them close as long as possible. And sometimes they are exhausted and unreasonable and they mistreat their children and make any number of mistakes they later regret. What they do not do is bundle up their youngest and haul her off to a Home for the Feeble-Minded never to see her again. There must be a reason, something that can explain why my father left me there forty years ago, when I was still called Verity. I am determined to find it.

I (Athena) begin my research here, in the remnants of Esau's childhood. The town newspaper, The Stenson Trombone, wanting for material, reports all sorts of local mundanities — science fairs, quarry swimming holes, children diving for a lost pair of spectacles — and eventually provides a window, however tiny, on nearly every person in town. It also reports final grades for each local student. (I am grateful for this material. But how many of those children, whose parents would otherwise have been content, were scolded for not being best in the class?) There is also a woman, Jacqueline Berlingue. She is old now, but in her day she cleaned house and did domestic things for anyone who needed help, and Esau and his family needed help. She talks about a new wheelchair and the knuckle-skinning drudgery of scrubbing walls coated in ink, about a framed picture in the vestibule, about old Mrs. Blessure's cupboards of sugar, about a deaf child and a china cabinet mishap. Other events are now a matter of public record. One need only dig for them.

There is enough, perhaps, to cobble together the story.

JUNE 1937
STENSON, ONTARIO

The boy Esau pried the top off the barrel with the side of the blade
and immediately jumped back — but not far enough. The stench
exploded from the barrel into his face and shot down his throat.
He felt the heave coming and ran out of the shed. His gut seized
and he retched into the alley gutter, clinging to a post for balance.

He gasped for air, waited a minute in case there was more,
and then straightened and wiped his face with his sleeve. With his
back to the window, where he knew his father would be watching,
he pulled a small jar from his pocket. A bit of camphor, salvage
from the doctor's trash, pocketed without his father seeing. He
smeared the grease under his nose and slid the jar back into his
pocket. Not that it helped much. He could smell the rot here,
across the yard. In winter, when things were frozen, the job wasn't
so bad, the stink didn't rise and cling to the body. But now, in
June, a vile steam rose from the barrel. Glossy-backed flies were
already swarming above it.

There was nothing to be done. He'd better get at it. The
neighbours complained if the shed door was open for too long.
Bent over and breathing through his mouth, he walked back into
the shed and settled on to the old stool by the barrel, knife in one
hand. He reached into the barrel with the other and clenched
against the feel of slime. He pulled out a hunk of dead animal
and slid the knife between the rancid tissues. A chunk of gummy
white fat tumbled into the tub at his feet and lay there, glistening
in the sunbeam from the open door.

He turned his head to the side and retched once more.

The following day was a Friday, and the first class was fine. But as the day warmed up, the reek of decomposition began leaching from Esau's pores. His classmates gagged and twisted their faces, and his own eyes burned. He had bathed after yesterday's chore, of course, but the reason he was salvaging fat in the first place was that they had run out of the strong lye soap his mother made from it. A good rinse with baking soda might have done the trick in winter — but not in June.

The teacher had changed the eleven o'clock lesson. Esau had passed by her desk on the way to his own and she had coughed. He sat down in time to see her swipe her eyes with a handkerchief and rise to her feet. She cleared away the arithmetic papers laid out on the table at the front of the room and pulled out jars and matches instead. They talked about flames and oxygen that morning. The repeated lighting and snuffing of tallow candles under canning jars filled the room with smoke and took the edge off the rank suffusing the room.

After lunch, when the schoolroom walls began to sweat and his own warmth intensified the smell, the teacher, who knew Esau would have little trouble catching up on missed material, sent him on errands and chores outside the schoolroom. He did them slowly, slowly, but by midafternoon the most unnecessary were finished. Esau slipped back into class, pressed his sticky legs into the grooves of the seat, sat low, and tried not to move.

He appreciated her effort, he did. But she and every pupil in the school room knew, though none spoke of it, that somewhere along his way home Esau would be ambushed. And who could blame them? Who could blame anyone for hurting something, anything, that smelled *that* bad?

His brothers could be no help. They had afterschool work mucking out livestock pens and it took them along a different road. Immediately after the end-of-day bell, Esau sought out a group of pupils much younger than he, and walked as far as he could in their midst. And when they ran to escape the smell of him, he ran along, easily keeping up. But soon they scattered, and he was left alone, unguarded, a long walk still ahead.

Somewhere in the alley behind the dime store, stones began to fly. One ricocheted off his head. Again he ran. His chin shot up, his bare feet left bloody tracks on the rubble — but his tormentors did not give chase.

He probably realized a moment too late that running from them had delayed the inevitable, nothing more. He slowed to a walk and pulled his lips back from his teeth to draw air in faster and cool his heaving chest. He dropped into a sidewalk bench and fingered the scars threading his scalp from previous encounters, searching for the fresh cut now leaking onto his hand from the single landed stone. They'd find him later, he knew, finish the job. Draw it out.

"Ah, slate. Bloody sharp, isn't it? The Inuit people use it for blades in their ulus you know. Have for thousands of years." The high school Science teacher Mr. Chavez sank into the seat beside Esau, tie loosened and shirt untucked in the heat. He carefully rubbed the dust off a blood-tipped stone.

Still breathing hard, the boy looked at him blankly, and wiped his hand on his pants.

"This, what they threw at you. I picked it up. A fine piece slices skin so beautifully that the Inuit use it for their knives. Wonderful stuff, slate."

Esau said nothing. Blood had pushed through a dusty crack on the ball of his foot where he hadn't yet grown summer callouses. A long bubble was forming.

"That smell. You work for the butcher?"

He shook his head, kept looking down.

"Ahh. You must be salvaging fat for soap. I transported decomposing animal remains from a killing floor in the old country when I was young. Not quite the same thing, but not altogether different. One eventually grows accustomed to the smell, you'll be glad to know. Took me about two years."

The boy scoffed — and the teacher sighed. "Come young man," he said, and helped Esau to his feet. "I too know something of bullies. I've found a conversation about geology and a foamy draught to be antidote to their worst effects. Brody's Drugstore has begun again to carry root beer, did you see? These hard times are coming to an end."

He handed Esau a large handkerchief. The two ambled down the street, the lanky, limping, eleven-year-old boy wiping his face and the tall disheveled teacher leaning a little to the left in a protective curve over his companion, lightly tossing up and catching the slate and a few other stones he had picked up along the way.

Saturday passed without attack. Then Sunday. By Monday, the smell had faded and Esau's neck began to ache from checking his shoulder for pursuers. By Wednesday, he just wanted it to be over. By the following Saturday, summer break had started and he had almost forgotten.

He and his sister had spent the evening in their cubbyhole of shrubs overlooking the quarry gravel pits. The heat wave hadn't let up. The sky turned orange and then red and then grey, and still the muggy evening air sank onto their shoulders like wet sand. He helped Mattie back into her wheelchair and kicked away the stones breaking the wheels. They had taken this path so often it had two distinct wheel marks all the way down the hill. Mattie chattered over the bumps and waved away mosquitoes with her hanky.

"Hey! Decomp!"

Esau froze. With Mattie there it would be worse than usual. That afternoon, eight days ago, he shouldn't have run.

"Why isn't your Drool Princess locked away?"

They stepped from behind bushes halfway down the hill, the five of them, and quickly encircled the boy and his sister. Their pockets, Esau noticed, bulged with stones. (Stones on this part of the hill, Mr. Chavez said, were mostly chalkstone, embedded with chert.) Mattie began to cry.

Georgia's fist came up, slowly and methodically, under Esau's nose. He shoved it away and hung on to the wheelchair with one hand. She jabbed him in the face with her left fist, punched him hard in the stomach with her right — her hip twisted with effort — and finished with her knee in his thigh. Esau folded in half and contorted to keep a hand on the chair. Ernie grabbed that wrist with both hands and corkscrewed the skin in opposite directions until it was the only thing Esau could feel. Walter and Jack wrenched the chair away and pushed it toward the other Ernie, and then they landed on Esau with stones and fists and knees. There were no wasted movements, not one hurried breath. It had been choreographed ahead of time. An elegant, well-executed bashing.

Esau couldn't straighten for some time, and when he did Mattie's chair was perched on the precipice over the south gravel pit. Ernie held it with a loose hand, and Mattie gripped the side arms frantically. Her precious eyeglasses slid forward off her nose and tumbled into the water forty feet below. She turned her head back to Esau — he could see the cold whites of her eyes — and she screamed, hard and hoarse.

"Hey Decomp! The family retard might like a free-fall."

Esau ran up the hill, still breathless. "Please don't hurt her."

"Aww, ya wanna keep her? Break a window in that house."

This, too, had been decided ahead of time. There were five of them; they could deny having been there and corroborate the story.

"That *would* be a nuisance," an adult voice said. "I just replaced a window from the last time someone broke it. Do I have you gentlemen to thank for that? Or perhaps you, young lady?"

It was Mr. Chavez whose house lay at the foot of the hill and who had quietly come up the path. The last bit he addressed to Georgia.

"And this sport," he continued, "I wonder if you might explain it. Why does one team have five and the other two?"

Caught, shamed, Ernie pulled the wheelchair to safety and the five of them dispersed as quickly as they had appeared, without saying anything.

Then it was just Mr. Chavez, Mattie, and Esau at the top of the hill as the bushes and quarry faded into silhouette and then darkness. Mr. Chavez handed Mattie a clean handkerchief to wipe her tears and invited them down to his house for root beer, but they had to get home. And Mattie could not stop crying.

The moment they got into the house, she shouted out everything, and their mother began the long process of calming her down. Their father, face now elastic with rage, confined Esau to the big chair in the living room and drummed his fingers on the doorjamb trying to think of a suitable discipline. The tall chair back dwarfed the boy. He leaned against the side, fingered the fresh bruises as they expanded like shiny flesh balloons on his arms and legs. His brothers watched from the tattered chesterfield and pretended to read. His father paced.

Much later, without so much as a tongue-lashing, he sent Esau to bed.

That night his parents' voices filtered through the thin wall, deadly even and controlled.

"Salvaging fat is too nasty for a child. And to punish him for something he could hardly prevent —"

"We all pull together, Ellie, however we can. He could have lain down in front of the wheelchair. He could have let them beat him. There are always options."

"They did beat him, Alvin. And if the ruffians pulled the wheelchair away, he couldn't very well lie down in front of it."

"Yes — well — I wasn't there, I don't know what the options were. But there are always options. He didn't think of one. He's supposed to be a smart kid!" (The vein on his father's head was likely thumping now, visible through the thinning hair.) "Ruffians. Five stupid kids from down the road. What if the boys don't find the glasses tomorrow? What if they broke in the fall? How'm I gonna pay for glasses, Ellie? I can hardly pay for food!"

Esau fell asleep with his head buried in hot, insufficient blankets.

The next afternoon, his mother paced the kitchen floor, wiped the stove and cupboards, wiped them again, checked on Mattie, who was spending the day in bed, and wiped the cupboards again, as Esau sat at the kitchen table. At his elbow, a stack of soft clean paper sheets she had made from salvaged scraps with a deckle. He sat and he wrote, four hundred eighty times, one line for each second his sister had been terrified, *I will find ways to protect my sister. There are always options.* His father would count the lines when he returned from work that evening. Esau's brothers were spending the afternoon with their friends diving in the quarry pit for Mattie's glasses.

Eventually, his mother pulled a bowl down from the shelf, built a fire in the stove, and used precious sugar to make cookies. She dusted the tops with egg white, more sugar, and pepper, and set a small extravagant pile on a chipped plate beside her son.

His father's reprimand came through the thin wall again that night.

"He was being punished. And you made him *cookies!*"

"Alvin" (Esau could hardly hear her) "one of us has to be reasonable. He's not a line in one of your blasted manifestos."

Mutterings then, unintelligible through the wall. She must have kept at it, for some time later Esau's door opened and then his father's hand stroked his head.

"I'm sorry, Esau," he said. "It wasn't your fault. I oughtn't to have punished you."

The local children dove for the glasses for three consecutive days. They were never found.

Later that week, Mr. Chavez knocked on the screen door and asked if Esau might come work for him. It was a big house he lived in and he was unmarried. He could sure use a hand.

On the first day of work, Mr. Chavez showed him a walnut cabinet four feet by two, curved at the top and with an ornate glass door — art deco, he called it — and it was full of books Esau could borrow, one at a time. Then he outlined Esau's duties, ended his days salvaging fat for soap, and set him to work in the shady garden.

A few weeks later, Mattie had new eyeglasses.

Everything Esau and his brothers learned in school, or from Mr. Chavez's books, they taught in turn to Mattie. A difficult birth had damaged her brain, and the local doctor had declared her too slow for school, though she was perfectly capable in most respects. Other disabled children in Stenson were kept hidden by their families, but Esau's father, who had named his sons after

23

relatives but his daughter for a queen, was determined she have every chance. "It'll help you too," he said to the boys. "The best way to learn to tie a difficult knot is to teach it to someone else." In the evenings, after their jobs and after dinner, each boy sat with Mattie for half an hour, trying to explain something he had learned that day. And whether it was the teaching, or Mr. Chavez's books, or something else altogether, no one could be sure, but it didn't take long for the town to know that the Blessure boys, who mucked out animal pens and salvaged fat from offal, were bright. In June 1938, the *Trombone* printed a photograph of them, cowlicked and gangly, under the heading "Three Blessure Boys, Top of Class But Don't Enjoy Studies." The oldest boy, Henry, was quoted in a short article alongside: "'No, sir, we don't enjoy studying. But we don't have no choice because we have to teach our sister (sic).'" Their father hammered together a frame from scrap moulding and hung the clipping prominently in the vestibule. It was the first thing visitors saw when they entered the house, and Mr. Blessure's usual line, to anyone who noticed it, was "Equal opportunity. Everyone benefits."

A year later, in April 1939, Esau made the paper again. Early one day, judges from Toronto came on the train and spent hours looking at Stenson children's science projects. They spent an especially long time in front of Esau's project. They passed around the piece of fulgurite loaned him by one of the quarrymen who knew of his growing interest in geology. They read his handwritten exposition that fulgurite was a rare natural glass created when lightning struck and liquefied quartz sand. They fingered a bit of quartz and donned the antique spectacles, loaned him by the undertaker who had once removed them from a body, all the while remarking over the explanation that the lenses they looked through were in fact a specially treated quartz stone.

And then the tallest and sternest of the judges folded his long body into a child's desk and wrote in calligraphic hand a letter of invitation to the Royal Agricultural Winter Fair in Toronto. He stood, and, with everyone watching, he handed the letter to Esau and shook his hand. He gestured and together they turned towards the reporter from the *Trombone* who snapped a photograph. Esau, spine preposterously straight and grinning widely, shaking hands with one hand and holding the invitation with the other. That news piece was also clipped out but never framed. It was pasted, along with a photo of Esau at the fair, discreetly inside a cupboard door. Esau was clever, no one could deny, but it wouldn't do to boast.

For the next five or six years, until Esau was a young man, eighteen years old, and his brothers long gone, he went to school, expenses paid by working for Mr. Chavez, and continued to teach Mattie what he learned. It became a game for them, one Mattie was likely to spend half a day preparing. Esau would sit down, open a book and turn the page, only to find it stuck to the next with flour paste. Or he would stand up after a lesson to discover his chair had been dusted invisibly with a teaspoon of brown flour, now spread evenly across his backside. Sometimes, Esau came to the table with a clean pair of underwear on his head like a hat and didn't crack a smile, though Mattie was pealing, snorting with laughter. Other times he taught the entire lesson in a French accent, or with the book upside down.

Esau was the only Blessure child to attend high school; his brothers had to work. If it hadn't been for Mattie and what he could teach her, he probably wouldn't have been permitted to go at all.

Writer's Note: *Jacqueline, who often helped out at the Blessures, says she wasn't convinced of the effectiveness of Mattie's "education" — she and Esau spent half their time being silly — but certainly, she says, it was heartwarming to watch. She also says Mr. Chavez was exempt from military duty because of flat feet. She says, in fact, that Esau and the teacher became fast friends. Esau, it seems, spent his free time either with the teacher or with his sister, and rarely with his brothers or other schoolboys.*

Esau's years following the Royal Winter Fair have left few records. News of the war takes over even small-town newspapers, and endearing stories about local children get shoved aside like other luxuries of peaceful times.

ATHENA'S JOURNAL
OCTOBER 22, 2003
(WEDNESDAY)

Imran, my Independent Assisted Living worker and friend, thinks I should journal about my other current project. No one has to read it, he says, but my description of the process might be "helpful at some point." My other project, then, is this: I have decided to try for custody of Arvo who was my companion through my years in the Facility. I went to the courthouse and now have a tall pile of forms here. I will begin filling them out on the weekend.

Imran says that, given my background, they will be particularly rigorous about my application and I should prepare for "a battery of tests, a litany of excuses, and a plethora of delays." I am not looking forward to more time under the microscope. And

I fear I will not likely succeed. But I miss Arvo and the possibility that we might live together makes it worthwhile.

Today is a visiting day. I wake to the sunlight just after 8:00 AM, make hot coffee, eat breakfast, and think about how I will reno-vate the apartment if Arvo comes to live here. A light flashes high on my kitchen wall. I look down from my window. My neighbour and friend Mr. Saarsgard is standing on the lawn one floor down with his mirror, signalling me. He waves that I should come down. I pick up a pen and notepad and jacket on my way down the stairs.

"Do you have a minute?" he writes. "I have a machine I want you to see."

Mr. Saarsgard does not know Sign. He is timid, mumbles, and does not look directly at me when he speaks. I cannot lip-read him. We converse through notes.

He loves machines as much as I do but he does not under-stand them. He frequently buys new sound systems, cash registers, and televisions for his XXX stores, but needs help install-ing them. And they often stop working because a connection comes loose or because he does not use them properly. He calls me then to repair them. I follow him to the back of his store now, expecting to find something to repair.

There, by the stucco wall, sits a vintage black BMW R68 motorcycle. He has ordered a sidecar, he says, but it will not arrive for a month.

It is ravishing. My mouth falls open. I drop the pen and paper and walk around the bike, stroking the elegant tank and curve of the seat and muffler and pipes and kickstand. Mr. Saarsgard picks up what I dropped and smiles as he watches me smile.

"Would you like to go for a spin?" he writes.

"Spin?"

"Slang for "ride." Would you like to go for a ride?"

I just smile. He hurries into his store and brings out two

helmets. It is a strange sensation to wedge my head into something so tight but I do not mind. I zip my jacket and clamber on behind him and we go for a spin around the neighbourhood.

He is not yet a good motorcycle driver, Mr. Saarsgard. He must often compensate for over-steering. And my balance is less developed than most women my age. Sitting upright on that narrow seat is hard work and sometimes we wobble. But I do not mind. The back of a speeding motorcycle, cold wind on my teeth, is a fine place to be. It is a sensation to file away and remember on sad days.

And then it is 10:00 AM, time for Mr. Saarsgard to open his store and for me to visit Arvo.

I gather my things and walk to the bus stop. The first time I took a city bus, ten years ago with a careworker, I was terrified. I could not maintain balance when the bus was in motion, not even while seated. Ten years ago, walking down a sidewalk seemed herculean. Others lifted their feet; I shuffled and limped. And fell. Often. Now I can walk and take the bus, "no problem," as Imran says. I take the bus frequently. Sometimes I jog to catch it.

When the bus approaches my stop by the Greyhound terminal, I pull the cord. Usually, the sign at the front of the bus lights up to say a stop has been requested. This time the sign does not light up. I pull the cord again. Still no light. It must be damaged. I am concerned the bus will not stop and I will be left in an unfamiliar part of town. I pull it again and again, many times.

Suddenly a man is in my face, inches from my nose. He is angry and he shouts so forcefully I feel his voice. I have no trouble lip-reading him.

"STOP RINGING THE FUCKING BELL! WHATSA MATTER WITH YOU? ARE YOU FUCKING DEAF OR FUCKING STUPID?"

"I am fucking deaf," I answer with my voice. "I did not know there was a bell." Imran says my voice sounds hollow and unused.

He says it is a sound distinct to deaf people.

Shame flashes across the man's face. Now he is ingratiating, saccharine, more irksome than ever.

"AW, MAN! I AM SO SORRY."

His neck veins bulge with the effort of shouting. My skin vibrates from the force of his voice and my nose fills with the smell of his digestive system. I want to get away. Thankfully the bus has stopped. I step around him and go to the door.

"HERE, LET ME HELP YOU."

He steps behind and shoves his arm under mine at the moment I step down. I do not expect this and almost fall to the ground. When I glance back, he has tucked his hair behind his ears and he wears the expression of a man resolved to be useful. I intend no affront, but buying a Greyhound ticket can be an ordeal. I will be unable to concentrate if he hovers nearby. I pull out my pad and pen.

"Thank you for your help," I write. "I am fine now."

"I'M GONNA HELP YOU. WHERE ARE YOU GOING?"

"Sir, you are making me uncomfortable. Please leave me alone now."

He looks hurt. I brace.

"FINE, BITCH. I WAS TRYING TO HELP. FUCK YOU."

He stomps away across the bus terminal parking lot, directly through a large puddle with a thin oil-film on top, to continue the journey he began before meeting me today.

I approach the wicket. Today, my ticket purchase is uneventful. I write that I am deaf and want to buy a ticket, the agent smiles and prints out the ticket, and I pay for it. I climb aboard the coach and settle into a seat near the front.

I nap a little on the trip, and two hours later, we arrive.

I disembark, catch a city bus, take it to the Arlington suburb, and walk to Arvo's Group Home. A pile of long fence posts lies on the front lawn. Five are already planted, shielding the suburb from the great brick house. A corner of a handmade picket sign sticks out of the trashcan by the door. I lift the lid. The sign reads "No nuthouse in Arlington."

I push the doorbell.

Arvo's Group Home keyworker opens the door — and Arvo is already there. Twitchy, gangly, hair flattened by constant smoothing, generous ears poking out sideways, and as tall as the door itself. He pushes her aside and then he is hugging me and crying a little and hugging me more. He is always happy to see me.

He takes me by the hand and pulls me inside. I smile at the keyworker on my way past. Her mouth stretches into a flat line across her face.

He leads me first to his room. He tries to shut the door, but she follows us and prevents him from closing it. He goes to the closet, then, and shows me a new T-shirt with a gear work print on the front, a new pair of running shoes, and a pen from the Sunshine Mountain ski resort. A tiny chairlift with skiers slides up and down the mountain when you tilt the pen back and forth.

I reach into my bag, and pull out the present I brought this week: a man in a tuxedo and top hat on a little bicycle with weighted poles in each hand. I pull over a chair, stand on it, and take the harlequin off the toy tightrope stretching from ceiling corner to corner in his room — I brought him the harlequin last year — and replace it with the man in the tux. Arvo is delighted. He runs to the corner of the room, reaches up, and pulls down the rope. The man on the bike cycles towards him. He runs then to the opposite corner, pulls down the rope, and the man cycles backwards. Arvo laughs and runs from corner to corner making the tuxedo man cycle back and forth for a long time.

"Where did you buy that?" signs the keyworker. "I've been looking for one for my niece."

"I made it," I sign.

"Oh." And then, a few minutes later, "So you made the doll, but where did you find the bicycle?"

"I made it all," I say. "I used balsa wood and fabric and tin. I have been working on it for several weeks. It is precision work. The bicycle must be perfectly balanced or it will not function properly and will fall off the tightrope."

"Wow. You did a good job."

"Yes. I know."

Arvo runs to his closet. He retrieves his black leather shoes, blows off dust, and slips them on. Rummaging through his dresser, he finds an old bowtie. It is turquoise and it sparkles. He pulls out his only hat, a green cap with John Deere on the front.

"Do you have some black paper?" I sign to the keyworker. She returns a moment later with black paper, scissors, and tape. I roll one sheet into a cylinder and cut another into a brim. I fasten them to his cap with the tape. Now he has a stovepipe hat like the dapper tuxedo man. He waves at himself in the mirror, and points, and says "look look" to me. He laughs some more and kisses my neck. He tries to push the worker out of the doorway, shut the door. She braces against the jamb and smiles, but will not budge.

"I would like to take him for a walk," I sign. "It is a beautiful day." Arvo is agoraphobic. I am the only person he willingly ventures outside with.

"I'm sorry, Athena," she signs. "I wish I could say yes but the neighbourhood has restarted the anti-Group Home campaign. We're afraid they'll throw things at our clients."

With this news Arvo and I retreat to the living room. I do not like the living room. It has framed Bible sentences about purity and holiness on every wall. Religion is one of those things I do not yet understand. The repeated phrases and intentional construction of belief seem duplicitous to me. But it is the only place we can sit.

Arvo cuddles into me, crying on my neck and then kissing the tears away. The worker goes into the kitchen and starts making dinner. Between moments of affection, we play Pick-Up Sticks — Arvo has his own rules, I do not mind — and we sign in a language no one else understands. She keeps an eye on us over the bar. I am so tired of being watched and not seen. He eventually falls asleep on my shoulder, slouched down with both arms around me.

In the late afternoon, I stroke Arvo's face to waken him, and I say goodbye. He cries a good deal and I leave to catch the bus. On the long ride home, I count light poles (4,287). A distraction to bridle my tears.

At home, I reheat some dal for supper. Imran joins me as he often does on visiting days; he knows I long for comfort after leaving Arvo. To the meal he contributes fresh naan from the Indian grocer and his homemade mango pickle. After supper, we make chai and Imran shows me his new project.

Into a plain brown scrapbook, he has stapled bits of typed and torn paper. They are excerpts, he says, from the *Book of Judith* pertaining to the maid. He took an interest in her after an evening a few weeks back when he and I looked at a library book of famous paintings of Judith decapitating Holofernes, a general under King Nebuchadnezzar.

"I can't stop thinking about the maid," Imran says. "She does this astonishing thing: she assists her employer in seducing a General and then sawing off his head. She's in nearly every paint-ing made of this story and yet we never learn her motives, nor even her name. A person doesn't go along with sawing off a General's head out of obedience. She would advance her station in life faster if she were to report her employer and save the

General." He slurps up chai. "No, there's something in the act for her. She wants to participate, to feel the saw working through bones and the vibrations running up her arms. She wants his blood on her hands. Perhaps she wants to swing his head around by the curls. I snipped out these passages and stuck them here, out of their context, so I might consider when I have the time: what exactly is in it for the maid?"

We talk about it for a while and conclude nothing, except perhaps that Holofernes and Nebuchadnezzar were vestiges of an old and doomed regime. Their time had come. If it hadn't been Judith and her maid with a saw at Holofernes's neck, it would have been someone else.

And then I show him the painting *Les Demoiselles d'Avignon* in a *Modern Painters* book from the library. After Mr. Picasso completed this painting, the book says, it so shocked his friends that he hid it, this magnificent piece, for ten years. To create something so inviting and then to lock it away. We think it must have been unbearable.

Now it is time for bed. I plan to fall asleep thinking of the wind in my teeth on the motorbike this morning. Maybe one day I can drive the bike and Arvo can be my passenger.

Writer's Note: The next documented event takes place in Esau's last year of high school. He is eighteen years old now, and has been at the top of his class every year of secondary school.

MARCH 1945
STENSON

Dear Mr. Blessure,

We are pleased to offer you acceptance to the

Geophysical Studies program at the University

of British Columbia beginning on the fourth of

September, 1945. Additionally, we are pleased

to inform you that you are this year's honoured

recipient of the General Scholarship for Promising

Students of Geology. The program focuses on

aspects of geology useful to the war effort . . .

Esau skimmed the remaining paragraphs, leaned against the wall, sank to the floor. The rest of the day's mail lay unopened at his feet. He lingered in the silent vestibule of his parents' house for nearly an hour, reading the letter again and again, holding the possibility in that moment for as long as he could.

That evening, Mattie, whose health in recent years had been so robust that she had not needed her wheelchair, walked door to door, telling his news. Soon the kitchen filled with neighbours stopping by to congratulate him, a local celebrity, and to revel in a young man leaving town for something other than war.

The next day, Esau worked out an arrangement with his parents. That summer, in addition to working a few hours weekly for Mr. Chavez, he would shovel gravel at the quarry and would give them all he earned. In return, they would buy his train ticket to Vancouver. Mr. Chavez had written a friend in Vancouver who agreed to hire him for a few hours a week to staff his bookshop and earn pocket money. Everything was secured.

Esau packed his bag weeks before it was time to leave, and then emptied and re-packed it six times more. He had two pair trousers, five pair underwear, two pair long underwear, five pair socks, two undershirts, two short-sleeved shirts, three long-sleeved shirts, a red tie, a thick wool cardigan, a jacket, a warm hat, a muffler, one pair of mittens, and a heavy coat. Mattie and his mother had sewn or knitted everything but the coat. It had been pulled from the wooden box once belonging to his grandfather. His father's employer, the bank manager Mr. Sorenson, had given him a soft leather folder with a notepad inside, and nearly every business in town had pushed into his hands a pen or a pad of paper with their stamp at the top. He would leave well supplied in stationery.

Esau's evening walks with Mattie that summer took on a feeling of gentle winding down and unhurried farewell. He wouldn't have given up a single one.

JULY 1945
STENSON

At the end of July, two weeks before Esau's departure for Vancouver, Mattie sat at the kitchen table writing letters to her older brothers now at war. Without warning, she fell sideways off the chair, and there, on the floor, had a series of severe epileptic seizures.

In the days that followed, they realized that, for the first time in years, she was too weak to walk and needed her wheelchair. Esau pulled the old thing down from the attic, wiped off the dust, oiled the wheels, and tried to help her into it — but she had long ago outgrown it. Her knees rested comically in the vicinity of her forehead. They couldn't help but laugh.

Esau half-carried her back to a kitchen chair, then turned the wheelchair upside down and studied it. Surely, by adding a piece of leather to this or a copper pipe to that, he could enlarge it.

A while later, he called their father who also put his mind to the task.

Several hours later, they both stepped back from the chair. These joints, this design, they could not bear the weight of an adult.

"It won't work," his father said.

Esau blanched. He knew what it meant. He stood and walked directly out the front door, leaving Mattie and his parents sitting in the kitchen, blinking at the screen door clattering in his wake.

He didn't return until after midnight. The next morning, he left for work an hour earlier than usual and came back long after dark when everyone was usually asleep. But when he opened the screen door, his father sat in his usual place at the table, elbows in their grooves, waiting.

Esau inhaled and sat down. His mother set a plate of reheated food before him but he crossed his arms and locked eyes on his father.

And then his father looked away, dragged his lips, said times were still tight: they had to renege on their promise to buy his train ticket. Mattie needed more medication *and* a new wheelchair.

His mother leaned against the stove, plainly uncomfortable.

"It's not the end of the world, you know Esau," he said. "Historically, many great social movers had very little schooling, less than you. What matters —"

But Esau was gone. The old screen door clattered behind him.

He ran first in the direction of the quarry, then turned abruptly back towards the Science teacher's house. Perhaps Mr. Chavez had a solution.

When the house came into view, Esau slowed. All lights were on and extra lanterns lit. Light even from the basement windows that were always boarded up. And dozens of people. A few human silhouettes on the hoods of two police cars parked on the path by the house. Others standing in clusters on the verandah, in the yard, squeezed into the bench swing under the burning porch lantern. Young Jacqueline Berlingue, curls tied back sensibly, balanced a round tray on one hand and handed out cups of something. Father Matthew rocked in the chair in the verandah corner under the wind chimes; he looked blankly into the night and didn't seem to notice the cup in his hands. More people milled about inside the house and leaned against furniture or doorjambs. Dr. King was visible through the front window and sat at the table writing.

A strange mix of people. Something was wrong.

Tentatively, Esau stepped around plywood from the basement windows that now lay on the lawn, nails hammered sideways for safety, and approached the house.

A local constable intercepted him. The fabric on either side of his shirt placket stuck to his skin, soaked in the night heat. He had long ago abandoned his hat.

"Hello — Esau, isn't it? You're looking for José?"

"I want to talk to Mr. Chavez." Esau leaned to the side, looked around the policeman's bulk, scanning the front porch.

"Ah." The policeman pulled a handkerchief, already wet, from his pocket and wiped his brow. "As it happens, we are also looking for José Chavez," he said, more to his handkerchief than to Esau. "If you should see him, you're obliged to tell a policeman."

"I don't understand."

The policeman folded his hanky, looked the boy in the eye, and repeated everything he had just said. "I'm sorry, son," he said. "José tricked us all."

Esau's arms hung at his sides. Tricked? He fixed on the fact he could grasp: Mr. Chavez's first name was José. Had he never known his first name? Wasn't José a Spanish name? Was Mr. Chavez Spanish? Or perhaps Mexican?

"Son, why don't you sit here?" The policeman took his stiff arm, pulled him elbow first through knots of people to the front steps of the house where another boy, Michael Vinterburg, sat alone leaning against the wooden rail. Michael's twin brother Gabriel had fallen off a roof that week and lay now in a coma. The policeman pushed gently down on Esau's shoulder, so that the boy's knees bent automatically, and returned to his work. Esau sat on the step beside Michael, upright and rigid in the still air.

After a long while, he said, "I don't understand."

"Gross indecency," Michael said. "Someone reported him."

"Oh." Then, "Why is everyone here? Where's Mr. Chavez?"

"Snoops and meddlers" — Michael drew a flat circle in the air — "savouring the gossip. And he's gone. I hope they never find him."

This much Esau understood: Mr. Chavez could not help him get to Vancouver. Mr. Chavez was gone.

Jacqueline brought them water with ginger slices in it. They took the cups automatically, drank mechanically, set them back on the tray, saying nothing.

After a while, a housefly landed on Esau's leg. It didn't move in the usual way of flies. Esau began to rock back and forth, still rigid, clutching his stomach, watching the fly. The rocking forced the air to move and the step to creak, but the fly stayed, motionless. Eventually Michael laid a hand on Esau's arm and stopped him from rocking.

Esau flicked away the fly. "I can't stand this," he said.

"Wanna leave?" Michael asked.

And so the boys (young men, really) left. Not in the direction of town, but up the dirt path once marked by wheelchair ruts to the cubbyhole of shrubs.

Here, away from the listless yard at the foot of the hill, the air was clearer. Here, the day's heat slipped off their backs. They stretched out under the shrubs and rested their heads on a low, flat rock. Michael pulled something leafy from his pocket, something his uncle had sent from the war, and they rolled it and smoked it and with each draw they pushed the day aside for a while, slightly.

They spent the night on the bank, drawing what comfort they could from one another and from the reliable old moon plodding across the sky as the quarry pits rested below.

The headline in the *Trombone* that week read "Tragedy Strikes Again." Beneath the local casualty reports still coming in, though the war in Europe had ended, the front page showed a photograph of Gabriel Vinterburg squinting into the sun. A tall, handsome, freckled young man, musculature revealed by the hang of his shirt, with fair hair and a mischievous look about him. The Vinterburgs, it said, had relocated to Stenson from the dustbowl prairies seven years earlier, farmers whose bus tickets were paid by the government. Gabriel, who was known on the schoolyard for his ability to draw, had fallen off a granary roof, coincidentally the tallest structure in Stenson, and suffered a severe head injury from which doctors predicted he would never recover. The article cautioned that Gabriel was a twin, virtually indistinguishable from Michael, and if readers were to see Michael on the street, they ought not to congratulate him on a miraculous recovery.

Beneath that, in a small box, a short statement that the police were still looking for high school teacher Mr. José Chavez. His car had been found, abandoned and with a flat tire. Should readers see him would they please contact the Stenson police desk sergeant immediately.

Esau awoke first, wakened by the industrial coughs of machines in the quarry below.

Yesterday's events slammed to the front of his head and his mind began to race: *a packed suitcase, a child's wheelchair, a sweaty policeman, his provincial life, a packed suitcase, a child's* Michael's even breath inches away caused the hairs on his arm to wave in the morning light. It altered the slow downfall of dust filaments. Esau lay still, and a calmness returned.

Eventually Michael awoke, smiled at Esau, and said nothing.

After a while, he stretched, letting his knee fall to the side against Esau's and his arm rest above Esau's head. The movement, Esau noted gratefully, disturbed nothing. His mind remained calm. They lingered on the bank of the quarry as late as they dared, yielding to last night's intimacies, while the machines continued their noisy repast of biting and chewing and spitting out the earth.

When there could be no more waiting, Michael got to his feet.

"I've had about enough of Stenson," he said. "I'm off to Toronto to sign up for war cleanup. You comin'?" He held out his hand to help Esau up.

Esau stood, dusted his clothes. The idea held a world of allure.

He looked at Michael as long as he dared, saw risk and the ache tighten his face, then pinned his eyes on his feet.

"I wa—don't th–." He exhaled and tried again. "My brothers are in the Navy. My mom — all her boys gone — it's too much."

Michael looked away, neck suddenly slack. "Whaddya gonna do?"

"Uhmm. Maybe I still have my quarry post."

The instant Esau said it, the succession of thoughts erupted again and slammed to the front of his head with such intensity *wheelchair, a sweaty policeman, his provincial life* that it forced a quick gust from his lungs.

Of course Michael noticed. "Esau. You sure?"

And when Esau nodded *(push it away)* Michael shrugged. "Well, this is it then."

Michael leaned in — and Esau, awkward, held out his hand. Under the solemnity of a man departing for war and the glare of the Stenson sun, he could manage nothing more.

They parted ways for a short time, Michael heading west and Esau heading north down the hill, with the understanding they would look for each other here, under these shrubs, another midnight. As many midnights as they could manage until Michael had to leave.

The sun was high, the air beginning to bake. Esau peeled off his shirt as he walked. He paused at the bottom of the hill, before Mr. Chavez's house. Everything quiet now, everyone gone. It was a big house for one person, the sort to raise a family in. The clapboard siding showed none of the rain streaks that fell from the eaves of his father's house. Mr. Chavez must have scrubbed it recently. The garden hose, probably used yesterday, stretched across the lawn warming in the sun. These domestic leftovers, the serenity of this day, they seemed inappropriate in a week of suffering. Better that the wind wail like the rabbits his brothers had shot when they were young (he could never do it, not then, not now), or that the sun veil itself properly behind a cloud. Better that the eaves weep soot.

From now on, Esau would be just another Stenson young man, like all the small-town boys, fossils, who had come before and who would come after, those who jabber on the schoolyard about what they'll do and where they'll go and who, in the end, never leave. He too would have to grow into the conviction, as one grows into a coat bought for next year's winter, that sometimes it's best not to dream larger than the routines into which one is born *(push it away)*. That there is no such thing as a birthright.

Esau wiped his sweating face with the shirt in his hands and turned towards home *packed suitcase, a child's wheelchair, a sweaty policeman, his provincial life (push it away)*. No point in wallowing *(push it away)*, others had it worse *(push it away)*. He had Michael now, who had reached for him as eagerly as he had reached for Michael, and who would surely not leave for a month yet. It was time to focus on something else.

Anything else.

His mother and Mattie sat at the worn kitchen table, canning Niagara peaches. They wore their thinnest summer dresses, sleeves rolled up onto the shoulders and fastened with safety pins. Their hair pasted to their necks and perspiration ran in Vs, disappearing behind their bodices, though all the house windows were thrown open. Mattie smiled to see Esau and stood and hugged him. Juice dripped from her knife down his neck and she pressed her sweat into his.

"I'm thorry about your train ticket," she whispered into his ear.

"It's not your fault, Mattie."

His mother looked at him meaningfully *A packed suitcase, a child's wheelchair (push it away).* No doubt she would scold him later for staying out all night. She pointed to the counter, where four sandwiches sat on a plate under a glass bowl to keep flies away, and turned back to work. She and Mattie each reached into a large basin of hot water and pulled out a warmed, floating peach. In tandem, each grasped her peach in one hand and used the other to slide the knife under the skin up by the stem, and pull down in one swift motion. Loosened by heat, the skin pulled away easily, exposing the flesh, oozing and raw, which they sliced into sealer jars that already had a small mountain of sugar at the bottom. Then they reached into the basin, pulled out another peach, and did it again, as they had last summer and the summer before that and the summer before that. Fifteen seconds a peach. There were at least two hundred peaches to go.

Esau leaned against the counter (the table was crammed with sealer jars) and watched them work as he ate. He listened to their chatter, saw the roughness, the dark acid lines in their hands. His mother had once confessed she'd wanted her own shop, "a little *Stube,*" part bakery, part pantry-and-preserves. And Mattie used to rant, beg, weep to attend school. They gave no signs of resenting their paltry lives. They had learned to enjoy snug routines and each other's company. The jars gradually *a sweaty policeman, his provincial life* filled with peach slices.

He would be resolute. He set the empty plate on the counter and went to his room. He pulled on a fresh shirt and underwear and socks and slid again into his dirty pants. On his way through the kitchen, he tripped on the linoleum, recovered, then stuffed one peach in his shirt pocket where it wouldn't be crushed, and gripped another in his teeth. Between bites, he stuck a kiss on his mother's cheek. "I'm off to the quarry," he said, his head in a fog *(push it away)*. "I'll be home for dinner."

And he stepped, left foot, right, searching for any wisp of resignation that might ease this letting go, this transition from one kind of life to another.

Late that night, Esau lay in bed, his winter post at the quarry secured, not shovelling mere gravel but assisting the surveyors. What exactly was *gross indecency?* Who could he ask? He heard Mattie trying out her new wheelchair in her room down the hall. One of the wheels needed grease. He'd fix it in the morning. His eyelids dropped. The wheel squeaked, the wheel squeaked, each squeak a rumbling thunderous shockwave *(push it away)* the wheel squeaked, the wheel squeaked —

Suddenly the darkness burst into a flailing, racing, cycling machine against being pressed back into this stale life. It caught him completely off guard. His pulse tripled, his sheets were doused in sweat.

He did the only thing he could think to do. In two strides, he was at his desk. He reached down into the suitcase by the desk and pulled out a pad of paper and a pen. Leaning forward in the chair as if he'd be there for just a minute, he wrote, hundreds, thousands of times:

I do not hate my sister. I must not blame my sister. I must protect my sister.

I do not hate my sister. I must not blame my sister. I must protect my sister.

I do not hate my sister. I must not blame my sister. I must protect my sister.

Next morning, when her calls to breakfast produced no response, his mother opened the door to Esau's room.

It was sinking in paper. Compulsively, throughout the night, he had filled pad after pad of paper and any reachable writeable surface — desk, walls, bedpost — with the same three sentences. Esau slumped over the desk in the midst of the paper sea, so fast asleep she couldn't wake him. She called her husband and together they hoisted him onto the bed and tucked him in. The pen in his right hand, covered in dried ink and blood, had clotted firmly to his fingers. They turned then to read what Esau had written, she with hand over mouth and he standing upright, yielding nothing.

Esau slept for two days and nights, visited daily by Dr. King. While he slept, his mother and Jacqueline (hired for the task so Mattie might not see) scrubbed the walls and furniture. Could they just finish the wretched job, Esau's mother said when Jacqueline expressed alarm, and leave the assessments to the doctor. They burned all the paper but for one piece which Jacqueline squirreled away in her apron pocket.

My therapist, who is paid by the government not to mind his own business, peers at me overtop his spectacles, and asks if I might be interpreting the materials to cast Esau in the kindest light. Even after ten years of coming here, there is something about this man, curved shoulder and pointed face, that reminds me of a bird.

"Kindest light?" I ask in Sign. "He does things of which no person could be proud."

"What I mean — I hear you, these past few weeks especially, representing him as a victim," the psychologist says through the interpreter. "A man from whom choices have been taken. This man suffers. Bullying, poverty, mental breakdowns, misfortune. Each week, your descriptions amplify tragedy more than the week before and I'm concerned for what this says about responsibility. Is it possible that his circumstances were no more difficult than the thousands of people who had to look after their siblings or who never got post-secondary or, for that matter, secondary schooling? In the forties, such things were not disastrous. They were merely common."

I hate that these sessions are a condition of my freedom, but I will admit they have helped me a great deal. Here, in this room, I have worked through fear, rage, and crippling jealousy. Here, I generally feel validated.

But recently there has been a shift. Years ago, when he first suggested I research Esau and the others, he said only that I might find the process interesting and "perhaps helpful in recovering memory and in coming to terms with abandonment." And then, for a few years, as I uncovered clippings and letters, it was

"Fascinating!" as his watery eyes betrayed stifled yawns. "Why do you think he did that?" But last week, he shifted uncomfortably in his chair and asked if, "before continuing further on the victim trajectory," I might consider other explanations. Could we talk, for instance, "about whether Esau might have been reluctant to deal with the pressures of university away from the security of his home? Or whether he might have preferred quarry work over studies and whether that preference or something else altogether turned him away from university?"

"Look," I signed. "Look at these documents. These clippings of children diving for spectacles, of Esau topping his class. This photo of him holding a Royal Winter Fair invitation. He was accepted to a prestigious university program — was offered a scholarship! — but did not attend. Look at this bank stationery, with three sentences written many times like a child. Look!"

"I see them," he says. "But I'm questioning whether his father was so unyielding and the poverty was so severe. Whether Mattie's epilepsy had anything whatsoever to do with Esau's decision to stay. For instance, words spoken or written during psychotic breaks generally reveal, well, psychoses. They can't be taken for hidden truth. I'm questioning whether he was trapped at all.

"Now Verity. Verity was trapped. She was prevented in a decisive way from following a great many of her dreams. But in my experience, most people who never follow their dreams are not prevented. They simply *allow* life to nudge them in directions which they might not choose for themselves, but which offer little resistance. With the material you've shown me, I'm questioning whether Esau was in such very bad shape. Could you talk more about this? Do you think, especially in light of the Elora document, there might be other explanations for his decisions? Or for why you might go to such lengths to render him victim?"

I look at the ceiling and consider his words.

Of course I am especially alert to events in Esau's life that tinted his view of Mattie or that bent Esau's posture or weighted his step, that made the slightest increase in burden impossible to bear, that left him no choice but to leave his daughter at the Home. I do not deny my bias. But my bias, Esau's "victim trajectory," as he says, nevertheless provides the most lucid account of events.

My therapist, however, does not see the evidence. He has not done the research I have done. He does not know Esau as I know him.

I say nothing.

And then there is the interpreter. A pale somber man with thin moustache and no lips who sits to the side in a straight-backed chair and signs with too much precision and not nearly enough emotion. It is like signing to a toaster. Without fail, he wears a starched striped shirt, collar crisp enough to slice fruit, with one of three ties (burgundy, navy, or grey), and pinstriped trousers (dark grey or light grey). The vertical lines and edges make him appear stiffer than he already is. The therapist hired him for his background in psychology. I wanted to bring Imran, my IAL worker and friend, to interpret. Imran has no hard edges; he is comfortable to be with, he signs beautifully, with clarity and jubilance, and he smiles often. But the psychologist said he would be inappropriate because we might have to speak about him (we never have), and the government would not pay Imran if another interpreter had already been provided.

After all these years, I know nothing about this straight-edged man that I have not said here. And yet, I am to sit in this chair every week and expose my most visceral intimacies. I cannot help but wonder: is he translating correctly the things I say in Sign? Or what the psychologist says verbally? Is there any way to know?

If we were writing everything instead of speaking then I could know. But the therapist prefers speech and the facial hair on both men makes them difficult to lip-read.

Still I come each week, undergo the rote of self-revelation, only to be permitted to live independently.

At the end of each session, I remind myself that yes, they are kind men, they have helped me. But together they form a cog in a massive institutional machine, the same machine that has rationed my life. For all their good intentions, they are always already corrupted.

On that note, I have completed the custody forms. I have sent them off to the appropriate offices.

Now I wait.

SEPTEMBER 1945
FRANCE

Young and strong, Esau appeared to recover quickly from his nervous collapse. As soon as he felt well enough, he walked to the quarry and abandoned the winter post he had secured. Then, despite earlier misgivings, he rode the bus to Toronto and signed up for the war that was nearly done. He and Michael sailed together on the RMS *Queen Mary* on one of the last voyages transporting Canadian troops to the war. The Germans had already surrendered and the Japanese surrendered a few days after Esau and Michael set foot on the continent. Their battalion re-imposed order and government on areas that had none, helped families reunite, distributed Red Cross kits, and cleaned up the refuse of war.

What things Esau must have seen. Walking bombed-out roads, each mile, each footfall deeper into a gutted landscape. Burning the last beams of homes now too splintered to restore, parting tall grasses under swarms of flies to uncover animal carcasses or a half-human corpse to bury, confronting groups of bandits who ignored the roads and crossed forests and fields on foot and looted as they went. Piling up rubble (limestone, one grain of sediment and another and another, collected over time, then hardened slowly under an ocean and later handcut into walls of a tenth-century chapel, or a hunk of feldspar that had crossed the whole of Europe in a glacier) into a fence. A static mundane boundary marking ownership and the containment of cows.

At one point, Michael and Esau's unit came upon an old man and his granddaughter, a thirteen-year-old girl who looked like she was fifty, hiding in a cellar that had been dug in a pasture a hundred feet away from any building, where the soldiers had not thought to look. There they had hidden for months, starving, along with their starving dog. Every few nights they snuck up, outside, to uproot a turnip from a village garden or scrabble a heel of mouldy bread from someone's trash. They hadn't known the war was over and didn't believe Esau's lieutenant until they were each, including the dog, given a hock of salted ham and a Red Cross kit of sardines, biscuits, and chocolate. The gratitude in their eyes, their joy over a sardine squishing in the teeth nearly overwhelmed Esau. The lieutenant urged them to eat slowly for, unlike their dog, who could scarf food without concern, they had systems that needed time to recover.

The old man had once been the town postmaster and was needed again at his post, so Esau and Michael were assigned to stay with him for a while, get the post office running, and help him re-inhabit his old house. They borrowed a wheelbarrow and tools from a farmer and began in the post office. They hauled out the rubble and dismantled a crumbling wall that had taken a mortar hit. Then they rebuilt it and repaired the roof, constructed a counter and window and, since the door had been ripped off, they brought one over from what had once been a haberdashery. A top hat and fascinator were still painted on the face of it. The mailboxes and slots were gone too, and the old man sorted the first bits of post in tidy piles on Carnation Milk crates and weighted the piles with spent shell casings his granddaughter found. Then, with the help of the granddaughter and her dog, Michael and Esau cleaned up the old house, hammered together a new outhouse, re-dug the garden, and cleared the path.

"Why didn't you eat your dog?" Michael asked the old man one night. The girl had gone to bed and the three of them were sharing a mug of cheap wine.

"She had lost too much already," he said, gesturing towards her bedroom. "And look at the poor mutt, still so skinny. What would it have given us? A single meal?"

Best of all, the nights up in the chilly attic. A small room with round window, oak wardrobe, iron bed, and only a thin quilt, over which Michael and Esau piled their coats to stay warm. The place had been empty of people for a while and the surfaces were covered in dust. Sweaty, breathless, Esau and Michael pressed into one another on the narrow bed, against the wall, onto the hand-braided rug that warmed the floor. In the morning light, after their first night there, Esau saw in the dust on the wardrobe his own spine and shoulders with Michael's handprints — and one knee — on either side. He looked at it for a while, reliving the moment. And a few minutes later, when both of them got up for the day, Esau leaned against the wardrobe as he dressed and wiped the prints away.

They would do it again that night anyways, he didn't need the record. Michael wasn't a claim to be staked.

After rebuilding the post office, Esau and Michael rejoined their battalion in Douai, a village in Northern France that had sustained a great deal of damage. Late one evening, in an old underground pub just beginning again to serve patrons, they told the bartender about their hometown, Stenson. In turn, he told them a remarkable story about five of their fellow townspeople who had come through Douai earlier in the war. Ernie, Ernie, Walter, Georgia, and Jack — the same fast friends and ruffians who had years earlier tormented Mattie and Esau — had joined the war effort together, four as soldiers in the same unit and one as a nurse.

All four of the men were hit in the same attack. Ernie and Walter were killed instantly and Jack and the other Ernie were delivered quickly to the Aid Station nearby, suffering severe phosphorus burns.

There, Georgia was waiting for them. She tried fiercely to block out their screams and to nurse them back to health, or at least to functionality. Jack was the last to die, gurgling, in a grease-stained cot. She closed his eyes and kissed his forehead, and then calmly took his bag from under his cot. She found a private corner in the hospital tent. She reached up with her bandage scissors and, without looking in a mirror (none was there), she sheared off her hair and threw it in the trash. Next she cut off her nurse's uniform now soaked with Jack's blood and sputum and tossed it into the bin for soiled bandages. With a clean cloth, she wiped herself down, and stepped into the street clothes Jack carried in his bag as reminder of who he really was. She used her bandage scissors one last time to poke extra holes in the belt that had been his. Confident the trousers would stay up, she stepped out of the corner, kissed the foreheads of each patient she had been caring for, handed her scissors, handle first, to an open-mouthed medic who later reported this story, and strode away from her unit.

She was never seen by anyone from her old life again.

Michael, an aspiring journalist at the time, listened carefully to the bartender, asked a few questions, and wrote up the story of the five bullies who developed a camaraderie so powerful it was remembered amongst thousands of forgotten stories of men and women who came through Douai. The story said that, before leaving for war, the five of them had made the rounds of Stenson and apologized to the children they once terrorized, as if they had known they wouldn't return. It was a moving tribute. He mailed it to the *Stenson Trombone* and to families desperate for more information about their lost loved ones.

Two years after the war ended, their hometown of Stenson unveiled a monument, a simple iron oak leaf, commemorating these five war dead, setting their camaraderie on a pedestal as a symbol for the town. Georgia's family said in the newspaper that it was easier this way, with closure and honour, than to spend their lives and meagre bank accounts looking for her, or to think of her wandering that war-shredded continent, crazed with grief.

(I wonder about Georgia sometimes. Where did she go? How did it feel to walk away from her old life? Did she look back? What kind of person did she become? Years later, Michael confessed in an interview that they never had apologized for the bullying of children. He made that bit up so their families could think well of them. I wondered then about those who had been bullied by these five youth. Did they feel belittled every time they walked by the monument? By the ways their ugly realities had been forged and recast — an elegant, well-executed rendering — into something grand? Was that oak leaf their stuff of nightmares? Or did they alter the story in their own memories so that they, too, could have something to lionize, something to admire?)

Writer's Note: When Esau returned from war, he and Michael parted ways, he married a girl named Jude Ahluwalia — and their courtship is a part of the story I (Athena) find difficult to tell.

I thought I might piece the narrative together from archival records and news photos of public events around town. But the photos show dance floors and community halls too crowded to ferret out one couple's story, and the newspapers and archives never tell which courtship rituals (of thousands) a couple followed nor how they were paced. Most often, the first recorded measurement of romance is the announcement of engagement. Even Jacqueline, who has filled many gaps for me, does not know details of Esau and Jude's romance, and she sheds only the faintest light on his separation from Michael. "My dear," she says, "any romance worth having is worth keeping quiet about." She has certainly kept quiet about her own.

To make matters worse, my background prevents me imagining a credible courtship. I have done research. I watched romantic movies from the sixties (those I found with subtitles) and wrote a draft of what might have been their courtship based loosely on Casablanca *and* Breakfast at Tiffany's. *Imran read it. He tried not to laugh, but the vein on his forehead began thumping like the arms of a wind-up drummer. (One of my roommates at the Facility had a toy drummer in her personal effects drawer. Most nights, after lights out, she wound it, set it on the floor, and the thirty of us watched it march between the bedposts. Drumming and drumming in red-paint uniform, it marched in circles in the light spilling into the room through the square window in the door.) I shredded that draft.*

Not to be put off, I returned to the library and spent weeks reading romance novels to determine conventional romance trajectories. In my second draft, I followed the Harlequin blueprint, though in a condensed format. Imran said, in the most diplomatic way, that Harlequin could benefit from my expertise, but the formula had given my project "a touch of the preposterous." I shredded that draft too.

Let me explain how vexing this is. I have been out of the Facility for a decade. I have spent that time trying to integrate and have learned a great deal in a short time. I am adept at behaving properly in a store and in a restaurant and at a party. I know how to tell which vegetables are fresh and what to do with cheese when it grows spots and how the juices that run clear let you know when chicken is cooked. I know when to clean the bathroom and why to use bleach solutions on white towels and tea strainers but not on black pants. I can dress a minor wound. I have learned to watch folks without staring (a difficult thing to do) and why to touch someone's hands but never the head. I can walk outside without bumping into people, and I know what direction traffic flows. I have completed Secondary School Equivalency, I have exceeded the expectations of every analyst and psychiatrist to assess me, I have spoken through interpreters at conferences and people listened to me.

But, like the purity sentences on Arvo's living room walls, romance rituals elude me altogether. They appear fraudulent and I cannot see the point of them. Young children understand them; twelve-year-olds, barely into puberty, try them out on school-yards, plying one another with seductions and jealousies, some of them sooner than that, say the drugstore magazines. Surely, after a decade of study, I should have some of the understanding an adolescent with a quarter of my years has! Evidently not. "There are many kinds of intelligence," Imran often says.

In the Facility, there was no wooing. Those of us who wanted to — given the pharmaceuticals it was not many — got down to the business of sex or masturbation when the urges came. There was nothing more to it. The staff looked the other way.

Imran said I ought not say more about this here. Treading on the inappropriate again, I am, apparently.

"Why?" I asked, over breakfast at my kitchen counter. (He had brought fresh rye bread, still warm, with seeds in it. It goes especially well with butter and marmalade, or with Jarlsberg cheese.) "I mention no genitals nor explicit sexual activity, not even in euphemisms. The romance books have many euphemisms: the one I am reading now speaks of the 'ready moistness of her thicket' and his 'ramrod raging need' of her."

Imran squirmed on my kitchen stool. He stirred his coffee, pushed marmalade back and forth on his bread.

"Romance books are uh fiction, Athena," he finally signed. His articulation was hesitant, slurry. "Actual uhhrm intimate relations come across as too uh personal on the page. Folks prefer intimacy to be evoked. They don't want uh detail."

"Mr. Saarsgard's XXX store is full of detail," I say. "He drives a car with a low belly and haunches. It cost more than I get in subsistence cheques all year. Would people not have to want detail very much for him to afford that car?"

"You see ahem what I mean is people usually read pornography for a specific reason. That is, they uhhh they want errmm —"

Poor Imran. He never could have made it through that sentence. Every few seconds, he looked at the window as if hoping a tin drummer would come through and distract us.

"Perhaps we could watch some films from Mr. Saarsgard's store and you could show me which parts ought to be evoked," I said.

Imran's eyes closed, uneasy. And then he realized I was joking and relaxed.

Joking is difficult to do. It is not a Sign problem. It is another thing I do not yet fully grasp and most often get wrong.

I abandoned the topic and turned my attention to the fine

dark bread. These social niceties, ill-fitting uniforms to attract one kind of attention and deflect another, the codes are still too complex for me. In the Facility, we said what we wanted. No one thought we could say anything worth listening to.

Unfortunately, after all this research, I am no further ahead. I still cannot write convincing romance, and I do not know if this material is inappropriate or if Imran is simply uncomfortable around such talk, the way some people are uncomfortable around talk of money. After two failed attempts and several conversations with a writhing Imran, I have decided not to try imagining Esau and Jude's romance.

These are the facts.

Together, Esau and Michael remained in France for fifteen long, wonderful months. Esau planned upon return to move to Tilsonburg with Michael and his brother Gabriel and continue their life together. Those plans fell aside and he instead returned to Stenson and to his quarry post as Assistant to the Surveyor in late 1946. Not long after, in spring of 1947, he met Jahida Ahluwalia. She had been named for her paternal grandmother (also Jahida Ahluwalia) but she went by Jude. Her parents were both second-generation Torontonians, but from different ethnic communities: her father grew up in Scarborough in a Punjabi-Scottish-Canadian family, and her mother in Don Mills, in a German-Norwegian-Canadian family. Tired of the city, they moved to Stenson after their appliance repair shop in downtown Toronto burned to the ground (a spectacular fire that made the front page of the *Globe and Mail*) and took ownership of the old Chavez home the January two-and-a-half years after Mr. Chavez's disappearance. Jude graduated from Dalhousie University and joined her parents in Stenson in 1947. Esau married

Jude approximately three years later, in 1950. That is all I know of Esau's courtship.

As for Jude herself, the Stenson Ladies' Circle learned she was schooled in History and set a series of events in motion. In 1948, at each monthly Ladies' Circle meeting, Jude gave a short summary about an Ontario woman of history, beginning with Laura Secord. These summaries were so well received that the following year, in 1949, she presented a series of Autumn Sunday Afternoon Lectures, open to the public, called "Suffrage Struggles in Other Lands." They took place in family parlours around town and a bonnet, passed after each lecture, collected proceeds for an organization providing assistance to unwed mothers.

A week after the final lecture, Dr. King, in the first recorded indication of tensions with Jude, wrote this in his weekly *Trombone* "Health in the Home" column: *"Readers ought not be concerned by the rising tide of brutish women bawling and brawling for rights, for the biological inferiority of the prettier, weaker sex always shows itself eventually and guarantees women's eternal dependence on the half of the population to whom leadership comes naturally."*

In the months that followed, Jude cross-stitched the entire passage onto a full yard of evenweave and mounted the sampler in an ornate gilded frame that further exaggerated the size of it. Esau and Jude were married around that time, in spring 1950, and shortly thereafter moved into one of the tiny three-room bungalows built after the war on Arnhem Road.

Jude hung the sampler over the loveseat in the living room, where it dominated the wee house, and invited the neighbourhood to a housewarming party.

"Esau, what are you doing?"

Jude walked lopsided into the living room, leaning back under the weight of the cutlery drawer in her arms. She set it at the edge of the sideboard and began laying cutlery out for the party.

"Oh. I thought maybe I'd hang our wedding photo here," Esau said. "We paid for it, it'd be nice to show it off."

Esau had the enormous sampler already off the wall. It lay on the loveseat.

"Sure. You could set it on the little shelf there and leave the sampler on the wall."

"I could . . . You look stunning, by the way." A compliment to distract her from the sampler.

To no avail: "Thank you. Darling, are you uncomfortable having the sampler on the wall for the party?"

"I-it's big, don't you think? It fairly overtakes the room. We could move it to the bedroom."

Esau held the much smaller wedding photo over the nail in the wall.

"It *is* big, you're right. Had the comment been more concise, the sampler would be smaller."

"Right." He laughed quietly and lay the wedding photograph down. "Jude, I applaud your audacity. I wish I had more myself. But you invited the whole neighbourhood! What if the doctor shows?"

"What could be *less* audacious than a feminine, cross-stitched sampler that takes the doctor's advice to heart?" She set aside the spoon she was polishing, lay a hand on her heart, and curtsied. He smiled unsteadily and slumped.

Then he straightened: "Seriously Jude. Don't you think it's best not to provoke?"

"Nnn — Maybe. Listen, I'll take care of it. If anyone says anything about the sampler, send them to me."

Esau sighed and rehung the huge thing as the doorbell rang. Minutes later the house was full.

Shoulder to shoulder, through the three rooms, guests milled, eyes flitting to the sampler, then to Jude, then back to their plates of stuffed eggs, melba toast with crab-cucumber salad, broiled grapefruit eighths, and warm ginger snaps. Jude swung this way and that, filling plates and punch glasses, always smiling. She wasn't stunning, though he often said she was. Certainly she was attractive enough — her dark curls combed back off her face and resting on her shoulders, the full skirt and fitted jacket with cinched waist that were (she said) the latest fashion, her shapely hands and ankles — but others in the room were more handsome still. Jude had a steady forward motion about her, though, that drew people and they jostled now to get near her. As if she knew who she was, as if she had inside herself none of the fearful search for judgment that Esau seemed unable to shake off.

To Esau's great relief, Dr. King did not show. However, after an hour or two, old Mrs. Klippenstein from Normandy Street approached him.

"Have you noticed, Mr. Blessure, that all eyes here dart to that remarkable bit of cross-stitch on your wall, attributed to our good doctor I see, but no one seems to be discussing it?"

"I expect the party lines will buzz tonight," he smiled. "Jude says I'm to direct any questions about it to her."

"I have no questions." The old lady laughed. "I think it's marvellous. Stenson has so much *affect* these days; some impertinence does us good. I'm going to refill my punch glass and admire it once more. Doctor's orders." She winked and set out through the elbows.

"How's married life?" A low voice in his ear. It could only be Michael Vinterburg.

Esau stiffened. He hadn't seen Michael since they were mustered out of the military and went their separate ways. Would he be sore? But Michael grinned and lifted his glass. An elbow knocked them both and punch splashed from Michael's glass onto Esau's shirt. Then they were laughing and sopping up the fluid with napkins.

"My father says to tell you these houses are shit. The wood wasn't properly dried and they'll warp and look shabby inside a year. Sell, he says, as soon as you can."

"Thanks for the advice, I think."

The conversation was effortless. No, caring for Gabriel wasn't always easy, but they had a routine and it left Michael time to write. He was working on a piece about poker tournaments aboard transport ships, did Esau remember them? Yes of course Esau still thought of higher education but now he had a mortgage to pay — and Jude wanted children. He was considering private research to keep the mind active, but had nothing firm yet.

(There, on Michael's hand around the glass, the curved scar from when they'd cleaned up a bombed airfield outside Toulouse and a scrap of fuselage had sliced through his glove. Esau had bandaged it.)

Michael asked about the strange embroidery on the wall and Esau told the story. Michael shook his head and smiled. He and Jude were alike, Esau could see it now, each their own Lydian stone.

"She met me at the door," Michael said, looking into his glass. "She's lovely. How did you meet her again?"

"My father introduced us."

"This was before or after you told him you were moving to Tilsonburg with me?" Quietly spoken, without resentment.

"I said you needed help looking after Gabe. He said" (and here Esau mimicked his father) "Son, camaraderie is important. It gets men through awful times like war. Wouldn't you like a *family* now that the war is done?"

Esau meant it as a joke but Michael met his eyes, not laughing.

"Evidently you agreed."

"No — You don't understand what it's like, Michael."

"I guess I don't. Anyway, she's lovely, Esau. And smart."

"Yep," Esau said. "She's someone I can feel safe with."

He'd intended no slight, but Michael looked down, then away, and then excused himself. He and Gabe had come to Stenson to visit their parents, and he ought to spend some time with them.

Esau would have hung his head and looked at his shoes, but it was so crowded he couldn't see them.

Much later that night, still uneasy from his conversation with Michael, Esau opened a drawer in the empty kitchen and pulled out an envelope that had lain unopened on the counter for three days — the response to his latest attempt at private research. It was stained with onion juice and hamburger blood. He fished a knife out from among the party dishes drying upside-down on tea towels and slipped it into the crease at the end.

"Dear Mr. Blessure," the letter read, "We are pleased to inform—" His paper on the surprisingly low pressures under which some rocks can metamorphose into entirely different rocks suited their journal and readership, the letter said. His research was sound, the paper well penned. If Esau agreed, they planned to publish it in their upcoming volume. Incidentally, professional geological journals such as this one preferred to print work by credentialed writers. The editors were wondering — had he considered a formal education?

The tension disappeared from Esau's face. A publication, this small thing, so satisfying. He never would have picked this Stenson life, but it was a rich life still.

He walked to the desk against the kitchen wall and pried a copper tack off the corkboard above it. He pinned the notice under the tack, beside the stack of rejections that had come before, and that curled around their own tack, foxed and growing brittle with age. He blew off the dust, tidied the stack, and made a note to write Michael and apologize for his insensitivity and to tell him the good news. It was time for bed. Jude had pulled the light chain an hour ago.

Jude's Sunday lecture series the following year, 1951, was called "Influential Women of War" and took place in the Town Hall. Dr. King provided no commentary.

(Evidently, however, the strain between the doctor and Jude didn't lessen. Twelve years later, in May 1963, when Jude already had four children, the doctor slipped a comment into his health column, that week on the topic of preventing food poisoning, about "the appalling dangers of *women motorcyclists* on Stenson roads made all the more treacherous by the addition of *children* straddling the seat in front!" And there was a photograph of Jude astride her grandfather's old Yamaha with Verity on the seat in front of her. They both leaned forward in the picture, mother and child, grinning widely, hair flapping in the wind from beneath their helmets.)

Writer's Note: I (Athena) made the trip to Ontario to interview Jacqueline Berlingue last summer. Imran, my Independent Assisted Living worker and friend, came with me. I can book an IAL worker for trips if I fill out enough forms in advance. Jacqueline lives in Toronto now, just north of Bloor Street. I wanted to meet in a café but she would have none of it. "In my flat," she said, "I'll make tea."

Her flat is the main floor of her Edwardian house — she bounds around it with energy to spare and a tea towel around her waist for an apron. Imran and I arrived mid-morning. The kitchen was sunny and the teapot steaming. (Hot tea still feels luxurious to me. In the Facility, when I was still Verity, our drinks were never more than lukewarm for fear we might burn ourselves.) We stayed for lunch and talked through the afternoon. We left at 4:30 PM and every day that week we did it all again.

On the flight back, Imran said he had never interpreted so much in one week before. "It is good for you," I said. "Signing burns calories." He laughed and said it was inappropriate to comment on someone's weight, you know. Imran is tall and slender, but recently he pointed out to me a new, thin pad of softness at his belt and said he wished it were not there.

I showed Jacqueline the doctor's columns.

"Well, this was after the war," she said. "It was an awkward time for everyone."

She closed her eyes in a long blink and explained. Small towns had been trying to find comfortable ways again, making place for wounded men and war brides, jostling the workforce to re-slot veterans into posts held for years by women. Women who had run everything without men, who surprised themselves with their reluctance to return to old ways. Jacqueline's mother had expected once again to be a housewife; she had looked forward to fewer responsibilities. But when the moment came, she could not do it. Her parents learned to manage the farm together, neither one boss of the other.

"My father," she said, "saw no sense in working above or against her, but it took time for both of them to get used to having a partner. Other husbands tried to re-take their former authority by force — even if they were too wounded to work — as if they were still fighting a war. The women whose husbands had died at war were the lucky ones. It was not an easy time," she said, "not for many years. In Dr. King's mind, I expect, going back to the way things were was about restoring order."

Familiarity as antidote to loss.

She told me then about Jude's huge sampler. (And looked at me expectantly. I believe she meant for me to ask after Jude and the other children, an expectation I did not fulfill.)

Back to Esau now, thirteen years after that party. He has published six more articles, and he does much of the surveying work for the Stenson quarry but, without formal education, his position is still that of Assistant to the Surveyor. Jude writes History textbooks for a Toronto publisher of educational materials. He and Jude have moved into a larger house on Normandy Street and have four children: Edward nine, Samantha eight, Alexander six, and Verity four.

APRIL 1963
STENSON

Mrs. Klippenstein, the neighbour across the road, opened the door wide for Esau, who paused to straighten the mud scraper on her porch, then shuffled in wearing Jude's slippers. They were soaked in dew. Jude's leopard-print housecoat was tied over his pajamas, the top of which he had not bothered to button.

The wind chimes tinkled above the door, a gust of chill night air, when the old lady closed it. The clock chimed 3:00 AM.

"She rang the bell — in her thin nightie and bare feet — and asked for cocoa! I gave her a quick bath to warm her up and telephoned you. No no, don't be sorry. I haven't had such fun since Ralston was here."

Ralston, her son and only family, was killed at Dieppe twenty-one years earlier. She had lived alone since. A satisfied grin intersected her wrinkles.

"I already installed a heavier gate latch to keep her from running into the street," Esau said. "Evidently it's not enough."

Mrs. Klippenstein waved Esau through the vestibule and living room into the kitchen. Four-year-old Verity had already placed a cushion on a chair and climbed up to the table. She waved to her father coming into the room. The old lady chortled at the sight of her. Using a spoon to hold back foam, she poured hot milk into mugs. Then she flicked off the light, pulled a kitchen drawer, and drew out a packet. She unfolded the parchment. The moonbeam settled on long, thin, wine-dipped cigarillos. The old lady grinned conspiratorially and struck a match to the candle on the table. She lit a cigarillo from the candle and passed it across the table to Esau.

Esau's mouth puckered briefly, no he shouldn't, and then his fingers reached of their own accord. Mrs. Klippenstein fetched a china plate for an ashtray and reached again into the drawer for a fat half-smoked stogie for herself.

"They're never as good the second day," she said, but immersed it nevertheless in the flame and puffed until a perfect circle of orange sat three inches from her mouth.

"I haven't smoked anything since the war," Esau said. "I hope she doesn't remember this," and they both looked at Verity. The candle flame swayed in her eyes. Esau closed his eyes and pulled air through the cigarillo reverently. His face slid into an expression of relief and a small cloud rolled over his lower lip.

Mrs. Klippenstein watched him and smiled.

"It's a terrible habit," she said. "I quit for years. Then, when Ralston was fifteen, I caught him smoking on the porch in the middle of the night. I wanted to thrash him, big boy that he was. But he had this expression, like a kid stealing candy, and he said, 'Aw Mum. Midnight sins don't count.'"

She tapped off the ash.

"It was from a children's book, *The Clock Strikes Twelve.* Stories of magic at midnight, laws of physics rendered impotent. I reached out to slap him then — and he stood, a foot taller than me, and slid his arm around me as if he were my sweetheart. He slipped the cigarette from his mouth into mine so smoothly I hardly noticed and, with one hand, wedged another between his own lips and lit it, arm still around me like a lover's. Cheeky thing."

She shook her head.

"I hadn't smoked since before he was born — but there was a lit cigarette in my mouth. It was so *quenching!* I did slap him then, after finishing that cigarette and another two. We smoked together in the middle of the night every few days after that. First cigarettes, and then cigars and pipes and other things. The midnight smokes, we said, never counted."

She sipped her cocoa.

"I miss that, you know. Something illicit, however inconsequential, after the town is asleep. Your girl, wanting cocoa at 3:00 AM, she has the right idea."

Esau eased out another puff. Verity fought to stay awake, tried to catch the curlicues unwinding through the room. When her head sank to the table, Esau balanced his cigarillo on the plate's edge, carried her to the chesterfield, and tucked an afghan around her. He returned, picked it up again. When he sat, the housecoat fell open and ash floated gently down and landed on his chest hair.

Esau and Mrs. Klippenstein finished the cocoa and cigars and then a pot of tea, until the candle snuffed out and the kitchen window turned golden. Before Esau left for breakfast, toddler asleep in his arms, Mrs. Klippenstein promised to keep an eye out for young Verity Blessure from across the street who was always going somewhere.

ATHENA'S JOURNAL
NOVEMBER 19, 2003
(WEDNESDAY)

My therapist asks to see the 1963 clipping of Jude and Verity astride the motorcycle that so agitated the doctor.

"Look at that bike," he says when I show him. "It *is* a Yamaha. From the twenties, I'd say. What a beaut! And this is Jude. She looks unstoppable. Thank you for showing me."

He passes the photo to the interpreter who glances at it politely and hands it back to me.

"Athena," the therapist continues, "I wonder if here the doctor doesn't make a valid point. Verity can't be more than three or four, much too young to ride a motorcycle safely. The helmet doesn't fit her at all."

"She was not hurt," I say.

"I suppose she was something of an adventurer too —" he looks directly at me "— such a young child leaving the safety of her bed at night. Esau must have worried terribly when he picked her up from the neighbour's house that night."

"Probably," I say, though I haven't considered it before. In fact, I am not certain if it was Esau, Jude, or someone else altogether who picked Verity up that night, though I recall that someone wore leopard-print and sat and smoked with the old woman. (What happened to her, I wonder.)

The room is quiet as the therapist skims his earlier notes. When he speaks, his expression is gentle, but his thumb and forefinger come together in a way that suggests focus and urgency.

"I can't help but notice," he says, "that Esau once again is prevented from his preferred life, a life with Michael, by external forces. This time, the father. Did Jacqueline advise this interpretation?"

"She thought the father's disapproval might have been a factor."

"Did she mention other factors?"

He is fishing for something again, though I cannot see what.

"She thought Esau felt it vital to be seen as one kind of person and not as another. By comparison, Michael, she thought, had craved approval in his youth, but after his brother's injury seemed no longer to care about it."

"Aha!" he says, pausing as if to say something then changing his mind. "Did Jacqueline have other insights?"

"She sent me to meet a man named Andrzej who had been an adult in Stenson when Esau was young."

"And Andrzej, did he see Esau as" — he sees the challenge in my eyes and selects words carefully — "as someone from whom choices were removed?"

"He told stories about people in small towns who are always being watched."

"Interesting. Certainly you know something about being watched."

"Yes. People who are watched must modify their behaviour in ways that consume a great deal of energy," I sign. "It makes one feel rather desperate."

I stare at him pointedly. What are these meetings for if not for him to watch me? But he seems not to catch my implication. I continue.

"Andrzej spoke of going to extraordinary lengths to live a double life under the scrutiny. Gabriel, Michael's twin, he thought had permanently injured himself."

The therapist listens thoughtfully as the interpreter signs this. His hands have relaxed.

"Well. A quest for approval and an atmosphere of being monitored certainly complicate things. Do you think they shed light on the Elora document as well?"

Again, with the Elora document! Truly it is breathtaking the variety of ways he finds to peck at what Esau signed at Elora Home for the Feeble-Minded.

I want to say Look, no father would abandon his child without considerable external pressure and *of course* I want to determine what those pressures were. But he would only rattle off a list of historical fathers who did exactly that and ask why I believe such things about fathers. The thought of that conversation exhausts me.

"I do not know," I say instead. "I will think on it."

ATHENA'S JOURNAL
DECEMBER 08, 2003
(MONDAY)

Today, months before I expected, a letter arrives from the Department of Support Services of the Province of Alberta. The letter is typed on generic Department letterhead.

Two processes were set in motion when I applied for custody of Arvo, it says. First, the process of considering custody reassignment. Persons are assigned to the Public Guardian only after an extensive search finds no family unit or private guardian available. The Province has no precedent for a developmentally disabled person under the Public Guardian being adopted into a family unit. After decades of activism, developmentally disabled people still move from family units to institutions or Group Homes, never the reverse. Because this request is so unusual, the letter says, I should expect the process to take longer than other custody processes. No doubt they will invent some forms for me to fill out.

And the second process. I must prove that I can make a family unit successfully, and that I am capable of caring for Arvo. This will not be the usual assessment done in custody cases: I discover, this morning when Imran makes a telephone call on my behalf, that I am still under the Public Guardian myself! Because of my history and because I receive subsistence from the government, I am not considered independent. My ability to care for someone, especially someone with "special needs," is being questioned. My competence will be evaluated and presented to a panel in a hearing. This panel will determine our fate.

I walk over to the XXX store to show the letter to my friend and neighbour, Mr. Saarsgard. He reads it carefully and thinks I must be "outraged" and wants to know do I feel like "fighting back or giving up?"

"You do not understand," I write on the pad. "What I want is to live with Arvo. There can be no talk of giving up nor of fighting back, certainly not of outrage. These are luxuries for those not under observation."

Scarlet Fever is a type of strep infection. The name comes from the scarlet rash that later peels off the face and torso. Under the most favourable conditions, the fever, which can be shockingly high, runs its course in about a week and the infected are none the worse for it. More often, recovery takes weeks, sometimes months. People can regain their health but lose their sight or hearing or have permanent throat damage. Sometimes it evolves into Rheumatic Fever which can damage the joints, heart, or brain. Scarlet Fever has its own glamour, its own canon. The boy in *The Velveteen Rabbit* lost his playthings because of it. Mary, in *By the Shores of Silver Lake,* was blinded by it, Beth in *Little Women* and Victor Frankenstein's mother both died of it. And Mozart, whose resistance to authority was as legendary as his music, could not resist Rheumatic Fever and finally succumbed, they say.

When Scarlet Fever came to the Blessures, Aunt Mattie was looking after the kids because Jude, their pregnant mother, was in hospital with toxemia. Esau leaned against the doorjamb of the kitchen watching Mattie fix lunch at the counter.

She was on her feet that day. She laid out and buttered bread. Judiciously curling her fingers away from the blade, she sliced cheese, three kinds, then onions, then basil, and finally, tiny garlic cloves. She scraped the garlic shavings into a buttered pan, raised the flame — the smell overtook the room — and slowly layered the other ingredients on the bread slices. Using the flat of the knife, she lowered each sandwich into the spattering pan. Esau's jaw still clenched when she worked with blade or flame — what if she fell? But she hadn't had a seizure in ten years. Phenobarb, mephobarb, and more recently diazepam had changed her life. They had also exacted a toll. Her curved posture over the pan, her cautious gestures, the grey pallor to her skin, the strange jerky movements of her eyes, especially now, when she was tired.

"Ethau, can you phone Mom, and call everyone to the table?"

Esau stepped backwards to the hall telephone and dutifully called his mother, now a widow for six years.

"Oh I'm fine," she said, as he knew she would, "Apart from missing Mattie, of course."

From the hallway, he could look into the spare room where Mattie slept. The bed was mussed from her morning nap and her wheelchair sat empty beside it. Her balance would be shaky by dinnertime, though, and she'd probably be in the chair by evening. Years ago Esau had widened the spare room door and lowered the closet bar. She visited them often and he wanted everything within reach from her chair on any days it was necessary. The books on the night table were the same books Mattie had brought last time, and the time before that. She read when her eyes allowed, but she had difficulty retaining new information — and knew it. That made it worse.

He summoned the kids to lunch. They took their places lethargically.

Mattie doled out hot sandwiches, listened, asked the right questions, teased them a bit. Above all, Esau missed her constant chatter. Phenobarbital had stopped it almost overnight. She was still the most reliable person he knew. She never missed a family birthday, her fried cheese sandwiches tasted superb (and provoked heartburn) as they had a hundred times before —

"Wh —?"

"You're thtaring at me," Mattie said. "Look at your children."

"Uh —"

His attention shifted. His four children had lifted their shirts and stuck their tongues out at him.

"They're hardly eating and they're all thpotted! I'm getting the thermometer."

They *were* spotted and their tongues, now bright and knobby, might have been ripe strawberries. He laid a hand on Verity's forehead. Much too warm. Soon the thermometer removed all doubt.

Esau stepped back into the hallway once more, this time taut with concern. He telephoned the doctor, then carried his children one by one upstairs to their bedrooms, sandwiches abandoned without protest.

By evening, their lives had changed. The children were ill. Esau and Mattie were forbidden to leave the house, even for work or to visit Jude or their elderly mother. And on the front door the doctor had secured a heavy sign with thick black lettering: "QUARANTINE: Scarlet Fever: Keep Out of This House."

The first weeks were the worst.

Esau and Mattie worked in shifts so that each might seize a few hours' sleep. They applied compresses and spooned fluids into unyielding mouths, they wiped up the mess when someone didn't reach the toilet and later returned to scrape hardened particulates off walls, they laundered fetid bedding and pajamas, and they fought back alarm at crusted skin and walnut-sized throat glands. Soon Esau couldn't bear to watch the mercury stretch up the thermometer and Mattie took over measuring temperatures. Then the hallucinations began, and the night lamp in the hallway outside the kids' bedrooms lengthened shadows into fever-dream ghouls, and Esau knew nevertheless the fevers were dangerously high.

He was no good in a crisis. Jude was the one to look after the kids. What if he did something wrong? What if the children didn't pull through? How much more could Mattie take?

Twice a week, someone at the hospital wheeled Jude to a telephone, and Esau could talk with her. He craved her assurances, but on the phone he kept his voice even, downplayed the kids' symptoms and Mattie's pallor, wanting not to worry Jude for she was as sick as they. He knew from the *Trombone*'s incomprehensibly long obituary section that others had it much worse.

In rare free moments, Esau looked out the front window. The world moved on without him, without his kids. What he would have given for a quick conversation with the grocer's deliveryman or the paperboy. On muggy evenings, when torpor descended with sundown, Esau drew himself a cool bath and curled up sideways in the tub, reciting ordered rock taxonomies or longing for Jude or thinking back on a cubbyhole of shrubs.

One night, the mugginess relented, and Esau sat at his desk working on his next article: could it be that, of two pieces of sandstone with the same physical composition, apparently subjected to the same pressures, one would metamorphose, the other would not? A few nights later, he did it again. Those evenings sat upon the others like a life preserver on water: he was a published research geologist, strata and history awaited him.

And then a weak voice would cry out, startling him back to the present and he rose from his desk to tend to the needs of a child.

The Stenson epidemic lasted five weeks. In the third, the Blessure fevers lessened. Verity developed Rheumatic Fever, prolonging her illness, but the older kids were better able to care for themselves. Another week and Verity was recovering too.

Soon they would be free.

By the time Dr. King came to the house for final checkups, he looked grey and pinched from short nights and difficult days, and he had picked up a summer cold.

"The worst is past, I think," he said and sneezed into his sleeve. "Excuse me. The Cardinal boy is blind, the Njo girl is deaf" — Esau took his hat — "six children on this street alone have heart murmurs or lung damage, several have brain damage, and" — he shook his head — "so many deaths." They headed for the kitchen. "The Flores family on Kursk Street lost three children this week. And I can't lift quarantine for a proper funeral. Their youngest is still sick."

"We're all alive here," Esau said. He pulled out a chair for the doctor.

Mattie put on a pot of coffee, and set water to boil to sterilize the doctor's instruments. She offered him a fresh handkerchief and the three of them sat at the table. They sipped coffee and watched while the children, all four of them, played in the sunny backyard. They lacked their usual energy, played listlessly. Sometimes they lay back on the warm grass and watched the clouds.

"They mith their mother," Mattie said.

"A slow recovery is normal for this disease," the doctor said. "After the sick children I've seen, I think yours look wonderful. Is Verity having trouble breathing?"

"No sign of that," Esau said. The Rheumatic Fever had left her quiet, they'd noticed, but her breathing was fine.

When the instruments were sufficiently boiled, Mattie put away the coffee and the doctor moved to the dining room and laid them across the end of the oak table where Jude usually worked. At the other end, he spread brightly coloured toys, a sock monkey, and noisemakers he had stuffed into a second medicine bag. Then he called for his first patient.

Nine-year-old Edward came indoors and warily approached

the doctor. Mattie brought a bowl of apricots to the kitchen table to pit and slice for pie. Esau stepped into his office, from which he could see both Mattie and the doctor, to do paperwork.

The doctor spent a half hour with Eddie. He shone a light into his mouth and ears and probed under his arms. He swabbed his throat. He had the boy jump several times and then listened to his lungs. He examined skin inch by inch. He showed him toys and fabrics and asked questions about colour. He covered his eyes and made noises and asked what he heard. He handed him a wooden puzzle and watched him logic it through. Then he drank a glass of water, gave Eddie a lollipop, sent him out to play, and smiled across the room at Esau.

"Edward is perfectly well," he announced, and wiped again his raw, oozing nose.

The doctor put the next two children through the same routine. Both were healthy, if still sluggish, and with each pronouncement of recovery, the doctor looked more refreshed, and Esau nodded. It would be okay.

With Verity, he took twice as long as he had with the others. In his office, Esau looked at his papers but listened only to the doctor gently asking questions and running tests again and again. After forty-five minutes, Mattie rolled in with another glass of water. The doctor accepted it gratefully and turned his attention back to the girl who giggled every time the cold stethoscope touched her chest.

Mattie returned to the kitchen. From his desk Esau saw she had given up on pie and sat looking out the window, straining to hear what was happening in the dining room. He abandoned his paperwork and his view of the doctor, and pulled up a chair in the kitchen. She brewed more coffee and they drank without speaking, listening to the doctor's quiet voice and to the relentless ticks of the clock on the wall.

Finally, Dr. King gave Verity a lollipop and sent her outside. He walked heavily into the kitchen and asked for another glass of water, which he gulped in two huge swallows.

Esau and Mattie waited.

"Physically, she's healthy." He sank into a chair. "No sign that her heart or lungs are worse for wear. She's certainly not blind. No throat problems of any kind."

Esau and Mattie waited.

"But — the fever has destroyed her hearing and left her with some brain damage. The way these things go, we'll have to watch for epilepsy. She might yet recover. If not, if there's no change in a month — well, there's an institution in Elora you could consider. It has a children's ward." He pushed out these last sentences quickly, getting them over with, and wiped his brow with the already-wet hanky. He looked haggard again, old.

First Mattie then Esau sat back in their chairs. Outside the children continued to play.

Esau said nothing. His arms flopped down at his sides.

Mattie was first to speak: "She lookth fine to me. Why do you thay brain damage?"

"She didn't respond to a single prompt. Each time I asked her to lift her arms or stick out her tongue, she looked confused. She didn't respond to mental stimulants the way a four-year-old ought. Not to puzzles, not to pictures nor games nor toys nor sounds." One meaty finger unfurled with each item.

Mattie was right of course, Verity was fine — but what fat fingers the doctor had, Esau hadn't noticed them before. Sausages.

"She didn't take the sock monkey when I presented it to her, let alone hug it to herself the way normal children do. Every time I offered it to her — I tried several times — she pushed it away. She plainly didn't know what it was. Excuse me —" The doctor blew his nose.

Of course he had misdiagnosed. The poor man was exhausted, anyone could see. An honest mistake.

"She has excellent coordination and reflexes," he continued, "and is as mischievous as ever, I'll grant you, but the brain is damaged. If it recovers in a few weeks, wonderful! If not, this, what we see today, is how far she'll develop mentally. Her reflexes and coordination will probably regress. She won't be fit for school at six years. She'll not learn nor judge properly. She might be a danger to herself and to the baby that's coming. Mark my words, things will go badly with a retarded child in a crowded house. I've seen it before."

Mattie pushed her chair back from the table. "Doctor, thank you for coming. I'm going to my room now. Good day."

She rolled away.

Esau watched her go. Of course Mattie was insulted. The doctor needn't be such a brunt. Even for a tired man, it was uncalled for.

"Do you have questions, Esau?" Mattie's door clicked shut. "Esau?"

The doctor expected an answer. Jude would clear this up later, of course, but Esau had to look after things for now.

"I—I mean no disrespect, Doctor," he tried, "but your uh diagnosis seems uhh extreme. You're not well yourself today."

The doctor didn't seem surprised by the implication.

"Esau, I've been a doctor for a long time. I was there when you were born. This is not an easy thing to diagnose, and, as I say, in a month she might yet recover." He reached a comforting hand across the table toward Esau, whose arms still hung uselessly. "But I'm not optimistic. Let's hope for the best and prepare for the worst."

"I'll discuss it with Jude. But she'll nn-never agree to Elora."

"Well." The doctor leaned back in the chair. "It's not my

business. Your wife is very sick, however, and she might get worse. If Verity doesn't recover, I recommend you take care of it without telling her, without adding to her strain — and before she returns."

"I — don't understand."

The doctor stood and stepped into the dining room to collect his things. Cupboards obscured his head but his voice carried across the countertop that divided the two rooms.

"Esau, Mrs. Blessure is an intelligent woman, but she doesn't know her limits. She'll have a new baby after a toxemic pregnancy. She'll be in no shape to care for an infant and Verity, who's as good as an infant now herself."

"We'll hire help. Jude is her mother." Esau couldn't raise his voice and had to say it twice.

"Yes, well. Childbirth — affects women's minds. The hormones."

"There's never been a problem."

"I understand. But with a woman like Mrs. Blessure, it's — Esau, it's probably just a matter of time until her nervous collapse. You can take a lamb out of the barn and dress it like a wolf but it will not long survive in the wild."

He fastened the clasps on his bags and walked back to the kitchen.

"Sometimes, Esau, making decisions alone is the kindest thing a husband can do. If you should take care of it before she returns, Mrs. Blessure will be so rapt and busy with the infant, she'll hardly notice Verity's absence. She'll be grateful, I warrant, that you never troubled her with it. You have, what, two months yet if she carries full term?"

An old familiar tension at the back of Esau's head, wheeling, forcing air from his lungs.

"I don't think I can do that," Esau whispered.

The doctor sneezed — that poor, soaked hanky — and approached Esau again, lowering his voice.

"I've already said too much. But please, think back on your life, Esau. Perhaps to a night the walls were covered in writing. Sacrifices must always be made for children like this. I'll see you in a month. Six weeks, if you prefer."

He walked to the entrance, donned his hat.

"I'll alert the people in Elora in case Verity doesn't recover. I have one more household to examine now and then my day is done. I'm lifting quarantine. You can visit Mrs. Blessure again. My best wishes to her when you see her."

He opened the door, ripped the quarantine sign off, stuffed it in the porch trashcan, and stepped resolutely down the street, on to the next house, oblivious to what he had just done.

The vile sock monkey, reeking of stale saliva from dozens of children that he with his summer cold could not smell, hung from his bag and bobbed as he walked.

Esau still sat at the table. After some time, he wrapped his arms around his stomach and began almost imperceptibly to rock.

It had been a long and difficult month. That evening, Mattie, who had been well for years, went to bed early complaining of feeling poorly. Esau was upstairs tucking in the kids when Mattie's bed began banging violently against the wall.

He knew immediately what was happening. He ran down the stairs, three at a time, and threw open her door. She continued to spasm in her bed as he loosened the top button of her nightgown and checked to make sure she wasn't choking.

When it finally passed, he took the glass of water from the night stand and raised it to her mouth. Then he wiped her face with a cool cloth. She had dirtied herself during the seizure and began crying when the humiliation of it dawned on her.

"I thought they were done," she said, choking a bit, not yet breathing easily.

"Shhh. Take a bath and then you can sleep. Tomorrow, we'll call the doctor."

After a few minutes, Esau helped her to her feet and into her bathroom, where he turned on the taps to fill the tub.

"I'll change the sheets and wait in the bedroom," he said, "in case something else happens."

As he turned to leave the bathroom, he saw his four children, backs to the wall, silent tears coursing down their faces in fear of things they couldn't comprehend. They had seen it all.

That night, Esau stayed up all night long, sitting at the kitchen table, listening, thinking, making lists, and drinking tea from a Meissen china teacup.

"Mattie, it's time to go."

The door opened slowly. Mattie sat in her wheelchair wearing a loose, beige dress and her most comfortable shoes. Her suitcase was packed and beside her on the bed. She looked grey, depleted, like a wet cardboard box.

"I don't want to go."

Esau closed the door behind him, keeping the kids out.

"I know. It's a few days."

"I'll thtay. You need help."

"We'll manage."

Mattie looked down at her ankles. She had rolled her stockings down to the feet so they wouldn't press the fresh bruises where her shins had hammered the bedpost during the seizure.

"You have to check on Mom. Today. I worry about her," she said.

"I'll take you to the hospital and drive right over."

"Call her now. Tell her you're coming."

He went to the hallway, placed the call, returned, picked up Mattie's suitcase.

"What if I never leave the hothpital?"

He set the suitcase down again.

"Mattie, they're just going to watch you. Maybe tweak your drugs."

"You're too confident, Ethau. They hardly underthtand epilepthy at all."

He sighed and drew up the desk stool and settled beside her, arm across the back of her chair. Her head fell silently onto his shoulder. He comforted her now, but she was right. All that she had done. Well, perhaps their mother could help out.

After nearly a quarter of an hour, Mattie nodded.

Esau stood, set her suitcase in her lap, and wheeled her out of the room. The four kids had lined up in the hallway, backs to the wall, waving silently at Mattie as Esau wheeled her by. She waved back, feet pedalling the ground, until Esau turned the chair around so he could wheel it gently backwards down the front steps.

Esau knocked on the front door of his mother's house. The paint on the doorjamb was peeling. An eavestrough had lost its mooring. Some of the planks were loose on the steps and bobbed under his weight. More things to do. They'd wait. Now he would check on his mother quickly, update her on Mattie, ask her to look after the kids next week, and hurry home.

He could see her through the lace curtain, sitting in the old tall-backed chair, eyeing him, not answering the door. He rapped again. After a worryingly long time, she opened the door.

"Oh, it's you. Come in."

"Are you okay Mom?"

"Fine, dear. Just cautious about that door. I was looking at you standing there and deciding whether to answer. I'll put on the kettle. You should telephone before you come. So I know to expect you."

"I did tele—"

There was a smell. He sniffed discreetly and swept his eyes around the kitchen — and laid them on the sink.

It was spilling dishes and filth he wanted not to identify. Flies buzzed above the stack. His mother shifted a plate to slip the kettle under the faucet and knocked a tumbler loose. It fell to the floor and shattered. Unconcerned, she bent down, from the hip as if her knees didn't work, picked up the larger shards, and placed them carefully on top of the trash under the sink. The trashcan had long ago overflowed and they slid to the cupboard floor. She left them there and tried to shut the cupboard door. It didn't close, hadn't in a while, and batted her shin. She had a bruise there, as if she had banged it many times. Through the crack, he could see a mouse caught in the trap under the sink. By the looks of things, it had been dead for some time. He had to turn away —

— and laid eyes upon the table. It was covered in tall stacks of paper, a skyline of newspaper high-rises. His mother didn't get a daily paper. This was salvage paper, pulled from nearby trashcans, now growing mould in her kitchen. A paper sack of groceries stood on the table, in a little clearing at one corner.

He fixed on that, the one clean thing, and unpacked it while they waited for the kettle to boil. The sack held three five-pound bags of white sugar. He took them to the dry goods cupboard to put them away. Inside the door was the old newspaper clipping of Esau and his Science Fair project. The cupboard itself was full, top to bottom, of identical bags of sugar, neatly lined up, row upon row upon row. He opened the next cupboard. More rows of sugar. And the next, sugar. All cupboards but the two for dishes and pots, sugar.

"Where would you like me to store this sugar, Mom?" He kept his voice even, unconcerned.

"Just in the cupboard there, dear."

"The cupboard is already full of sugar."

"Take out the bags at this end. The old ones go in the trash."

"But the old sugar is still good."

"Yes dear. It goes in the bin. Someone will pick it up."

He studied his mother. Her clouded eyes didn't meet his the way they once had. For years now, she and Mattie had come over for dinner every Tuesday, Mattie always bringing pie. He hadn't seen her for a few weeks, but by the look of things she had been slipping for some time. Why hadn't Esau noticed? He ought to have noticed. He ought to do something now, his father would have expected it. But do — what?

The unanswered mail rested on the kitchen counter against the old cookie jar. He thumbed through it. Bills, mostly, that Mattie would pay when she returned.

Mattie.

Mattie was why he hadn't noticed. She had been running this house, covering for their mother so proficiently there had been no need for him to be told. To ask her to move into his house and care for his children, a request she would never refuse, was to place his mother in peril. Every day of quarantine Mattie had fretted about their mother but he dismissed her concerns with decades-old examples of their mother's competence, had not thought to ask why her anxiety was so severe. All this time he had depended on Mattie and yet had not really seen her.

His mother carried the teapot to the table, then fetched two cups and saucers from the cupboard. The cup she handed him looked clean, but he couldn't stop himself from taking it to the sink and rinsing it under the tap again. She didn't seem to notice and filled his cup with tea when he returned to the table.

There they sat, at the one empty corner of the old kitchen table, ignoring the squalor and flies, sipping tea in the most cultured of ways, while he gently asked questions and peered into her state of mind.

The old screen door clattered. Jacqueline Berlingue, local Jill-of-all-trades, stumbled in and set a cardboard box on the floor.

"Sorry to be late, Mrs. Blessure. Here's your food for tomorrow. Do you have everything?"

"Oh yes dear, thank you. You're very kind."

Jacqueline looked around the kitchen helplessly. Esau, squinting overtop a newspaper tower with questions on his face, caught her eye.

"Mattie signed your mom onto the Scarlet Fever Assistance List the first day of quarantine," she said. "I've been coming ever since."

She pulled two covered casseroles and a jar of cream from the box and placed them in the refrigerator. She took out the half-empty cream jar, smelled it, and poured its contents down the drain between the haphazard dishes. "The day after tomorrow I'll have time to start cleaning." She opened the dish cupboard and counted enough clean plates for the day's meals.

"I — I had no idea," Esau said. "If I'd known —"

"I'm sorry Mr. Blessure. I'd love to chat but other families are waiting. Would you empty the trash before you go? Your mom should be okay until Mattie gets back."

"Mattie had a seizure —" he said.

But she had already heard. Mattie had telephoned her from the hospital at the first opportunity. Jacqueline murmured a quick goodbye and left. The old screen door clattered in her wake.

That Mattie would set this right soon enough should have comforted Esau — but the wheeling at the back of his head didn't lessen a bit.

The head of Jude's hospital bed was partly raised and she leaned back against it. A manuscript was spread across her blanket. She had been working, though her eyes betrayed the kind of pain she was in that day.

Esau kissed her gently and handed her the quarantine notice pulled from the trashcan. "Perfect!" she laughed, and tucked it into her bag. Then she set aside the papers, moved over heavily, and patted the space beside her.

He probably settled in against her, and slid carefully down the bed where he curled into a fetal position around her pregnant belly, his head on what remained of her lap. Her swollen fingers twined through his curls. The baby kicked against his face.

"It's a relief to see you," he said, squeezing in tighter.

"Tell me," she said. "I'm too tired to talk myself."

"The kids are better. They ask about you every day. Mattie had a seizure but she's doing okay. Mom's house needs repairs."

"What else?"

"Alex has grown an inch. Everyone needs haircuts. Samantha ripped her red skirt. My paper was accepted for publication. Eddie wants a lizard."

Jude laughed. "Who's publishing it? That's thrilling! And we'll have to help more at your mom's," she said. "We can't leave it all to Mattie."

He filled the air with details but said nothing about Verity's diagnosis nor the pressures now upon him. Instead, as Jude leaned back wearily, he snuggled against her belly and drew comfort from her skin. This perfect moment, the warm dark cavern of her lap. He still had Jude. Later she would decide about Verity. She would set it right again.

When he left, he had instructions for roasting a pork rump and making soup from the leftovers, and a bag of gifts for the kids.

A few days later, Esau kept an eye on his stock pot and on the children in the backyard, and he sat at the kitchen table, sketching. Housework garments needed a redesign. Aprons, for example. Practical, necessary, but ruffles and prints had no place on anything worn by a published geologist such as himself, and the fabric wasn't durable. He sketched a new design on a scrap of paper — it resembled a canvas carpenter's apron. He named the sketch "Kitchen Apron Suitable for a Man, by Esau Blessure, July 28, 1963." When he got up to stir the pot, he slid it into one of Jude's cookbooks, where it would be out of the way.

At some point shortly after quarantine's end, there would have been a scene like this one:

Esau parked the car in a clearing, left the kids in the backseat with toys and crayons, and walked in the ruts towards the quarry office, a temporary building half a mile down the road. He had in hand a brown envelope containing notice the contagion had passed and he could be back on site. Not today, he hadn't found anyone to look after the children, but maybe tomorrow.

He kicked up gravel under his feet, bent his knees into the familiar shuddering of the ground as the machines began the day's first rumbles. The fine dust particles that settled on his tongue, he didn't mind them as much as usual. It was a relief to be out of the house and in work clothes, even if it meant being grimy. He whistled a bit and waved back to the kids. Verity had pressed her ear to the window glass.

He paused by the worksite. He could hardly see the huge press that pounded the earth, loosening limestone from its mooring and commencing the great production line. But there was the first boulder of the day shuttling up the conveyor into the vibrating feeder. The side facing him was half dolomite and pinker than the rest of the rock. It would travel through the jaw crusher, drop from the chute a hundred smaller pieces, then through the impact crusher, a thousand further pieces. By the time they had made their way up the last conveyor, through the last vibrating screen, by the time they were tipped (miscellaneous, uniformly greyish) into waiting dump trucks, they had moved just five hundred yards from where they began.

The vertical jaw crusher began without warning to sputter and lurch. The operator quieted it, opened the cab door, and swung down like a dusty gorilla to the engine platform. A dust puff rose from his boots.

All operations halted. Everyone watched.

He opened the engine hatch — it opened too easily, Esau could see — and reached into the compartment with gloved hand. An animal, cat or possum or raccoon, now too mangled to iden-tify, caught up in the belts. He tugged at the sinews and half of it came away. He tossed it to the ground, dozens of feet below. He reached in again, a different angle, and pulled out the last remnants, a tail, a leg, some organs and fur. He motioned to someone on the ground to tell the boss, and gave a thumbs-up to operators on both sides and below. He climbed back into the cab, rasped the crusher into gear, and the great production line began again to produce.

Ah, they were good guys, all of them. Generous, knowledge-able in their own ways, up for a beer and a laugh after work. But there was nothing attractive about them; for all the equipment around them, nothing refined. Just forward-sloping backs, bellies drooping over belts, loose grubby necks and bowed legs, hands more coarse than grindstones. Here was none of the romance of geology, no whiff of eons compressed into stone. This, this was manufacturing, petty vandalism of prehistory, capitalism at its most crass.

But for the debts.

Esau turned toward the office, dusty, set on cinder posts, a concrete block for a step. As he neared, he could hear voices inside, over the noise of the crushers, laughing, whooping. Someone made farting sounds with his armpit. Esau opened the door, trying a smile —

The laughter dwindled, and the men, awkward now in the cramped space, turned and hunched their huge bodies through the narrow door, one at a time. Each one slapped a "welcome back" on his shoulder on their way to the pits.

"Hello Boss," Esau said. "What's the good news?"

"Blessure!" the boss said, drinking loudly from his thermos and thunking it on the desk as if misjudging the distance. "I heard! Didja know yer gonna be the first in the whole company to be published in that swanky journal? Some of the other guys ha' been tryin' fer years."

"Really! Well. I'm pleased." Esau gestured to the door through which the men had gone. "And what of the company? What news here?"

The boss dropped his eyes and lowered his voice.

"We're shuttin' down here. Not enough limestone left to make quarryin' worthwhile an' that kaolin deposit we thought we had," he laughed under his breath, "we never found it. We're movin' north to crush stone for the Trans-Canada highway. Some of these guys are comin' along" — he pointed at the door —"but unfortunately they're bringin' surveyors from the States. I don' think there'll be work for ya, Blessure."

Machinery rumbles filled the silence and the floor underneath them shook. The boss spoke first.

"I suppose ya could try up Kipling way in James Bay. They found enough kaolin there for ceramics through the country. Started weeks ago. They might have a full crew, but it couldn't hurt to try."

Esau had missed his chance. He took a breath.

"I can do labour. Set me at a jackhammer" *(push it away)*.

"Blessure." The boss laughed. "Yer wife's arms're bigger 'n yours. If I putchya at a jackhammer, they'll accuse me o' murder."

"I could do it."

"Esau, I'm sorry. Yeh've been a reliable worker fer a long time, but we bin gettin' along without ya for six weeks and we're shuttin' down fast. If the company needs another surveyor up north, I'll put in a word fer sure. But I won't recommend ya for labour." He looked directly at Esau, frank and kind at once. "The fellas like you. Everyone knows you do fine work, and they'll be proud as all heck when that paper comes out, but they sometimes feel they hafta look out for ya. We can't have that up there. Men lookin' out fer you, not minding their own work in those conditions."

Esau fell silent. He looked down at his dusty work boots, suddenly fond of them. His arms hung at his sides.

One of the pit men knocked, came in, told the boss about the animal, left again. The boss made a note and tacked it overtop the survey, Esau's survey (though the credit went to the Head Surveyor) hanging across the wall behind him.

"Look, Esau, I'm sorry. I didn't wanna tell ya that, ever."

"I didn't know. I thought —"

"Why do ya *want* this? Yer always wipin' yer hands. You'd hate labour."

"You know. Kids, bills."

The boss was quiet for a while, picked up the thermos again.

"What I can give ya is night machine cleaning and maintenance fer the next six months or so, while we wind the place down. Our guy isn't keeping up. That's the second engine this month jammed up by an animal. They're after the warmth. It'll get ya some cash while ya figger things out."

Cleaning and maintenance? Had it come to this?

Esau took the position though it paid less than surveying and offered fewer hours. In six months, something would surely work out. And they still had Jude's pay. At least he wouldn't have to find someone to look after the kids in the daytime.

Since it wouldn't interfere with her other duties, Jacqueline agreed to sleep at his house, in Mattie's room (for a small fee) so the kids might not be alone at night.

SEPTEMBER 1963
STENSON

With that began the weeks of watching.

Verity had stopped speaking altogether. More worrisome yet, she had stopped crying. Tears sometimes coursed down her face over inexorable confusion, but when she hurt herself she didn't bawl in the way of a healthy child. Perhaps this was what the doctor meant by regression, by her being a danger to herself.

Esau began checking her limbs and digits for injury at night before tucking her into bed.

For several weeks after the diagnosis, whenever Esau found a moment, he picked Verity up and set her on his knees, facing him. He spoke slowly, directed her eyes to his lips. Sometimes, he placed her fingers to his lips or throat or jaw so she would feel the vibrations his voice made.

She hugged him and kissed him and smiled wide as she could, but she made no sound. Twice she seemed to catch his intent, opened her mouth, and willed out a tentative, guttural grunt. Both times, she swiftly clamped it shut and that now-familiar glazed look took gruesome pride of place on her face. Esau's stomach lifted when he saw it — but the older kids seemed to have forgotten there had been a time when she had chattered more than any of them.

He came out of the washroom once to find her with head pressed against the refrigerator. Her eyes had a faraway look about them, her mouth was open, her lips lacquered with spit. In the days following, he saw her with the side of her face pressed against nearly everything. The sofa, the hutch, a book, the fence, the grass, her stuffed animals.

Once, he came upon her sitting atop the kitchen stairwell to the basement. She had taken his smallest screwdriver from the toolbox, and had removed the back of the electric kitchen radio. She was studying the wires inside. She was about to lift it to the side of her face when Esau noticed the cord — still plugged in. He lunged, yanked it from the outlet before exposed wires touched her face. Then he crumpled to the kitchen floor, palms suddenly wet. When he opened his eyes, a bewildered wet-lipped Verity stood over him, looking at him more strangely than usual.

Another day that week, this column appeared in the *Trombone:*

On Tuesday evening, at 7:30 PM, a curly-haired four-year-old darling girl named Verity Blessure climbed over the fence of her front yard on Normandy Street, and crossed the street, intent on paying a visit to her kindly elderly neighbour, Mrs. Klippenstein. While crossing the street, she was very nearly killed by a speeding automobile, driven by Mr. Bruce Carmichael of Thorold, Ontario, up in Stenson to visit his sister. Mr. Carmichael claims and neighbours verify that he honked the horn many times but the girl didn't appear to notice and continued on her merry way.

With enough swerving, he was able to steer around the child and stop the vehicle, after first running over the tail of an orange tabby. The tail has been amputated. No children were hurt. Mr. Carmichael has received a speeding ticket. Young Miss Blessure is known on her street for her friendliness and her unannounced neighbourly visits. Neighbours say the little girl's mother is presently in hospital, expecting another child and suffering severe toxemia. "I pity the father," a neighbour said. "He has a lot on his mind." No doubt he looks forward to his wife's return! All's well that ends well.

Esau installed a bolt on the outside of Verity's bedroom door the following day. He didn't want to imprison her, exactly. But he could not be everywhere, and could think of no other way to protect her.

Halfway through the weeks of watching, the doctor telephoned.

"Mr. Blessure, your wife is having a rough day. Her blood pressure is high and her kidneys are having trouble keeping up. Her case is atypical. She might recover completely, but women with early onset toxemia sometimes slip into a coma. I thought you should be aware."

"Thank you for calling," Esau said. His shoulders slumped.

"One more thing —"

"Yes?"

"Have you uh thought further about Elora? The Cilia family took their fever-damaged son to a Home and he's very happy there. Mrs. Cilia is positively relieved that the burden has been lifted from her."

Esau hung up the phone.

He needed air. He would tuck Verity in, leave Eddie in charge for a few hours, and go for a drive.

He pushed open the door to Verity's room — she wasn't in bed. Instead, she squatted beside the bed and viciously beat a stuffed animal against the bedpost, every muscle in her body hard and tense. At her feet lay another stuffed toy, disemboweled. A severed ear clung to the paper scissors on the floor, fluff from the stuffing floated through the air and stuck to her wet face. Even in fury, she was silent.

Esau sighed, walked in, and picked her up. She sank her face into his shoulder, and he sat down on her bed with her in his lap and leaned back against the wall. They sat in this way until the fluff in the air settled and she fell asleep. Then he tucked her in amidst the mess, squeezed into the small children's desk, and watched her sleep. When she slept it seemed as if nothing had changed.

Jude (how could she be so sick?) would look at their daughter and know immediately what to do. Mattie, now at home again with their mother, would insist that Verity was fine and the doctor be kept at bay. Michael, well, Michael had made his choice around Gabriel years ago. But as Esau watched Verity, serene, sleeping like every normal Stenson child, the diagnosis *bothered*, like a hangnail or a painting hung crookedly on a wall. Maybe she was fine. But a child who voices nothing, whose expression is nearly always of confusion, whose mouth is perpetually open, whose lips unfailingly glisten with saliva, who now inexplicably destroys things, well, the diagnosis did make sense of all that.

It became habit then for Esau to contort himself into the tiny desk in the evenings as his smallest daughter fell asleep. And when the thoughts began to overwhelm *seizures, strawberry tongues, lopsided ledgers, cupboards of sugar, epileptic seizures, strawberry* he calmed them as best he could by charting the household budget, or by slipping into his office to work on his research.

OCTOBER 1963
STENSON

The first Saturday in October was a rainy day and the children were playing indoors. Verity was reassembling a toy, Eddie mounted a tricycle too small for his frame, and the other two kids crowded together on the back of it. The trike became a chariot, the kitchen-dining room circle a racetrack, and they cycled around, hollering, racing imagined rivals.

Esau sat in his office fretting about Jude, now nearly inert, unrecognizably swollen, and charted again the household expenses. He didn't see that one of his children had picked up a fireplace poker for a spear. What happened next, he could never be sure.

Unwittingly, Verity moved into the path of the chariot.

The chariot swerved to avoid her and veered into Jude's enormous china cabinet.

The spear pierced the glass door, driving shards down on four collapsed children, jolting shelves off their brackets. And then one Meissen china dish followed by another and another — Jude's inheritance, worth a good deal of money — slid onto the heads and backs of the children and onto the floor, where they smashed, every last one.

By the time Esau reached the dining room, three children were wailing, four were bleeding, and a small fortune of glass and hand-painted bone china lay shattered on the floor. Smithereens. The "spear" leaned awkwardly against the empty back wall of the china cabinet that teetered now on three legs.

There was no point in getting angry. The kids were upset enough.

Esau closed his eyes for a second (push it away) and ordered them to stay put. He stepped into the hallway, summoned a breath, and considered what Jude would do now. He fetched a soft hand broom and carefully brushed them down. Then, one at a time, he extracted them from the heap and carried them to the tub off Mattie's room. Gently as he could, he undressed them, inevitably pushing some shards deeper. The shrieking intensified, made more shrill by the sight of glass embedded in one another, and quickly became unbearable.

Esau stepped out again, stuffed his ears with batting, and returned with a stool which he pulled to the dry tub. Patiently, with fingers and tweezers, he extracted shard after shard of glass and china from each child. Each extraction meant a new bubble of blood, a fresh round of wailing. And no sooner would one child pull out and drop a shard than another would step on it with naked foot. The voices grew hoarse. Eddie had the most cuts. Dozens threaded his scalp.

Once all visible shards had been extracted, Esau lifted the kids out of the tub, ordered them to freeze on the spot on which he set them, rinsed the tub thoroughly, and wiped it with a clean cloth. Then he lifted them back into the tub and bathed them. They calmed slightly in the warm water, as the dried blood washed away, but the relief was temporary, an eye in the storm. When he sterilized the wounds to bandage them, the alcohol on open cuts incited the highest pitches yet.

Verity's cuts must have burned as much as the others' but she stood naked and silent in the tub, letting the tears run. She plainly had no idea what disaster she had caused.

Afterwards, Esau carried the kids to bed and promised cuts would heal faster and there would be ice cream for dessert if only they all took a long nap. Then he plodded downstairs and swept *tongues, lopsided ledgers, cupboards of sugar, smithereens, epileptic seizures, strawberry* the dining room floor. The porcelain heap was ankle deep. Ha, he should survey it. There was probably more kaolin here, in this precious broken china, than the Stenson deposits had ever had. He fetched the Hoover to clean the last of it. The sound of collateral being sucked up the hose must have been agonizing.

(When Jacqueline arrived in the evening, the remains of the cabinet had been hauled, piece by piece, out to the garden shed. She found a flashlight and went out to look at it. It wasn't so bad. Just the glass and one leg were broken, it could be repaired. It was still a handsome piece of furniture. But Esau didn't want it in the house anymore. And there Verity's bed sheets flapped on the line. She must have wet the bed during her afternoon nap.)

Before a week was out, the children had filled the gaping wall where the cabinet had stood with crayonnings and water-colours and racquets and toys. One afternoon, as they played outside, Esau tidied the space in front of the wall. He dumped the toys in the toy box and hauled the racquets and birdies and balls down to the basement. He took down the drawings and watercolours, rolled them up, and placed them into a box he labeled "Drawings Done in Jude's Absence." He scraped off the Scotch Tape remnants with his fingernail, and then with a paring knife. He scrubbed the wall with a brush and soap and warm water. And then he stood and gazed at the empty space, a negative monument to what had been there before and to the accident that had destroyed it, for several minutes.

It was no use. The children filled the gap again with art and toys and the detritus of life in a shorter time than before.

Esau gave up and let the space fill.

Like a conveyor belt ferrying boulders to be crushed, the days kept lumbering on. Feeding and bathing and bedding of children, cleaning and groceries and cooking, strange hospital visits and night maintenance shifts and scrubbing machine grease out of coveralls, and paltry, broken sleep. The now-constant cycling in Esau's head (push it away) was eclipsed only by profound monotony. Once, late at night years ago, Jude had whispered of the implacable boredom of childrearing and housekeeping. She needed her work, she had said, to untether her mind from everlasting children's natter, from dishes and laundry and floors, from the swaying list and kilter of a household.

But knowing this, and knowing too she regretted nothing of the last ten years, Esau marvelled daily at her constancy. He had never been so tired, so irritable, and it had been a long time since he felt this unhappy. He just wanted it to end.

Then, on a Wednesday afternoon, the telephone rang.

Michael Vinterburg, his old companion, was in the area with his twin Gabriel for annual medical appointments. They hadn't seen Esau in a year and, if it suited, they would bring dinner, Michael said. Hot fried chicken, bread, coleslaw. An entire evening of adult company.

When the knocker clacked, Esau stood back and let the kids welcome the guests and direct them to the table. He leaned into the doorframe between rooms and watched. Watched Michael wheel Gabe's chair into place, watched Michael lift Verity onto the book-boosted chair, watched Michael slide his own chair in under his long thighs, watched Michael soak up and dish out attention, watched Michael glance back at him when the chaos allowed.

He was still the most vivid of men. Still tall, still freckled, still angular and strong, with none of the roughness of quarry men.

They tucked into the food immediately. Eddie passed Michael the coleslaw and Michael eyed it in outrage, as if it were a hammer or a hoe:

"Look Mac. Jutht what'th goin' on around here? Let'th get organithed, hmmm?"

His Daffy Duck was spot-on. The kids stared.

"It ithn't ath though I haven't lived up to my contract, good-neth knowthe. And goodneth knowthe, it ithn't ath though I haven't kept mythelf trim, goodneth knowthe."

Michael became the cartoon, stretched his lips into a duck-bill, so pompous, so animated. The older kids laughed harder than they had in months, the room hummed, and Michael slid spoonful after spoonful into Gabriel's mouth, dropping his own lower lip every time the spoon approached Gabriel. Verity sat silently on her boosted chair throughout the meal, smiled in a confused sort of way, and ate her drumstick.

"She doesn't talk," Eddie said, matter-of-fact.

Esau braced for Michael to take advantage, to write *"Sound please"* on his napkin. Instead, he looked at her and stroked her cheek with the back of his hand. He had never made fun of Gabriel either, Esau realized, nor Mattie. The entertainer of classmates and troops alike never mined the easy subjects for a laugh. No wonder so many were drawn to him.

Esau should never have looked away from Michael, should have never stopped basking in the company of his oldest friend. For once he did, he could look only at Gabriel. Gabriel was as tall as Michael, though you could hardly see it: his limbs folded into the wheelchair like an accordion and he slouched to the extent that his head bobbed, as if loosely tacked to his chest. His clothes were fashionable but his atrophied muscles, his joints and bones poking like clothespins, made them look ill-fitted. His face was still recognizably his own, but no longer had the luminosity that once compelled a priest to worship him nor the square symmetry of Michael's. The muscles on one side of it hadn't worked since the accident and that side hung, as if weights were fastened to the jowl.

When Gabriel chewed, he did so on the other side of his mouth with large exaggerated jaw movements. He never quite closed his mouth and, from his vantage point, Esau couldn't avoid a grotesque private viewing of chicken skin and coleslaw, half-chewed. His sour breath crossed the table and cut through the fresh bread and hot chicken; the kids didn't seem to notice, but Esau's appetite dissolved. And when Gabe wasn't eating, a stream of drool ran steadily from his mouth, landed on his bib, overran its edges. A horror-comic version of Michael.

After each mouthful, Michael gently wiped away the food that slid from Gabriel's open mouth with a cloth. He changed the bib several times throughout the meal, but the shirt was always soaked, the lips and chin glistening, the skin around his mouth bright and raw from years of unremitting moisture. Michael included Gabriel in conversation and assumed Gabe understood. Every few minutes, Gabriel made a guttural noise, a chuckle of sorts. It reminded Esau of something, he couldn't place it, and, though he tried to resist it, his stomach lurched.

After dinner, Michael asked to tuck the kids into bed, the sort of thing he never got to do.

Esau stayed downstairs with Gabriel, positioned him at the window looking out into the night, and washed dishes. He reached around now and again to wipe Gabe's chin. Upstairs, where Michael was, laughter and warmth:

"Do it again!"

"Lithen Buthter. Enough ith enough. Thith ith the final, the very latht thtraw. Who ith rethponthible for thith?"

When Michael finally came down the stairs again, the kitchen was clean, and Esau reached around to wipe Gabriel's chin, the millionth time. He smiled to lay eyes on Michael again.

"The apron suits you Esau. The ruffles especially. How fetching."

A look passed between them. Michael reached behind Esau and untied his apron, hand lingering, breath on his forehead, distance between them finally gone. With the other hand — he turned Gabriel's wheelchair around to face them and wiped a fresh wet spot on his chin.

Gabriel's diaper needed changing, Michael said. Esau nodded, pensive now, and they wheeled him into Mattie's bedroom and hoisted him onto the bed. Michael unzipped Gabriel's pants — instantly a stench so dense Esau tasted it. Michael had the changing down to a quick smooth system, rolling Gabriel this way and that to replace the soiled cloth with a clean one. Gabriel had never had a bedsore, Michael said. Gabriel grew less flexible each year despite range-of-motion exercises. Gabriel still eyed handsome people on the sidewalk. Gabriel still laughed at cartoons. Gabriel still liked to hold a paintbrush, especially if it was dipped in paint. When Michael looked at Gabriel, he saw his beautiful gifted twin.

Esau listened, helped Michael roll Gabriel, asked questions, noted how frail the bones felt, how immovably the legs had seized into one position, how Michael's attention never drifted far from Gabriel. But his mind fixed on the spectacle of that diaper. Esau had four kids, he knew diapers, but a soiled adult diaper was nothing like a child's. Too copious, too intimate. He knew something of this from Mattie's recent seizure, but one epileptic accident is a different thing from a life assembled around vigilance and nursing an adult *tongues, lopsided ledgers, cupboards of sugar, smithereens, adult diapers, epileptic (push it away).*

The three men returned to the kitchen where they turned the lights low, sipped Scotch from children's mugs and talked into the evening. Or rather, Michael talked, Esau drank Scotch, and Gabriel uttered that strange guttural laugh.

In all likelihood, Esau longed to have Michael to himself that night, to draw the comfort of warm nights in cubbyhole shrubs or on a continent recovering from war. But four children slept upstairs, and a man in a wheelchair bobbed and drooled and grunted here in his kitchen.

Will it come to this? Esau must have wondered. To massive loaded diapers and vats of stinking drool and hour after hour, year after year, of caretaking without respite? And what then of the others in this family? What of Esau?

Later that night, after the guests had left, after Jacqueline arrived for the night, while Esau was driving to work and the air through the open window cooled his face, he made the connection: Gabriel's guttural laugh reminded him of the grunt Verity had twice forced out on his lap when he'd urged her to speak.

He stopped the car and vomited into the ditch.

He waited, in case there was more, then wiped his mouth and drove on. His mind resumed its racing *seizures, strawberry tongues, lopsided ledgers, cupboards of* Surely Verity would become like Mattie, not like Gabriel. And anyway, he had already decided that Jude would choose Verity's future *sugar, smithereens, adult diapers, epileptic seizures* when she recovered, he was no good in a crisis. But he had a few minutes now *strawberry tongues, lopsided ledgers* Perhaps he would swing by the doctor's house. If a light was on, maybe ask a few questions.

Without Mattie there to defend Verity, with Gabriel fresh in Esau's racing mind, it probably took the doctor ten minutes to set things in perspective. Esau likely made it to work with time to spare.

Writer's Note: After all my research, I write this knowing I have more questions than answers. I am not certain of the dates, so many recorded events have no origins, some of the gaps are so wide. Sometimes, I long for the drug-addled days of the Facility when the possibility did not exist that there is no good explanation for what happened to that little girl.

This much is recorded fact: Friday, October 25, Michael and Gabriel, in town for medical appointments, visited the Blessure home. Monday, October 28, Dr. King re-examined Verity. His appointment book allowed fifteen minutes. On Tuesday, October 29, Esau signed preliminary papers. On Monday, November 4, he delivered his daughter to the Elora Home for the Feeble-Minded. Twelve days later, November 16, Jude returned home, weak but otherwise well, with baby Clara, to find Verity gone.

I (Athena) wonder sometimes when exactly Esau told Jude about Verity. Did he whisper it at the hospital, as they collected her things and prepared to leave? Was it on the drive home, a new infant daughter swaddled in her arms? Did he wait until they stepped under the lintel and only three children ran to greet her? Or when she saw the empty wall where the hutch had stood? Whatever the setting of full disclosure, the moment he finally told her would have been the moment he realized that he had taken bad advice and had grossly misjudged Jude.

She looked at him, seeing him for the first time, realizing what betrayal he was capable of. Levelly, coolly, she informed him that from this moment on she would sleep downstairs in Mattie's room. With the baby.

That week, Jude began her search. That week, she began compiling a scrapbook-journal, perhaps a simple brown coil-bound book. The ripped-up quarantine notice went on the first page, left hand side. Opposite it, on the right-hand side, the first handwritten entry: "November 16, 1963: Learned that Verity is now considered retarded and has been taken to an institution somewhere in Ontario.

Things to do: Find Verity."

ATHENA'S JOURNAL
JANUARY 16, 2004
(FRIDAY)

"Athena," says the therapist, "do you have any idea why Verity was silent?"

"I cannot be certain. It was long ago. I imagine, with her hearing gone, any vocalization felt unfamiliar or uncomfortable in her head and she avoided it. Some deaf people avoid vocal speech because it feels disconnected in the head."

"Ah. That explains it. You can see, though, why the doctor made such a grave error if the child made no sound at all."

"Perhaps you see it. I will not blame a four-year-old."

"I intended no blame, Athena. I intended to highlight the complexity of this tragedy."

I say nothing.

"Let me recount, then. There's an epileptic sister with a history surrounding her, there's Jude's absence, the stress of sick children, bills to pay, a failing mother, lost income, boredom, the disabled brother of an old friend, and a pushy physician. These are the factors contributing to Esau disowning Verity?"

I nod. "Especially the physician," I sign.

"Are any of these Esau's responsibility? Are his actions under these many pressures his responsibility?"

(This again. I maintain composure.)

"I have said it before," I sign. "Esau was manipulated by a disgruntled unethical physician capitalizing on extraordinary temporary circumstances. He is absolved."

"What about Jacqueline's point that he wished to be viewed as one kind of person and not another? Might it be a factor here?"

I shake my head no.

The therapist looks at me contemplatively, not unkindly.

"Okay. Responsibility aside, how do you feel about this? Sometimes emotions aren't altogether rational. I feel angry reading about Esau and Verity. Angrier still when I think of Michael, whose parents were also aging and who as a writer would have struggled financially, but who didn't consider abandoning his twin though Gabriel required much more care than Verity ever did. What do you feel?"

I think for a moment.

"I feel sad this happened. But poor Esau. What desperation to be driven to this!"

"If there are enough circumstances, then, and if these circumstances are severe enough, it's okay for a parent to stop being a parent?"

"It is understandable." I look him in the eye when I sign this. I know he will find it startling.

"Athena," he says. "I'm not saying you're wrong. But I want to try something. To take one brick out of the wall, ask a question, and then put it back: what would it mean, hypothetically of course, if it were more complicated? If Esau were partly responsible? If the Esau we see in the Elora document were the real Esau who — who seemed relieved to be free of what this child required of him? What would it mean if he had done, *of his own volition,* this one immature and irresponsible thing?"

(There it is again, the Elora document.)

"The question is moot," I say. "Records show Esau Blessure to be mature and responsible. He nurtures and provides for the other children under difficult circumstances. He cares lovingly for his mother and disabled sister. He is the only son doing this; his brothers are mentioned nowhere. There are two possible reasons for his actions around Verity: either someone tricked him into abandoning her or Verity herself is unlovable. So unlovable she must be disposed of."

Everything in the room is still.

"I see," he says eventually. "That is quite an insight. Unfortunately, our time is up. Next week, I'd like to talk more about those two options."

Writer's Note: I wanted to omit this story. It clutters things. But the therapist says it "complicates" my rendering of Esau and Imran feels it "relevant to custody." (I cannot see how.) I will leave it in. For now.

When Imran and I (Athena) interviewed Jacqueline in her Toronto home last summer, she recommended we travel to a nursing home in Pickering, north of Toronto, and visit an elderly man named Andrzej.

What I remember most about the nursing home is the acrid, sugary smell of cleaning fluids that leach metallic on the tongue. It smelled like the Facility and I halted the instant it hit me, mid-step, between the automatic front doors. But Imran gently pulled me to the desk, and asked for Andrzej. The receptionist mumbled into a phone and soon the metal doors at Reception unlatched.

Andrzej sat upright in his wheelchair in a fine white shirt and brocade vest, silver cufflinks, and a green silk scarf pinned at his throat with a silver pin. His white hair hung to his shoulders, thick and wavy, and his manicured hands looked like they had never held a carpenter's tool though by then I knew him to have been a licensed finish carpenter. On his lap rested a slim leather envelope. He was something grand, and in a place like this. I almost stopped noticing the smell. An orderly stood by Reception, watching.

"You're here about my Stenson years!" he said. "What a pleasure!"

He shook our hands with the strength of a younger man and guided us to a comfortable corner of the lobby. (I was relieved to stay in the lobby. I never would have had fortitude to walk through those latching metal doors.) Imran and I sat on a velvet sofa with curved legs that resembled the limbs of a dog. A brass plate on the arm said it had been donated.

Andrzej waited until we were seated, then snapped his

fingers like people do at restaurants in movies. The receptionist looked up.

"Honey, can someone bring us some Cognac here?" He winked at her, and she gave him such a look. "Well, how about coffee then?"

She rolled her eyes and picked up the phone. A few minutes later a pimpled boy brought a tray of coffee (hot!) and cookies with many walnuts in them.

"We're not supposed to do that," Andrzej said. "They want us to eat in the dining room. But it has no windows, the tables are laid with oilcloth which can never be clean, and the flowers in the vases are plastic. Here, we can look out on pansies and snap-dragons and you can sit on that elegant sofa." He looked right at me when he spoke. (People usually look at the interpreter.) "Now, young lady, what is it you'd like to know?"

I told him Jacqueline had sent us and asked what he could tell me about Esau Blessure.

"Esau Blessure," he said, and stroked the case on his lap. "Do you have time? May I tell you some stories?" He continued without waiting for an answer. "Esau did us a great kindness. You have likely heard by now that José Chavez, Esau's employer, was my lover for many years."

I had not heard this, but I nodded.

"In those days, two men, we had to carry on in secret. I lived thirty miles away, in another town, and visited no more than once a week. On Wednesday evenings, after the carpentry classes I taught at the Stenson High School.

"Each week, after the last student had left and my tools were packed away, I walked to the Sunshine Café, ordered a cheese-burger, and dropped a coin into the jukebox. Then I slipped on a confident smile, like I was pulling up my socks, and I scanned the café for the prettiest girl. I strolled across that café chest first" *(he puffed out his chest) "right up to that girl and invited her to dance. Of course, "the prettiest girl" was often not the prettiest girl there, but I told her she was. And she agreed to dance, always. Even klutzes can manage a waltz with a strong lead. After the dance, I ate my meal and paid my bill, and walked to José's house where I spent the night before driving home the next morning. If you walked by the house, you saw lamps burning in both guest and master bedrooms. The next afternoon, the guestroom sheets flapped on the wash line. I cultivated the Ladies' Man ruse, you see, so that José and I would not be suspected."*

A smile, rueful, stretched his mouth.

"But we had a room in the basement. Back in the corner against the foundation where most people had root cellars. You couldn't see in from outside. José had shuttered the windows with plywood. The door was blocked with brooms and spades and shovels, and we hung a heavy lock on it, the kind you might find on a toolshed. Inside, we had a small portable stove for heat, a mattress, muslin sheets, a warm quilt. It was — cozy. Beside the bed, on one of those wooden stools I taught my students to make, stood a silver-framed oil painting of me and José, kissing like newlyweds. You could make out our faces plain as day. On the back, written with a thin paintbrush, was this: "To my own Andrzej, on his thirtieth birthday. One day I will find a way to gather all the love in the world and give it to you. Until then, I give you this painting, which took me many weeks to do, and all my love, José."

"It was quite a risk," he said, "leaving the lights burning above every Wednesday, heading downstairs, lugging those spades and shovels out of the way, prying open the rusty lock, and loving one another to our hearts' content. Then, in the morning, lugging it all back. We believed that no one, not even young Esau who spent plenty of time there, knew about us.

"And then someone called the police.

"We uh we disappeared into the belly of Toronto."

He brushed cookie crumbs from the case on his lap.

"One December day several years later — '47, I believe — a fine young man stepped into the store in which I worked. Esau Blessure, back from the war. Taller, stronger, changed, but easily recognizable. In that moment I believed our game was up and prison a certainty. I turned to run but he quickly raised his palms. 'I vow,' he said, 'to tell no one I have seen you.' He had sought me out, he said, because he had something for me."

Imran's signing had become restrained. He was doing this, I know, to prevent his gestures from distracting the old man who now appeared lost in another time. The orderly had moved to the far north corner.

"First, Esau gave me news that José was presumed dead and his will, in which he left everything to me but for a set amount to help Esau through university, had been overturned and his estate handed over entirely to his brother Victor. That wasn't surprising. Those who didn't think homosexuality evil in those days thought it madness. My lovely José was declared unsound of mind. But it did irk — it irks still — to think of those men, Victor and his lawyers, sitting in José's house, drinking José's coffee, while dismantling his will and assessing the worth of his estate."

His nostrils widened. He sucked in a breath and continued.

"But along with the bad news, Esau brought me this."

From the slim case on his lap, he pulled the painting of two men kissing that had once rested upon a stool in the hidden underground room. He passed it to me. The inscription was exactly as Andrzej had recited it.

"I was overwhelmed. I didn't think to ask how he came to lay hands on it. He must have retrieved it from police evidence one hazardous way or another. I owe him a great debt for it."

I passed the painting to Imran who looked it over and handed it back to the old man. Andrzej slipped it inside the leather case and stroked the case again. The orderly was inching south, along the far wall, behind us.

"Once I recovered from surprise, Esau asked if we might speak further. He and I arranged to meet after my shift in a lounge we both knew. The walls were moss green, I recall, and hung with photographs of half-dressed women though the men clustered in the booths would have preferred photos of half-dressed men.

"Esau bought me a drink. We spoke awkwardly at first. We both had information we wanted to share but revealing too much could be dangerous. He told me that the circumstances sur- rounding our disappearance had always seemed strange to him. He and another Stenson man named Michael Vinterburg had been to war together and, over time, they had pieced together what might have happened that night. I expected him to ask about the room in the cellar or if José was with me, but he judiciously avoided both subjects. I think to protect us. What he asked, finally, was what I remembered of Father Matthew, the Stenson parish priest. That's when I knew he and Michael really had something.

"Father Matthew was not easily forgotten. He didn't like to wear vestments, I recalled, particularly not during the Depression or the war. He said their lavishness contrasted his parishioners' poverty too sharply and every few weeks, he showed up for service and gave communion in his everyday clothes and his stole. Some people thought he meddled. The school principal once complained to me that the priest had visited his office upon hearing that girls weren't permitted to wear trousers, even in winter — and thereafter girls and boys alike wore long underwear and trousers on cold days. George and Greta from the Sunshine Café, where I danced with young ladies, paid their immigrant cooks less than citizen cooks. He visited them too one afternoon,

and, by the time the sun set, Father Matthew had worked through several milkshakes, the cooks were paid on the basis of experience, and a statue of the Virgin sat in the window."

We smiled at this. Andrzej stroked his hair and continued.

"Stenson was a demoralized town then, shrivelling under the slow burn of poverty, and Father Matthew had a reputation for using sermon time to organize community solutions should a parishioner need help, to fend off collectors or dig a well or rebuild a barn. It was a matter of time, he used to say, until each of them needed a helping hand. Most people thought him an extraordinary priest. And oh my he was handsome. We all noticed.

"Esau said that Gabriel Vinterburg, an adolescent in the parish, noticed especially. Like his identical twin Michael, Gabriel was athletic, intense, unusually comfortable in his skin, and, above all, resourceful. Once, in confession, Father Matthew mistook Michael for Gabriel — and said much more than he knew.

"Apparently, Gabriel had made advances on the Father, who unfailingly rebuffed them. He even appeared one day at the Father's chamber door, requesting a conversation about Seminary studies. The Father stepped into the kitchen to make them coffee, and Gabriel slipped quietly up behind, caught him off guard with nimble hand, and pleasured him quickly, aggressively, competently. He was not a small boy; the Father could not have pushed him away without violence. But he could redirect Gabriel's attentions. After that first day, their liaisons were about Gabriel's pleasure. He never hurt him, never sought his own fulfillment, never made an advance himself. Each time Gabriel suddenly appeared, strong and insistent, all Father Matthew did, all he allowed himself to do, was to admire the beauty of God's creation, of the taut lines of a virile body, with his eyes, with his hands, with his reverent tongue. Perhaps he thought it a type of prayer."

Andrzej stopped talking and sipped at his coffee. He wore the expression of a man in a faraway place. Imran and I said nothing.

"Gabriel and the Father carried on this way for several years. The conflict within the priest must have been staggering. Eventually, it seems his vows won out and he broke it off. Gabriel, then seventeen, didn't take the rejection lightly and continued to stop by the Father's chambers and the Father continued to rebuff him. Then came the news that Gabriel had climbed the tallest structure in town and 'fallen' off its roof.

"What this had to do with José was that Michael, Gabriel's twin, was understandably upset. Gabriel had been working obsessively on a drawing that concerned the Father. Michael brought the drawing to my José, who was his schoolteacher and a local painter, ostensibly to ask about its artistic value, but really, I think, to seek advice. José was unfailingly kind to young men he thought might turn out like us. He drove out to show it to me and we talked.

"That boy, that Gabriel, he should have been a painter. With a crude charcoal pencil and the back side of an Arithmetic exam, he had crafted something delicate, muscular. The sketch was full of light and movement. Gabriel had drawn the Father wearing a light robe, head partly covered in a cowl. He was kneeling in front of a boy, presumably Gabriel himself, at a three-quarter angle, bent over him, eyes closed, mouth parted. One hand rested, splayed on the nearest thigh, and the other reached across the torso cupping the boy's far side. The boy himself laid back horizontally over a low ottoman or table. He was young in the drawing, twelve or thirteen, radiant and shockingly alive. His toes were pointed, his back was arched, palpable euphoria and mischief on his face even as his eyes were closed, even as the cowl-headed figure bent over his torso strategically blocking private parts from view. The boy's naked body, what one could see of it, fairly writhed on paper.

"We were both stunned. Such ability! But the image — we who had never visited an art museum where such images might be common — unsettled us. We decided it meant something, and that José would drive back that night and show it first to Father Matthew and then to the police in case they were looking into Gabriel's accident.

"José said the Father was taken aback. That he carried it to the light to see it better. I imagine he wondered, as we did, who had taught this extraordinary boy to draw.

"It must have taken great force of will for Father Matthew to wrench his eyes from the drawing and look at José. Even under scrutiny, he wouldn't have shied away — he'd have thought it unbecoming a man of the cloth — but the drawing would have pulled at him like a magnet, I think. Muddied his mind.

"José took the drawing back, said Father Matthew was his friend, he was not there to judge, but the boy lay in a coma. He was turning it over to the police the next day and had come to tell Father Matthew in case he wanted to prepare.

"Father Matthew stood under the lamp and wept. What could he have said? What could mere words say in the face of such a damning and gorgeous drawing, sketched by a golden boy who had climbed up on a roof and landed in a coma? José touched his shoulder, a comfort gesture, and left.

"I believe, in that precise moment, the Father broke his vows, placed a phone call anonymously, and reached for the vicar-age car key. He meant to follow José home, I think, and, in the hubbub he had generated, retrieve the drawing.

"In fact it was much simpler for him. José, driving home just then, swerved off the road to avoid a rabbit and punctured a tire. He left the car where it was and walked through the forest towards home for the jack. It wasn't far. By the time he got there, the townspeople had already gathered, broken the lock to our room, and pushed out the plywood covering the windows. *From the forest, José saw the crowd and the light from the basement — and surmised the rest. He stayed in the trees, walked to the highway, and stuck out his thumb. After about four hours and several rides in opposite directions to throw off any potential followers, he arrived at my house.*

"In the meantime, Father Matthew came upon José's empty car with sunken tire, saw José nowhere, reached through the window, and picked up the drawing from the front seat where José had left it. And made his way to José's house to join the others.

"Overnight, we abandoned our homes and careers. I worked in an art supplies store and José in a bookshop. For some years we used false names. We felt gratitude for the flat tire and we built a new life. A good life. A good long life."

Andrzej paused to nibble at a cookie. Imran and I sat quietly. The orderly moved slowly along the south wall towards us.

"Michael and Esau had worked out most of this," Andrzej continued, "though I'd often wondered who placed the call and where the drawing went. It had been extraordinary, you see, more remarkable than any car accident, and it wasn't mentioned in a single news article after our disappearance. It was as if it had vanished. Nor was Father Matthew mentioned, though José had just been to visit him. But Esau and Michael saw him at the house that night, and to get there he had to drive by José's abandoned car.

"It all fit. When José and I spoke of it later, after my evening with Esau, we agreed that it all fit."

"Do you believe," Imran asked, "that you could have kept the secret from the townspeople indefinitely? Or were people already suspicious?"

For a long while Andrzej didn't answer. He crossed his legs and folded his hands overtop his knees. The acute angle of his hanging shin revealed how very thin he was. Kitchen aides, all in uniform, walked through the lobby pushing stacks of steaming meal trays that smelled of beef gravy made from OXO cubes. The orderly moved closer, now in my peripheral vision.

"I don't know," Andrzej said, finally. "Small towns are — small. People talked about Gabriel's accident. What he was doing on a slippery roof, that sort of thing. I thought he had intended to 'fall.' The agonies of adolescence are often downplayed. But I don't know what they said about Father Matthew and I don't know what they said about us. Perhaps I'm being naïve and they all knew and were waiting for just such a moment."

A nurse walked by pushing a med cart, syringes and tiny plastic cups of pills lined up in rows. She signalled the orderly who nodded and glanced at me. I willed my heart to slow, but she walked away, through the metal doors. Andrzej was speaking.

"Years later, when Gabriel's medical costs became too great, Michael Vinterburg wrote a letter to Father Matthew's bishop and included a copy of Gabriel's drawing. Apparently he drew dozens trying to perfect it. Soon after, Michael Vinterburg received a sizable cheque to help with Gabriel's care, no questions asked. I'm sorry, though —" Andrzej leaned forward and touched my hand "— that young Esau Blessure never got his schooling. I believe he would have enjoyed it."

At that moment, the metal doors unlatched and the nurse backed out again with her med cart. The last thing I recall is that she paused before the doors, looked directly at me, and calmly filled a syringe. The orderly, I recall, pushed back his sleeves and came at me from the other side.

But Imran says that never happened. He says the nurse waved at us pleasantly and kept going — and I disappeared.

He and Andrzej searched and soon found me under the side table (adorned with a crocheted tablecloth and a vase). I had *moved there so swiftly and silently, without disturbing the vase on top, that they had not noticed. This fact impresses me. The side table was petite and spindly; I am not. They coaxed me out, Imran says, and my pulse was quick and thready, my face wet and ashen. I remember none of this, nothing but that syringe and the orderly and a mountain of fear.*

Andrzej was lovely. He said he had never heard of a phobia more reasonable than that of a nurse filling a syringe, and I ought not to think for a moment that there was anything wrong with me.

For days after hearing this story, I marvelled. At Gabriel, of course. At his artistry. (I would like to see the drawing.) At the ways he was able to generate a love so intense a priest could not resist it despite laws and vows and taboo, so intense that Gabriel himself likely rather stepped off a roof than consider an approved life without it. But more, I marvelled at Esau. What was it about this story, these men, that compelled him to steal from police evidence? And to track Andrzej down? Such risk. Such effort.

Verity could not even convince him to keep her.

Writer's Note: Young Verity, deposited by her father at the Elora Home for the Feeble-Minded, lived in institutions for three decades. She was in Elora, Ontario, a few weeks before being transferred to the Holdstock Facility in the Canadian Rockies where she was kept for the next thirty years. My memories from that time are scant, and Verity's official file covering those thirty years (not including the Elora intake form that came West with her) is two pages long. A few intake notes, a list of med changes, a note about her first menses, some height and weight measurements, and other perfunctory scribbles.

One cannot gather a credible thirty-year story from two pages of crude half-science scratches.

My therapist suggested I (Athena) check public record and legal files surrounding the Facility: "A place that size, running for that long, there must be public record somewhere." And indeed, I have uncovered two relevant sets of records, both substantial. First, orderly Ruby Rojas's civil suit for wrongful dismissal dragged on for years, producing an abundant volume of notes before being settled out of court. Second, Nurse Harriet Caulle gave several detailed interviews as part of a mid-1990s investigation into possible human rights abuses at the Holdstock Facility. The interviews, which included descriptions of daily life in the Facility, were transcribed by graduate students in Social Sciences at University of Calgary. Both the audio and transcribed versions are held in the Archives of South and Central Alberta. They are a lucky find: Caulle was the person most consistently present through Verity's thirty Holdstock years, her next keeper, and she is the Holdstock employee whose choices I want most to understand. How is it she could spend so much time with Verity and not see who she really was? Perhaps in her testimony will be an answer for why Verity was so long abandoned.

What I find both distressing and curious is that some Facility files have been destroyed. Nurse Caulle mentions making notes that are nowhere to be found — and remnants of ripped pages peek out from the binding seams of report books. What could have happened? Most of their charges were human discards. People outside wanted only to forget they existed. What could possibly have happened that required the obliteration of evidence?

Because the public records are hundreds of pages long, and because evidence has been destroyed, the therapist thinks I ought to "explain my method" for this section in case I wish someday to craft this material into a book, an idea I like very much. My method, then, is this: I have chosen selectively those few events from the Rojas or Caulle records in which young Verity is a player, or which affected her in some way. I have drawn also on sparse references to the Holdstock Facility in the local newspaper, on some administrative notebooks kept by Dr. Molner Holof Vestidge for his accountant, and on minutes from Holdstock Board of Directors' meetings. I have limited myself to telling recorded events, to witnessing persistent corporeal testimony. That is enough. I have not tried to imagine what stories were torn out along the way.

On another note. These last weeks I have been reading about the art and architecture favoured by despots. The photographs in the books I fetched from the library show buildings in which henchmen carried out torments ordered by men like Mr. Stalin, Mr. Hitler, and Mr. Pol Pot. The structures themselves appear remarkable only in their ordinariness. The captions tell of great suffering within the walls and yet, to look at the photos, I cannot see it.

DECEMBER 1963
HOLDSTOCK, ALBERTA

People say the most wretched things. Confidences are divulged.

Well. Harriet Caulle was *glad* to step off the train in Hold-stock, Alberta, a half continent away from where she knew anyone or anyone knew her. She had at her side a four-year-old girl with whom she had crossed the country. The girl had recently under-gone a growth spurt and the arms of her coat were an inch too short, though the long knitted mittens kept her warm never-theless along with the red blanket piled around her neck like an overlong scarf. Harriet stroked the girl's hair. She had been surprisingly well-behaved on the week-long journey, a comfort to Harriet, she would admit, and not a single toileting incident. Perhaps, though, she hadn't known it was a journey. One could never tell how much this population understood.

With confidence Harriet set her boot onto the platform of her new town — and it shot forward on the icy step. She wrenched her torso, caught the rail (also icy), regained her balance but ripped her glove, and stepped down more gingerly after that. Then she glanced to both sides and over her shoulders. Everyone was busy. None but the child had seen her lurch and she would never tell. In Elora, whence she'd come, that step would have been sanded!

Harriet reached for the child who was sliding gleefully around the icy lot and hailed the only taxicab she could see. She stood in one spot, legs planted and slightly bent, tightly gripping the child's collar, while the conductor passed her bags and trunk from the platform to the driver who hoisted them into his cab. The yard resembled every small-town station yard they had passed through. Trucks parked haphazardly across the road and parking lot. An assortment of locals, swaddled against the cold until they all looked alike, collecting relatives who had come with the train or stacking parcels atop a toboggan. Children and their dogs running the length of the platform and then chasing down the tracks after the locomotive as it vanished once more into the conifers.

Harriet's trunk was bigger than it looked and now it needed some wielding to fit into the taxi. The driver unloaded her bags again to reinsert them in a different sequence.

"They'll fit, doncha worry," he assured. "I've hauled more'n this! Wouldncha rather wait in the car? It's warm!"

"My legs want stretching," Harriet said, though she would have preferred the car. She remained planted, gripping the girl's collar — and keeping an eye on her bags.

In those few minutes, the station yard emptied, the commotion of moments ago suddenly absent. The weekly arrival of the train that drew the community into a shared space the way a village well might have done a hundred years earlier was now over and a few hours still left in the workday. The stationmaster was shuttering the depot. It was nothing more than a pitiful temporary shelter, Harriet could see that now, smaller still than the station at Bowmanville, Ontario, where her grandmother had kept a cottage.

A blast of wind brought an abrupt end to the snowsquall. Now the mountains, invisible a minute ago, were *there*, more present than Harriet had prepared herself for. Nature, red in tooth and claw, Tennyson said, and yet they seemed not savage but calm, intelligent, disallowing the sunset. She could make out the town buildings now. A grocer, a hardware store, two churches, a school house. Strange that in all its years of existence, the town had not managed to carve out a niche for itself. It seemed, at most, rubble in a hollow valley, all space belonging to the hills. Harriet hated the out-of-doors, every inch of it unpredictable.

Thankfully, it could be avoided. She had been avoiding it all her life.

She inhaled sharply. The air hit her windpipe and she coughed. What cold! A breath too deep could score your throat!

"Naahh," the driver said when she asked. "Nobody bleeds from the cold. Ya jes need some good woolens is all. Them stock-ins yer wearing aren any good. They'll fix ya up at th'Institushun. You shoulda waited in the car. Yer from down East. I take it?"

He laughed at her then, making no effort to conceal it — and in that moment it was all a bit much. Harriet took the only self-ministration she could manage with driver and child looking on: she clamped down on the inside of her cheek and savoured the familiar taste of blood.

She looked sidelong at the girl. Her lips were as red as the blanket around her neck and wet again. Harriet fished in her bag for the jar of petroleum jelly and smeared them. The girl hardly noticed. Her eyes were fixed on the rosy mountains in the twilight outside. Wonder spilled from her face.

Harriet twisted the lid shut, slipped the jar back into her bag, and huffed. If a feeble-minded child could see beauty here, certainly she ought to manage it.

As for the cold air. Well. Fresh air, fresh start.

Thirty minutes later, Harriet stood uncertainly on the rubber mat in the front hall of the Ladies' Staff Quarters, the child at her side clutching the red blanket. The kitchen was to her left.

A few teacups on the counter needed washing, a tin of cocoa wanted putting away, but otherwise it seemed clean and orderly. And warm. In this climate, the house was warm.

Her shoulders relaxed. She unbuttoned her coat and boots.

"Coming!" The voice came first, a lady's voice. The person

tripping down the banistered stairs, however, in greasy trousers and close-cropped black hair and wielding a pipe wrench yet, she looked — not altogether ladylike. Still, one compliments another woman.

"Hello! Welcome! You must be the new Head Psych nurse. May I call you Harriet? I'm Ruby Rojas, please call me Ruby. I'd shake your hand, but I've grease on mine. I was fixing a drippy faucet."

"Hello, er, yes Harriet is fine if we're to be housemates. And what a lovely curl in your short hair. I've always longed for curls myself."

"How nice of you to say, thank you. Is this our new resident? Hi there, my name's Ruby." She crouched and looked the child in the eye.

"This is Verity. She's deaf and mute and feeble-minded. And rather a delight."

The girl smiled silently, reached forward, took the heavy pipe wrench firmly, laid it on her blanket, and sank to her knees to play with the guide.

"If she likes a pipe wrench, we'll get along fine." Ruby pulled out a large handkerchief and wiped her hands. "Here, let me take your bags, Harriet. A week on the train — you must be dying for a bath and a good bed. Your room is upstairs beside mine. We share a loo. I was thinking Verity should stay with you tonight in the trundle bed. She might adapt better to the ward after a good night's sleep, don't you agree?"

It was a merciful thing Harriet did agree for she was momentarily muted watching Ruby muscle her heavy trunk up the stairs. They did things differently here, clearly. Well, that was to be expected.

She ran her tongue over her bitten cheek, picked up Verity, wrench and all, and quietly followed.

In the middle of the night, suddenly Harriet was awake. The silence, after days and nights of the train's rhythmic snare on the tracks, must have wakened her. She rolled over, about to close her eyes against the moonlight escaping the curtain's borders, and glanced at the trundle bed.

Empty.

She was out of bed more quickly than a woman her age ought to move. Was the front door bolted? She couldn't recall. She ran from the room.

"It's okay. I've got her." The Ruby girl sat cross-legged on the wide window box at the end of the hallway — in men's pajamas. The child stood on the box beside her, wrapped in her red blanket, looking out the window.

"I think the moonlight wakened her. I heard her footsteps on the boards. You were sleeping, I didn't want to rouse you."

"This is what she wanted? To look outside?" Harriet stood barefoot and disheveled in her nightgown and shook her head.

"It's worth taking in. See for yourself."

She hesitated — Harriet preferred windows from a few yards back — but then clenched, approached, and peered over Verity's head into the valley below. The snow reflected and amplified the moonlight. The night was more light than dark, the clouds whiter, harder, sharper than they would be against an afternoon sky. And the mountains, layers and layers of colossal crooked dominoes, at least a hundred glossy peaks and their reaching shadows, full of intent, constricting the field of vision. She turned away.

"Isn't it beautiful?"

"There's no horizon," Harriet snapped. "She's still clinging to that blanket?"

"Wouldn't let go through her whole bath."

"At least she's safe."

Harriet shuffled back to bed careful not to glance in the direction of the window again.

She had been surly. It wouldn't do. Ruby was appealing in her offbeat way, and Harriet might yet need her: the social landscape, its strata and allegiances, had not yet revealed itself and Harriet did not yet know where it would be most beneficial to stand. She would have to apologize to Ruby in the morning. She could blame the long journey.

Mind now, she was going to love it here. Fresh air, fresh start.

"What a perfect place for an institution," Harriet said to Doctor Vestidge in the doorway of his office the following morning, child in tow. "Isolated, spacious, natural barriers from the public."

The office, which could be accessed only through the Infirmary, had no windows whatsoever. What luxury! Now, mid-morning, he was working by lamplight.

"You must be Miss Caulle! You've arrived! How splendid!"

The Doctor spun in his chair, clapped his hands, beckoned her in, shut the door, and vigorously shook her hand. "I do hope you feel welcome."

He had thick spectacles in front of smallish eyes, a dispro-portionately small head, and very little neck. His body seemed a padded cylinder, his head a mere extension of it, and he toed in as he crossed back to his desk. He motioned to a chair by the desk and Harriet sat. The girl stood beside and leaned against her.

"I fear the telephone might ring at any moment," he said, "and if it does you'll have to excuse me. We're in something of a crisis here."

A pica patient on a recent outing to a diner had grabbed an armful of Heinz bottles and dived under the table. He had swallowed all the ketchup before staff were able to extract him. Four telephone calls from onlookers so far and one from the editor of the *Carabiner*. A publicity nightmare.

Harriet clucked sympathetically.

"So this is our new patient?" He reached for her blanket. The girl did not let go.

"Yes, she's been gripping that thing since we left Elora. Even in her sleep."

He exhaled slowly, then nodded. "They do suffer, our charges. So many things they can't control."

He reached into the drawer of the med cart beside his desk, pulled out a syringe already filled — Harriet saw the bottle sitting beside — and sank it quickly into her little leg.

The dose was massive, Harriet noted as the plunger depressed, enough to fell a grown man. Verity folded in half like a sock monkey. Her grip and her bowels loosed immediately. He caught her before she hit the floor and took the blanket away.

Harriet remained still. She must not show alarm. They did things differently here, she already knew. And he was not wrong, a sedated patient suffered less.

"What an — effective solution."

He smiled, nodded. "We'll keep her under for a week. Here, she's dirtied herself. Clean her up, put her to bed. With a green blanket. Our patients have green blankets. She'll be most comfortable on your floor for now, we can move her later if we need to. Then come back and I'll give you the tour."

The telephone rang. He eyed it grimly and loosened his tie. "Do bundle up," he said, "It's cold outside," and reached for the receiver.

Harriet carried sleeping Verity to her ward, introduced herself to the two nurses there, and asked for directions to diapers and to Verity's bed.

"I'll do it," one of the nurses said, and reached for Verity. "You're Head Nurse, and anyway you don't start 'til tomorrow."

"No no," Harriet smiled. "Verity knows me and this place is new. If she wakes in the changing, a familiar face will be a comfort." Of course the child wouldn't waken, not for days, but the nurses should see that Harriet didn't consider herself above the lowliest chores.

Harriet changed and diapered Verity and, checking first that no one was watching, cupped the girl's face in her hands and stroked back her hair. How perfectly awful to diaper a toilet-trained child. But now she couldn't waken and toilet herself. At least she wouldn't understand enough to be humiliated. Sometimes feeble-mindedness was a blessing.

Harriet tucked the green blanket gently around her, put her little shoes on the night table shelf and her soiled clothes in the laundry bin, and hurried back to meet the Doctor.

The conversation in which the nature of Harriet's alliance with the Doctor was cemented must have been shortly after her arrival on the grounds, perhaps during the outdoor part of the tour. In the unbearable cold, the Doctor would have guided Harriet along levelled paths in and around outbuildings.

"Now here we do maintenance and repair." He nodded to a man with a torch who stopped welding and pushed back his face shield long enough to wave. "You can see how the forest closes in," gesturing now to the trees. "If a patient were to get lost in it or, worse yet, find a way down to town, the public reaction —" He shook his head. "I daresay we'd be beheaded."

He led her further out, past more outbuildings, pausing to explain each one, through a gate and away from the grounds.

"Privately, Miss Caulle," he bent his head towards her as they walked, "I long to relieve our charges of the burden of outdoor activities altogether. They *suffer* so! But ignorant taxpayers want to think of them in a distant and benevolent place, wind and sun on their faces. What they consider kindness is in fact disruption of routine. They can't grasp what it costs them!"

Harriet, regrettably outside again, soon lost sensation in her feet, and not long after lost control of her jaw. It began to shudder.

Only when they were a half mile from the last outbuilding, behind a cluster of evergreens, did the Doctor stop and face Harriet to say what he could not utter inside an institution with thin walls and hollow ventilation shafts.

"Now, Miss Caulle, you and I, we have our own mountain to climb. You see ahh — funding cuts are coming down the pipe. This government understands institutions better than most — I suspect that's owing to the Premier's son being at the Provincial Training School in Red Deer — but still, redundancies must be eliminated. I see this as an opportunity. We can make our Holdstock more efficient! State of the art!"

He swung his fist up a few inches in excitement — his gloves were much thicker than hers, and lined with fur! — then continued.

"But the staff, you see. I *fret* about them. This is a time to adapt and they are set in their ways. I fear they might find changes of this uh scale unpleasant. Something of a crucible. Perhaps they will resist."

Heavens, he could go on. Harriet strained to remain still.

"I've hoped you might do me a favour. Indeed, this is partly why I hired from across the country. I need to build bridges with the staff, you see, and I'm not adept at that sort of thing myself. Would you uh assist? Inform me of what they say when I'm not there? So that I can better connect with them? Ruby Rojas, for instance. Our best worker. She holds sway with the staff. But she's swiftly hornswoggled! Unions, Group Homes, whatnot —"

Ah.

There were the lines of allegiance, ever-present, ever exacting. Harriet forever caught between them.

At least they were plain now: the Doctor here, Ruby and the staff there. At least Harriet wouldn't have to guess from jibes and glances.

She needed a minute to think. So difficult to weigh implications here, out-of-doors in the frightful cold.

Ruby she lived with, the staff she worked with. And the Doctor wanted her fealty. More than that, he wanted her to report the very things Ruby and the staff meant him not to hear — they would surely consider it betrayal.

If they found out.

She ran her tongue over her bitten cheek.

Was it betrayal, really? Just some context, wasn't it? A small thing. Transitions needed managing. And how could she say no, here, alone with the Doctor who had hired her and now looked at her expectantly, and then walk with him all the way back to the Main Building?

What was one to do?

Behind the stiff wall of her scarf, she nodded. Of course she could be counted on to help. The movement sent a shudder of cold through the length of her.

"Wonderful! Thank you Miss Caulle! I'm so very grateful. We shall be crackerjack, a first-rate team, you and me!" He clapped his (warm) gloves together. "Now. One can see you're not yet prepared for the climate. But I've bought something for you and best you open it here, before we return indoors."

He pulled from his pocket a white bag of thick cotton, heavy for its size. Harriet could not keep herself from shaking as she opened the drawstring with gloved hands and pulled out a long, weighty chatelaine, silver and visibly expensive.

What risk! Such a gift, and to a woman yet, might be misconstrued. Risk to Harriet too. One didn't like to curry favour, it had a way of coming back.

But he had thought of that too:

"Thank you Doctor! I hardly know what to say!"

"Yes, well," he smiled toothlessly. "Perhaps best to say nothing at all. Especially not to the staff. They'll think you arrived with it."

She opened her coat in the chill air and slipped the chatelaine around her waist. Her fingers refused and the Doctor had to pull off his gloves and fasten the clasp. A brief awkward moment for both of them before the decadent heft of silver settled onto her hips.

At least she could feel her hips.

Tonight, after a hot bath in the blessed indoors, she would attach her nurse's timepiece to it. The cloth bag she slipped into her coat pocket.

They turned back, the Main Building soon in view once more. In a city, it would have loomed, a reinforced-concrete barricade against urban chaos. Here, at the foot of the mountain, it seemed frail. A balsa wood plaything.

Later, after the indoor tour, Harriet wandered back up through the Main Building, opening closet and cupboard doors, checking each key on her ring, assessing for order. The halls were wide with sturdy wooden handrails, the corkboards had schedules neatly posted, secured by evenly cut pieces of tape. (So many disasters prevented, so many disorders calmed right down, if only everyone knew what was coming next.) No thumbtacks, staples, or other sharps to be seen. The beds on the wards were neatly made, the spaces between them might have been measured. The diamonds on the bedspread prints lined up and you could follow a single diamond column across twenty beds on one side of the ward. The baseboards in the stairwells were dust-free (she ran her finger along them), the ointment lids on the med carts were wiped clean, the suction equipment state of the art. She could read her breastpin ("Miss H. Caulle, Head Psychiatric Nurse") in the reflection of the enormous soup cookers in the kitchen, they were that shiny. And everywhere the comforting smell of carbolic acid pushing away reminders of intimacy.

At one point, a young woman sharply dressed in starched blouse and pencil skirt approached her, said her name was Gracie and she was a patient on Harriet's ward. She had been properly let down, she said, that Harriet's summation of work experience, posted on the corkboard, showed no study of structuralists nor philosophy of any kind. She had been wanting for "an intelligent conversation every now and then" and had been "hoping for someone around here who was well read."

Harriet nodded politely and kept a rigid face until Gracie walked away, and then smiled discreetly into her fingers. One thing you could count on: this population was never dull.

The single Holdstock irregularity was the mountain itself. The Main Building was lodged in it, rock intruding right into some rooms. In Laundry, the stone face regulated heat from the washing, had some use. But the Great Room was crowded with patients circulating around one activity or another, and what you noticed, what drew your eye, was the rock. Oh, there was a primitive beauty about it, but — well, you go to such lengths to keep the place clean, and there you have a great dirty *stone* in the busiest room looking right at you. The pests and vermin drawn to stones, to nest or cocoon in the crevices! And the room was too chilly now in December. All the radiators and fireplaces in the world aren't going to warm up a mountain.

Still. A purpose, a routine, a tidy set of rules, the child safely sedated upstairs. And of the workers she had met, none wore a chatelaine of any kind. She might not love it here, but perhaps it would be all right.

(Many years later, Harriet whispered into a tape recorder of the acute apprehension dominating her first days at the Holdstock Facility and how it was the Doctor, his demonstrated appreciation of her, that finally set her at ease.)

Holdstock Facility Daytime Duties Manual, 1963, excerpt:

6:30 AM	Night staff wake patients. Ambulatory: toilet them. Bedridden/wheelchairs: change diapers. Scrub your hands with yellow soap between each diaper. Bedridden/wheelchair-bound: brush teeth in bed (glasses in kitchen, toothpaste, toothbrushes in night table drawers). Ambulatory: brush teeth in Wash Room. Bedridden: reposition. Sign out.
7:00 AM	Day staff arrive. Sign in. Bedridden/chair-bound: feed in bed. Ambulatory: take to Dining Room in their pajamas. (Breakfast is the stickiest meal).
	Nurses: Distribute morning medications with breakfast.
	Immediately after breakfast, bathe all patients, no exceptions. Ambulatory: walk to Shower Room, undress in Dressing Room, shower, then dry and dress in Dressing Room, and walk to ward. Bedridden/chair-bound: undress in bed, cover with draw sheets, transport to Tub Room on stretchers. Orderlies lift patient into tub, and out onto stretchers after bathing. Dry them in Tub Room, cover with draw sheets for transport to ward, and dress on ward.
	Pay special attention to patients who dislike water; they might act out. Should someone self-stimulate, clean up fluid but otherwise ignore. Should someone urinate in tub, ignore it. Should someone defecate in tub, drain water, lift solids with scoop hanging on south wall, give to custodian to dispose, and re-bathe patient.
	Orderlies: Tubs are deep. Lift patients carefully using legs, not back.
	Immediately after bathing, shave men (razors are locked in cupboard at Nurses' Station), perfume girls. Dress all patients in day clothes. Ambulatory/chair-bound should be up either on their feet or in wheelchairs.

10:30 AM	Mid-morning snack. Tie bibs on all patients before snack. Clean up snack, change patient's clothes if necessary.
	Nurses: Distribute mid-morning medications along with snack.
11:00 AM	Bedridden: reposition. Change diapers of all who need it. Scrub your hands with yellow soap between each diaper. Wheel or walk patients to Vocational or School Activity area in Great Room. Ambulatory: toilet in Great Room Toilet Enclosure. Chair-bound: check and change diapers, if necessary. Stretchers for changing are behind doors. Scrub your hands with yellow soap between each diaper. Activity area staff will tell you where to leave each patient. If you are assigned to assist in Activity area, follow Activity staff instructions.
12:30 PM	Lunch. Ambulatory/Chair-bound: take to Dining Room and eat lunch with them. Bib all patients. Bedridden: feed in bed.
	Nurses: Distribute noon medications. Must be taken with meal.
	Immediately after lunch, Ambulatory: toilet them. Chair-bound/bedridden: check and change diapers. Scrub hands with yellow soap between each diaper. Bedridden: reposition.
2:00 PM	Ambulatory/Chair-bound: return to Activity area.
2:45 PM	Mid-afternoon snack. Bib every patient before snack. Clean up after snack. Ambulatory: toilet in Great Room Toilet Enclosure. Chair-bound/bedridden: check and change diapers of all who need it. Scrub your hands with yellow soap between each diaper. Bedridden: reposition.
	Nurses: Distribute mid-afternoon medications along with snack.

3:00 PM	Day staff: Sign out. Evening staff: Sign in.
Notes:	- <u>Never</u> take your eyes off patient in Toilet Room.
	- <u>Never</u> take your eyes off patient in Dressing, Bath, Wash, or Shower rooms.
	- <u>When feeding, never</u> leave patient's side until all food is swallowed: aspiration is a frequent cause of death in bedridden. Each Nurses Station has an aspirator on a wheeled cart. Call nurse immediately if patient aspirates.
	- Some patients resist eating or dislike medications hiding in their food. Cajole, distract, and find ways to make meal a pleasant affair. As last resort only, pry mouths open with spoon, <u>being careful not to cut skin or hurt teeth</u>. Do not, under any circumstances, pinch nose shut to compel patient to open mouth. This method has caused more aspirations than any other.
	- Dining Room staff behind counter will spoon out ketchup if required. Under no circumstances should ketchup bottles be on tables.
	- Extra pillows for repositioning are in cupboards above doors.
	- <u>Nurses:</u> Set up <u>triple</u> medication checks on cart every time. The wrong drugs can kill someone.
	- Laundry bins are now categorized. Please sort laundry as you drop it into bins: RED bins for diapers (Drop whole diaper into bin, feces and all. Laundry staff will dispose of feces), GREEN for linens, YELLOW for towels and bibs and other terrycloth, BLUE for patient clothes.

Of all units, Harriet's had the fewest diapered patients. Even so, by the end of her shifts, the harsh yellow soap had left her hands crevassed and seeping, longing for the distant memory of skin. Then she would return to Ladies' Staff Quarters and immerse them in petroleum jelly or mineral oil. Once, when no one was watching, she tiptoed down to the kitchen and sank them into a pound of soft butter.

The day of the last Christmas Skate and Open House began with the snarl of a chainsaw as maintenance workers in leather gloves and aprons cut fallen trees that had been dragged to the site of the Facility lake with tractor and chains. By 11:00 AM, the stack of dry wood was taller than the outdoor privy and the bonfire flames reached twenty feet in the air, keeping the serrated cold at bay.

The rink itself, Harriet learned from Ruby, had been built by Irwin Coffey, an ambulatory patient. Back in October, Ruby had retrieved Irwin's old carpentry toolbox from Storage and brought it to him. He opened the lid, laid out the tools on a table in the Great Room, wiped and oiled each chisel and hammer and saw, and took them outside. Their weight slid into old grooves in his hands once more as he carved felled trees and stumps into benches and bolted them into the ground around the lake. In the evenings, after the day's work, he sat at a table in the Great Room and rubbed lanolin into his tender hands, muttering quietly that his callouses were returning, it wouldn't be long now until he moved home again.

But when the woodwork was done, two days before the Christmas Skate, he pushed his tools into the Doctor's arms and asked they be put away. The Doctor passed them along to Ruby who returned them to Storage, found Irwin looking searchingly at his lighters, and gave him a long, quiet embrace. There would be no recovery this year.

The next day, Irwin and Ruby together hauled a long hose out to the lake and Nigel Crowfoot, the custodian, transported a generator on the back of a truck. Irwin sawed a hole in the far end of the lake and pumped water up from below to flood the ice on top. The thin coverlet of snow and cracks and ridges in the ice melted and refroze into a pristine green slab. Thus far it had been a winter of extreme cold and very little snow, but a shovel leaned against a bench in case of a squall.

On the day of the Skate, just before noon, Harriet hurried to collect patients from their early lunch and dress them for the outdoors. It was her day off but she was expected to attend nevertheless. Verity, awake again after a week of sedation and already bundled but for her hat, sat on her bed, quiet and dozy, not yet buzzing in her usual way.

Harriet carried her to the window and stood her on a chair to watch the town cars winding their way up the icy mountain road. They could already see tire chains on those at the front of the line.

She turned away to attend to others. Every few minutes, she had to approach the window again — Verity had motioned or pointed at something — and each time, inevitably, there were still more cars. By the time Ruby came to escort ambulatory patients outside, it seemed that most of the town was down in the parking lot.

"Why on earth so many people, Ruby?" Harriet asked.

"Best ice rink in the area and it's the only day all year they get access," she said, guiding a patient away. "It's an occasion — you'll see!"

Harriet hoped not to see. She hoped for an afternoon in the blessed indoors away from windows altogether. With so many people, she would not be missed.

The Doctor's car pulled into the lot.

Bother! It was unavoidable. He would surely look for her outside and must not see her unrest.

She huffed, and tugged Verity's toque onto her head and sent her with Ruby, then returned to her room. Clenching against the aggressive scratch, she pulled on a double layer of woolen stockings, an extra underskirt, undershirt, and sweater, then her coat, two scarves, warmest hat, and boots. (Why had no one warned her of the great inconvenience of cold?) She braced, stepped out the door, and made for the ice rink.

The Presbyterian ladies had set up a food station near the fire and doled out beef sandwiches and Christmas baking and poured hot cider from vats hauled from the Main Building. Harriet took a green blanket from a woman in an elf cap whose arms buckled under a stack of them. By the bonfire, she wrapped herself in the blanket, eyeing the mountains and ice on one side and the safe Main Building on the other. At one end of the rink, a hockey game was underway, at the other an obstacle course for children. Someone called Harriet's attention to an official, there from Calgary to investigate rink quality; the town of Banff, an hour away, was bidding for the '68 Olympics. Should the bid succeed, they would be interested in using the Facility lake for rehearsals. He tied on skates and skated solemnly around the lake, beef sandwich in hand, ignoring the festivities at the centre, ignoring the mountains, concentrating on each stride, on how blade met ice.

Leading a group of locals, Ruby ran past Harriet towards the Main Building. Minutes later they passed by again, now pushing patients in wheelchairs, and (heavens!) wheeled them onto the ice. One by one, they lined up the chairs, locals on skates behind them. Someone blew a whistle, and the whole row pushed off. The patients, every last one, stretched forward for the finish line, hollering, nearly falling from their chairs into the path of speeding blades.

Then followed a race for women pushing male patients, another for men pushing female patients, another for skaters and patients over fifty-five years, and so on.

Through them all, Verity and a boy named Arvo, the two youngest Facility patients, held up the finish line made of blue Christmas garland. Every few minutes, they became enthralled by fish swimming below the green ice, and knelt to watch them. And when the line dropped, people called out. Arvo quickly stood again and waved to get Verity's attention and they returned to finish-line duty to the cheering of the crowd. Minutes later, they were on their knees again, watching the fish below, their hands and feet splayed on the very ice the blades skimmed.

Harriet watched the races through gloved fingers.

"Uncover your eyes Harriet!" Ruby said, skating by. "Isn't it spectacular? Don't you just love it? Look how happy they are!"

Harriet lowered her hands. If people here loved it, she would love it too. But the blades, the watchful mountains.

She looked away — at chimney smoke on the distant ridge ahead, at the bonfire, at the blessed safe Main Building — and recited to herself the proper sequence of steps in emergency treatment of deep wounds such as those caused by the blade of a skate.

"Merry Christmas, Miss Caulle. What do you think of our publicity event?" Dr. Vestidge spoke quietly to Harriet. He was so short he had to stretch up to speak directly in her ear.

"Doctor! Well, honestly, I can't stop thinking each of those ice-skates is a blade. And that everything would surely be safer indoors."

He pulled out a hanky, already soaked, and wiped his face.

"It taxes the nerves. Indisputably. I hate it myself. But the public wants *Currier and Ives*. Today we give it to them. Thank you, Irwin."

Irwin the rink-maker had handed him a cigarette lighter and another to Harriet. "Present," he said, in a gruff and quiet voice, without meeting their eyes, and moved on to the next group of people.

"Doctor! That patient has a sack of butane lighters!"

"Yes, well, last week he had a hammer and saw." He wiped his face again. "If he's true to form, he'll collect them shortly, carry them back to his room, and stand them up like dominoes in his personal effects drawer. Which is locked, by the way. He asks for the key when he wants to look at them."

"But whyever allow him any at all?"

"Miss Caulle, I'd dispose of them if I could. But Irwin and his lighters were here years before I arrived and there's never been an incident. I emptied the fuel of course, that caused uproar enough, but I haven't sufficient cause to remove them altogether. Thankfully, he never wants to light them. He's a brain injury. A beam fell on his head in a carpentry shop fire. Now, lit candles or fireplaces frighten him. Look how he avoids the bonfire."

Irwin was collecting the lighters again. And when the townspeople handed them back and thanked him for making the rink or told him they still used the table or cabinet he once built for them, he tucked his hands under his arms and said, "'Lo," in a deep voice, as if it were expected, nodded, and didn't meet their eyes.

The *Carabiner* photo shows the mountain-circled rink, Verity and Arvo at the centre holding up the Christmas garland finish line, and skaters pushing people in wheelchairs who are shouting, laughing, reaching for the line. The spectators, cheering in white and black, exude a Victorian lithographic charm. Harriet is in the photo. She stands by the fire, wrapped in a blanket. She covers her face with it and is identifiable only by her distinctive cloche hat and fashionable heeled boots (which stand out in a crowd of toques, fur-lined caps, and heavy boots obviously designed for warmth). The caption mentions that the Christmas Skate of 1963 was a particularly loud one; the snowless ice, rimmed by mountains, became a drum. If someone dropped a rock or shouted, the sound reverberated off the hard surfaces in echoes, boom rumble boom.

Deaf-as-a-stone Verity wouldn't have noticed. What she later recalled was a dog off its leash, licking her face when she knelt on the ice. Her mouth open in silent laughter.

After the Skate, after the short Holiday Open House, after everyone was safely inside and the public far away, the patients changed clothes for their Christmas party. Someone in Administration, who never worked front line, had decided a patient could be Santa Claus this year and had told him so. But within days many patients wanted to be Santa Claus. A few of the orderlies had spent much of December sewing up thirty Santa Claus suits for those patients who wanted them. A reasonable, equitable solution.

Harriet sat in the Great Room beside the snapping fire and across from the beribboned spruce under which Ruby was stuffing presents. The orderlies rolled the bedridden into the Great Room first. Even Julienne, the girl with hydrocephalism so severe it was dangerous to move her, was wheeled in on a stretcher. It had been piled high with pillows held in place with stretcher straps. An orderly sat behind her, resting a hand on either side of her enormous head to catch and steady it if it should slide in any direction. Her hair, more scalp than hair, had been washed and combed and a red ribbon had been tied across her forehead. She was wearing lipstick. She looked pretty and smiled widely.

Verity ran in, saw Harriet, smiled, and made straight for her lap.

Harriet began to lift her off and onto the chair beside, when Ruby said, quietly, "Harriet, she's four years old and you're the one she knows best. It's Christmas."

"Other patients don't sit on my lap."

"They're not four. The Doctor left an hour ago. He won't know."

Harriet said nothing, but allowed the child to relax against her. After a minute, Verity turned in Harriet's lap, took Harriet's face between her tiny hands, and kissed her nose. Harriet shifted her chair so that she could see who came through the doorway before they saw her, then gave Verity a quick squeeze and kissed the back of her head.

Wearing a Santa Claus suit and navy slippers, a tall thin man named Bernie walked in. He picked up a stacking chair and carried it to the wall, away from other people, sat down and started to rock quickly, intensely, hands curled inward and a stiff smile on his face.

And then the second and third and fourth Santa Clauses walked in and sat down. Soon the chairs were full of red felt.

It took half a minute for realization followed by anguish to set into their faces like cooling wax: each Santa Claus had believed he or she would be the only Santa Claus. A moment, however brief, of distinction.

Another half-minute and thirty Santa Clauses sat in the Great Room, wailing, thirty white pom-poms over a sea of red felt, bobbing as they cried.

Ruby, Nigel the custodian, Harriet, the other staff, they looked at one another helplessly and quietly began to laugh.

Harriet was in her element now.

She lowered Verity to the floor and strode to the intercom on the wall. She called all available staff — custodial, kitchen, laundry, grounds, medical — to the Great Room. She directed three staff to stay there with the non-Santa patients and Nigel's grand fire, and the other staff to take two Santas each back to their rooms to dress again in everyday clothes.

Harriet herself escorted Bernie and a Mongoloid fellow named Stephen back to their ward. Verity followed behind. Harriet sat the men side-by-side on Bernie's bed and reached to undo both waist buckles, one with each hand. In tandem, each man took her hand in both of his and gently pushed it away. She pulled off Stephen's hat, and, when she reached to remove Bernie's, Stephen's hat went back on his head.

Harriet stood back from the bed then and surveyed the ward.

Everywhere, staff were having the same battle.

A power struggle with a patient is already lost, every Psych nurse knew.

Harriet left the young men there, on the bed, and hurried to the Nurses' Station where she had seen a plate of sugar cookies for the staff. She took four and returned to the room. She gave one to Verity who stood by the bed quietly watching, she sat on the bed beside Bernie, and she began to eat.

"Cookie?" Stephen asked. Bernie didn't speak. He ate the crumbs that fell from Verity's cookie onto his bedspread.

"Certainly, Stephen. After you take off the Santa suit. If Verity and I were wearing Santa suits, we couldn't eat cookies."

Bernie's suit came off without further coaxing. Stephen complied only after Bernie motioned a request to eat his cookie.

With two Santa suits off, the other patients in the room began to relent, one at a time. In the afternoon's distress, though, Bernie and Stephen had wet their pants and neither wore diapers. The red of the felt was bleeding onto the white and green bedspread. A similar bleed was growing on bedspreads nearby and the room was smelling unmistakeably of warm urine.

Harriet threw hospital policy about decency aside.

She took Stephen and Bernie by the hand, not a stitch between them, and walked them down the hall. They paused at the Nurses' Station, one exasperated nurse out of uniform with two naked men — Stephen began jumping to watch his genitals swing — and Harriet called Laundry and had them deliver extra diapers to all wards, including those where patients weren't diapered. And then they marched forward to the Toilet Room, Verity marching behind.

It was a full hour before the party got underway again.

Santa Claus suits forgotten, they gathered in the chairs and sang carols at the top of their lungs like there was no tomorrow, none louder than Ruby. To Harriet, it sounded terrible. Only a handful could keep a tune. But here they were. Inside, warm, safe, none slashed by skates, none eloped into the hills, and so happy.

Since the patients had been promised, the staff decided that afternoon that each could be Santa for one week of the year. Someone wore a Santa suit nearly every week that year and Christmas music played every month of the year.

(The following December, when Harriet went looking, the Christmas music records were gone. She did not file a complaint; if she had known who'd removed them, she would have thanked them.)

Holdstock Facility Evening Duties Manual, 1963, excerpt:

3:00 PM	Day staff: Sign out. Evening staff: Sign in.
4:00 PM	Help patients clean up Activity area (pick things up hand-over-hand and return to cupboards). Assist Activity staff as needed.
	Maintenance staff: Build fire in Great Room fireplace. Fasten grate firmly when finished.
4:15 PM	Bedridden/wheelchair-bound: check and change diapers. Scrub hands with yellow soap between diapers. Bedridden: reposition. Ambulatory/Chair-bound: take to Great Room Relaxation Area. Ambulatory: toilet in Great Room Toilet Enclosure. Play records and set games and books within reach of patients. Books, catalogues, board games in right cupboard under window. If weather is nice, patients may be taken outside on paths. Those in motorized wheelchairs can drive themselves provided that a staff is also outside in the area. Outdoors, patients must wear hats and be warmly dressed.
5:30 PM	Supper. Bedridden: bib and feed in bed. Ambulatory/Chair-bound: walk or wheel to Dining Room. Bib before eating.
	Nurses: Distribute dinnertime medications. Must be taken with meal.
	Immediately after supper. Ambulatory: toilet them. Chair-bound/bedridden: check and change diapers. Scrub your hands with yellow soap between each diaper. Ambulatory/Chair-bound: return to Great Room, or to wards if they prefer. Bedridden: reposition.

7:30 PM	Prepare patients for bed. Examine skin carefully. Treat any new scrapes or sores. Apply petroleum jelly to all feet and lips, and do any other treatments as required. Ambulatory: toilet them. Chair-bound/bedridden: change diapers, put on nightgowns and pajamas. Scrub hands with yellow soap between each diaper. Bedridden: reposition.
8:15 PM	Night Snack. Give snack in bed. Bib all patients. Nurses: Distribute nighttime medications with snack.
8:45 PM	Ambulatory: toilet them. Chair-bound/bedridden: check and change diapers. Scrub hands with yellow soap between each diaper. Bedridden: reposition. Immediately after diaper change: Lights out.
10:15 PM	Check and change diapers of all who need it. Scrub hands with yellow soap between each diaper. Ambulatory: if awake and asking for toileting, toilet them. Bedridden: if awake, reposition.
11:00 PM	Evening Staff: Sign out. Night Staff: Sign in.

The evenings of the weeks following the Christmas party, Harriet later said, were among her favourite Holdstock memories. After their evening shifts, she and Ruby lay on cushions before the fireplace in Ladies' Staff Quarters. They sipped wine from goblets, they raised their aching feet to the flames, they played checkers and Sorry!, they listened to Ruby's records, and Ruby worked on a cigarette.

One night, she told Harriet about the patients:

Irwin Coffey, the carpenter on one of the General wards, hoped to move back into the house he had built with his own hands. "He made an oaken front door and still plans to woodburn into it a lone spindly spruce bent by the wind. He'll show you the sketch if you ask."

Lily Pitt had left her children with her husband and had checked herself into Holdstock seeking a cure for her Sapphic longings. "She's strong-minded, plain-speaking, sensible. The breadwinner in the family — her husband was shell-shocked in Korea. She thought she'd be here a month at most."

Arvo Herzog, the mute eight-year-old, loved making things roll. "He's on a program to stop rocking. When we see him rocking, we gently redirect him with a soccer ball keychain."

Elsa Sibelius painted in Activity Time. "I've hung her most recent canvas in my bedroom. I think it's revealing." Harriet had seen it and thought it horrid: a woman, body parts misaligned and angular, eyes oriented in opposite directions, limbs attached in absurd places, and a machine beside, funnelling sludge into her head, her pathetic spindly arms too short to reach and remove it, the whole thing done in tones of ochre and charcoal.

Gracie Lee, the scholar on Harriet's ward, always had to know what was coming next. She had abandoned her graduate studies when the uncertainty became too great to bear. "She still reads her books but now she studies the schedules posted on corkboards every day for hours. It calms her. Years ago —" Ruby settled onto a pillow "— on my first day of work, someone forgot to post the new-staff announcement. Gracie was in the lobby and saw me, a stranger in staff uniform, crossing the grounds. She must have squatted behind a sofa and done her business. When I stepped through the door, she let fly at me with a handful of fresh feces."

"Heavens!" Harriet's fingers covered her mouth.

"Instinctively, I caught it. Well, some of it. And — old softball reflexes — I threw it back. Smack into her chest. A bit splashed up onto her face."

Harriet's lips turned down and palm turned out, but Ruby persisted.

"I walked right up to her, put out my filthy hand, and said, 'Hello, my name's Ruby. I'm your new orderly and I'm pleased to meet you.' Gracie fled. The Med Charge Nurse happened to be in the lobby. She looked at me and said, drily, 'You'll do fine,' and sent me to Laundry for a fresh uniform. Since then, Administration has posted staff and routine changes most diligently."

Together, they laughed and laughed.

"Now Harriet. Tell me about Verity," Ruby turned to face Harriet and rested her head on her hand. "We never get young residents anymore! They're usually sent to the Training School in Red Deer where there's a farm. She likes machines and magazines but you travelled with her. You must really know her."

"Uh —"

Harriet scrambled. Verity was mute and deaf and feeble-minded. What else was there to *know*? She liked machines and magazines? A revelation to Harriet.

To buy some time, she pretended a sneeze.

"Well, let's see," she said, wiping her nose and folding her handkerchief back into her pocket. "When her father left her at

Elora, she clung to his leg pitifully. For weeks after, the staff had to coax her away from windows. I suppose she was watching for him." (Harriet hadn't supposed it at the time, but now it seemed the sort of conclusion Ruby would draw.)

"Oh myyy, that's awful," Ruby said, suddenly sober.

"Also," Harriet said, wanting to lighten the mood, "that girl has permanently chapped lips, no end of energy, and always wants affection!"

They laughed then and refilled their goblets.

Yes, those were the best times.

Now that Ruby had asked, Harriet began to watch Verity differently. Strange how often she placed her ear against walls, speakers, floors, windows, the vertical beams. Against nearly everything, it seemed. Well, perhaps the girl lacked sensation in her hands. Some kind of nerve damage? But then Harriet saw her approach a hot radiator, try it with tentative fingers, and back away. Clearly the nerves were intact. It had to be a kind of feeble-minded self-stimulation then. At least it wasn't violent.

Since the train journey, Verity had attached herself to Harriet, and each time Harriet left the ward, the child tried to follow. She was so quick and so quiet that Harriet had often moved a great distance, to another floor or another building, before she noticed Verity behind her, mimicking Harriet's stride and posture as exactly as she could, and with an entitled expression yet. As if she belonged there behind Harriet and nowhere else.

As part of Harriet's orientation as Head Nurse, she was to spend a week working each of the shifts so that she might know the routines of the evening and night shifts as well as her own day shift. The first night, after the patients were asleep, she and the night orderly were folding laundry in the lit hallway by the cupboard just outside the swinging, wooden Psych Ward doors. The doors had a solid bolt and latch up at eye level and a narrow glass pane running nearly the height of them.

Someone tapped the glass. There stood Verity in her nightgown, peering out the vertical pane. Harriet opened the door, picked her up, and again tucked her into bed. But when she slipped out, latching the doors behind her, there was Verity, so quick, already out in the hall, already snug in the wheeled bin of clean blankets. Back onto the ward then, where Harriet tucked her in again and walked out backwards so as not to take her eyes off the child. No sooner had the bolt and latch clicked shut than Verity was at it again, tapping gently on the glass.

"Leave her be," said the orderly. "She'll tire soon enough."

But she did not tire.

Tapping, tapping, tapping, she stood there for one half hour, then another, accusing face turned on Harriet and the orderly as they folded laundry for the ward.

Finally Harriet could bear no more and left, ostensibly to fetch something from another floor.

When she returned some time later, Verity had dug a long nail into the bevelling in the door at the edge of the glass and was working to pry the pane loose from the other side, dismantling the door!

Quickly Harriet unlatched it. Verity's nightstand now stood lopsided. She had unscrewed a leg to access the long nail. How could — Well, it must have already been unscrewed and Harriet too busy to notice. Verity herself was wrapped around Harriet's leg, clinging fiercely, as she had clung to her father's leg in Elora.

Harriet bent down then and lifted her. Verity cuddled into her neck and relaxed. With the girl on her arm, rocking as she walked, Harriet unlocked the nurse's desk, and pulled out leather restraints. Verity played with them as if they were toys as Harriet carried her back to her bed. She pulled at Harriet to join her under the covers and, when Harriet instead tied up her little hands and feet, Verity's expression changed to one of disbelief and then the tears began silently to well.

Inhuman to tie up a child, any child. But what was one to do?

Then it was Harriet's turn to watch through the door. The moment Verity was asleep she hurried in and removed the restraints, snuck a wrapped candy beneath the pillow for Verity to find, and penned a request that the girl be transferred to another floor.

ATHENA'S JOURNAL
FEBRUARY 27, 2004
(FRIDAY)

The testing has begun.

Imran, my friend and IAL worker, asked if I wanted him here when they test me. At first, I thought yes, it is always nice to have Imran around, but I asked if I would then appear dependent. He said probably, but I should do that with which I felt most comfortable and not worry about how it looks to the tester. I told him to go, I would look after myself.

He is being supportive, I know. But the system will not willingly relinquish custody of Arvo. Every moment of dependence will count against me. I reminded Imran that I have often been uncomfortable in my life. It is not a great tribulation.

The tester, at least, is lovely. She is overweight. (Imran will chide me for that word, but the tester herself says "Fat! I am fat. There is no shame in taking up space.") She is jovial and friendly —

and perhaps a little nervous. She laughs a moment too soon, I find, and a little too hard. And when she does not realize I am watching, she chews her hair. And by that I mean that she chews it off: the section over her left ear is an inch shorter than the section over her right ear. The layered haircut hides the asymmetry and, if I did not look for it, I likely would not see it. But nervousness is nothing to worry about. She signs nicely, with crispness and happy disposition, she takes an interest in me that I feel is genuine, and she does not patronize me. She shows me her credentials when I ask, and, when I tell her about this project, she is interested and encouraging — but asks that I not mention her by name. I will call her Cheery Psychometrist.

She begins with a meticulous tour of the apartment. She opens every cupboard and drawer, including the tiny ones on my desk, lifts the toilet seat, and examines the fire extinguisher. She sits on each stool and tries to make it wobble, she checks that the kitchen knives are safely stowed, she checks expiration dates on food and Rolaids, she checks under the bed. She explains, when I ask, that she is assessing my organizational skills, my cleaning skills, and my safety skills, and that these evaluations are part of the Daily Skills Inventory. And then she says she is "peeking at my naughty secrets" and immediately laughs very hard. I believe it is meant to be a joke.

I was concerned about the paintings. (These are cheap prints from thrift shops. My subsistence cheques do not allow for real paintings.) Last week, over a fine ciabatta and bowl of olives, Imran suggested that I take down the Lee Krasner and Elaine de Kooning and recommended Robert Bateman and Norman Rockwell instead. They would make my apartment appear "more conducive to custody."

"How is that possible?" I asked. "Abstract art is popular around the world."

"Yes . . . but panels deciding custody want guardians to be absolutely predictable so that they can know the people being taken care of are safe."

"I am predictable," I say, and chew on an olive. "They can predict I will do everything I can for Arvo, and they can predict I will prefer impressionistic and abstract art over art that is realistic or anaesthetic."

"Yes, but if they don't understand modern art themselves, they can't help but wonder about the psyches of those who do. They might assume that your methods of looking after him will be unconventional, like the art on your walls is unconventional, and consequently suspect."

"Mr. Hitler was like that, you know, Imran. He believed impressionistic art was insane and therefore corrupt. He had many wonderful paintings burned on large pyres. Perhaps I ought to tell them about Mr. Hitler."

"I don't believe that would help your case." Imran smiled and stopped signing to slide his bread through olive oil.

"I have some acrylic paints. I could supplement a Rockwell painting to include leather restraints and syringes."

"Athena," he says, "Political commentary *of any kind* will not be conducive to custody. To appear normal is to appear mainstream. Content with the way things are. What you want here is a pretty picture."

Once again, I wonder if Imran's tastes interfere, if his personal discomfort with modern art influences him now. Nevertheless, after he left, I hung one Van Gogh reprint. *Starry Night.* I thought it a good compromise.

"Look," I said, when Imran next stopped by. "This is a "pretty picture" and I have not altered it. That is a moon. That is a church. That is a star. You can identify everything in this painting."

"Real stars," he said, "do not look so, so turbulent. But yes, this picture is at least recognizable and certainly makes your apartment more conducive to custody." (I believe I will tire of the phrase "conducive to custody" before long.)

"This is a Van Gogh. Mr. Hitler outlawed paintings by Mr. Van Gogh, you know."

"Athena. Promise me, please, that you won't mention Hitler at any point in these proceedings."

I promised, of course. Poor Imran. He is a good friend to me and I torment him so.

I decided to leave the Krasner and de Kooning on the wall. I am willing to do a great deal to acquire custody, but pretending to appreciate art I merely condone would fire back on me: if Arvo does come to live here, I will have sudden visits from officials, some unannounced. If I hang a Rockwell for the assessments, the officials will expect Rockwell when they drop in. They will think me deceptive if they find de Kooning instead. (I could not bear to leave Rockwell on the walls. It would be like entering sedation all over again.)

But I digress. I worried about the paintings and am relieved to report that my concerns were all for naught: Cheery Psychometrist has wider tastes in art than Imran and owns a Van Gogh print herself.

She stands for some time in front of the only original painting I own, by Elsa Sibelius. It was a gift from the artist long ago. At first glance it looks like a Krasner or Pollock drip painting in the early stages. A mess of black lines on white canvas on one half, and a mess of white lines on black on the other half. But if you keep looking, you can see faces in the lines and between the lines, faces of every expression imaginable. Rage, delight, delirium, naiveté, longing, despair, and so forth. Cheery Psychometrist likes that painting very much, it is my favourite too, but she has never heard of the painter. I think it wise not to enlighten her and change the subject.

"Which Van Gogh do you have?" I sign.

"*Vase with Fourteen Sunflowers.* Some of the sunflowers are dead. It's much more realistic than still-life flowers frozen permanently in bloom. Flowers have an unfortunate habit of dying." And then she laughs very hard.

"I like the *Sunflowers* series," I say. "Have you noticed the vase has more than fourteen sunflowers in it?"

"No! Really? I'll count them when I get home."

We sit at the table. She says her job is not to advocate for or against anyone. She must be objective and collect as much information as possible to pass on to the panel. The panel decides custody, she does not. I say nothing, but I suspect her recommendation influences the decision a great deal. Why else these tests?

I show her then that I can make a budget and balance a cheque book. She asks what I eat and I describe my meals in a way that sounds like the *Canada Food Guide.*

Halfway through the Daily Skills test, the mirror light of Mr. Saarsgard, my neighbour and friend, flashes on the wall.

"Will you excuse me for a moment?" I say. "My neighbour is calling."

I let him in. He sees Cheery Psychometrist, apologizes for interrupting, and writes a request that I repair his oven. He has been preparing mincemeat for months, he says, and wants now to bake it into a pie. I am certain he came to ask me to go for a spin but does not want to jeopardize the interview; I repaired the oven thermostat for mincemeat pie last week. Nevertheless, I say I will come along with my toolbox in the evening, after the day's tests are done. All the while, Cheery Psychometrist takes notes.

After we finish the Daily Skills Inventory, she says I will be taking the Peabody Picture Vocabulary Test, the Stanford-Binet Intelligence Scale II, the Wechsler Adult Intelligence Scale, Revised ("it's unwise to rely on one IQ test"), the Wechsler Intelligence

Scale for Children ("not because you are a child, but because it assesses vocational aptitude"), the Wide Range Employability Sample Test, the Minnesota Multiphasic Personality Inventory, Revised, and the Myers-Briggs Personality Assessment.

"Do you have questions?" she asks.

"Yes," I sign. "I have been researching these tests in a library book. I understand their importance for guardianship. But none assesses whether I am able to calm someone during a lightning storm or coax an agoraphobic person onto a crowded bus and into a shopping mall to buy new pants. These are important skills for living with Arvo. Will they be assessed in another set of tests?"

"We could observe them, Honey, and describe them to the panel, but I don't think we could measure them on a standard-ized scale."

I ask her then about the individual tests I will be taking and point out the criticisms levelled at them in the library book. She says she will compensate for the verbal dependency of the Peabody by modifying it for signing and by not measuring the speed of my responses. She will not, however, compensate for the gender and cultural biases in the Stanford-Binet and the WAIS and the WISC. The panel, she explains, will take special interest in questions about mainstream culture because they are looking for whether I have sufficient understanding of it to be guardian to Arvo in this culture.

"I wrote a letter about the sexism once," she signs. "Us girls have to show the boys a thing or two about smarts." She laughs here and touches my arm in what I believe is meant as camaraderie.

I begin to tell her about the creators of the Myers-Briggs who never studied Psychology when she touches my arm to interrupt:

"Athena," she says, "I expect each of these tests has failings, though I've never researched beyond gender inequity. You are right to raise them and consider their implications, but analyzing the failings of each test will take a long time, time we don't have. My answer to you then is this: we will do these tests because I have to submit a report in June that includes this information. And at Arvo's custody hearing, I will be asked about the tests and how you ranked. All this information will be taken into consideration when the panel makes its decision about custody."

"These are excellent reasons to take each of these tests," I say and nod. "I will not resist. I hope my questions have not jeopardized my ranking."

"Not at all," and she pauses her signing to touch my arm again. "I'm impressed you're interested in the process and not just the outcome."

We set times for the remaining tests. I refrain from asking if other guardians have to take them. I know the answer.

After she leaves, I sip English Breakfast tea (hot) and wonder why someone who administers tests every week would not research them extensively. Still more astonishing, how does a person look at the Van Gogh every day and not notice it has more than fourteen flowers? What is she looking at when she looks at the painting?

I am off to Mr. Saarsgard's now. I am taking my toolbox. I am also taking a jacket and scarf in case we go for a spin.

Note: Mr. Saarsgard reads this journal entry and points out that "fire back" should be "backfire" — "This isn't German; we rarely split our verbs like that" — and "all for naught" is a phrase no longer in common usage. How regrettable. I like that phrase.

I also like the word "pie" spelled "p-y-e." I learned a few years ago, when I tried to make a pumpkin pie, that the p-y-e spelling is no longer used at all. I could not get the pumpkin flesh and egg and cream and spices to set. The mixture swished about impudently there in the perfect crust. I went to Mr. Saarsgard for help, and he said pumpkin pie is difficult to make from scratch because it uses no corn starch nor any of the usual thickeners. He suggested I purchase pie filling instead, and informed me that the "p-y-e" spelling I had used was obsolete.

I will make the edits later.

FEBRUARY 1964
HOLDSTOCK

Harriet sat at the back of the Dining Room with the other nurses, trying to blend in. Dr. Vestidge rocked on his toes at the front, red and sweating.

"We have a real opportunity here, folks," he said. "With fat-trimming and belt-tightening, Holdstock can become a svelte institution. We can weather the storm, and emerge stronger than before. We'll be an example. More with less. An exciting gauntlet to take up!"

Harriet looked around. The staff seemed undeceived. They knew what his words really meant. Jaws set, knuckles grew and whitened, the volume of air became insufficient. The room clenched.

"Here's how we'll proceed. No new purchases other than food and medications and absolute necessities for a year. At least. If things break and can't be cheaply repaired, we'll not replace them, so let's safeguard what we have. No further special events or patient outings. Holdstock patients are from this point confined to grounds.

"A bit of restructuring now. Medical and Behaviour Wards will collapse into one, and three General Wards will collapse into two. We'll push beds together for room. And all uhh non-essential staff — Activity and Vocational, for instance — will be laid off. The rest of us will pick up their duties. Postings are on the corkboard."

On the list went, long, obscene, and through it all the Doctor looked up at the lights or down at his notes but never at Harriet nor anyone else in the room. When people glanced her way, Harriet pretended ignorance, furrowed her brow, and shook her head along with them.

The Doctor left the room without taking questions. Harriet followed the others, bruised and silent, out of the Dining Room and alongside the corkboard to read the lists of layoffs and extra staff assignments.

And promptly made for his office.

The door stood ajar. He was leaning over his desk and tugging back and forth at his tie.

"Doctor, I'm a nurse," she said without knocking. "I have no Vocational experience."

"Yes, Miss Caulle, I know that." He sawed at his neck, finally loosing the tie, and wiped under his collar.

"The corkboard says I'm to pick up six School Activity Area hours weekly with the child patients "on account of considerable expertise in Vocational training." I've *no* expertise in it. I've not even observed Vocational staff working."

"Yes, I understand. Please close the door." He was sweating still, profusely, his neck so inflamed as to appear altogether absent. "I, er, I must justify to the board and the staff that I hired you in the face of deep cuts. And I combined Behaviour and Medical wards. It would make considerably more sense to combine Behaviour and Psych wards but would do you out of a position, and in fact I need you. It occurred to me you'd have little trouble picking up where Vocational staff left off. Certainly their work cannot be difficult and the material not terribly challenging."

He smiled at her now, in sweaty camaraderie.

"Oh."

Her presence meant others more senior than she would be let go, that was now clear. Transitions did need the right people. But — how awkward.

"You're right Doctor, I'll manage. I wanted to be certain you knew I had no Vocational training."

"Certainly, certainly. Er — no one else need know that."

She reached into her pocket and handed him a fresh handkerchief.

That weekend, before her new shifts started, Harriet went down to School Activity to gather what it was that she was supposed to do there. In a locked cupboard she found binders of records and carried a few to a table to read.

Today, Sophia picked up the empty spoon without staff assistance. She placed food on her spoon with staff assistance.

Today, Freddy went twelve minutes without slapping his face, an improvement of seven seconds. His chart received a star.

Today, Salvatore applied glue to a popsicle stick with staff guidance.

After first assessing each patient — a surprisingly involved undertaking — staff had written "programs," (Ruby had mentioned programs), step-by-step methods to repeat daily, sometimes for years, so that patients could learn individually, "in ways best suited to each," and they had carefully recorded their pupils' progress.

The Sophia girl had learned to feed herself after three years — three *years* — of daily hand-over-hand, of teaching her muscles to close around the spoon, to scoop up a specific amount of food, to guide it to her mouth. After four-and-a-half years of gentle redirection, Freddy had stopped the self-abuse altogether. And the Salvatore patient had eventually constructed a popsicle-stick cube one hand-over-hand stick at a time; a photograph was affixed. The shelves sagged under dozens of notebooks and binders, each meticulously documenting progress. One patient printed her name after six years of coaching. Another had learned to read. Many never showed any improvement whatsoever.

Heavens.

Harriet stood to shut the curtains and switch on a lamp, then sat again.

She had heard of schools for the feeble-minded in Elora, mostly run in somebody's basement by well-meaning parents who spent their evenings lobbying school boards. She had lauded their efforts, donated to their cause. But the day-to-day of it she had imagined to be something more akin to babysitting than to the rigor she read here.

A stack of books sat at the corner of the desk: *Positive Reinforcement in People with Mental Retardation, Encouraging Speech in Mutes, Agoraphobia to Zemmiphobia: An A-to-Z Guide to Panic Disorders and Treatments, Evaluating Literacy in the Mentally Retarded.* She flipped through them. They seemed as thoroughly researched as any nursing text, though the science was different. Two books had been authored by someone just laid off here at Holdstock, someone she now replaced.

Faking a vocational background was not going to be easy.

One thing at a time, one thing at a time. Rushing in never did anyone any good. She would spend her first shift observing.

The following afternoon, Harriet opened the relevant binders before her and watched.

Elsa was painting something horrid again. She was a teenager, old enough for the Adult Activity area, her binder said, but the school area painting program "better suited her post-electroconvulsive therapy recovery."

Arvo hefted shelves down from empty bookcases around the room — Harriet locked her knees together to prevent herself interfering — and assembled them into a ramshackle series of linking ramps around the School area. He reached to the top of the highest ramp, let go a sponge ball, and sat down to watch it pick up momentum and roll from ramp to ramp. He rocked slowly as he watched. When the ball finally trundled to a stop halfway across the Great Room, he retrieved it and did it all over again, wholly absorbed.

Verity sat on a child's chair, looking at a magazine and moving her lips, imitating people who could read. She had not been sleeping well of late. Bed-wetting, tossing in nightmare, sometimes crying. "Did anything like this happen on the train?" Ruby had asked. "Not once," Harriet said. "Then she's in distress." "No Ruby, it's common in this population. The Doctor says so." And Ruby had given her such a look, as if seeing something in Harriet for the first time. At least the girl had given up following Harriet. That was a blessing.

Suddenly Verity looked up and dropped her magazine: Arvo had abandoned the ramps and pushed towards her an empty broken med cart that had been standing by the janitor's closet for repair. Something was wrong with the castors; it lurched and clacked across the floor. Deftly he and Verity overturned the cart, laid it on its back. She had a screwdriver in hand — from where on earth had it come? Harriet watched quietly. A few minutes later, the cart was fixed, Verity raised her arms in momentary triumph, and Arvo pushed it in circles around the School area as if it were a toy truck, peeking around the sides since it was taller than he. Verity returned to her magazine. The screwdriver was nowhere to be seen.

Harriet made a note about the screwdriver. Verity had no programs yet and it was her job to invent one. Where to begin? What kind of "programs" did one construct for a persistent, sleep-disturbed, profoundly retarded, deaf five-year-old who stole tools and Lord knows what else? More to the point, what kind of programs to convince the staff that Harriet had vocational expertise? An uncomfortably complex deception.

The Shift Change bell rang. Well, she would come up with something.

She helped the children tidy the area and tucked a program-writing book and the panic-disorder book into her largest pocket. Maybe they would help her patch something together.

In the end none of it mattered. With the sporadic staffing, programs couldn't be maintained and Vocational record-keeping was abandoned. If other staff noticed Harriet's dearth of vocational training, they were too busy or too intimidated to say. Elsa spent her days painting since that was what she liked to do. Arvo rocked and played with ramps and balls, and Verity looked at magazines and books and tinkered with whatever contraptions she could find. At least once a week a staff member wouldn't show for an Activity shift, and the children were sent to Laundry to fold sheets and towels.

It became, Harriet noted later, a version of babysitting after all.

The cutbacks were severe; things at the Holdstock Facility did not go well for some time. For weeks, Harriet was suddenly called to assist in one crisis or another on the collapsed Medical-Behaviour Unit where the quietest, most fragile patients now lived with the noisiest, most aggressive, and staff trained in one field now worked in another. A worker originally from the Behaviour Unit changed the diaper of Ivan, the rigid-legged brittle-boned Med-Unit boy, before having time to read his file, before learning his knee joints had never functioned. When Harriet came to set the leg, the orderly said he had *heard* it break from across the ward. Another time, two workers rather than the necessary three tried to change Julienne, the hydrocephalic. Her heavy head slipped, the worker reached — and pressed a frantic hand into the enormous soft spot on the top of her head. Harriet came running, but the damage was permanent and the girl would never recover enough to smile. One of the Cystic Fibrosis girls who needed chest physio six times a day received it now twice, and aspirated badly. Harriet arrived as they were beginning artificial respiration. Dr. Vestidge sent the girl to an Urgency and Emergency Unit in Calgary where she died a month later. (He reminded the staff that she had outlived most CF patients and had not died on-site, it was not their fault.) A Spina Bifida boy — what was his name — broke a finger, presumably in a bed frame, and no one noticed for days. By then the finger was shiny and swollen and Harriet was called to help re-break and re-set it. There was no longer time to check every quarter hour on the girl whose twin got the entire placenta and to wipe her face and neck. By mid-morning each day, cups of gelatinous rank-smelling sputum pooled on her sheets and pillows and hands. Her fingers and chin grew raw and abraded from constant moisture. Harriet started to check on her once a shift and to smear her chin with the petroleum jelly she still kept in her pocket for Verity's chapped lips. Each time Harriet stepped on that ward, she noticed Medical patients deteriorating, probably from sleep deprivation, wakened every few minutes by one or another Behaviour patient calling out, wailing, or hitting his head against the bed railing.

Harriet's own ward became so fragile she didn't dare take her usual days off for a month. Stress-induced seizures and self-abuse were up — she led one psychotic or another to the padded room nearly every day now — and the patients learned coping mechanisms from each other. Those who had never pulled or eaten hair now did both. The two Praeder-Willi patients, without the surveillance of a full complement of staff, ate everything in sight and vomited soon after. Harriet told her staff not to return the bucket and mop to Janitorial. They were mopping up vomit daily anyways, it may as well stay on the ward. Gracie's nightly obsessive door checks became feverish. If she couldn't test each lock thirty-three times (rather than three), she trembled and wept and chanted self-protective rhythms. One night, with Harriet beside her, she flipped the deadbolt back and forth and listed obsessively species of pine trees by their Latin names.

"Number one *Pinus monticola*. Number two *Pinus cembra*." Harriet waited patiently. Perhaps at number thirty-three (*Pinus contorta*) Gracie could let go the lock by herself. But when she reached thirty-three, Gracie started over again. Harriet gently pried her fingers off the bolt then and led her away. Another night, she listed every patient on the Psych Ward, followed by their medications and dosages. "Gracie, how do you know their prescriptions?" Harriet pressed. "That information is locked up." But Gracie continued to chant until Harriet finally sedated her so she could rest. In the frenzy, the announcement of permanent cancellation of the Christmas Skate and Party went unremarked. Perhaps not even noticed.

The Doctor strolled the wards with loaded syringes in his pocket. If a patient seemed disorderly, he'd inject her.

"It makes them comfortable," he smiled.

Most of the staff cringed to see patients sedated and quickly minimized problems or covered them up if he was in sight. Ruby's method was gently to redirect him; she kept in her pocket a list of things around the Facility needing minor repair, and if she saw him coming and patients were about, she'd call to him urgently. Harriet saw the two of them at least once a week, heads bowed in low conversation about this loose railing or that jammed stretcher wheel.

Ruby, self-appointed advocate of the feeble-minded; Ruby, who encouraged patient risk-taking; Ruby, now fretting about safety? She had probably sabotaged the thing herself. Harriet had no proof, though, and when the Doctor thanked Ruby appreciatively for her vigilance, unaware of the rift that openly gaped between them, Harriet fingered her chatelaine. Twice, she almost told the Doctor her suspicions in one of their meetings — but then with whom would she play fireside board games? The other women staff were married and Gracie, bright as she was, wouldn't exactly be appropriate company.

Two good things came of the changes: first, Harriet took advantage of reduced staffing to discard Irwin's lighters. The staff assumed the Doctor had done it. Second, all the rocking and drumming gave her an idea. She had Nigel drive her into town where she bought a small radio. Her ward had music then from dawn to dusk. They could pick up just two stations here in the mountains, but two were better than none. The improvement in patient disposition was marked, and soon all wards had radios, purchased by the staff out of their paycheques.

"Well done, Miss Caulle! Crackerjack!" the Doctor said.

Harriet beamed.

APRIL 1964
HOLDSTOCK

The afternoon after Elsa's electroconvulsive therapy, one of Harriet's nurses reported that Elsa's humerus had broken in treatment.

Harriet stared at her in alarm, ran to Elsa's bed, reached for her arm — and stopped. The ungainly angle, the impossible alignment. It was obviously broken.

There was no excuse for broken bones anymore! Either the dose was too high or the anaesthetic too low. Someone had been careless.

Harriet left the nurse in charge and ran down to the Infirmary. She glanced around for the Doctor.

"He went into town," the orderly said.

Harriet picked up the ECT log.

Ah, here was the problem: routine treatments like Elsa's were being administered by a technician-in-training. The licensed technician, who had treated her for years, now came on-site only for special cases. Cost-saving measures.

Harriet sank into the chair in the waiting area. It was unacceptable, she had to do something.

A minute later she smoothed her skirt and quietly laughed at herself. What had she been thinking? To speak her mind to the Doctor? In this immediate and unreasoned state? At worst she'd lose her post, at best his confidence.

She shook the fuzz from her wits and judiciously filled out the form with as much dispassion as she could muster. It was just a broken arm.

She left the incident report with the orderly to file, took a splint and went back upstairs to set Elsa's arm.

Elsa seemed a different person after the ECT. The agitation and rages of past weeks were gone, and the strange frozen postures distinct to her schizophrenia were replaced by an awkward limpness in the wheelchair. Her unsplinted hand wrapped around her jaw, pain vivid in her eyes.

She could have no more painkillers now, so Harriet wiped her face carefully, applied ointment to the faint burn mark at her temple, and wheeled her to the School Area. Perhaps distraction would help. She set up her easel and paints, wedged a paintbrush between her fingers, and tried to help her to stand. Any movement would coax blood to her muscles, relieve some pain. But Elsa went slack and heavy in the chair and shook her head. She wanted to sit and cry.

Harriet could not bring herself to insist. She drew the curtain shut, set a cup of water within Elsa's reach, and turned to the desk to do paperwork. Verity, she noticed, looked unusually concerned.

When next Harriet looked up, Verity and Arvo were collecting cushions from the sofas and easy chairs by the fireplace. Verity laid them carefully along the wall in a long pile. Then she and Arvo approached Elsa.

Verity gestured something.

Elsa nodded and the two children helped her to her feet, across the School area, and to the heap of cushions. Verity sat first, and then Elsa lay down carefully, Arvo gently taking as much of her weight as he could. She stretched out on the deep softness, her head on the girl's tiny lap.

Young Verity sat like that, motionless, for the remainder of the afternoon, cradling Elsa's head and stroking her forehead, carefully avoiding her jaw and splinted arm, until she finally fell asleep.

(Arvo, meantime, colonized the wheelchair, and propelled himself along the length of the Great Room. Back and forth, back and forth, back and forth, squealing, elated.)

Both Harriet and Ruby mentioned this scene and its remarkable tenderness later in their records. Harriet also noted that Elsa appeared to be picking up Verity and Arvo's strange gestures.

They weren't cooperating. It was mimicry. Surely.

I am returning from another frustrating session with the therapist when Mr. Saarsgard pulls alongside atop his BMW R68 motorcycle, extracts a pen and paper from his jacket, and asks if I might join him for dinner. I hurry inside to change my clothes, he fetches his low-bellied car, and we drive to an Ethiopian restaurant we both like.

He first brought me here several years ago after I had complained about Imran's latest program that forbade me eat anything but bread and fruit with my hands. It is an intimate restaurant with muted lighting and fine linens. In which every person eschews cutlery and eats with hands.

And the food! That *berbere* spice mixture, roasted in the sun, embeds in the chicken dish the slightest knife point, and the slippery goat *tibs* and lentil *wot* are smooth and rich. The first time we ate here, I expected to push aside the bitter greens with white curd but I now find them necessary to the platter, as if the other dishes would cloy without the greens to offset them. I wonder, on these evenings, how my system never seized with the slop of decades past.

I have one complaint about restaurant meals thus far: I would prefer to finish them with tea, a lighter taste than coffee, but I have not yet found a restaurant that serves *hot* tea. Some bring you warm water and a dry teabag and these combine into something frightening, reminiscent of Facility swill. Consequently, I enjoy properly steeped hot tea at home and have coffee with restaurant meals (and lie awake then at night).

Mr. Saarsgard and I always split the bill. He can afford to pay for us both, but he knows that I prefer to pay my own way now that I am able. It is cumbersome to eat with hands and simultaneously converse with pen and paper, and it requires many napkins, but we manage it nevertheless.

"If it's OK to ask, why was therapy difficult today?" he writes. "Did you finally tell therapist about applying for custody?"

I cannot help but sigh.

"Not yet. A man in my project, Esau. Verity's father," I write. "I feel finished with his part of story. Therapist disagrees. Will not let it go. Says I see him too much as victim of tragedy. Implies I assuage his responsibility, romanticize him, ignore evidence."

"What evidence?"

I pull from my bag a copy of the Elora document (Verity's intake form) and we examine it together.

While Mr. Saarsgard reads, I again admire Esau's penmanship. It is calligraphic and economic, elegant and precise. It slants gently to the right, and is written with the most delicate point, each stem surprisingly narrow. He must have carried a special pen with him. Near the end of the form, the slant of the writing increases as if he is hurrying to finish.

"This note," Mr. Saarsgard writes, and points to a sentence in the margins in Esau's handwriting, requesting no further contact with the Home *even under circumstance of death.* "And this one." He points to another in the Comments section, written by the nurse: *Father unattached to child. Hurried away light in step, whistling a tune.*"

"Harsh!" he writes. "You romanticize this man?"

"I understand him," I write. "He did not intend to abandon her. Was coerced."

"Doesn't sound coerced," he writes. "Doubt that explanation would work even in porn."

"Long story," I write. I put away the document and wrap *injera* around a goat piece.

"Athena," he writes, after a while, "Isn't Verity you?"

I nod.

"Why say *her?* Why not *me?*"

We eat as I gather my thoughts. Eventually, I wipe my fingers and write again.

"I know I was Verity," I write. "Am not trying to avoid it. But project is not about that. Is about how these things were able to happen in first place. About that randomness in a sea of records and precision. About people making choices without seeing the person before them."

"Then it should be easy to speak of Verity in the first person: I, Verity," he writes, and underscores.

I grasp a potato piece too vigorously and it pops out of my *injera* and lands on the floor. Mr. Saarsgard smiles and hands me a fresh napkin to pick it up.

"You sound like Therapist," I write. "I worked hard to build new life, shuck old one. That ineffective girl discarded like empty can is not who I want to be. Not even in a sentence. Unpleasant."

"Athena. You are a remarkable person," he writes. "I marvel at you. And Verity, more than this Esau chap or anyone else, she made you. Give her credit. Haven't read it all, but what you describe sounds like deeply personal story about Verity. About *you*. 'Randomness' bit sounds like bilge."

"Bilge?"

"Delicious word, suitable in many contexts. Look it up." Mr. Saarsgard is always teaching me words.

"Am neither psychologist nor judge," he continues. "But if I were deciding custody, would not grant it to someone who explains away Esau's actions. Nor to someone who won't admit her given name and personal history. She'd seem unreliable.

Would always wonder if she might deny Arvo's history or explain away mistreatment of him."

I read his words and look at him.

He is right. I feel certain that every person at every table in this fine-linened restaurant would agree with him.

Suddenly I am aware of my great weariness. I am *so tired* of seeing everything from the perspective of the system without them and their great machinery ever seeing it from mine. It is a deep exhaustion that fills the spaces in my bones. Mr. Saarsgard sees the expression on my face and graciously moves on.

"I have bought you new motorcycle helmet," he writes. "Had flames painted on the side."

After dinner, back in my flat, with large black Xes I cross out the sentimentalized account of my (Verity's) last day with Esau. In all likelihood, he drove me to the Elora Home unceremoniously, not stopping for lunch nor to play with me under trees in soft grass. He was probably neither unkind about it nor particularly moved. Most likely I was another item in his day that needed looking after, that needed checking off a list.

Thinking this way feels lonely. I prefer my earlier crossed-out version and cannot yet shred it.

But I admit the revision feels true. There is relief in it.

I have been holding this admission at bay for a long time.

Writer's Note: There is one more story to tell about Verity's first year — my first year — in the Facility. It comes up briefly in the records of Ruby Rojas as taking place October 16, 1964, ten months after my arrival. Weather records report the night was clear, early snow lighting the mountains, and the moon nearly full.

"Harriet, wake up! We have to take care of something. Here. Put on your coat. Here are your boots."

Too sleepy to demur, Harriet plodded behind Ruby downstairs, out the door, around the back of Staff Quarters. Her bed had been warm, her curtains drawn against the autumn moon. Now she was outside in the bright and the cold, anxiety beginning to surge. She looked away from the mountains, down at her boots, while Ruby fumbled with the lock on a door marked "Storage." Harriet had never before noticed it. The mud underfoot, frozen in the night air, had been trampled by small feet.

Ruby groped for the light string and then pulled Harriet into the glare.

Harriet blinked. It seemed, at first glance, to be an abandoned kitchen. The low table was made of stacked catalogues and magazines, a red blanket thrown over for a tablecloth. On the table sat three grimy mismatched cups, an empty candlestick holder, a pot with clotted remainder of something that looked like cocoa powder mixed with cold water, and several chewed cigarettes. An empty cocoa tin lay in the corner. Ragged cushions surrounded the table in place of chairs, and more were thrown into a corner beside a wheel that had a long stiff wire attached to its axle. The wheel had been pushed around and around the table and had left marks in the dust on the floor.

"Is this your private smoking lounge," Harriet asked, "now that you can't smoke inside?"

"No, the kids have been coming here," Ruby said. "This is from resident storage in Laundry. That's the blanket Verity arrived with."

"The — kids?" Harriet turned slowly to look at Ruby.

"Verity, Elsa, Arvo. They sneak out the Main Building delivery hatch in Laundry on days they're sent there."

"But how do they get in?"

"I've only ever seen them come out. Verity probably picks the lock, all three probably carry stuff over."

"Impossible." Harriet tried to think it through. "Feeble-minded can't cooperate like that. Someone has found a key. The Laundry staff are supposed to *watch* them."

"They do watch them. But they have to do laundry. It's hectic and congested and hot down there."

Dubiously Harriet eyed Ruby.

"Harriet. Don't get the Laundry staff in trouble. They work hard. I don't see how you expect them to do their work *and* look after a bunch of hyper kids."

Harriet smoothed the placket of her coat. "They could die in here Ruby."

"Enough with the melodrama," Ruby's eyes rolled. "No one's been hurt. Come, we'll cart the stuff back to Laundry and shutter the hatch so they can't come back."

"The cleaning staff can do it. I'll requisition it."

"No, Harriet. No requisitions, no reports." Ruby's gloved fist thumped the doorjamb. "If there's a record, he'll sedate them for a year. He was standing by the hatch today. A matter of time until he puts it together."

"Fine," Harriet waved her hand. "No records. But crossing the compound is —"

She stopped. She had almost told Ruby of her increasing out-of-doors anxiety.

"Is what?"

"Er, the night watchman has to report all movement."

"I've arranged for him to look elsewhere."

"Ruby! That's —"

"It's necessary, Harriet."

It took several trips to clear the storeroom. Harriet had to brace for each one. And then she returned to her sheltered bed, leaving Ruby to pour hot water over the small footprints in the mud, re-trampling it with her own feet, and to nail shut the old delivery hatch as quietly as she could in the night air.

The following day Harriet slipped down to Laundry storage to examine in daylight the kids' means of egress.

Fast asleep in the corner, between the blockaded exit and the cupboard with pillowslips, lay Verity, her old red blanket both pillow and cover. A wobbly stool leaned against the shelf; she had climbed it to retrieve the blanket from the high reaches where Harriet had stowed it. Her hands were scraped from trying to wrench the plywood from the hatch and dried tears streaked her face. The fluff from a pillow — torn to shreds, probably beaten against that plywood until it burst — stuck to her face.

Harriet was Head Psych Nurse. That sleeping child needed comfort but she could not show favourites. And what if Verity began to follow her again?

She turned on her sensible heel and ran up to her floor. She grabbed her coffee cup from the Nurses' Station and headed for the linen cupboard where the pillowslips lay neatly stacked, folded side out. She poured the coffee over the stack, direct- ing the stream to soil every slip. She picked up the soiled slips and dumped them, still folded, into the laundry bin. Over the intercom, she paged: would Miss Ruby Rojas kindly fetch a few pillowslips from Laundry for the Psych Ward? For some reason, theirs were dirty, every last one.

The next night, after midnight, Harriet, again in coat and boots, braced against the outdoors, and tried to hurry quietly across the compound. She avoided the floodlights and tried to slip through the shadows, but the noisy autumn mud slowed her down and forbade any hope of stealth. With every step, it squished and sucked loudly, tugging at her boots. She waved back at the night watchman who waved first at her (and dutifully recorded her movement in his log), and she let herself into the west door of the Main Building.

She slipped out of her sticky boots, carried them in hand, and rushed in stockinged feet along darkened corridors and down-stairs to the Infirmary. There were no overnight patients and the Doctor's office was dark, the place empty. She crossed, let herself into Pharmacy, and took, without recording, nine benzodiazepine pills, three from each bottle, and wrapped them in a tissue in her pocket. From another pocket, she pulled a cotton swab and bottle of mucilage. She dunked the swab and resealed the bottles she had opened.

Her near-slip with Ruby the night before had been too close a call. Having a few pills on hand was a sensible precaution.

On her way out, she grabbed an empty folder to wave at the night guard so he would think she had crossed the grounds to retrieve a forgotten file.

As for the kids sneaking out of Laundry: Harriet was not one to keep secrets from the Doctor, but the hatch was now sealed, the problem solved. In her conversations with him, the matter never came up.

With time, Holdstock settled into a new routine. Elsa continued her monthly electroconvulsive therapy sessions and Arvo and Verity continued to comfort her after. Irwin continued to avoid fires, and Gracie continued to obsess. Harriet and her staff learned to cope with fewer people to do the work, as colds and fevers increased from reduced hygiene and fewer cleaning staff, and as patients became more likely to act out from boredom.

A handful of patients on the Medical part of the Med/Behaviour Ward, Harriet noticed, seemed to prefer the assurance that each day would be exactly like the one before and to enjoy the relief the Doctor's syringes provided. A life of strict routine, without so much as a holiday party to liven it. Each time Harriet grew frustrated with an acting-out patient, she reminded herself: some patients on the Med Ward seemed happier than ever.

Sometimes, on her way back to Ladies' Staff Quarters, Harriet cut through an old disused wing. There she might see a ball abandoned in the middle of the dusty hallway. Or a wall painted with the strangest of images. Or some medical contraption no longer used, dismantled or in a stage of repair. Month after month, year after year, each time she cut through, something on the wing would be different than it had been the time before but it was always empty of people so she thought nothing of it.

Had she explored further, around a corner to the left and another to the right and into a small abandoned room, she might have realized — as Ruby did — that Verity, Elsa, and Arvo had set up another private space now that their storeroom was closed to them.

This time, they left the items from resident storage where they were to avoid rousing suspicion. When Arvo's wheels and balls finally wore out, they together fabricated new ones from remnants of builder's Styrofoam used for inexpensive wall repair around the Facility. When Elsa's paints ran out, Arvo and Verity brought her near-empty cans of wall paint from storage: over time her paintings became less colourful with access to fewer shades, and more textured as her brushes wore out and she used any kind of plastic, paper, or wooden edge she could find to apply paint instead. Now and then novels disappeared from the Main Building or Staff Quarters and reappeared in the small room. An old dolly became a wheeled sled on which they pushed themselves around, construction scraps became toys, and worn mattresses were heaped together for a comfortable place to relax. The worn holiday decorations — a string of blue garland with tinsel mostly gone — found new use and brightened the corner.

They usually managed only a few hours a week there, away from watchful eyes, but those few hours, Ruby speculated years later, probably meant everything. Here, she noted, they revealed themselves. Elsa's most interesting paintings. Arvo's most complex rolling ball mazes that, with the addition of Verity's springs and contraptions, became sculptures. (The most complex, I recall, allowed a ball to roll unceasing for a quarter hour.)

I remember so little. I'm relieved, reading Ruby's records, that I *did* resist. That I tried to make my own life with what few things were available. At least I did not self-betray.

ATHENA'S JOURNAL
MARCH 29, 2004
(MONDAY)

Finally I tell the therapist I am applying for custody.

He has known for some time, it turns out. The Province informed him that his "input will be required" at the hearing. He was waiting, he says, until I was ready to discuss it with him.

"Athena," he says, "I will try to support your bid for custody, but I'll have to answer what they ask. I won't lie."

"I do not want you to lie."

"May I ask you more about this? Your file speaks of Arvo, of course, but in ten years this is the first time you've mentioned custody to me. You've hardly spoken of Arvo at all. How long have you been thinking of this?"

"Any time I have not been with Arvo, I have been thinking about how to be with him. I think about Arvo many times each day and I have since we were parted."

"I-I had no idea! All these years. My goodness."

I take some pleasure in the bewilderment that slides across his face, but the visible hurt accompanying it catches me off guard.

He pauses, re-establishes his calm and steady expression, then continues. "Can you tell me something about what custody means to you? Are you doing this because you want to contribute in some way? To parent someone? To prove something?"

"I want to live with my lover. You live with your wife who, presumably, is your lover. I want to live with my lover."

In my peripheral vision, a rare smile flits across the vertical interpreter's face. The therapist shoots him a warning glance.

"I see. Are the two of you equals, do you think? In the Facility, it would have been Arvo and Verity, sometimes Elsa, a team working together against the Administration. But here, you would have *custody*. You would be a parent, essentially, and he would be in the position of a child. My wife and I, on the other hand, are equals."

I wonder if his wife would agree, but do not ask.

"We are equal. Perhaps you underestimate the emotional support I draw from Arvo. For example, when things began to go badly in the Facility, he taught Verity — er, me — to rock as a means of coping, of using physical momentum to enter another place."

"I'm not sure the panel will think that a beneficial interaction."

"Then they will be wrong." The therapist smiles at this.

"The thing is, Athena, on the one hand you claim he is your equal, but on the other you apply for custody. In the movement from public to private guardian — which is unusual to say the least — someone does have to be a *guardian*. These things you say contradict one another."

"I am saying nothing contradictory, but I understand the system cannot yet acknowledge the complexity of my situation."

"That's one way of putting it, yes. I think you'll find it difficult to convince the panel that you can be both lover and guardian. Have you spoken with Arvo about this? Do you know if he wants to leave the Group Home?"

"Arvo is agoraphobic. When he is in a building, any building, he never wants to leave it."

"Then how do you know he wants to come with you? As far as these records indicate, he doesn't speak."

I am uncomfortable speaking with the therapist about Arvo at all and more uncomfortable still defending these truths so primal to me. I think again, as I have before, of young Gabriel, who surely knew about love and approved categories and who might also have longed to flee this room. But these men are experts in body language, they wield authority in Arvo's custody, and they expect a response. For all my discomfort, I sit still except to sign and do not let my eyes waver.

"You know, Doctor, when they took me from the Facility, I did not know I was leaving. I thought we were touring the grounds. I did not say good-bye to Arvo. I missed the others, but I ached for him. Weeks later, it came time for Arvo to leave the Facility and he could not walk through the gate. He could, with effort, exit the building onto the grounds, but he would not leave. In the struggle, his gloves came off — it was winter — and he gripped the cold iron fence railings so tightly his hands bled, while around him social workers and staff tried to coax and bribe him out. They did not want to sedate him, that was no longer the way of things, but they could not convince him to leave.

"Eventually, they allowed him back into the warm Facility, drove all the way to the Group Home where I was staying at the time, two hours" drive at least, and fetched me and my keyworker. They could not yet communicate with me, and once again I did not know where I was being taken. When I saw the Holdstock grounds, for all my considerable trepidation, I became excited for I would see Arvo again.

"And there he sat, on a bench in the lobby with bloodied hands. Workmen were about, dismantling the place. I knew then I had been brought there to persuade him to leave. Which I did in less than ten minutes and without words that you know.

"They drove us to his Group Home. We held on to one another in the van and later on his bed in his room, and I rocked with him, I talked with him and ate with him, I watched him fall asleep. I thought I was to stay there with him, that we had come out the other end of Holdstock together and things had been set right. It was a great relief.

"The moment he was asleep, they scooped me up like a soiled diaper, belted me into the van, and returned me to my Group Home, several hours away. I did not see him again until after I left the Group Home permanently."

It is unmistakable. Anger flashes across the therapist's face.

"What I am saying, Doctor, is this: no, he will not initially want to leave his Group Home, but after a few minutes he will come willingly. He and I have managed transitions before. We can manage another."

"What a moving story. I didn't know you were involved in Arvo's departure from the Facility." He says this so quietly that the Vertical Interpreter must ask him to repeat it.

"What does that file say about me? It mentions Arvo but does not say I aided the transition?"

"It's the same file you have, Athena. It doesn't mention him by name, as you know. It says Verity, who's about eight or nine, is becoming sexually active with another resident. Children are sexually curious, of course. I inferred it to be Arvo."

"Oh." I consider that for a moment. I do not recall a time before sexual activity. "Does the staff who wrote that say anything about her own sex life? If not in this file, then in another file?"

"That would be inappropriate," he says, "as you know."

I think it wise not to speak my thoughts at that. He continues.

"Back to Arvo, then. Do you feel this is a good time for custody? I'm thinking of practical things. Who will do the cooking? The cleaning? Where will Arvo sleep? Is the apartment big enough for two? Do you feel you can care for another person?"

"Yes, of course. I will cook and clean. I cook and clean now. Arvo will help me. He will have considerably more space in my apartment than he currently has in his Group Home bedroom. And he will sleep with me."

"Has he ever slept in a bed with another person? Have you?"

"No, I do not think either of us has, now that you mention it."

"People usually find it difficult to adapt to sharing a bed."

"Then we will have to adjust as they do."

He pauses for a while, considers.

"Athena, why not go about this in stages? Why not start with, say, a dog? You could choose a dog, feed him, walk him, clean up after him, play with him — and see if you enjoy responsibility for an animal, let alone a person."

"A dog! I love dogs!"

"Yes, you've said so before."

"I would love to have a dog."

"Why haven't you gotten a dog before this then?"

"I did not think I would be permitted a dog. It seemed something for other people."

"And yet you apply for custody."

I ignore his implication and say I will speak with Imran about a dog this evening. We can go dog-shopping at the SPCA.

ATHENA'S JOURNAL
APRIL 02, 2004
(FRIDAY)

I have a dog!

Imran says he is a "mutt." He is medium-sized and well-proportioned with agile ears and short hair of several colours. The people who last owned him severed and discarded his testicles. I expect he misses them. The SPCA representative says it is common practice. I have named him Vincent because of the purposeful, organic way he moves in circles. Like the purposeful organic circles in some of Vincent Van Gogh's paintings.

Imran's hands wrapped around his head. "I have to write a dog-training program for you now!"

"Imran," I said, "have you ever had a dog?"

"No. That is precisely the problem."

"Imran, why not *not* write a program, since you know little about dog care, and I will learn to look after him? He seems an intelligent animal already able to communicate his needs. And I have fetched a book from the library."

Imran agreed that made sense. I think he was relieved. I have not told him Vincent did defecate inside one day, the first day.

He did it in the bathtub and looked so ashamed. We had a conversation then, Vincent and I. I said everyone defecates. There is no shame in it. I thanked him for doing it where it could be easily cleaned up. And then I told him I am deaf and cannot hear him barking when he needs to go out. I demonstrated by walking around the flat on all fours and placing my hands on a chair that he should paw my knees when he needs to go outside. After many tries he began to mimic me. Once I was certain Vincent understood our communication must be visual, I went back to the tub and cleaned it up. I am not bothered by feces the way Imran is.

Vincent has had no further mishaps.

I introduced Vincent to Mr. Saarsgard — whose motorcycle sidecar has arrived! The next day, Mr. Saarsgard had goggles for Vincent and we went for a spin, Vincent and I in the sidecar, and Mr. Saarsgard on the bike. And then we traded places: I drove (keeping to back roads to prevent police encounters for I do not yet have a license), and Mr. Saarsgard sat in the sidecar with Vincent. And then Mr. Saarsgard drove, I sat behind on the motorcycle, and Vincent sat alone in the sidecar. Vincent seemed content with each of these arrangements and rode along in the sidecar, mouth agape, tongue flapping, leaning into the wind.

This morning he brought me not his leash but his goggles. I believe he wanted to go for another spin. I understand entirely.

He is the ideal dog for me. We shall get along famously.

APRIL 1971
HOLDSTOCK
(Seven years have passed.)

After supper, Harriet quietly knocked on the Doctor's office door and went right in. He was already pouring the Port. She tossed her cloak over the coat rack, he passed her a small goblet, sipped from his own, and, at the end of the room, they settled into the hollows they had worn into the armchairs and in tandem rested their feet on the ottoman, bookends. His tie was off, and the tension in Harriet's chest beginning to release. Firesides with Ruby were infrequent these days, and her meetings with the Doctor the highlight of Harriet's week.

They could speak freely here now. Mol and Irwin had lugged soundproofing from a padded room dismantled in the '64 cutbacks and Irwin had installed it. The room was acoustically dead and tremendously peaceful.

He took up a pen and paper from the side table. "Anything new on your end?"

Harriet reached for her notes. "I believe a romance is brewing in the kitchen — Wilf and Juanita. Nigel's son has fathered a child out of wedlock and Nigel's wife thinks Emmett ought to marry the girl, but Emmett wants another. Adele in Medical has insulted Bronwyn in Laundry by refusing to attend her own birthday party. Her religion forbids it, she says. Adele has also taken to praying over sick patients and this offends at least half the care staff who are preparing to confront her. Jojo in Grounds is having an hysterectomy next month. Her mother disapproves and her husband is relieved. And Alberto on my floor is vacationing without his wife this summer. Divorce, I hear, is imminent. Nothing that concerns us."

The Doctor noted everything she said, then turned a fresh leaf.

"I have bad news, Harriet," he said. "The integration claptrap means institution funding is going to Group Homes. We received notice of cutbacks today."

In her chair, Harriet deflated. "How much?"

"A lot."

"We haven't yet recovered from the '64 cutbacks."

"I know. I really did think that would go better than it did." A little smile, sheepish, pleading and then the skin at his throat slackened. He'd aged ten years in one minute.

They drank in silence.

"We'll manage resentment more effectively if we bring staff into the process," Harriet said. "Make them feel they have influence. Give me the numbers. I'll work with Ruby. We'll consult others and choose what to cut."

"Fine, if you think it will help. I won't hold it against you if it fails." He picked at lint on the armchair upholstery, and then lifted his chest. "Well. Shall we get on with something we can actually affect?"

Harriet took her cue and opened a different notebook. "I've been combing literature for precedents," she said. "It's not safe to sterilize Verity. She's too young for the procedure."

"The problem is this could be our last chance. Lougheed's Conservatives are looking to use the Sterilization Act as an election platform. LeVann thinks if we lose the current Premier it'll be repealed within the year." He waved a letter, presumably from Mr. LeVann. "I warned him years ago to sterilize frugally. He was drawing attention."

Harriet leaned forward to fill the goblets.

"What about that Bernie fellow?" he asked.

"His family would never approve. They take him to a harlot every month."

"Ah. I'd forgotten the family. And that they still visit. The Arvo boy?"

"Yes. He's old enough, active, and we've no means to care for infants."

The Doctor made a note.

"Anyone else?"

"Well, Lily. The homosexual aversion therapy isn't working."

"You're thinking radical hysterectomy. But total surgeries make no difference in that population, Harriet, I'm certain. The problem rests in the mind."

"You've said so before. Nevertheless, she's begging for it on the chance it might help. Her children are growing up without her, yet her longings still overwhelm, she says. I believe her."

On they went, late into the night, deacons of benevolent extinction and of the patients' most private parts.

Writer's Note: Later that month, Arvo and three other Facility men made a day trip to the Provincial Training School in Red Deer, three hours away. They appeared before the Eugenics Board in the Administration building for five minutes each, and were then led across the grounds to the clinical building. They undressed in a waiting room, and were taken from there, one by one, into a small, spotless operating theatre with pale green walls. That evening, not yet fully conscious, they were transported back to Holdstock and woke up the following morning in the Infirmary where their recovery was monitored.

In the Provincial Training School Sterilization Program books, each man's vasectomy gets a single line, one of 4,728 sterilizations the Board approved. Official Holdstock files note only that the men went on an outing to Red Deer and that the Infirmary needed a second nurse for a few days. There is, however, a hasty scribble about costs surrounding four vasectomies in the Doctor's book-keeping ledger under a line confirming receipt of two hundred pounds of potatoes. I (Athena) have been unable to locate the sterilization forms the Eugenics Board would have had to sign.

I told Arvo the last time I saw him (staff lurking in the Group Home hallway). "I know," he said in our sign language, "I remember." There had been someone there, he reminded me, an older man with silver hair and brown skin and cigarette lighters who tried to stop us from being affectionate and who had tears in his eyes. He was warning us, Arvo said.

And he cried and he kissed me and he said it would be alright.

JUNE 1971
HOLDSTOCK

Though a handful of clouds had finally broken the worst heat of the day, the crepuscular rays piercing them continued to warm the grounds throughout the long evening. Harriet and Ruby sat at a picnic table (of course Ruby wanted to meet outside) under the faded "Drink Nesbitt's Orange" awning that had once adorned the town pharmacy and now shaded an area to the side of the Main Building. They sipped Ginger Ale, Ruby smoked cigarettes behind huge sunglasses, Harriet waved Ruby's smoke away ("It staves off mosquitoes, Harriet. You should be grateful.") and they massaged the Facility budget to yield up its gristle.

"To recap. We don't compromise resident care. Agreed?" Ruby asked.

"Agreed," Harriet nodded.

"We safeguard the workforce as much as possible. We cut extras. Agreed?"

"Agreed."

"Can we go after the Doctor's pay?" Ruby lit another cigarette and eased the smoke over her lip. It was the fourth evening of budget reductions.

"He's already arranged for a pay cut."

"Has he really?"

"Yes, he really has."

Across the angled cigarette, Ruby surveyed her thoughtfully.

"Harriet, are you sleeping with him?"

"With the Doctor? That's revolting."

"It's the seventies. We're all getting it somewhere."

A ground squirrel approached their table. Harriet shooed it away with a fly swatter, and set her back again to the mountains, eyes forward on the blessed wall at Ruby's back.

"I am not a hippie, Ruby. My relationship with the Doctor is professional. I don't see any way around paving the flowerbeds, I'm afraid. They're too dear." Harriet made a note.

"It's the clout you're after then." There was no edge to her voice.

"Pardon me?"

"Never mind. If we give up the flowerbeds, where will Stephen do his gardening?"

"I'd hardly call digging fingers in dirt 'gardening.'"

"He calls it gardening and I'm not going to argue. Where will he do it?" Ruby tapped off the cigarette ash.

"Give him something else to do. Would a keychain satisfy him?"

"He likes gardening."

Harriet pointed to a potted geranium. "We could give him a flowerpot of dirt. We have flowerpots. And dirt."

"I don't think it's quite the same, sinking your fingers into a flowerpot of dirt." Ruby gripped the cigarette in her lips and mimed fingers in a crowded pot.

"Nonsense. He'll hardly notice."

"I used to be proud of this place," Ruby said.

She unfolded her legs from the table, flicked ash from her cut-offs, got up to prop open the nearest door to cool the indoors, then sat again.

Verity appeared at the door, then joined them at the table. She stayed a few minutes before running back indoors.

"See," Harriet said. "Even Verity prefers to be safe indoors. We should consider ending all patient out-of-doors time."

No sooner had she said it than Verity appeared again, this time with Arvo, alternately gesturing and tugging his arm. As he approached the door, his inflated ball that rolled effortlessly on the smooth floor hit the grass and stopped, all momentum vanished. His face flattened in disappointment. He gestured. Verity kicked the ball back inside, gestured something, then tugged his arm again.

"Look," Ruby said. "They're signing. She gestures something, then he gestures a response. It's a conversation. She's coaxing him outside."

"No Ruby," Harriet said. "What you're seeing is confirmation that this population can't cooperate. She pulls one way, he pulls another."

They returned to their budget, Ruby shaking her head.

Five minutes later, Ruby smiled widely. "I win," she said.

Harriet looked up from her notes and forced herself to turn and look out. Lily and Gracie now sat on a bench nearby, Irwin and Elizabeth behind them, and Verity and Arvo rested quietly on the grass, looking at the clouds. Arvo lay stiffly, the picture of unease, glancing often at the ball just inside the door, but clinging to Verity and relaxing visibly with every passing half-minute. From time-to-time Verity pointed at something — a squirrel, a glowing ochre mountaintop — and Arvo nodded. Eventually their eyelids dropped and they fell asleep on the grass. Altogether oblivious, Harriet couldn't help but note, to the looming hills.

After several weeks, Harriet presented their list to the Doctor in their weekly meeting.

"Crackerjack, Harriet! I'd have never thought of half of these! We'll implement them all."

He looked best here, in his office, sitting in the upholstered chair, a pen in one hand, a glass in the other. Something about the position of these chairs made his head looked properly proportioned to his body. Perhaps it was the angle.

"Thank you, Mol."

"It's not enough."

"What do you mean?" She lowered her glass without drinking.

"I mean it's not enough."

"But — we cut what you said needed to be cut!"

"And you did so beautifully. But it's a quarter of what we *need* to cut. For pity's sake, Harriet, pick up your jaw. I thought it kinder not to say."

"Really Mol, it's much easier to do my work when you are forthright with me. Ruby will think I lied!"

"Yes, I — I didn't think of Miss Rojas, to be honest. I wanted not to overwhelm you."

Harriet smoothed her skirt. How like him not to consider — Leave it. Move on.

"Mol. We cannot cut that much three times again without seriously compromising patient care."

"I know." He met her gaze directly.

"Can't we do something? Drive to the city and talk to someone in Provincial Government?"

"That's what LeVann did."

"What happened?"

"They closed up his wards, dismantled his buildings, and moved his patients off-site. Now they want to come here, let me see" — again he extracted a letter from his breast pocket —

"'to observe Holdstock Facility clientele and select some for pilot projects in relocation, empowerment, and de-institutionalization.'" He handed her the letter and rubbed his neck as if it were in pain.

"This is impossible."

"Indeed."

"What do we do now?"

"I thought I'd beg a measles outbreak to hold off this inspection. Then we make cuts. Apply uh flexible paperwork. Compromise patient care. Try to stay unnoticed until the foolishness passes."

Harriet stood from her chair, straightened her back. The letter was in her hand but she looked straight ahead and not at the letter at all.

"What if we remodel an outbuilding as a type of experimental Group Home? We could gather data and prove our patients too impaired and needing more structure and protection than Group Homes allow."

"That last paragraph there —" He pointed to the letter and recited from memory.

"— about 'movement towards *off-site* Group Homes for maximum de-institutionalization.'"

"I-I don't understand! All that work and study and cost to make an institution state-of-the-art, why move them into *houses* now? They're not siblings!"

"They think us old-fashioned, Harriet. That we prevent patients from 'meaningful social roles.'"

"*Of course* we preven — How insulting." She set the letter down gently, straightened again, and clasped her hands together, her fingers turning white from the grip. "We rescued them *from* homes and and and *we're* being made out as as as as scoundrels! We're not Farar wanting to to to euthanize defective children for 'good mental hygiene.' Nor LeVann getting rich off his inmates' labour!"

"Harriet, sit down already. You're beginning to sputter. You needn't convince me."

Bit players in a lesser tragedy.

Everything hurt. The fine Port didn't help. Harriet cried herself to sleep that night, grieving the end of assiduous nursing.

"You *are* sleeping with him!" Ruby ran to Harriet's station when she caught wind of the true extent of the cutbacks. "If you'd just rip off your clothes and throw back your head you might really come for once but don't think for one second you're not in bed with that asshole, grinding away!"

"*Ruby!*"

"Send them to the fucking Group Homes, Harriet. You're not meeting basic needs! It's monstrous!"

"Miss Rojas! Collect yourself!" Harriet stood and drew herself to full height, hands clasped, but Ruby turned and left the room.

The staff on the floor pointedly looked away. Of course they had heard everything. Of course they would talk. Why did people always blame *her?*

She sat again, keeping her posture, and bowed her head into the *Duties Manual* where she had been reducing comfort attentions.

In times like these, Harriet likely thought back to that boy, that barn, where had that been? She was a student then, assisting two senior nurses in scouring rural towns for people no one wanted to admit existed. They found them, in dark and hidden rooms, in cellars, in attics and sheds. But that boy — that was Gravenhurst.

On a tip from a neighbour, they had found him in a *barn*. Naked, malnourished, covered in filth, tied up like a cow. His legs had fused into bent positions, Harriet recalled. He couldn't straighten up; all of his long bones had been broken at one point or another and not properly set. From across the barn, in a weak sunbeam filtering through a grimy window, she had seen his penis was infected, shiny and misshapen with pus. When they unchained and guided him out, he wouldn't step into the sunlight. He'd been terrified of that which he had never seen, the warmth he had never felt, and had gripped the barn door with closed fists and tightly pressed knees until they backed the van to where he stood. Usually families were ashamed, so ashamed, believing feeble-mindedness was their fault, a weakness in the bloodline, and they cried with relief when they learned about the services a good institution could offer. But this family had no shame; they had gazed on Harriet with eyes of steel, each one of them, as if beating that child and withholding food had been their God-given due. She had used her last bit of fortitude not to grab the shotgun leaning against the barn door and puncture them all while her colleagues led the boy to the van. Inside the van, under the senior nurse's approving eye, Harriet had wrapped a blanket around him, a protective membrane, and he'd shuddered when her hand brushed his shoulder.

If not for places like Holdstock, how many of their charges would be chained up somewhere, sitting in their filth, naked and frothing at the mouth?

The morning after Ruby's outburst, Harriet's pillow was again wet from her weeping, her hand grooved from the chatelaine, and shame still lay bitter on her tongue.

Once more, the Facility locked down and slashed at itself.

In the first month, August, they implemented Ruby and Harriet's suggestions: Grade A fruits and vegetables were no longer purchased; the kitchen used seconds ordered directly from farms and bought cases of dinted and rejected canned goods from factories. As plates and glasses broke, they were replaced with metal trays and plastic cups. The floors were washed less frequently and with a cheaper, more acrid disinfectant. A rougher toilet paper went into Toilet Rooms. Unused outbuildings were dismantled, the materials reused or sold, lower quality materials used for repairs. The grounds were either paved or covered in gravel that didn't need mowing. Staff uniforms were no longer provided nor laundered, and cheaper medications and creams filled the med cabinets.

On the first Monday of September, for the next wave of changes, Harriet made a point of being on her ward though it was her day off. Along with her staff, she accompanied patients down to the Dining Room for breakfast. Instead of the usual sweating jugs of milk and juice in the centre of each table, a half glass of each sat by every plate; the remaining patient liquids for the day would be tap water and warm tea or coffee. Instead of fragrant loaves of crusty brown bread, the breadboards held stacks of paper-white squares, each one-third inch thick, of pasty manufactured starch to be greased with plain margarine — butter, honey, and jam nowhere in sight: the baker had been laid off. The pots of margarine and breadboards were nearly as full after the meal as before, and the patients still complaining of hunger.

At day's end, when Harriet crossed back to staff quarters, a truck in the loading bay was picking up the sewing machines and mending supplies to be auctioned in Calgary, and sacks of special occasion clothing for the Sally Ann. The seamstress, menders, and two Laundry staff were laid off. Mending would be done by the Presbyterian Ladies' Group as part of their charity work, and all laundry would be washed in the great industrial machines that quickly dissolved delicates.

Most of the October changes didn't affect Harriet's ward a great deal. All visitations ceased, and the reception area closed, the receptionist laid off: contact with the public in this climate could be only dangerous. Patients with family who visited regularly (Harriet had none on her ward) were transferred to other facilities. Those patients with electric wheelchairs (most of Harriet's patients were ambulatory) had them taken away and sold. Patient time out-of-doors was permitted only when an entire unit and its meagre staff could go outside. Consequently, the Medical/Behaviour unit, half its population bedridden, no longer went outside. (Harriet's unit went out when she was off-shift.)

But the changes that did affect her ward were unbearable. The Doctor had ordered that liquid in patient diets be rationed, resulting in fewer diaper changes and lower laundry costs. "It's not good for them to lie in their urine," the Doctor reasoned when Harriet pressed. "All that ammonia. Better they urinate less." Linens were changed half as often, and then half as often again. By month-end, the place smelled unmistakably ripe. Once, Harriet herself stepped outside for a lungful of air.

The November changes brought grit and headache. The elderly senile and others likely to deteriorate had been sent from Holdstock, where they had lived out their lives, to seniors' homes and hospitals. The death of a patient might draw public attention. With fewer patients, more wards were collapsed, patients moved from one floor to another, and beds crammed to make space. Walls between wards were knocked down wherever structur-ally possible (in this way two night staff could monitor eighty patients) and demolition dust drifted through the Facility. Grit accumulated and gummed up every surface, and this while the staff were learning a new record-keeping system (quantitative instead of qualitative, allowing for two clerical staff to be laid off) and stacks of dusty new forms laid about. Worse, the dust provoked no end of coughing. Finally, Ruby broke out a box of procedure masks and masked all patients, and no one rebuked her for the expenditure.

Harriet looked up once to see the Laundry staff emptying the cupboards of patient clothing. Finally they would launder out the dust. But a half hour later the clothing cupboards were again full. Of generic pajamas and gowns shared among all patients, a different colour for each ward, ordered in bulk from a hospital-supply warehouse. Her staff looked upon the open cupboards and then at her, bald disgust refiguring their faces. They blamed her, clearly.

Verity, now twelve years old, refused to wear the hospital garb. Somehow she got into the staff lockers in Janitorial and donned someone's housedress. An orderly forced her back into hospital clothing — both were bruised in the attempt — after which Verity marched to the Toilet Room and locked the door. A few minutes later she came out naked but for underwear, socks, and shoes. The hospital garb had been shoved into a toilet which had then been flushed. The toilet overflowed, a dreadful mess.

But December. December was the worst. The Doctor prescribed combined oral contraceptives for all menstruating women patients, including those already sterilized. All women on any given floor menstruated at exactly the same time each month, and each floor's menstruation time landed in a different week of the month. Harriet's ward was the third week. One worker rotated through the units, adding extra hands during bloody weeks to deal with changing and cleanup; three workers were laid off.

He also prescribed mild sedatives for all patients. "It helps compliance," he said. After one woman aspirated briefly from newly relaxed muscles, he ordered all patient food, including the pasty breakfast bread, to be pureed. Within a few days, then, patients were fed in bed or in wheelchairs in the Great Room.

Regardless of how well patients had once eaten on their own, all were now spoon-fed; pureed mush slid down their throats in four or five efficient scoops. Meals went quickly and four staff could be laid off, the Dining Room became a staff lunchroom.

Lily, Gracie, and the other high-functioning patients, affronted at being spoon-fed, shouted their helpless anger every time Harriet walked by.

"Oh for heavens' sake, I don't have time for this!" Harriet mumbled, and assigned another nurse to their direct care for a few days. It would soon blow over.

But after several days of pureed food, Gracie defecated into her hands and walked about the ward, smearing any surface she thought Harriet or the Doctor might touch. Harriet donned gloves until Housekeeping staff could do their work.

Nighttime snacks were cancelled altogether and lights extinguished two hours earlier, immediately after dinner. The electricity savings were considerable (though the crumbs clinging to Verity, Arvo, and Elsa's linens each morning proved how impossible it was to enforce. Harriet pretended not to notice).

Bedridden patients were repositioned half as often as before. All patients received laxatives to counteract constipation induced by sedatives, less water, and less repositioning. Suppositories were administered preventatively to non-ambulatory patients on alternate days at exactly 2:00 PM. The dirty diapers would be changed in that half hour at the three o'clock shift change when there were twice as many staff. And if there wasn't enough time, or if someone's bowels loosed thirty minutes late, well, they'd get to everyone eventually.

Regulated menstruation and bowel movements, sedation and withholding water — oh, it wasn't ideal but it would be okay. They did things differently here is all. And what if it was a mistake? Hadn't bone ash first been added to fine china from a Jesuit missionary's mistake? Change was trying, of course — Harriet was affected too — but the staff ought to be grateful, really. They still *had* work. He could have fired the lot of them.

But when it came to bathing, Harriet wouldn't budge. The Doctor introduced a directive to decrease bathing and order still more salve and bandages for consequent pressure sores. Harriet ordered her staff to disobey. Over the intercom, he called her to his office.

"Did Miss Rojas put you up to this?" he asked.

"No, Mol. Ruby isn't speaking to me yet. I doubt she ever will again." She leaned back against the closed door.

"Oh Harriet. I'm sorry to hear that. You could have fired her, you know."

"I don't believe firing her would have salvaged our friendship."

"I meant —"

"I know what you meant, Mol. I shouldn't be curt." She rubbed her temples. "Ruby does the work of two and she's well-liked. Firing her would make it worse for everyone. It just gets — lonely."

"You look exhausted and we're still short of funds," the Doctor said. "And the expensive private institutions bathe their patients twice a week at most."

"I don't care. Bedsore ointment is expensive and I haven't the staff to administer it. Less bathing means more skin maceration and less repositioning. Pressure sores are already up and the place smells vile. I'm not withholding baths to save a few pennies only to spend those pennies on ointment —" if Ruby could hear her now "— and you can fire me if you'd like."

"Well," he sighed, pulling at his tie, "the money has to come from somewhere. We'll have to get creative."

(That Christmas, Harriet hosted a little do in the Ladies' Staff Quarters. After the cutbacks, it would do the staff good to indulge. By post, she had ordered cheerful cocktail napkins with a sprig-of-holly print on them and laid them strategically at each corner of the table. She lit candles and built up the fire, and she served aspic salad, a cheese ball with crackers, cocktail meatballs, eggnog, and White Russian cocktails. None but Mol showed up and he stayed a short while. Pointedly, Ruby used the back entrance to avoid passing the kitchen altogether.)

Writer's Note: Mr. Saarsgard has experienced a catastrophe. At some point after midnight, a customer forced a loonie into the quarter slot of his vintage peepshow booth. The booth is a beautiful antique (with ornate metal detailing and a Projecting Kinetoscope) of which Mr. Saarsgard is especially proud, but the projector inside is fragile. Early this morning, he discovered it and ran over straightaway, flashing his mirror light on my ceiling repeatedly until I (Athena) wakened, looked outside, and saw his anguish. Promptly I fetched my toolbox, and in my slippers and pajamas I followed the thin curls that bounce against his neck, and Vincent followed me.

My cursory inspection revealed the projector untouched but the coin slot components must be replaced. A minor repair. I will be unable to do this before the store opens today because Mr. Saarsgard must first telephone for parts. Vincent sniffs the booth most vigorously, confirming that it is very popular indeed.

As relief settles in, Mr. Saarsgard wipes his face with a handkerchief — and a moment later is visibly pensive again:

"Last time this happened," he writes, "culprit was not eager customer but vandal. Warm-up to picketing."

(Picketing, he has explained before, is unpleasant. It boosts his income dramatically but brings with it attendant distress.)

Vincent and I return home. It has rained in the night, and

Vincent takes his leash in his teeth and runs to and fro, cavorting, seeking out puddles, until he smells thoroughly of wet dog. Our return indoors Vincent feels is premature, and, before we enter, he turns to me and drops his front legs in a clear invitation to play.

Something very old, vintage, snags in my brain.

I oblige him, of course, but for the rest of the day, as I go about my chores, I push and pull, judder and jostle it. Of what does that moment remind me?

Twice, I coax Vincent into the shower to rouse again the wet dog smell. I recall disparate images, but nothing cohesive. Water stains on Holdstock ceilings. A janitor's mop in tatters, wet threads everywhere. A puddle on floor tile patches that do not match the floor. Standing on a chair before a locked door.

The third time I summon Vincent to the shower, he collapses heavily in the hallway outside the bathroom, crosses his front paws and looks steadfastly away from me. I cajole. I assure that it will be worth his while, that memory recovery is difficult and requires sacrifice, that there will be treats in the offing.

Vincent is an intelligent animal, not easily wheedled.

I take a fresh approach and re-read Ruby's notes. She mentions no dogs.

In Harriet's interviews, however, I find exactly four sentences.

HC: Once — around '68, I think — a staff who volunteered at the pound brought up some dogs for an afternoon. One reminded me of my childhood pet, and somehow it got inside for a short time, but what disarray! I called it over, gave it a good rubdown, led it outside, and cleaned up that evening. A lovely simple thing, to pet a friendly dog.

Gradually something emerges.

Dogs! Eight or nine of them, out on the grounds!

Anyone who could ran outside to greet them. Verity immediately attached herself to the biggest: it was lean and short-haired and would probably grow into a mastiff or something else enormous and muscled but was as yet a haphazard and oversized puppy with outsized paws.

Two other dogs quarrelled over something and a dogfight erupted, drawing the attention of everyone there as they tried to gain distance from snapping jaws.

In that moment, Verity guided the puppy indoors. It stood nearly as tall as she and licked her rigorously, happy to comply.

First they hastened to the Great Room to gather Arvo from his hiding place beneath the cushions under the window that had been replaced with plywood. (Verity broke it when the room smelled too strongly of urine.)

Arvo raised his arms! She had managed it! This one they would keep. Soon they were all three a wriggling heap of limbs in the cushions.

Elsa sat nearby in her wheelchair, awaiting something, and the puppy half-climbed her lap to lick her ears. She laughed (and froze). He ran to the janitor's bucket, with a great paw overturned it, and rolled in the spreading pool of water. Immediately, Arvo and Verity followed suit. Everyone was wet, everyone laughing, everything wonderful!

The dog found a rubber toy, shredded it efficiently until the squeaker was between his teeth, and then frolicked in tight circles.

"He is squeaking and squeaking," Arvo signed and laughed until he cried.

Verity laughed because Arvo was laughing. The dog dropped the squeaker and ran to the suction machine, there for cystic fibrosis patients, grasped the hose in his teeth, yanked quickly, and separated it from the machine. He turned and dropped his front paws in a clear invitation to play. *(There it is!)* Verity and Arvo gave chase, trying to grab at the hose in his mouth, and the dog led them round and round and down the hall and back again.

Abruptly he whipped his head so that his ears flapped against his nose.

"Nurse Harriet whistled," Arvo said.

The puppy ran to her and she bent on one knee to pet him — and he forgot the children, following her willingly down the hall to the door. Verity saw hands outside reach for his collar.

They could not keep him after all. She was despondent.

Then — Elsa's arms stretched out in front, her head shook, and she shrank into her wheelchair. Fear.

Verity followed her gaze: Harriet striding back down the hall, speaking. She ignored Elsa's distress. She ignored the dog wreckage. She unlocked the brakes on Elsa's chair and pushed her away.

How alarming! Carefully, Verity followed from behind. The nurse rolled Elsa down one hall, then another, through a swinging door. In an empty wing, they entered a room.

Verity snuck up and pulled a nearby chair to the door. She climbed and peeked through the window near the top.

Elsa lay on a table. Her face and shoulders were blocked by someone but Verity saw that her feet were strapped down and cords led from a machine to Elsa's head.

Someone injected her — she sagged, instantly slack — and a few seconds later someone else flipped a switch.

Elsa lurched. Her body lifted right off the table.

Understanding and horror all at once. In the surprise of it, Verity almost fell.

She must not be seen.

She climbed down, returned to chair to its place, ran to the Great Room, where she crawled under Arvo's cushions, and cried. Later, when Harriet rolled by with slumped Elsa, she neither saw nor heard her.

Writer's Note: Strangely, I am both shivering and sweating. And bewildered. This cannot be a memory for there is the window, already broken for relief from a urine smell, but Harriet says the dog visit happened in '68, three years before the urine smell. I am certain of dog mayhem and of standing on a chair — but altogether uncertain of what I saw. Another romantic invention. Most likely.

FEBRUARY 1972,
HOLDSTOCK

First came a sound from down the hall, and Harriet, who was working at a med cart, felt panic rise in the Great Room before she looked up. Then she saw Verity, Arvo, Irwin, and the other patients part, instinctively clearing a path. And then there was blood everywhere and Lily was brandishing a pocketknife — at least a dozen leaking wounds — and raising to sink it once more into her own flesh.

"Cut them out, Caulle!" she screamed at Harriet. "I wanna go home!"

Harriet dropped everything, focussed absolutely on Lily.

The two orderlies crouching, circling, inching closer to her, they would do their job. There, in her peripheral vision, came Ruby, sprinting down the hall. Harriet kept hold of Lily's gaze, talking quietly, as Lily extracted the knife — another wound — and raised it to plunge again. There Ruby vaulted over a table, there she ducked behind a sofa, she came up to Lily from behind and below, she grabbed and pushed her wrists up her back, simultaneously pressing her head down between her legs. The orderlies pounced, she was restrained, and Harriet grabbed the loaded syringe from the top drawer of her cart and lunged. The needle vanished through Lily's pant leg into the thick flesh of her thigh, the only large muscle she could reach through the bodies.

Lily bellowed in protest and slumped to the ground.

The crisis was over.

Blood trailed across the Great Room and down the hall about ten feet, where the knife had first plunged.

Harriet dismantled the syringe for sterilization, called for a First Aid tray, and knelt by Lily. Beside her, Ruby took the knife from Lily's limp hand, snapped it shut, and stepped away. An orderly brought the tray, tossing Ruby a towel for her sweat, and wheeled Harriet's med cart away to lock it up. Harriet dunked a swab in iodine, lifted Lily's shirt, and bent to the ordinary task of cleaning and bandaging.

"Good thing she's plump," someone behind Harriet said, "or she might've punctured something."

Patients had begun to gather. Some had blood on their clothes.

"She wants the radical hysterectomy," Gracie said. In Harriet's peripheral vision, Gracie's fingers began to rub something in her hand, probably that ribbon she liked to carry. "She wants to go home to her kids. Lévi-Strauss says children —"

"She can't have it, Gracie," Harriet said. "They don't do that operation anymore for people like Lily. It doesn't help with . . . with what she has."

The blood pools at her knees were not spreading across the checker-tiled floor. No serious wounds then.

"Jane Addams, Edward Albee, W.H. Auden, James Baldwin, Tallulah Bankhead —"

"Gracie, please try to stay calm. I have to concentrate."

Nigel wheeled in a mop and bucket, coaxed the patients back from the blood, and began washing the floor. Gracie's fingers moved faster.

"— Djuna Barnes, Roland Barthes, Aphra Behn, Benjamin Britten —"

Wound after wound, Harriet disinfected and bandaged.

"— Lord Byron, Willa Cather, Noel Coward, Leonardo da Vinci —"

The Doctor arrived, knelt heavily at Lily's other side. "That's too bad," he said. "I thought she might yet recover and go home. We'll have to change the diagnosis now."

"— Mazo de la Roche, Marlene Dietrich, Lord Alfred Douglas, King Edward ii, Ralph Waldo Emerson, E.M. Forster —"

"What do you mean?" Harriet sat back on her knees. Ruby was leaning against the wall, still wiping sweat and watching neither Harriet nor the Doctor but Gracie's flashing fingers. Some of the patients had gone back to their activities.

"She's become self-destructive. She's trying to cut out her ovaries, I expect. We'll keep her tranquilized. Chlorpromazine." He pulled a notebook from his pocket and jotted it down.

"— Greta Garbo, Federico Garcia Lorca, Radclyffe Hall, Richard Haliburton, Marsden Hartley —"

"Oh dear. Do you think we *should* have . . . ?"

He shook his head. "The surgery couldn't have prevented this. Any major wounds?"

"— Magnus Hirschfield, A.E. Housman, Sarah Orne Jewett, Frida Kahlo —"

"No, she was careful and the blade is short. Miss Rojas has it. Scars and muscle damage, I expect. We'll watch for infection."

The Doctor stood, called for a stretcher, and left. Nigel took the bloodied swabs. With her chatelaine scissors, Harriet cut open Lily's pant legs and started on the leg wounds.

"— Michelangelo, Yukio Mishima, Laurence Olivier, Joe Orton, Wilfred Owen —"

"Gracie," Ruby asked, "are you listing those names alphabetically?"

Gracie's chin jerked down in the corner of Harriet's eye. She continued, compelled: "Walter Pater, Cole Porter, Francis Poulenc —"

"Do you *have* to list alphabetically?"

She nodded again and began to rock. "— Robbie Ross, Jane Rule, Vita Sackville-West, Marquis de Sade, Sappho, Siegfried Sassoon —"

"These are people like Lily?"

Gracie nodded. "— Socrates, Valerie Solanas —"

"Why do you need to list right now? Is it Lily's self-abuse?"

Gracie shook her head no. "— Gertrude Stein, Lytton Strachey, Pyotr Tchaikovsky —"

"Is it the blood on your blouse? Does it make you feel anxious?"

Gracie nodded, her fingers slowed. "— Alice B. Toklas, Siegfried Wagner, Alice Walker, Andy Warhol —"

"Miss Rojas, please don't encourage her," Harriet said without looking up.

"I'm not encouraging, Miss Caulle. I'm trying to understand the anxiety. You, on the other hand, you hear all this, you see it, you kneel there and clean up after it, but you don't begin to understand what it means."

Harriet stayed bent to her task, didn't meet the eyes of staff witnessing once again her ignominy. Gracie's rocking stopped.

"C'mon Gracie, let's get you a clean blouse."

"— Walt Whitman, Oscar Wilde, Thornton Wilder, Tennessee Williams, Virginia Woolf —"

"Gracie, the Doctor must never know you now have to alphabetize. It's important. Do you understand?"

And Ruby led her away. When Harriet looked after them, Ruby had the ribbon in her own hand and Gracie didn't object.

What no one noticed, in the clamour and long hours it took to re-establish routine, was that Verity, now thirteen years old, still the youngest Facility patient, was nowhere to be seen.

The next morning, an hour before shift, Harriet woke Elsa Sibelius for her bath. She was booked for electroconvulsive treatment. Harriet had discovered that an unpaid hour to pamper Elsa before made for faster recovery after.

Elsa was already awake, tense and agitated. Harriet helped her into a bubble bath, massaged her face and scalp, and felt her gradually relax under the ablutions.

At 7:15 AM, as the Facility woke, Harriet pushed Elsa in the wheelchair down the hall toward the elevator, sensible shoes making hardly a sound.

At the ECT room, Harriet fished for the key. The technician-in-training would come along shortly, but she'd get things ready in the meantime. She pushed the door open with the wheelchair —

It was an enormous room, it had once been a ward, and the electroconvulsive therapy machine should have been at the south end of it. But the machine, the entire room for that matter, had been dismantled. The machine itself, the table, the technician's stool, the light fixtures and switch on the wall, everything was neatly laid out in unbroken pieces on the floor. Perfect rows of screws arranged in order of size. Long bits of wire, delicately untwisted and laid out between the larger slabs of metal and glass, also arranged neatly, evenly. Even the glass from light bulbs had been extracted from their metal bases, the internal wires deftly stretched out alongside wires from the machine. Nothing appeared to be missing or dented, but not one of those pieces could be broken further down.

A monument to precision and symmetry. A work of art.

Elsa gasped, clapped her hands together, and laughed until she lost control and froze into a posture her disease demanded. Harriet stared at the floor (the magnificent floor), for a long while.

The Doctor assigned Harriet to find the vandal and take repair money from that person's paycheque. She determined quickly that it must have happened during Lily's self-abuse episode when all their meagre Security was in the Great Room, but every staff member could be accounted for then.

After her investigations, some weeks later, from her hollow in the armchair, she said, "Either we've been burgled, Mol, or it's a patient."

"The patients aren't capable."

"I know. Though some say the Verity girl picks locks."

"Pfft! Don't believe it for a second."

"Of course not."

In the Facility records, the Doctor recorded the incident as a burglary. He filed no police report.

On her desk the following morning, Harriet found a file with a note attached. The Doctor had done an unscheduled checkup on Verity — and pronounced her severely epileptic with moderate psychosis. It said she had seizured in his office for two full minutes with no prior warning. He prescribed for her a concentrated regimen of anticonvulsants carbamazepine and phenobarbital, and haloperidol, an antipsychotic.

Harriet read the note again, and then re-read Verity's file. True, Verity had lived on another ward for years now, but Harriet still saw her in the Great Room nearly every day. How curious that she had never witnessed a single symptom of epilepsy at all, let alone one so severe. And Verity was the last patient in whom she'd expect psychosis. Had Harriet not been paying attention?

Had the Doctor —

Well. Harriet had neither time nor will to challenge a diagnosis.

They never found a guilty party. The Facility couldn't get another ECT machine nor have this one rebuilt without admitting to inadequate security and subsequently losing more funding. The parts were reused around the Facility as much as they could be.

Elsa Sibelius was sent away to another institution where she could receive monthly ECT. She was gone by month's end.

ATHENA'S JOURNAL
APRIL 08, 2004
(THURSDAY)

I had asked the therapist to show my Holdstock pharmaceutical record to specialists and inquire about the likelihood of regaining full memory of my Holdstock years. The news is not encouraging.

"They expressed surprise at the ever-increasing doses, to put it mildly," he says. "Perhaps it was even dismay."

In times like these, I appreciate his candor. He resists getting caught up in sentiment or pity which I would find insulting.

"One psychiatrist thought with hard work we might yet uncover a few more memories, but the pharmacologist said we ought not to hold out hope. She could imagine 'no better recipe for oblivion.'"

The room is still as I absorb this information.

After a while, he asks, "Athena, I've been wondering. How did you know about the ECT machine at all?"

"I have been wondering the same," I say. "I do not remember." I do not mention dog-pound day.

"Do you recall anything of dismantling it?"

"A glint of satisfaction at first understanding and then disembowelling something so big," I sign, "and at doing some-thing — anything — to modify Facility life. I had proven it possible. But these recollections are granular. I cannot be certain they belong to this event."

"Don't you think your memory is as reliable as these sparse documents you're working from?"

"No," I say. "Even I do not believe that."

He releases a long sigh. "Memory is not a photograph. It exists to protect us, to warn of danger, not to archive our lives. Sometimes the subconscious also protects us by blocking memories we are unprepared to deal with, but your subcon-scious had no choice in the matter. A loss of so many years is no small thing."

We agree to work further to uncover what might be there, he assigns me some exercises to that end, and we move on to another subject.

"What about Harriet," he asks. "How do you feel about her? You write her as a competent nurse who, for all her compassion and intelligence, didn't see you."

At this moment my patience with Harriet is wanting: "I feel her intelligence was in short supply. She did not comprehend I was putting my ear to things to try to hear them. What intelligence you see in her here is harvested from my own imagination."

The therapist and interpreter smile briefly.

"As for her compassion, I am practising restraint," I sign. "In fact, I believe her blithe attention to duty was a wilful focus away from our well-being, away from our humanity. I see that she was troubled and lonely, yes, but she meted out single drops of kindness over scratches while looking away from killing fields." I am on a roll, signing quickly. The interpreter can hardly keep up. "I blame her much more than Esau. Esau made a bad decision under great pressure after several months. Harriet had thirty years to correct an obvious error and she did nothing! Not even acknowledge the error. I want to represent her as something vile. Something mythically malevolent."

"Why don't you then? Why practise restraint?"

Behind the therapist's head is a window. It is too high for me to see anything but sky from where I sit, but I pretend to gaze out nevertheless. I must choose words carefully now or the subject will drag on interminably.

"I would be doing what she did," I say. "Reducing a person to something less than she is because I want her to be that. Harriet is someone on whom I hope never to model my life." I feel my face reflecting my disgust and I force it to even out again before continuing. "Also, the evidence does not support it. Even if it were convincing on the page, I would know it to be inaccurate. Eventually it would trouble me."

I do not say that any simplistic representation would result in him pecking at me to complicate it, as he did with Esau. I am bereft of energy to endure that again.

"Athena, you've come a long way," he says. "Interesting term, killing fields. Is that how you see Holdstock?"

"Today I do."

"Indeed!" he says, and nods as the interpreter spells it out letter by letter. "Knowing what you know now about your memory loss, what would you say to young Verity, the child inside you, if you could speak to her?"

"I would tell her to fight it," I say, "Every cell in her body should fight it."

"I think she did," he says. "With each further story you tell, I think she did."

ATHENA'S JOURNAL
APRIL 10, 2004
(SATURDAY)

"Killing fields?" Mr. Saarsgard writes. "Who died?"

On this fresh spring day, we are out for a spin to celebrate the early snowmelt and to visit another city where Mr. Saarsgard is considering establishing a second XXX store. En route, we stop at a roadside rest area to provide Vincent an opportunity to stretch his legs and to urinate. The latter he did immediately but the scents emanating from the legs of the picnic table at which Mr. Saarsgard and I sit (drinking steaming tea from a shared Thermos) are proving distracting to his leg-stretching.

"I did," I write.

"Oh I see!" he says. "This is metaphor. Rhetorical comparison."

"No. It is how I feel when I think of Harriet," I write. "Literal."

The pencil lead snaps under the force of my underlining, and I must pull out my sharpener. As I rotate the pencil under the tiny blade, I feel Mr. Saarsgard watching me thoughtfully.

Vincent runs over. Ever so gingerly, he tugs the red handkerchief from the pocket of Mr. Saarsgard's new leather pants. ("They are motorcycle pants," he told me. "I like to do a thing properly.") Away Vincent prances, cavorting a circle around the park. We are meant to give chase and retrieve the handkerchief.

Gamely, Mr. Saarsgard and I lumber after Vincent with faint hope of attaining our goal. Mr. Saarsgard's leather pant legs adhere to one another preventing both long strides and quick movement and the ground is too uneven for me. Separately, we collapse on patchy spring grass. Immediately Vincent abandons the handkerchief, forgives our insufficiencies, and vigorously welcomes us to the grass with licking. He moves on to inspect the parking lot trash bins, and we return to the picnic table.

Again, Mr. Saarsgard takes up the pencil: "Can you be specific? Didn't Harriet care for V on long train ride? Why 'killing fields'? Violence?"

"Don't know about violence. Can't recall," I write. "On train, H was caring, attentive. On train, V existed. But later, H was just nurse, V a nameless duty in her day. A child needs good deal more than dutiful nursing."

I underline carefully this time to protect the lead point.

"Ah," he writes. "I see. I don't know the first thing about children."

Afterwards, back home, I feel out of sorts. I do not know why, for it was a wonderful day, complete with excellent food (we stopped for baked halloumi and warm pita with a side dish of olives), prairie views, and wind in my teeth.

I attribute it to reading Harriet's interviews. To think that all this wonderful food existed then.

Imran opens my cupboards.

"Let's go dish shopping," he signs. "Your dishes aren't conducive to custody."

"They are colourful and unchipped," I say. "Arvo is sure to
appreciate them."

My plates are painted with pictures of interesting places
I have not yet visited. There is a *Buckingham Palace* plate, a
Taj Mahal plate, a *Victoria Falls Hotel* plate, a *Mount Rushmore*
plate, a *Leaning Tower of Pisa* plate, an *Alaska Dog Sled* plate,
an *Angkor Wat* plate, a *Dalhousie University* plate, a *Minnesota the Gopher State* plate, a *Cologne Cathedral* plate, a *Lake
Louise* plate, and an especially colourful *Chichen Itza* plate. The
paintings are not to my usual artistic taste, but they in no way
resemble Holdstock metal trays. Thrift store shelves offer up
many such treasures.

"They're unmatched," Imran says. "They're not the same size.
Angkor Wat isn't even round. An assessor might think you can't
yet budget for a proper set."

"The thrift store has several plates identical to this one." I hold
up Lake Louise. "We can purchase a matched set."

"Athena, these plates are tourist souvenirs. They are for
hanging on a wall, not for eating from. I don't even know if they're
food safe. Let's go shopping."

Already I know my plates will not affect custody, but I have
not yet been outdoors today and am glad for a trip. I tell Vincent
that I will return shortly and we will visit the dog park this evening,
no matter the weather, after Imran has left.

The spring rain falls steadily. Imran and I don rubber boots and raincoats and travel by bus to a Department Store. There Imran walks directly to the Kitchen Goods Area and, without browsing, hefts a large box of Corelle dishes down from a shelf and rests it on a nearby counter.

"Look Athena!" he signs, between pulling back the flaps. "These are perfect! They are light and strong and uniform with a beautiful pattern. On these plates, all food tastes of comfort and warmth."

The plates he lifts out have, skirting the rim, a repeated pattern that I fear is meant to resemble a congealed-OXO-gravy flower beside a congealed-OXO-gravy moth. It fails utterly. Yet Imran signs with such certainty and enthusiasm that I cannot help but ask:

"Imran, do you have these dishes?"

"No," he says, "but my mother does! Along with nearly every wonderful cook in our family!"

His glee is uncontained and spills from his fingers and face.

"Imran, does your mother know these dishes are used in Group Homes around the province?"

"Oh." His jubilance evaporates. "I see. I expect she would appreciate the uh practicality of that, but I see your point."

He closes the box. Before replacing it on the shelf, he asks: "Wouldn't familiar plates bring Arvo comfort?"

"Arvo fears the out-of-doors," I sign. "He does not fear plates. Further, Cheery Psychometrist examined and approved my plates. In fact, she is bringing me one from her *alma mater.*"

Imran labours to suppress his disappointment but his shoulders betray him and roll forward.

He is my friend. When he visits me and eats from my plates, I want him to do so in comfort. For this reason, I decide against reminding him of the perfect uniformity of Facility trays and purchase four Corelle place settings. They are plain white with a blue stripe on the rim.

I am pleased to see his shoulders lift.

With the dishes, we return to my flat and, after rubbing Vincent's belly and taking him outside to urinate, we make falafel. Imran crushes the chickpeas that I soaked overnight, I chop parsley and cilantro, we dry-roast garlic and cumin and coriander seed, and we toss it with ample amounts of chickpea flour and green chili. Then, in our clean palms, we press the mixture into balls. The kitchen is a glorious mess indeed, and soon we must pause our efforts to tidy and make space for deep-frying.

"Imran," I sign, as we wait for oil to heat. "Why did Harriet do those things? She spent time with us. She knew what the doctor was doing and she helped him to do it. She says she calculated calorie reductions as he increased sedation to compensate for lessened mobility. She appears to have done so calmly, without remorse or regret or hesitancy. We had only food to anticipate and she reduced even that."

Imran picks up a crumbling raw falafel, crushes it back into shape, and sets it down again to sign.

"Athena, what you endured was savage. The more I hear, the deeper my horror. A shameful blemish on our history, agonizing to think about."

Inwardly, I balk at the toy word *blemish*, but do not interrupt.

"What saves me is you," he continues. "You and Arvo and Elsa, building a community. Making a life despite it. With your games and your art and your stolen snacks and private cozy spaces. You did this on your own. As children! Harriet and the Doctor had power, but, in a strange way, Athena, you had more."

"Imran," I say, "the therapist disapproves of romanticizing distressing events. And you have not answered why a nurse would do those things in the first place."

Imran sighs not once but twice. He has balanced a raw falafel on the spoon, ready to submerge it in hot oil, and sets it down again to sign.

"I can't speak for Harriet," he finally says. "But it was a different time. Maybe her heart was in the right place. Maybe she didn't know better. Maybe she believed the Doctor, or wanted to please him. Or — a woman in those days, to be taken seriously — Or maybe she had bills and needed her job. It could be any number of things, really."

Vincent could have given a more sufficient reply.

I try another approach: "Like the maid in your scrapbook? Sawing off a head because it was a different time and her employer asked her to?"

"Oh! Wh — Hmm. What you endured was savage, Athena," he says. "But perhaps not decapitation."

"When the therapist and I spoke of Harriet, I said "killing fields." He said "Indeed." And I do not see how placement of her heart or any organ is relevant."

Imran turns his attention to the falafel. He will never contradict the therapist, I know. In my peripheral vision, his sideways glances reveal his awareness that I am still out of sorts.

One by one, we immerse falafel into hot oil. We eat the first while still cooking the last. I burn my tongue but do not mind for they are, despite the loathsome conversation, delicious.

Addendum, 4:00 AM. Whether by oily food or troublesome conversation, sleep evades me entirely. I have brewed some tea (hot) and have returned to Harriet's interviews — where I have come upon this document. Later I will add it to my Writer's Notes.

Interviewer: Miss Caulle, records show that when you moved to Alberta from Ontario you brought a child with you. Why was that?

HC: The consulting physician at the Elora Home where I had worked was a Dr. Neb King. He and Mol Vestidge were chums from Medical School and had stayed in touch. I was looking for a change in scenery just then and applied to nursing advertisements across the country. When King learned I had been hired here, he wrote Vestidge and asked if his institution might consider an inter-province transfer. A child needed to be separated from her family. The father had already signed the child over to the Province, so it was just a matter of paperwork.

A matter of paperwork. I do not know how to respond to that. The discovery does not help me sleep at all.

ATHENA'S JOURNAL
APRIL 22, 2004
(THURSDAY)

The therapist has given me an assignment. I am to write Harriet a letter.

I complained about Harriet concurrently using and erasing us for no adequate reason. He asked if, in my reading of atrocities, I had found adequate reason for a single one. I have not.

"The thing is," he said, "minions and clerics have for centuries carried out heinous acts to further their careers. Or to balance the almighty budget. Or to feed a belief they are 'helping' someone." Writing a letter in which I articulate my frustration, even if I never mail it, he thinks, "might bring resolution" to my emotions.

Three times already this week, I sat at my desk, cradled a pen in my fingers, and diligently began writing. After a few paragraphs, I paused to sip tea or to turn a leaf or to scratch Vincent's ears, and I glanced at what I had written — and invariably destroyed it.

The trouble is this: I feel intense things. On the page, however, they seem trite. Unreasonable. Responsibility is not concomitant with need.

The failing seems to be that no one in the Facility was assigned to parent a child, or just to care for her emotional state, and therefore no one did. For me, an emotional gauntlet. For them, a minor administrative oversight. I imagine the stiff interpreter struggling to hide the roll of his eyes at the insignificance of it.

But this life is the only one I have.

I am too out of sorts for this exercise. I summon Vincent for a walk.

NOVEMBER 1975
HOLDSTOCK
(Three years have passed.)

"Harriet," the Doctor said, at her Nurses' Station, "Have you seen my *Physiological Effects of Mental Disorders* lying about anywhere?"

"I don't think so." Harriet looked up at him from her desk.

"It's a textbook, hardcover, mostly grey, green lettering on the cover."

"Doesn't sound familiar."

"Oh dear. I've misplaced it. Very unlike me to misplace something. I've been looking a few days now." He came around the counter and began to rummage through her shelves.

"I really don't have it, Doctor," she said.

He nodded and left.

But later that evening Harriet did see the book. In a stack of books at Ruby's bedside.

"Nurse Caulle. What are you doing in my bedroom?"

Harriet spun.

"Oh. Uh. The door was open and I saw this book —"

"The door was locked. I heard you fiddle for a key on your chatelaine just now. For how long have you had keys to staff bedrooms?"

Ruby's intensity filled the doorway.

"Oh. Well, where did you get this book?"

"Miss Caulle, please answer the question."

"For heaven's sake, Ruby. It's been years. Can't we put it behind us and call each other by Christian names like civilized people?"

"You trespass into my bedroom and speak of civility."

"Well, this book —" Harriet held it up.

"— is relevant to our line of work."

"Uhh the Doctor is missing his copy of a book with this title."

"Ah," Ruby said. "You're searching my room because you believe I *stole* it."

The unmistakable tone of recrimination.

Harriet sat, beaten, on Ruby's bed.

"You're right, I shouldn't have come in. But why do you have it, Ruby? It's nothing you would normally read."

Ruby ignored the implication. "Page 271. What do you see?"

Harriet opened the book. That — *that* was a close-up photograph of Lily's vulva! The unmistakable white scars on her thighs from her '72 self-abuse incident stood out on the page. And beside it, another photograph of Lily taken from farther back. She was naked, splayed on a table with leather straps restraining her hands and pulling apart her knees. Her flesh welled up around the restraints and her tendons strained. Underneath, a caption: *Photograph of self-inflicted scars on female with Ego-dystonic Homosexuality.* In the tiniest print, credit for the photo was given to Dr. M.H. Vestidge of the Holdstock Facility, Canada. Over the page, Albert's scrotal hydrocele — and the scrotum much larger than it should be permitted to grow, easily the size of a cantaloupe, skin shiny from stretching. A year earlier Albert's Head Nurse had complained daily: the Doctor was refusing to drain the hydrocele on schedule and it was growing. Albert bawled whenever they changed him. It had gone on for months. Another page, another patient, another photo. And another, and another. And always, the leather restraints visible, always the welling flesh.

Harriet released a slow breath. "So that's how he's doing it."

"Doing what?"

"We're not making operating budget but he stopped mentioning it a while back. As if it weren't a problem anymore."

Left out again. Harriet ought to have realized. What else was he doing without her?

"Oh. What do you think of these photos?" Ruby asked.

Harriet smoothed the bedspread beside her. She must not reveal her devastation.

"Well — it *is* — coarse. But the Facility needs funds, Ruby. How else can we protect the patients?"

"This does *not* prot — forget it. I'm not having that conversation with you. Open the cover."

At the top, beneath another name crossed out, Ruby's name was written. This was a second-hand copy. It had never belonged to the Doctor.

"I'm sorry the Doctor can't find his book, Miss Caulle. That copy is mine."

"I see. I owe you an apology. I'm sorry, Ruby. I overstepped this evening."

What relief to be talking with her again, even under hostility.

Ruby's features slackened, and she swept her palm up, gesturing Harriet out the door.

Harriet stood, but continued, every additional second with Ruby a delectation. "I don't want to pry further. But can you tell me how you found out about this? He hasn't mentioned it to me."

"Verity took me to his office and showed me the book. I went to the city and bought my own copy."

"What do you mean Verity 'took' you there? How would she know?"

"I don't know. She took me by the hand to his office when he was off-site, pulled the book down from the shelf, and opened it to this chapter. We put it back exactly where we found it. It took a long time. She can hardly stand on these meds but she was determined that I see this specific book."

"Did you break in? Do you have a key?"

Ruby looked steadily at Harriet. Harriet the trespasser.

"Please leave my room, Miss Caulle. I think you'll agree it's in Verity's best interests you don't mention this to the Doctor. And that you, as Head Nurse, are obliged to protect her best interests."

On the way back to her room, Harriet took a deep breath and approached a window. Outside, at a picnic table, bundled against the cold sun, sat the cleaning ladies, drinking from steaming Thermoses and laughing. As wretched as the out-of-doors was, it did afford companionship to those who could endure it.

There was no need to report Verity to the doctor. The next time Harriet was in his office, she spotted the book there and pointed it out to him. It was on his desk, folded into a newspaper. It had been there all along.

Later she walked to Verity's ward and watched her sleep. Never had she seen someone mentally retarded who was quite like Verity.

*W*riter's Note: *For years now, I (Athena) have been dreaming the same dream several nights a week. It goes like this: I am a teenager in the Facility. One summer's night, I feel more clear-headed than usual. I put on daytime clothes. I take my handful of tools from their hiding place and tie them in a cloth diaper. I sneak down to Arvo's room and we pleasure each other. Then I kiss him goodbye. I have pills in my pocket, I am supposed to swallow them, but I give them to Elizabeth, who loves taking pills. I sneak down to my old Laundry exit, I take my red blanket from the shelf, and I tie it around my neck like a cloak. I am much bigger now than when I last used the exit and have little trouble prying off the plywood cover (though it is harder to climb out). Once outside, I refasten it as best I can with the tools I have. I cross the grounds in the dark, avoiding floodlit areas, and climb over a fence.*

I am Outside.

The night is clear and warm, the air tastes of trees, and starlight bounces off the grey Facility buildings. I strike off in the direction of a place on the mountainside where I have sometimes seen curls of smoke — and immediately fall to the ground. I examine the dirt path underfoot. It is bumpy and gnarled, entirely unlike the smooth Facility floors and paved grounds. I will have to take enormous steps to keep from falling.

The path to the place I have seen is long and uphill, the ground uneven, the starlight insufficient to light a wooded path. The giant steps make for hard walking. I must often rest. But I do not get lost, I do not get confused. I need only look up at the ridge above to get my bearings. The sky is pink when I reach the place of smoke, which turns out to be a cabin.

I am hungry and thirsty. Beside the cabin is a fast stream of water colder than any I have touched before. I squat and drink with my hands. It hurts my hands to cup it, it hurts my teeth to drink it, it is cold all the way down to my stomach, and my head aches when I swallow it. A surprising sensation. But I have arrived, I am alright, and I am no longer thirsty.

The cabin door is padlocked and takes a minute to open. Inside is one room. The furniture is made of barkless tree trunks and is coated in dust. Against the wall stands an iron sink with no water or tap, and an iron box with legs and a door. I open the door. It is a small fireplace-stove. Different from the fireplace in the Facility, but the ash pile inside gives it away. A tin can with long matches sits on the shelf. I can burn things. There are old newspapers in a crate by the wall for reading and burning. I open the plywood cupboards above the sink and find a pot, a pan, some plates and rows of tin cans. Food. The cans have no labels, I will not know what I am about to eat, but I do not eat labels, it will not matter.

Satisfied and exhausted, I lay on the bench and sleep.

When I wake, my head feels clearer than I ever remember. I find a can opener and eat two cans of food — tomatoes and pineapple. An acidic meal. Soon I must go outside and choose a place for a toilet and then I collect wood. There are no stacks of evenly sawed pieces like in the Facility and the wood I do find is off the path where the walking is difficult. I fall often and the vegetation removes sheets of skin. But I collect a small pile by the time evening comes.

For years I have watched the Facility custodian build fires. It takes a few tries, and my fire has too much smoke, but I manage soon enough. I fill the pot with water from the stream and set it on the hot stove and wait until it bubbles. I pour it into an empty tin can, I wrap a corner of my blanket around it so that I can hold it, and I sip carefully so as not to cut my lip nor burn my tongue.

What luxury. A hot drink in a room by myself, in a cabin I walked to with my own legs. I sleep deeply that night.

My days go on like this, fire, food, water, wood, fire. Every day, my head is clearer than the day before. This small cabin, this clean air, this unstructured ground, this is my new life. I begin to think about how to bring Arvo here, how we would love this place together. We would clear a dirt path for his balls to roll unobstructed. This part of my dream I want never to stop.

One morning in my dream, I awaken suddenly terrified without knowing why — until I smell the Facility. Carbolic acid and vile, fusty saliva. I hide under my red blanket and lay perfectly still. But someone peels it back and they are the Facility people and they smell so awful and they have huge meat hooks and although I resist they grab first one arm and then another, first one leg and then another, and then those meat hooks sink through my pants into my thighs and my beautiful clarity vanishes. I slide helplessly again into paralysis and nightmare.

I hate this dream. I wish I could stop dreaming it. I try to waken myself at the good part but I never can. The meat hooks keep sinking and paralysis overwhelms me every time. My therapist and I have spent many bewildering sessions on it.

And then I found this passage in the interviews of Harriet Caulle.

The interviewer asks about Miss Rojas's dismissal:

HC: She was dismissed because the youngest Holdstock resident, a teenager, eloped. Rojas left a door open and that poor disoriented girl walked out and disappeared into the forest. We searched the Grounds for days. If the public got wind we had lost one of our own, we'd have been shut down. A merciful thing it was summer and she wasn't freezing to death. Finally Dr. Vestidge drove to the Provincial Training School and fetched one of the Indian patients LeVann had scooped up from the roadside and was still there. He could track. He stepped out of the van, looked up at the mountain, pointed to smoke wafting from a chimney a mile or two in the distance — and we all felt rather foolish. We set off then, the Doctor, me, and four orderlies through the woods. I rather dislike the out-of-doors but the trip to the cabin was short, perhaps forty-five minutes. And there she was. She fought us but the orderlies knew their work and I injected her in the leg and sedated her straightaway. I looked around the little cabin then. Someone had cleaned; it was tidy and quaint. No sign of seizures.

Interviewer: Was the girl punished?

HC: Punished! [Laughs.] No no, you treat this kind of thing. Confusion is part of the disease. We sedated her fully for a month after that, then reduced the meds slightly and kept her moderately sedated for the remaining Facility years so that she wouldn't have to relive her days as an animal in the wilderness. In the old days we might have sent her for a lobotomy to relieve pressure on the brain, but that sort of thing didn't happen anymore. The drugs were better by then. Sometimes I thought that girl had become a repository for needles.

Interviewer: And Miss Rojas?

HC: She had left a door open. She was immediately dismissed. The Doctor gave her a good reference despite the incident and recommended she find work in a Group Home. The wrongful dismissal suit came soon after. She had left no doors open, where was our evidence, and so on. The court deemed the evidence inadequate but everyone knew it was her. Rojas had a rebellious streak. Sometimes she turned a blanket upside down on a bed, so the diamonds still lined up across all the beds in a ward, but if you looked carefully, you'd see the fringe that should be down by the feet was up, under a pillow! "Ruby," I would say, "It's authority. If you buck it, it will crush you." And she would say, "It's the principle of the thing, Harriet." Always pushing, that's Ruby Rojas for you.

My dream of all these years appears to be a suppressed memory! This was real! And if it is accurate, I exited the building — my own undertaking — while Rojas was hard at work.

I suspect my elopement was convenient for the administration, however, and the real reason for Rojas's dismissal had to do with a letter, dated 18 May 1976, which Rojas sent the Doctor and the Board of Directors.

She said that care was declining at the Facility and pointed to the textbook photos as an example of "complete abnegation of human rights." She said the sale of motorized wheelchairs "amounted to an act of theft": They belonged not to the Facility but to the residents. The sale she thought "in truth an effort to reduce resident mobility and to thwart independence." (Indeed, Nurse Caulle's interviews betray frustration with "people in electric wheelchairs" who "move from the place where you set them." Which, I think, would be the point.) She also said the Holdstock Facility was "once a home, now a warehouse" and listed Group Home organizations in the province that she thought offered better care. Two other Facility staff signed it as well. Rojas was dismissed approximately ten weeks after she submitted this letter, in August 1976, and about two weeks after my excursion into the woods. The two other staff who signed it disappear from the duty roster within the year.

And I am left to ponder the workings of my mind. How I laboured to hold on to the memory of dismantling the ECT machine, deliberately returning to it every day for decades, still losing parts of it, but here, despite a river of pharmaceuticals, my brain lodged this event without conscious effort.

My therapy appointment of the week is a weepy one. Even the vertical interpreter has an emotion for a second or two. We again try to recover other memories, using this one as a launching point, but the only moment I recall is that, at one point when sedated, I fell out of bed. I recall being jarred awake first by the noise of falling, then by the pain of impact, then realizing I was on the floor, seeing a nurse come running, and falling asleep again.

Soon after that, they replaced our beds with adult cribs. The cribs were a further indignity, but I recall, after the time of heaviest sedation, that wondrous sensation of having again affected institution life.

I existed. The world interacted with me.

1979

HOLDSTOCK

(Three Years Have Passed.)

Harriet, the sole nurse at Holdstock, still the only staff with a chatelaine, began her shift in what had once been the Med Room of the old Psych Ward. Now that all beds were in two long rooms on a single floor, it was the only remaining Med Room in the Facility. She loaded her cart with the necessary pills, bottles, and syringes and pushed it out past the Nurses' Station and into the corridor that ran between the two long rooms. Through a doorway, she waved hello to the two staff who were chattering in some other language — Harriet didn't know which one — and changing diapers and repositioning patients. They were on their first round of the day. On Wednesdays and Saturdays, they helped the bathing staff, but today was Tuesday. After changing each wet diaper in the Facility, it would be lunchtime. Another diaper-changing round and their shift was finished.

Harriet pushed the cart into the room opposite and braked it by the feeding staff who had already begun. One was setting up enteral feeding and the other was spoon-feeding those who still ate by mouth. They worked quietly, coaxing patients to swallow or shift, and Harriet administered meds alongside. Sedatives were kinder on stomachs that had something in them, and all patients needed them. (With Verity's escape of years ago highlighting the need for augmented patient surveillance in face of a diminishing budget, sedatives had been increased throughout the Facility. Not all at once, nothing so calculated, but one acting-out patient at a time.)

Some time later, after first rounds, Harriet locked the cart away and assembled a tray of creams, gauze, and bandages. Out on the wards again, she moved bed to bed: wound care happened in patient beds now that the Infirmary stored filing cabinets. A few new bedsores today wanted her attention. And of course the stoma sites. Most patients had Gastrostomy-tubes or Jejunostomy-tubes feeding directly into their stomachs without the bother of eating and swallowing. Aspiration had all but ceased but the stoma sites tended to infect. She treated them with barrier or antibiotic cream when she could, but with so many stomas and she the only nurse, she rarely kept up. Inevitably the tissue granulated, and she debrided and cauterized it with silver nitrate (watching carefully for burns).

She finished before the feeding staff were ready for second feeding. Back to the med room then to assemble a tray of callous removers, files, and creams. Then she set out again, bed to bed, measuring and trimming the callouses that grew on whatever body part bore the brunt of a patient's self-abuse, so pervasive in recent years. The bedridden were never got up, and the wheel-chair-bound spent most days in bed, so she wasn't a quarter way through the beds when the feeders called for her again.

No matter, she would continue tomorrow. This week it was callouses; next week she'd do toes. Without staff for complicated pedicare, toes with ingrown toenails had been amputated and the little stumps wanted looking after.

Harriet refreshed her med cart and pushed it into the Great Room where the second feeding was beginning, braking it by the filthy rock that still jutted into the room. The few remaining ambulatory patients sat on worn sofas throughout the Room, too sedated to interact much with anyone. The feeders were tying onto Verity and Arvo plastic bibs that curved out to form a bowl. They scooped their meals quickly into their mouths, then took the bibs to the sink, rinsed them, and tied them on Lily and Gracie. Patients swallowed willingly, then went back to watching television, drooling, rubbing ribbons or flipping socks in their hands, rocking rocking rocking all the while. From time to time, one of them stood and shuffled slowly back and forth across the smooth floor.

"Miss Caulle!"

It was the Doctor, striding the hallways again, thrill in his step no longer suppressed. He motioned her to follow. Harriet asked the feeders to keep patients away from the med cart (protocol, but in truth an unnecessary request) and ran to catch up.

He stood by Irwin's bed. She took her place on the other side of it. He reached forward and cradled Irwin's head in his stubby red hands, Irwin's drugged motionless head with fixed eyes and dribbling mouth agape. Then he turned to Harriet with saltwater cheeks:

"The suffering is gone from him, Harriet!" he said. "All those years. The suffering is finally gone."

These moments warmed her heart. When Mol's humanity glowed, when he saw her worth and wanted her to share in the accomplishment. In these moments, she saw him most clearly.

"Truly wonderful, Doctor," she smiled. "A real achievement." He lay Irwin's head down again.

She was as proud of Holdstock as he. Together, despite unconscionable decreases in funding, they had wrestled it to the pinnacle of efficiency. No breaks in routine, no demanding individuals. No crises, no outbursts, no laughter or tears. Very few staff were necessary, no one worked overtime, nothing unexpected happened. Never had precision and routine been so completely achieved.

They spoke for a few minutes about Irwin's chart, then Harriet returned to rounds in the Great Room.

Oh sure, it was all a bit dull. Now she was a nurse. Once she had been a teacher and a masseuse and a singer of carols, once she had rescued a boy tied up like a cow. But this version of Hold-stock was kinder to the patients, no doubt about it. Safer. And that was the purpose, wasn't it? To bring about kindness and safety?

Sometimes, with so few staff, Harriet became lonely. She had long used her clout to avoid the outdoors altogether — an awning from an outbuilding covering her path to staff quarters, a sched-uling adjustment to stay indoors on dog-pound day — but the cost! The more she evaded the outdoors, the greater her appre-hension. Her years of avoidance only exacerbated the problem. Once, the feeding and changing staff invited her to a bonfire by the lake. Harriet planned to attend, awaited it all week (once she had attended an outdoor Christmas skate for hours!) but when the bonfire day came she couldn't even dress in outdoor shoes. She *had* learned to knit: each Holdstock patient now had a pair of handmade woolen socks. But yarn and socks were not company.

Nerve callouses. Harriet needed nerve callouses. If the Arvo boy could sometimes face the looming hills, surely she ought to manage it.

Drawing on books she had once found in the Vocational area, Harriet used her after-work time to plan a schedule for bolstering strength against the looming hills. She began with a fifteen-second step outside and worked up to a short walk from the Main Building east door to the west door, fingers never for-saking the wall. Then to an outbuilding 217 steps away from Staff Quarters and from any wall whatsoever. And eventually to the lake where she forced herself — this was important — to gaze upon the mountains and not at the blessed Main Building. First for a whole minute (it felt like an hour) adding a minute every other day until she could last a full half-hour.

Pharmaceutical inventory, one of her duties now, permitted her a clandestine daily benzodiazepine and under it she had once walked to a nearby cabin to retrieve a patient, and had twice walked all the way into town, not in Nigel's covered car but on her own two feet. There, she went straight to the knitting shop, positively revelling in the company of the cashier, a woman her own age, and returned to the Facility before the med wore off. A triumph indeed. She halved the pills, kept the dose low. If the Doctor suspected anything, he never said.

(As for Verity, it was not always a bad thing to be oblivious. There were days when the smell pouring from her mouth was so foul, so inescapable, she retreated gladly to oblivion. Arvo helped. The two of them rocked together, among other things. The smell was the worst of it, of those years and years and years. Arvo was the best of it.

And yes, oblivion helped.)

Writer's Note: After writing this, I (Athena) stand from my desk and walk to my front door. I slide the deadbolt shut and insert the chain into its slot. I march to my living room and lower the blinds, I sit in a solid chair and anchor my feet — and I rock. I rock like Arvo taught me, from the waist with a straight and solid back, feet planted, abdominal muscles tight, mouth slightly open, eyes half-glazed, head bobbing like a fowl. I have not done this since Imran told me, years ago, that normal people do not rock.

And oh, I have missed it! What a wonderful thing to escape, to disappear through my own momentum, no medication involved.

I had thought that here, in the story of Harriet and Mol, I would find at last an enemy. Or at least an edict made by people who yearn to exterminate those whom they do not like. I do not want to discover, as I have, that a worm larder like the Hold-stock Facility results from people making do, trying at best to protect us, at worst to protect their careers. I also do not want to discover, as I have, that for all my anger towards Harriet I carry also some admiration for her extraordinary flexibility and self-preservation. She made herself indispensable.

The rocking soothes me and after a while I can stop and go about my day.

If I get custody of Arvo, we will rock a great deal, I am certain.

As part of further memory recovery, the therapist has asked me to list those "glimpses" I remember about Holdstock life in later years. Here they are, in no particular order:

1. Shuffling in the Great Room. I tried always to run or to pace aggressively, but my legs were heavy. It took all my strength to shuffle.

2. Rocking in the Great Room, looking at nothing but finding escape in repeated movement.

3. Staring at one thing, a leaf, a crack in the floor, mud from an orderly's shoe, for hours, appreciating what was beautiful about it. With enough attention, the most ordinary of objects could carry me away.

4. The week they installed heavy latching metal doors on the wards with tiny reinforced-glass windows at eye level. They replaced the wooden swinging doors.

5. Nurse Harriet's mouth always moving in time, it seemed, to the swing of her chatelaine. Arvo says she sang as she worked, sometimes about a bobbing robin, sometimes about a boy named Danny, sometimes about other things. He enjoyed her singing.

6. Coming out of heavy sedation that I now know followed my adventure in the woods. The world seemed under water and I could not maintain balance. Once I fell and chipped a tooth on a handrail. Another time I broke a bone in my left wrist.

7. A great deal of self-stimulation. I looked around the Great Room once and realized every one of us had a hand down the pants. It made bearable the sitting for hours with nothing to do.

8. The end of fires. After the man whom I call Irwin in this text had his lighters confiscated, he could not bear the sight of fire. If anyone approached the Great Room fireplace, he grew agitated and would hurt himself until the person stepped back from the fireplace. This continued until they wired shut the fire grate and set a television in front of it. He was eventually sedated into immobility, but the television stayed where it was.

9. Cartoons on the television. Once the TV arrived, it was always on and usually showed cartoons. Sometimes Arvo would tell me what was being said. It is difficult to lip-read Daffy Duck.

10. A tall man who wore a Santa Hat year 'round.

11. Early, I was bothered by a girl who would defecate in her pants. The feces got on her hands and she would smear it on something. Eventually, someone cleaned it up, but in the meantime there were feces on a wall or a chair. In due course, the medication made it so that I could no longer feel when I needed to defecate. I did then what she had done as I waited with a loaded dragnet of feces trawling behind, sometimes for an hour, sometimes for half a day, until a

worker was available to help me clean up. They diapered us, of course, but diapers rarely contain the full volume of an adult bowel movement. And they feel terrible. Any moisture next to skin feels terrible.

12. Realizing one day that the most incapacitated of us received the most affection. I began studying the others then, trying to copy their lopsided gait and other mannerisms. Eventually, I succeeded — and would have my diaper changed sooner.

13. The day the nurses began wearing slacks.

14. Gracie's orderly pastiches and lists stuck up in alphabetized mayhem on the Great Room walls. One in particular held my attention for weeks: she had torn up her university degrees into long strips of text, soaked them in coloured water, and affixed them with mucilage overtop a magazine picture of an angry crowd. At first glance, one sees a child's messy collage, but soon emerges a face made of words, with oblong mouth and hands at either side pressing it into place. Because in fact the face is in the process of exploding, revealing in the cracks the angry fists and faces beneath. Just the glue, which cannot be seen, and the hands at the sides hold it together at all.

15. Reading magazines. Popular Mechanics and Good Housekeeping were my favourites. There were novels too, many of them, but with covers ripped off or hundreds of pages missing. I read them, fifty pages from this one and seventy from that, and their stories ran together. A graveyard boy named Pip floated on a raft with a man named Jim and they visited an old soldier in a jungle who severed people's heads and affixed them to posts. As the medication increased, it took longer to read a page, sometimes hours.

16. My saliva getting a rank, stale smell.

17. Watching the nurses, often the only movement in a room, and smiling when they dropped or tripped over something.

18. The coral glow reflecting off the mountains at day's end. The iron bars on the windows, the most battered furniture, the bleakest rooms all seemed lit from within. Nearly every eternal afternoon had a day's-end glow to anticipate.

Writer's Note: The therapist and I work for weeks to recover more memories, to lengthen the list. We use a wide variety of approaches and exercises.

We do not succeed.

APRIL 1992,
CALGARY
(Thirteen Years Have Passed.)

Well now, wasn't this a treat!

Silk damask curtains, the thickest mattress Harriet had ever seen, and there, on the dresser, an electric kettle, a powder blue china tea set (the dearest sugar bowl) and three wee tins of tea that smelled divine. She was about to brew herself a cup to celebrate her first off-site vacation in nearly thirty years when that *delicious* mattress beckoned. Like a child Harriet pushed off with her feet, flopped back onto the bed, giggled, and let her eyelids fall.

She had done it. Under a single benzodiazepine, she had walked into town, taken the bus into the city, disembarked, and walked — walked! — eleven unfamiliar outdoor city blocks to the guesthouse.

She would love it here. And stay for two whole weeks.

She had a plan. Breakfast and dinner she would take at the guesthouse and, between them, she would visit exactly three places — a shopping mall, a university library, and the Alberta History Museum — but visit each several times. If she could limit the number of new environments, her apprehension ought to be manageable. Three new settings were three more than she'd had in years. She planned to map out her walking paths that very evening, after dinner.

Harriet woke when her eyelids warmed from the morning sun streaming into the room. She still wore her coat and shoes, and lay atop the duvet. She had slept in her clothes! And missed a scheduled dinner! How naughty!

Again she giggled and tripped to the bathroom. A slender cut-glass bottle of green bath foam sat on a ceramic ledge beside a grand claw foot tub. She hadn't soaked in a full tub of water since the last round of cutbacks. Three-quarter hour yet until breakfast.

Harriet ran the taps, slipped off her clothes, and eased into steaming scented froth. She would visit the library first.

Several hours later, after a bus ride in a strange city, a *twelve-*block walk, cozy in a noble leather chair under a green reading lamp, with newspapers on her lap and bookstacks on all sides, she had another milestone to celebrate.

That day and the next, Harriet spent at the library browsing newspapers (long ago cancelled at Holdstock) and catching up on world events. She thumbed through card catalogues — what pleasure, so many books at her fingertips — and borrowed a novel to read in her guest house room after hours.

The following two days she walked to a nearby shopping mall with high glass ceilings. Naturally, a mall had some chaos about it. Startling neon fashions for one, and store shelves crammed with goods Harriet neither recognized nor fathomed. She bought two pairs of shoes and a green eyelet dress, along with a bottle of thirty-year-old Tawny Port for sessions with Mol, but mostly she strolled the wide hallways, window-shopped, and watched people go about their days. It was exhilarating.

Still. Old terrors threatened to rise. Both mall days, Harriet returned early to the blessed safe guest house.

She began thinking about skipping the museum altogether and returning a week early to Holdstock — but how to explain it to Mol?

Instead, she returned to the familiar, ordered library.

This time, before settling into the noble leather chair, Harriet explored the library. Four storeys, curved walls, wings curling this way and that. Mol had recommended she visit the medical stacks in another building and check for pharmaceutical breakthroughs.

Mol wasn't here. The med stacks could wait. She rode the elevator to the second floor, and wandered every row of bookstacks there. Music journals, art books, photography, textiles, so many delights. She had been absent from this world for so long. Then up the stairwell (dusty baseboards! They could learn something from her Holdstock!) to the third floor. Novels, poetry, philosophy, and literary criticism. Up the dusty stairwell again to the fourth floor: anthropology, geography, history, sociology. And then Harriet stopped in her smart new shoes.

Society and Handicap Quarterly. American Journal on Intellectual Disability and Housing. Integration and Community Living.

Around her sat journals and books that seemed to concern the feeble-minded. No no — *people with disabilities* is what they said now. The corners of Harriet's mouth began to stretch. Usually Mol was the one returning from conferences with news of this sedative or that anti-psychotic. Wouldn't he be pleased if *she* returned with news in the field? Together they could strategize Holdstock's future — surely the Group Home claptrap had passed — and chuckle over the rights activists Mol so despised, how they'd been put in their place.

There were too many books to cart down to the main floor noble chair. At row's end stood a table. Beyond it, a window overlooked the campus and showcased distant mountains. Once the window would have prevented her but Harriet wasn't put out. Windows she managed effortlessly now. Making several trips, she carried armloads of volumes to the table and settled into a chair. She selected a journal with a cover article on Ontario institutions and began to read.

Condominiums, the writer said. Elora Home for the Feeble-Minded, where Harriet had once worked, had been emptied "in favour of Community Living" (another term for Group Homes, Harriet surmised), the buildings converted to condos. Other

Ontario institutions, which "prevented thriving," were also shuttered amidst "the quest for people with disabilities to be full citizens." Office buildings now, mostly.

With considerably less enthusiasm, Harriet reached for another volume.

Barbaric, this writer said. The very techniques she and Mol and their dedicated staff had used daily for decades. This article called them "Cro-Magnon. Barbaric."

Heavens.

She reached for another volume. And another.

Three hours later, she had not found a single article pushing against claptrap. Everywhere, accusations and denunciations. Segregated institutions, "once thought safe haven for the vulnerable," were in fact cruel, criminal, or somesuch. It left a bad taste in Harriet's mouth. She fumbled in her handbag for a mint.

Why had Mol never let on how the field had *changed?* Had he purposely kept her uninformed? Had he known all along that the tooled efficiency of their Holdstock was anachronistic? If *only* she had been kept abreast. The decades of weekly *tête-à-têtes,* all the times she had held down the fort. She was his poultice, drawing out the rancour of the staff, slaking on calmness, bolstering his might with her loyalty. What about *her?* These books, she had never felt so ignorant. It was humiliating.

Or — perhaps he concerned himself only with pharmaceutical advances? Yes, that was more likely. How like him, oblivious to all else. Had he ever noticed her apprehensions? Likely he'd never set foot in this library, though he'd visited the medical library dozens of times. Would he have any idea, for example, that eugenics had become a filthy word balled up in rumblings of lawsuits? Harriet smiled briefly to picture him sitting by her here, reading, yanking his tie back and forth. He would lose his head at these books.

Well. Lucky for both of them that she had taken this trip. She'd see him soon enough. They'd sort it out over the fine Port she had bought.

She stood to carry the books to a nearby library cart for re-shelving when a slim volume slipped out and fell to the floor: *Report of Canadian Disability Advocacy Council 1991.*

On the cover was an older photograph, taken with shaky hand, of an institution ward. Harriet picked the volume up. It could be any institution really; telling details like bedspreads or wainscoting were blurry. A woman in a nursing uniform walked away from the camera, pushing a med cart, between two long rows of beds with people in them.

She thumbed through. It wasn't fifty pages long. Definitions, lists of practices now considered unacceptable, bake sales for fundraising, marches for awareness-raising, college night classes for education. Provinces across the country systematically investigating their segregated institutions for adherence to human rights criteria and laying a blade at the necks of those falling short.

Near the back of the booklet, Harriet's eye seized on a list, disturbingly short: "Segregated Institutions Still Running in Canada." Sitting third from the top was "Holdstock Facility, Alberta." They had not escaped notice after all. Beneath the list, a short phrase. *"All to be assessed in the coming months for closure."*

An imminent inevitable assessment. There was a list. A published list.

People say the most wretched things.

Harriet's stomach, now an iron plate.

Suddenly the window terrorized her.

Swiftly she abandoned the remaining books piled haphazardly on the table and walked, almost ran, to the Ladies' Room.

Not the one with seven stalls, but the private one near the entrance with a wheelchair sign on the door and a stout deadbolt, which she slid into place.

She sank by the toilet and relieved her stomach of its breakfast. She waited, in case there was more, then flushed, rinsed her mouth, settled on the toilet seat, feet firmly planted, and had herself a proper, full-fledged, cold-sweat panic attack.

Those advocacy people didn't understand! The old ways didn't harm anyone; they did things differently is all.

"In the coming months." Whatever did that mean? When were those wretched assessors planning to visit Holdstock? April already and it was a '91 report. What if they were driving to Holdstock at this very moment? While she luxuriated here in bath foam?

She could telephone Mol. Warn him. He could hire dozens of staff this afternoon, modify the *Duties Manual,* reduce meds, set up privacy screens —

But the logistics! There was no time to train new staff. A sudden reduction in medication could be lethal. A simple change like reintroducing unpureed foods overnight could bring about death by aspiration, and an onsite death would make them look worse. And from where would the money come? If she returned to the Facility today and they began immediate improvements, there was neither time nor funds to address all the ways, deep systemic ways, Holdstock would fail the new assessment criteria laid out in these pages.

What was one to do?

Their Holdstock, paragon of safety, could not be saved. Somehow, somewhere along the way, Harriet had gotten herself on the wrong side of things. She had been protecting the wrong people.

But it wasn't her *fault,* Mol hadn't kept her abreast. If she had *known*, she could have done things differently. After the first few months, after the silver chatelaine, had he ever really appreciated her worth? How she could make things go one way and not another? At the very least, one wants to be appreciated. For all their conferences, all the Port, had she ever been in on the real secrets? *I wanted not to overwhelm you,* he had said.

She needed something. Surely she had *something*. She dumped the contents of her bag on the bathroom floor, fingered through the pile. There. A nail clipper. She raised her skirt, lowered a stocking, and eased a strip of tender thigh flesh between the clipper blades and — closed.

Spike of pain, rush of blood — it had been so long — ohh.

Harriet's pulse slowed. It really wasn't her fault. She had done her best. *She* needn't endure the scandal.

She sat for another ten minutes, clotting her thigh with a wad of toilet paper.

Then she got to her feet. She wiped her underarms with paper towel, she rinsed her mouth again. She washed her face and smoothed her hair, touched her toes and reached for the sky. She returned to the table, the books were still there, and she jotted down the telephone number of the Disability Advocacy people who had published the booklet.

She would place the call herself. If Harriet reported abuses, no one would think she had once enacted them. Her pulse slowed further.

She would move to a city. One with plenty of covered walkways and a properly restrained landscape. She ought to look up Ruby. They could gossip over wine and a cozy fire about Mol Vestidge, that beastly doctor under whom they had both worked.

Fresh air, fresh start.

Writer's Note: It took nearly a year to empty the Holdstock Facility. Community Living representatives from across the province turned up to gawk at the site of atrocity and to shop for the most attractive, normal-looking residents. Gracie and Lily and I were the first to go followed by Arvo and Irwin, the bed-ridden and most dependent the last.

No charges were ever laid.

ATHENA'S JOURNAL
MAY 05, 2004
(WEDNESDAY)

After many attempts, I believe I have assembled a note to Harriet.

Early on in this exercise, I abandoned the articulation of emotions in favour of listing moments she should have seen me. This approach I also abandoned for I cannot know which moments truly happened. Finally I arrived upon this short note:

Dear Harriet,

I should feel compassion for you. I know from Arvo the torment you suffered. But Arvo, with all his fears, harms no one.

I suspect you meant solely to obey, for obedience allows one to amass power while dodging the cargo of responsibility. But obedience requires a moral flexibility, a willingness to cruelty, that I do not understand.

Also, Harriet. It reveals that you have no self. You betrayed it away.

Compassion is not forthcoming.

Cordially,

Athena (who once was Verity)

It is a visiting day, and, strangely, Arvo does not meet me at the door. The Group Home keyworker instead opens the door and signs to keep my coat on.

I look around her, into the Dining Room, and there is Cheery Psychometrist testing Arvo!

Arvo's face stretches vertically with surprise, then horizontally with delight, then forward as he jumps to pull me into the room and kiss me. The tuxedo man he is holding gets caught in my hair. The psychometrist laughs at our embrace and his extraordinarily mobile face as he extracts the tuxedo man from my hair.

I turn to the keyworker: "I'm glad to see Arvo and Cheery Psychometrist," I sign, "but I booked this time with him."

"Oh it's just a mistake," she signs. "I'm sorry you made the trip."

"Again?"

Cheery Psychometrist interrupts. "What do you mean 'Again,' Athena?"

"Every time I have visited in recent weeks — I am careful to book in advance — Arvo has been unavailable. Last week, they pushed an enema into him before I arrived and let me stay only a few minutes. Arvo told me he had defecated that day already, and twice the day before. The enema, he said, made his intestines cramp."

The psychometrist lays down her pen, amazed, and looks at the worker. "You would administer a powerful medical procedure unnecessarily to prevent them from meeting?"

The worker says nothing.

"I believe it is because Arvo and I have sexual history."

"Is this true?" the psychometrist asks of the worker.

She turns and speaks to the psychometrist with her voice. Cheery Psychometrist interrupts her and insists she sign because "Athena is part of this conversation. It affects her a great deal."

The worker's shoulders roll forward in the manner of someone profoundly uncomfortable. "We do not prevent self-stimulation, no. But sexual activity between clients goes against house policy. I have to follow policy."

She fetches a Group Home policy manual and points to a statement that says any sexual activity must be limited to people married to one another.

"We are happy to marry," I say. "Arvo was talking about it a few months ago. That is why I made him the tuxedo bicycle man." Arvo holds up the tuxedo man.

"*You* can't mar—"

"Ah, tuxedos," Cheery Psychometrist interrupts. "I always wanted a life of formal wear, but now my neck is too baggy."

She laughs very hard, as if she expects us to laugh along. An oblique attempt, I think, at preventing the keyworker from speaking her mind.

"Arvo has told me many times that you *do* prevent masturbation," I say. "He says that any time you see him touching himself you hold his hands in yours and pray until the urges pass. It upsets him."

"Arvo doesn't speak, Athena."

"Arvo speaks to me. How else might I have known that he had defecated before you gave him an enema?"

Her cheeks take on the flush of exasperation. "Every time you visit," she says, "Arvo goes off his programs, out of control. Masturbating. Rubbing himself against cushions, the furniture, his bedpost. You don't understand. That Holdstock place messed him up —"

"I think I underst —" I start.

"— his life is *hard*," she continues, looking now only at Cheery Psychometrist. "He gets dry skin and plantar warts. His agoraphobia is severe. He tries hard to overcome it, then *she* comes, and he steps outside like it's nothing, and then he won't leave the house without her. We're back to square one. I wish her visits made life better for him but they make it worse."

"I'm sorry," Cheery Psychometrist interrupts. "Can you go back to the part where you restrain him and pray to prevent self-stim? You mentioned a bedpost. This takes place in his bedroom?"

She is caught — but does not yet know it.

"The union meeting last year," the keyworker says, pushing up her chin. "We asked the Provincial representatives about people masturbating in our place of work. They said we were being harassed."

"Did they know your line of work? Did they know you were in his bedroom?

"They said no one should have to endure it."

"And this is now policy here?"

The keyworker nods. I see no sanctimony on her face. She is convinced of the rightness of her way.

"May I keep this policy manual?" Cheery Psychometrist says, "for my report?" And she slips it into her briefcase without waiting for an answer. The worker leaves the room with a relieved expression and the three of us look at one another.

"Look what they are doing to you," I say. "You are a decent man, a fine lover, a bit of a coward — but they are making you over in their image and it is nothing like you!"

The psychometrist laughs her distinctive laugh and Arvo kisses me until I say to him in our language that we should finish the tests.

At the end, Cheery Psychometrist says that he scored much higher on everything the moment I was in the room, and she will emphasize this in the report. Arvo and I both smile.

Perhaps this is a sea change. Perhaps that benighted keyworker has helped my cause.

Three

Mr. Saarsgard and I are feeling depressed, we are drowning our sorrows in root beer.

I am depressed from my most recent visit with Arvo. He was wearing a new т-shirt which he had received as reward for stepping out of his house onto the patio. He liked the picture on it of a boy on a bicycle, but he is unable to read and did not know what the shirt said. I told him it said "I'm a child of God" and he began to cry. "I'm not a child of anyone," he signed, "Why would it say that?" He wanted to change his shirt then. I had to ask him to leave it on so that suspicion is not laid on me and my chances for custody.

Mr. Saarsgard is depressed because he is being picketed again. A neighbourhood well-being organization has several factions, he says, and when tensions flare, the members come together by picketing Mr. Saarsgard's XXX store. This time the placards in front of his store read "We shall overcome" and "Repent that you might enter the Kingdom of Heaven" and "No to Noodies." Mr. Saarsgard serves the picketers fresh-pressed lemonade and welcomes them in his awkward way, but they are angry and aggressive and do not appreciate his neighbourliness.

Nor do they know, evidently, that "Noodie" is not a word.

"I'm getting a tattoo," he writes. "It's my therapy when picketers depress me. Would you like to come along?"

He has several tattoos already, I see, when he removes his shirt in the tattoo parlour. They sit in a tidy row across his abdomen and each is small and intricate. One is an apple with a bite taken out and lipstick remnant on the white flesh. Below is written, in cursive font, "Taste and see that the Lord is good."

There is also an unclothed backside with "Turn the Other Cheek" curving under it like a bowl. The others I cannot make out. Today the tattooist is inscribing a phrase across Mr. Saarsgard's navel. It will say "The Kingdom of Heaven Is Within You." I recognize these phrases from picket signs and religious literature around Arvo's Group Home. Why would Mr. Saarsgard mark himself with phrases used by the people who oppress him? I say nothing and examine sample designs on the parlour wall.

At the far end of the room, beside a coffee percolator, stands a tin chicken in a transparent glass cage. The sign says "Circa 1905." When I insert a penny, the chicken lurches in a circle and pecks at tin feed on the ground as it has been doing for a hundred years. I easily determine from the pace of the lurching what kind of small apparatus, clacking beneath the grooves at the chicken's feet, compels it forward. It is the most depressing thing I have seen in a long while and makes me think again of Arvo.

I turn then and write to Mr. Saarsgard, who is wincing from the needle, that I would like a tattoo. Delighted, he asks to pay for it because I have done so many unpaid repairs for him. After the tattooist finishes with Mr. Saarsgard, he inks across the crease of my back, between the blades, a simple engine, dismantled and neatly laid out in a row of unbroken pieces, and, beneath it, a perfect row of screws arranged in order of size. He bandages my tattoo and gives me a cream to apply the next day. I am not as flexible as other women my age and so he also provides a small paddle with which to apply it.

Later that evening, in my kitchen over dinner (a pork chop with a sliced baked apple, steamed asparagus, and a buttered potato), I consider Mr. Saarsgard's tattoos further. While waiting for Arvo, I have often marvelled at literature lying around the Group Home. I can see it centres upon a reward system not unlike the one in which Arvo acquired his T-shirt: behave a particular way now and enjoy reward later. Arvo's guardians must reward him because he does not value being outside. But rewarding kindness and justice and ritual and so forth in an afterlife — does it not suggest they have little worth in themselves?

Nor have I determined the motivation for belief: Why would someone consider incarceration in an unpleasant place the result of misbehaviour, or of not saying the right phrases, or of the whim of a deity? Is it perhaps something like rocking? A self-soothing choice to not look life in the face and instead look elsewhere? That, that I might understand.

At this moment I notice my hands have become fists, and Vincent is eyeing me strangely. I unclench and sigh and return to my meal. Perhaps I ought to consider a more traditional approach and discuss this matter with the therapist. And as I contemplate broaching the topic with him, the vertical interpreter there to my right, I return again to Mr. Saarsgard's tattoos — and begin to fathom their cunning, layered meanings.

Oh Mr. Saarsgard.

I cannot help but laugh.

Writer's Note: With Verity safely out of Holdstock Facility, I (Athena) come now to the Group Home phase of my life. Around the world, people once segregated from mainstream society were integrated into it. In this country, that usually meant we lived with four or five others "of similar disability" in ordinary houses in ordinary neighbourhoods. With some exceptions, the homes had neither nurses nor janitors. The general staff gave us our pills and looked after the house in addition to their other duties. And recorded everything.

With the province's new privacy laws, I have access to all reports written about me in those months. There are thrice-daily reports from the Group Home, twice-daily reports from worksites, daily program charts, daily medication tracking, daily bowel movement charts, daily dietary records, weekly appointment records, weekly outing reports, weekly keyworker overviews, weekly worksite schedules, weekly occupational therapy reports, weekly physiotherapy reports, monthly medical overviews, monthly Group Home social schedules, monthly keyworker assessments, monthly financial reports and purchase requisitions as needed, Facility-to-Group Home transition reports, Group-Home-to-IAL transition reports, an outline for daily routine (also called the "Who Is Verity" form), and so forth. Boxes and boxes of paper.

"The policing makes me bristle," writes my friend Mr. Saarsgard when he sees them.

"No police," I write.

"Are and were many police," he insists. "Some look like Group Home workers who allow you no privacy. In my line of work, privacy matters."

Mr. Saarsgard is always giving me things to think about.

At the very least, the heap assures me I exist. But what am I to do with it all? This surfeit, this embarrassment of information surrounding seven short months, I find it more difficult to manage than the paucity of records surrounding my Holdstock years.

I call Imran for advice. He cycles to my apartment (he has taken up cycling to "whittle his waist"), and parks his new twelve-speed bicycle in the corridor. He steps around the boxes crowding my desk. Vincent is delighted for a visitor and licks his hand, encouraging Imran to pet him, which Imran does briefly before reaching for a file. Vincent realizes no further attention is forthcoming and returns to his cushion with a sigh.

"So many records," I say to Imran, "and no story."

Imran leafs through some files and asks how much I recall of my life in the Group Home.

"Not enough to tell the story," I say. "What I do remember is sporadic and untrustworthy."

He recommends then that I follow his method from the maid story in his scrapbook: select documents from a single perspective and gather a story from only them. I am taking his advice and have chosen to work from the Group Home Daily Reports written by my keyworker, Uly Banner.

What I know about Ms. Banner outside the Group Home comes from a local newspaper article, "Former Elite Athlete Now Champion of Disabled," which says that Uly had been training for a career as a professional Track and Field athlete (hurdles were her main event) when a car accident left her with a leg amputated below the knee and years of recuperative therapy ahead of her. The therapy process kindled in her a "yearning to work with other disabled people."

The photographs of Uly show a dramatic change in appearance at this time. She cut her hair short and began to colour it. She began also to tattoo her limbs with images of cartoon heroines, a way, she says in an interview, of marking and owning a body that had come to feel foreign to her.

Ms. Banner spent a good deal of time with me and documented thoroughly. These two reports, for instance, are from my first days there:

DAY SHIFT REPORT. Uly Banner. Monday, January 18, 1993.

Verity Blessure: V had a good day today.

V spent morning of her first day here sitting on living room sofa and getting up occasionally to pace. After lunch V looked at magazines and napped from 1:30 PM to 2:15 PM.

Staff tried to book a Dr's appointment for V today. Staff called four clinics that are advertising for new clients. Each clinic expressed interest in V until learning V lives in a Group

Home. Clinics were then suddenly not accepting new clients. One clinic said V's needs "were not the Dr's expertise." Staff asked if Dr had no expertise in renewing prescriptions, or if he had no expertise in 34-year-old women. Clinic said only that roster was now full. Clinics already called: Anisimova St, Balzer St, Bufanu St, Ehrhardt Ave. Staff will continue calling tomorrow (beginning with F in phone book).

DAY SHIFT REPORT. Uly Banner. Friday, January 22, 1993.

Verity Blessure: V had a good day today.

Staff took V to General Practitioner today at Schaller-Klier Ave clinic for first checkup since exiting Facility. Staff told receptionist that <u>staff</u> needed a physical and V was along for the ride. When Dr entered, staff gave him V's file, took out camera, and persuaded Dr to perform physical by informing him that refusal would result in staff taking photo of Dr and V and sending it, along with a report of Dr's refusal, to College of Physicians and Surgeons who might consider withdrawing his medical license.

Once thus persuaded, Dr looked at V's med regime (which includes anti-psychotics, anti-convulsives, anti-depressants, anti-coagulants, muscle relaxants, hypotension regulators, sedatives, laxatives, digestive aids, stomach acid buffers, anti-histamines, and birth control, and several other meds as needed) and said it was full of "inhumane contraindications." He asked staff if V had been subject in drug trials. Staff explained lack of files/history on V. Dr called specialist and sought advice. Dr recommended taking V off all meds for a period of at least four weeks. After that time, he will do complete physical, determine medical needs, and prescribe accordingly. Dr said there was "no point in doing a physical on a pharmacy."

V's prescriptions begin to taper off today. After 21 days she will take no meds. Staff are:

1. to make hourly notes on her condition. Record everything she eats and drinks, sleep habits, any unusual behaviours, apparent cravings, and every time she urinates or defecates. Record colour of urine and stool size (S,M,L) and texture (hard, medium, soft). Special record book for this in med cabinet.

2. to watch for seizures and psychosis. Seizure chart is taped to inside door of med cupboard. It describes seizure types and what to watch for. Dr said to expect severe seizures and psychosis as anti-convulsives and anti-psychotics wear off, beginning in about 48 hrs. Immediately after first seizure, staff should make V wear hockey helmet and keep it on until she is back on meds. Helmet (it's new! And pink!) for V is on top of fridge. Take it off for showers and sleep. Staff has wrapped her bedposts with pillows and duct tape.

3. to watch for sniffles/rashes/food reactions: we have no record of why V was on antihistamines.

Staff asked if V could go on solid food program. Dr said yes but we are to bring him all records of progress in this program; he wants to rule out food aspiration as reason for muscle relaxants.

And here is another, written two weeks and fifteen reports later. At this point, my med doses are greatly reduced:

DAY SHIFT REPORT: Uly Banner. Saturday, February 6, 1993.
Verity Blessure: V had a challenging day today.
Staff was called to V's room by V's roommate this morning a few minutes before wake time. V was still asleep, but in

early morning had defecated and wiped dirty hands on wall. V appeared surprised to be wakened by staff and to be dirty. Staff led her to shower. (Dr said to expect unusual bowel responses to reduced medication.) Dirty wall upset roommate who began to obsess (hand washing) and tantrum (see roommate's report for details) but V appeared not to notice. Staff left V in shower to attempt to calm roommate's escalation. V exited shower and entered bedroom (dripping) to watch roommate throw pillows at dirty wall. Staff encouraged V to dry off and get dressed and confiscated dirty pillows, upsetting roommate further. V and roommate watched staff scrub wall. Roommate did not calm. Staff got leftover paint can from cellar, and V and staff repainted wall patch (hand over hand) while roommate watched. Roommate calmed then and apologized to V for inappropriate behaviour and name-calling. V and roommate shook hands.

Again, V appears more alert, more awake than yesterday. STILL NO seizures, NO visible psychosis. It SEEMS meds were entirely unnecessary!

And one more.

DAY SHIFT REPORT: Uly Banner. Monday, February 15, 1993.

Verity Blessure: V had a fulfilling day today.

When staff woke V this morning, V sat up quickly, pushed staff aside, pulled up nightgown and removed her own (dry) diaper and moved quickly (for V) to bathroom and used toilet without staff assistance. Possibly V was once toilet-trained and recent incontinence a result of meds? Staff will write toileting program.

This morning V stood by window for nearly two hours, making shape with her hand. After a while, V began to huff and stamp foot, still making the shape. V appeared frustrated. Staff checked American Sign Language book. It was not the sign for outside or walk or cold or winter or window or squirrel or anything that made sense to staff. Finally, staff took V to closet and put on her knee pads and outdoor clothes (V did not assist with dressing) and took her outside.

V stood on porch, facing sun, with wide smile. Staff coaxed her off porch (V almost fell stepping down) and onto yard. V and staff took a few steps. Knee pads (and staff catching her when she falls) seem to be preventing injury successfully. Staff has scheduled daily outside time for V.

At lunch, when other clients were at worksites, V began solid-food program. V started with unpureed vegetable-pasta soup. V coughed out anything she couldn't swallow. She did not aspirate. After program was finished, staff gave her 1 c. pureed soup. (Very little unpureed soup had been swallowed; V was hungry. Noted in Dietary Binder.) Staff will introduce chewing gum tomorrow.

After lunch V assisted staff in washing down the walls and table and chairs soiled during solid-food program. At first, V was prompted by staff, but eventually V initiated wiping up spots of food wherever she saw them.

Because of progress in toileting program, staff and V went shopping for new underwear. A few times, V seemed to smile. V tripped when distracted but mostly walked well. V tried on underwear because staff prompted, but was more interested in looking around.

Unusual incident while shopping: V climbed into store window and took pose of mannequin beside her and held it for at least a minute (as long as it took staff to get in and convince V to exit window.) Store manager was understanding.

V and staff enjoyed looking in window of pet store. Perhaps V would enjoy SPCA volunteer program?

When V returned from shopping, she voluntarily took cloth and Windex and began to clean her own bathroom. V appeared to know what she was doing and to enjoy doing it. When finished, V went to front closet, took a cigarette from Staff jacket pocket, went to living room, pretended to light cig from unlit candle and to sit and smoke. Did V once smoke? If so, is right to be healthy more important than right to smoke now?

No seizures, no psychosis. Staff has arranged for V's "profoundly retarded" diagnosis to be reassessed and correctly categorized.

Uly watches me so carefully that I wonder how she found time for her other clients. She records every potential interest or preference or dislike. If something is measurable, she measures it. My legs, for instance, to determine if uneven leg length explains my shuffling gait. She notes, in nearly every report, that I show no signs of psychosis nor epilepsy. She barely restrains her horror at the practices of the institution from which I came. And she says, in dozens of ways, that I appear to be awakening. This impressive, detailed recounting goes on for seven months.

I remember little of these early months, I was just beginning again to retain information, but I am certain those were not decades of sleep from which I was finally waking. Yes, of course, there was the stupor under meds. But beneath the stupor, it was a time of the most vigorous thrashing against chaos and sludge, of almost always losing but sometimes retaining a paring of memory or logic, of being perpetually exhausted by the labour of it. I am no enchanted princess. What she calls my "awakening" is in fact the end of a great exertion, the commencing of rest. The antithesis of awakening.

As expected, I do find a story in Uly's notes. But it is the story of the notes themselves.

I (Athena) am not there after all.

I tell Arvo about Uly's notes when next I visit.

"You talked about her years ago," he reminds me. "I thought she was awful. That Ahmed boy and the touching." He leans against the arm of the sofa and rests his legs across my lap. We are in the room with purity sentences on the wall.

I need a moment to remember. Ahmed, a man who lived in the Group Home with me, had autism and was on a "Facilitated Communication" program. Daily, Uly sat beside him, a letter board on the table before both of them, and she supported his arm as he pointed to letters. Other people with autism or cerebral palsy who had previously been assumed too disabled for linguistic communication were now spelling out words when so facilitated. Uly and the others hoped Ahmed was another such person with hidden intelligence that could finally be accessed. But Ahmed did not like to be touched by anyone. Each session, Uly touching and patiently urging, Ahmed writhing and straining away from her, became more overwrought than the last.

At the time, the entire exercise bewildered me. In the Facility, the people who could not stand to be touched were touched as little as possible.

Arvo wondered the same. "What if he didn't want to break through? What if he wanted just to be Ahmed? She was awful," he signs.

"It must have been overwhelming," the therapist says, "to go from so little stimulation to so much."

The vertical interpreter is dressed, head to toe (even his shoes), in grey. Perhaps today is a neighbourhood costume party and he is going as a steel ruler.

"Yes," I say. "Even food. I was overjoyed to chew again but my throat ached from coughing. I believed I should eat quickly and in large spoonfuls. "Slow down" is the first sign I recall learning. I also needed much more sleep than I need now. A few minutes of sunshine on my face could be exhausting."

"Were you afraid?" he asks.

"Of what?"

"Any of it. Being in a much smaller house, or a regular bed. Staff watching instead of medicating. All the new sensations."

"No," I answer.

"More and more you remind me of Jude the adventurer," he says with a smile.

I do not see how living where others have decided suggests adventurousness. Nevertheless I nod.

"Speaking of Jude, would you like to meet her, do you think? Build a relationship with her?"

"No." My answer is prompt. (I do not say that I am curious about whether she has grey hair or is thick around the middle, and whether she enjoys olives and hot tea. About whether I take after her.) "Perhaps she cares less about my well-being than Esau did," I explain. "There is more hope in ignorance."

He winces. And changes the subject to ask how the Uly

research is coming along. (I expect we will return to Jude next week. Family matters he prefers to approach through slow, drawn-out pecking.)

In truth I have been unable to work on the Uly project for nearly a week, but I say nothing about that. Instead I pass him one of her notebooks and he thumbs through it.

"I liked her," I say. "She was interesting and she smelled wonderful and she was kind to me. She watched me but not in a way that restricted or confined. I liked having her there paying me attention. There is a — superiority in these reports I did not anticipate, but perhaps it is the report format." (I am not ready to tell them I do not see myself in the record.)

"Yes," he says, "I see it too. It is a difficult thing to look after people in the long-term and still see them as equals, particularly if they are silent. Uly doesn't quite achieve it."

"In addition, however," he continues, "I see here a vast support network. Physicians and nutritionists and physiotherapists and people who re-painted walls after you dirtied them and who coached you in socially appropriate behaviour because they wanted you to be comfortable in public environments and people who paid close attention to things that made you happy like animals and sunshine and unpureed food. I see people who worked hard to understand a stranger who spoke a different language. It took a good deal of time, but the effort was genuine. I see growing recognition of a great trauma done to you and that a powerful system failed you utterly. I see a lot of good will, however clumsily it was sometimes handled."

I nod. Sometimes nodding is the easiest way to end a conversation that goes suddenly in this direction. But he is not finished.

"Do you think," he says, "that the panel might see a vast support network currently behind Arvo? One difficult for any single guardian to match?"

Oh. _Oh._ A point of great consequence.

"I have not considered that," I say, "but I will certainly consider it now."

ATHENA'S JOURNAL
JUNE 14, 2004
(MONDAY)

Vincent has a blue rubber bone, and we have a ritual: we visit the dog park where I throw this toy and he runs and fetches it back to me and I throw it again. I do not throw well, but Vincent puts up with me and tries to be encouraging.

This morning, the park is nearly empty but for a man with a polka-dot tie and a three-piece suit, the pants of which are stuffed into galoshes. I marvel at his footwear on this dry sunny day in this dry sunny week when there is no puddle to be found in the city, until I realize it is not puddles he fears but dog feces. He is accompanied by a small white rigorously manicured dog. The dog's hair has been brushed and trimmed so unnaturally that I feel sorry for him. I cannot hear his barking, but I can see that it is constant and that he expends a great deal of energy on it. The owner is talking on a cellular telephone. He pauses momentarily to don surgical gloves from his pocket. He lays down a sheet of plastic food wrap and makes a hand sign. The dog dutifully trots over, squats, and defecates on the plastic. The owner wraps up the plastic sheet, disposes of it and the gloves, and pats the dog on the head before returning to his telephone.

The obedience of it makes me bristle. But the dog seems to think this the natural order of things and when the owner throws a white rubber bone, the dog dutifully pursues it.

When I throw Vincent's blue bone, however, the white dog quickly loses interest in his own toy and chases Vincent's. The owner seems not to notice. Vincent gets there first and the little dog begins again to bark and bark. I fear he will bark out a piece of his lung. I continue to throw the bone, Vincent continues to catch it, the dog continues to chase after Vincent's bone and bark, and his owner continues to not notice.

Eventually, the little dog runs forward and bites Vincent! I am appalled! Is this diminutive creature unaware that Vincent is three times his size, could easily chew him up, but is too mature to consider it?

Vincent eyes the dog, and then he collects both his own blue bone and the dog's white bone and drops them in front of the white dog. He turns his tail, caring neither about dog nor bone, disappears into the shrubs, and emerges seconds later with a long branch, twice his length. The weight makes him canter sideways and wobble and the twigs still attached drag on the ground and make the carrying still more unwieldy. He can hardly manage it. But his ears are laid back with pleasure, it is the undisputed prize of the dog park, and there is no way that small white dog could even pick it up.

The dog sees Vincent, larger now with his new stick, and picks up the blue bone and runs after his owner, leaving his own white bone behind.

The owner, still on the telephone, does not notice.

Vincent and I leave in the other direction, rubber bones abandoned and Vincent elated with his find.

"You are so fine, Vincent," I say, "So fine."

I am still unable to work on the Uly research, and my list of annual chores says this is the month for blinds. The vertical blinds covering the biggest window are the most difficult to clean, so I start with them. It is a tedious business. I stand on a chair by the window to unclip individual blinds before carting them to the tub, where I will immerse them in soapy water. I see across the road that the hat ladies have taken their places around the picnic table. They live in the seniors' home two blocks away. When the weather is warm, they all don lightweight brimmed hats and secure them with wide ribbons under their chins. They take the table in the shade, purses crooked in their elbows, they sit, and they play cards. Here, across the street, I see the ease in them. They behave like they have known each other a long while, perhaps from their youth. In the years I have lived here, I have often watched them through this window and considered their lives.

After some time, another local woman trundles by. She is also elderly, but I have never seen her near the seniors' home, I assume she lives elsewhere. She is alone today, as she usually is, and wears a baseball cap, a sleeveless plaid shirt, a flowered skirt, and fuzzy winter boots. She has tied a wide purple belt with a bow above her great round belly. She flops onto her bench aside the paved path and her skirt balloons from the movement. Usually people come and talk to her briefly — a young man who works in the convenience store, a bearded man from the cardboard shelter several blocks away, a young woman whose head is covered by the hood of her jacket, a truck driver seeking a flame for his cig-arette — but today no one approaches.

She unfolds a newspaper she has brought with her. As she reads the front page, she begins to laugh very hard. She sits on that bench by the path and laughs so that her face reddens and her belly bounces. No one pays her any mind. Even I can see that there is something off about her. She is interesting, but she is not comfortable to look at.

Is it enough for her? Her interesting life, alone?

Writer's Note: *After going to the dog park with Vincent this morning, and scrubbing blinds this afternoon, I lugged the boxes of copies out to the trash. I kept only the box of Esau files and two of Uly's report books to keep track of dates. Here, from my computer, through my window, I can see the boxes of files, affirmed and static records of seven months of my life, beside the bin. Still accessible, not yet hauled away.*

Looking at them comforts me. It has become safe habit to lean on documents for a story. The thought of telling it any other way is more overwhelming than I have let on to myself.

Why would anyone believe my memories of these events when I cannot always make sense of them myself? How can I be certain I am not again sentimentalizing events as I once sentimentalized Esau, thereby jeopardizing custody? I have so little credibility.

I feel I need permission.

But from whom? My therapist would say my reaction is common amongst traumatized people and would encourage me to remember what I can while simultaneously reading the documents for what they might reveal. He would tell me to record a memory when I am ready to take responsibility for it. Mr. Saarsgard would say that truth lies in the art, in story, in what works on the page or in the XXX film, and seldom in data or fact. He would advise me to craft it into a fine story and delete later if necessary. Imran would advise (and help) me to do what the therapist recommends. And Arvo would much rather hear my story than Uly's. I have their permission.

But to make a permanent record of challenging approved accounts terrifies me. And not only because the system still holds Arvo.

I try a sentence —

By the fifth word, my muscles are rigid with panic and a metallic taste has overtaken my mouth. I feel meat hooks slide into my thighs, I will certainly disappear —

I stand, interrupt the descent, walk around my apartment.

There are no meat hooks here, no nurses with needles. Not even people who would disbelieve me and insist upon an approved account. Here, within reach, are: me, a computer, art on the walls, bread on the counter (a sourdough rye), a jar of mixed olives, a sleeping dog, a door to the outside for which I have the key, and a fine neighbour with a motorcycle a short walk away.

I sit.

A good deal of time passes as I contemplate what and who is here now.

Mr. Picasso, I expect, craved permission and therefore hid away his wonderful Les Demoiselles D'Avignon painting. But Gabriel, with neither permission nor regard for taboo, sketched his unapproved record again and again.

I had intended here to try once more to understand, through stories mummified in documents, why yet another of my keepers did not see me. Why I was so long abandoned.

If I am to be truthful, it is not my absence from Uly's reports nor her superiority nor the unreliability of memory nor any aspect of Group Home records that puts me off. The fact is simply that my heart will shatter if I do this again. I, Athena, cannot face it.

Against the vast archive and documented cosmos of the system, my memory about my last days in the Group Home is a little thing.

When I consider telling my own memory, my own story, my feet get cold.

I shall have to buy some warm socks.

ALBERTA PROVINCIAL GROUP HOME

Let me begin again:

The first bit of clarity, the briefest glimpse of an unfamiliar doctor's office. I recall a blood pressure pump, anatomy diagrams on the wall, a *Compendium of Pharmaceuticals and Specialties* on the shelf. A woman (Uly) sat in the chair while I sat on the raised bed. Her skin was painted, her hair extremely short and striped, a curious feature, she smelled wonderful, and she had a removable leg, also curious. I wanted to examine it. I do not recall a physician at all.

Then came a gradual clearing, an easier balance, a more generous grip on space and sensation, a growing understanding with gravity.

Soon tastes, smells, textures began to emerge before me, within reach again.

A realization, gathered over days, that I no longer lived on a ward with dozens of people, but in a house. I slept in a snug yellow bedroom, windows ungrated, with one other woman (Sylvie). We had comfortable mattresses, beds without bars. We had our own slippers. We had our own bathroom, with one toilet, one sink, one shower. An incomprehensible luxury.

Three men also lived in the house, and one of them (Ahmed) stepped back every time anyone entered the room, as if establishing distance from an unpredictable force. During the daytime, the person with the interesting leg and hair (Uly) was always there. She appeared to be trying to communicate with me, to tell me what was coming next.

And then came the placards.

At first, I noticed a touch on the hand. Sensations rippled out from that point of contact. My arm moving, my hand holding something, a sharp smell, a bright splash of blue on the paper beneath me. I was moving in tandem with the person touching me, the person with the detachable leg. She was holding my hand and we were painting a placard, hand over hand.

Eventually my eyes focussed on the print. It said "Stop Compulsory Able-bodiedness." The only word I understood was "stop." I tried to stop moving then, but her hand overpowered mine.

In the next weeks, more placards: "Bring it on!" and "Disability is a failure of the social environment to adjust to its citizens." I enjoyed making them, the smell of paint, the comfortable weight of a brush in my hand. But I never understood them. I considered their words at length, and I wondered if language had changed, if words I once recognized and understood now held different meanings.

On the door to the staff office was a poster. One day I was able to read the sentence in large print at the bottom ("Which ones would you sacrifice") and, a few days later, I could read the twenty-four small-print rights listed above it (the right to go outside, the right to take risks, the right to choose your place of residence, and so forth).

I stood there reading the poster for a long while.

Never had I seen these words used in this way. I did not know what to make of them.

Soon after that, the protests.

Long afternoons, mostly Saturdays, of standing on steps before a large building which I now know was City Hall. Each time, people as far as I could see pressed against me. Uly with the detachable leg always stood beside me, shored up my weight. It is an exhausting thing to stand and hold a placard for hours even when one is shored up. Each time, a canvas sign as wide as a house hung between pillars of the building, preventing easy exit and entry. One Saturday, the sign said "Better Labour Laws Now!" Another week, it said "Homes for the Homeless!" And another, "Take Back the Night!"

At these events, the Uly girl and I would hold a placard. I could seldom read it because it was directly above my head, but I could read my housemates' placards on either side of me. I recall the pleasure of it, of standing outside, not alone, sun on my face, reading something. I recall "You need my disability to feel able-bodied," and "My disability is in your head, not my body." And one day a sign read "Go ahead. Stare. Your able-bodiedness is temporary."

My arms would soon grow flaccid, and then Uly supported the weight of the placard, but we would touch the post together, hand over hand. I recall little detail of the crowd. Bright colours, strange people, a kaleidoscope. Nothing specific or real.

The Group Home Outings Binder records the names of the protests we attended (termed "human rights volunteerism") and where they were held and how we got there and who the second staff member was.

Not once does it say that our placards never supported the cause of the protest; they had their own agenda.

One protest in particular comes to mind. The sign between the pillars read "Bring Our Soldiers Home!" Philip and Sylvie (my roommate) both held placards with drawings of men with rounded backs. I remember their names as Rich Three and Hunch Dam but deduced recently that they probably said Richard III and

Hunchback of Notre Dame. Beneath their drawings, both placards said "I am not a metaphor." I saw my placard that day, and it said "Watch Me Overcome!"

It began to rain. Uly tugged plastic hats and blue garbage bags with holes cut in them overtop our clothes. Soon the paint on my sign began to run. It ran onto my plastic hat, and spilled onto the blue garbage bag, and from there onto my shoes.

I looked down to see it streaming in runnels between the concrete slabs underfoot — and with that movement, the water that had collected in my hat brim surged into the gap under the plastic at the side of my neck. In seconds, every layer of my clothing was wet and cold and exceedingly uncomfortable.

I looked around then and saw that we still held our signs, now soggy and wordless, but most of the crowd had dissipated. I could see a clear line to a door in the distance with a gentle yellow light behind it.

I let go the sign and shuffled as quickly and carefully as I could across the large square, heading for the yellow light. Someone tugged at my back — I pulled away and nearly tripped over the seams in the concrete but managed to stay upright, moving forward.

Once across the square and inside the door of the yellow-lit restaurant, I pulled off first the plastic and then my wet jacket and then my wet shoes and socks and then my wet sweater and jeans and then my wet T-shirt and then, finally, my wet bra and underwear. Above all, I wanted nothing to do with Overcoming if it made my bra and underwear wet.

Eventually, Uly and the others in our group, who moved more reluctantly than I, caught up with me at the restaurant. By that time, I had disrobed entirely just inside the door. The other restaurant patrons carefully looked in other directions, and a flustered waitress held out my wet clothes and tried to persuade me back into them. The Group Home vehicle arrived then, the other clients embarked, and Uly covered me with her own (wet) raincoat and ushered me into the Ladies' Room, where she dried my clothes, starting with underwear, under the hand dryer.

That is as much of the day as I remember. Uly's report, however, goes further: when a patron came into the Ladies' Room and began to scold, Uly told her "to kindly go fuck herself."

Then, once my clothes were dry and again on my body, Uly says, we drove to a movie theatre and attended an afternoon movie matinee *(Cool Runnings)* since the vehicle was already booked. She says my housemate Philip especially enjoyed the movie and demonstrated this by shrieking and shouting throughout the duration. A Security man came then and asked us to leave, and she, Uly, stood up in the theatre and informed him and everyone within earshot that Philip had paid for his ticket and had the right to attend and enjoy a movie. She says that the Security man called the police, but the movie ended and we left before the police arrived. Uly calls it "a challenging outing for all concerned."

(After this passage in the report book is a long adversarial thread on the merits of social action versus those of client dryness and of not alienating local communities. Eventually a meeting was called for staff to air their grievances and develop Group Home policy on the matter. The records of that meeting are in one of the boxes that have now been hauled away.)

My first clear complete memory has to do with pens. In the Hold-stock Facility, pens and pencils were locked away from us to prevent them becoming implements of harm. We had crayons for a few years, but eventually they stopped being replaced. Consequently, even though I could read, I never had the chance to learn to print nor to write.

In the Group Home, pens lay around carelessly. In a cup in the kitchen, in the games closet off the dining room, in the office where staff would write reports, on the living room coffee table, on the kitchen counter, having escaped the cup.

I began to hoard them. To snatch a pen when I saw it, stuff it into my pants or bra, and then slide it later between my mattress and sheets. For a few nights, I woke in the night, opened a Group Home policy booklet I had found in the kitchen by the telephone, and, in the light from the streetlamp through the window, took pen in hand. On the first night, the pen never touched the paper on my lap. I had first to learn how to hold it. In a closed fist, and then between my thumb and forefinger, resting against my second finger, gripping too tightly at first and then relaxing. I aimed for the easy, thoughtless grip I had seen in my caretakers but it did not come easily. On the second night, I put ink to paper and drew circles in the booklet, overtop the print, round and round and round with the pen. I was not able to make the ends of a circle touch one another, but they still resembled circles. The ink on my face and hands made for a perplexed Daily Report.

My midnight undertakings came to a quick end on laundry day. Uly stripped the sheets from my bed — and found both pens and booklet. It became a long thread in the report book, as the staff tried to determine if it was pens I wanted or if I had pica and meant to eat the ink or if I was kleptomanic or if I was trying to obliterate policy by scribbling up the policy booklet or if there was any sense to the behaviour at all. Eventually, as a means of eliminating other possibilities, Uly took me shopping. We went to a stationery store and she bought a large colourful pack of crayons, a child's colouring book with pictures of people climbing mountains, and a pad of plain paper. She laid them in my night table drawer, making clear they belonged to me now.

I began to try to write. Slowly, a single letter at a time. Uly purchased a file folder, labelled it "Verity's Art," and dutifully placed each page of scribbled paper into that folder which was then placed in the same drawer as the colouring book. She never looked at what I had done.

Eventually, as dexterity developed, I could fit two letters onto a page, and then three, and, not long after, an entire sentence.

For months I wrote, a letter at a time, sometimes in the day, often in the night. Each paper was slipped conscientiously into my Verity's Art file, which grew fat and generous, and never looked at.

I waited for the perfect night. It had been years. Waiting another month or two was not difficult to do.

On a Wednesday in July, Sylvie had a *grand mal* (after which she slept deeply), I purloined a black Sharpie from the office pen cup, and the gibbous moon lit the night. My room filled with light.

I waited for the headlights of departing evening staff to shine briefly upon the wall, waited another hour for the night staff to fall asleep, and then I began to work.

I worked for hours.

And then I slept.

Uly's report book says that my roommate (Sylvie) alerted the night staff with early morning screaming and pointing at the wall. I did not hear her, and continued to sleep. The staff allowed me to sleep late, though it was a work day and by then I had a work placement stuffing envelopes, for they ascertained correctly that I had been up most of the night. They ascertained this partly from the ink on my hands and face and nightclothes, and partly from the wall above my bed.

On which I had written in large, shaky letters:

"I verity I rod tran mny das I liv huse whr rvo wy fathr leve opsitl I mis rvo mntins rvo ples"

What I meant to write was this:

"My name is Verity. I rode on a train for many days. I live in a house now. Where is Arvo? Why did my father leave me at the hospital? I miss Arvo and the mountains, but especially Arvo. I want to see him now please."

Uly and the night staff worked together to decode it while I slept. They solved most of it — but the "rvo" word stymied them utterly, though Uly had actually met Arvo back when she watched me coax him out of the Facility.

In capital letters in her morning report, the night staff asks what it means if I am not developmentally disabled after all, if I was misdiagnosed and institutionalized only for hearing loss.

Uly's report at the end of her shift is warm and congratulatory and has a tone not of surprise, but of fulfilled expectation, as if my wall message were inevitable.

And then she gets down to business. She sets up the Independent Assisted Living appointment that will bring Imran into my life who will help me contact Arvo. She informs Administration that another bed will soon be available, is there "another client for us to empower?" And she records her intent to look into pressing charges against Elora and Holdstock. Neglect, at the very least. Failing to provide — something.

When finally I woke, late the next day, it was as if the earth itself had shifted, so profound were the changes in staff behaviour.

Their gazes, now stolen, seemed to leak guilt and pity and curiosity. When I reached for jeans to put on the day's clothes, the staff discreetly left the room. When I deliberately chose mismatched socks, no one corrected me. When I scooped sugar into my coffee, the staff made no attempt to limit the amount. When I used the toilet, no staff followed me into the bathroom to take notes about what I did there.

One staff asked in writing what I would like for dinner — and when I showed him the roast beef and Yorkshire pudding recipes in a cookbook, he took me to the butcher and we bought a roast and he cooked it. Gravy, pudding, and all.

Another staff wrote, "Verity, I assumed you were developmentally disabled and I treated you as if you were because I believed the file. I should have paid closer attention. Please accept my apology."

I still have this note. I appreciate it now, but at the time, I felt bewildered.

I had wakened that day, and not for the first time, to a world I did not recognize.

ATHENA'S JOURNAL
JULY 13, 2004
(THURSDAY)

I have been thinking about Mr. Saarsgard's tattoos, about the therapist's observations, about Uly's quests and clever placards, about all the ways in which our lurching forward is automated and people watch through the glass or lay down plastic for our defecation. I fear that if I am to achieve custody of Arvo I will need a love more cunning, more strategic and conniving, than the one I have thus far practised.

I fear this because cunning love is not what I have.

$\mathcal{W}$*riter's Note:* *Most of the letters written by Jude Blessure to Michael Vinterburg, Esau's old companion, are gone. My therapist wrote to Mr. Vinterburg on my behalf explaining my project, he mailed a copy of everything he still had from Jude, and the therapist handed the package to me.*

I, Athena, open the brown package at the kitchen table in my apartment. Five letters in their envelopes slide out, along with a note from Mr. Vinterburg addressed to me. He wishes me well and says he and Jude corresponded regularly over thirty years, but, because he was obliged to keep track of professional correspondence, he "never bothered to hold on to much in the way of personal letters." Thinking back, he remembered the bulk of correspondence as the two of them encouraging one another and comparing notes on matters concerning people with disabilities. He kept these few letters because they reference Esau, with whom he was once close. He also mentions a fond memory of meeting me when I was very young and is gratified to learn I am well and undertaking this project.

The letters have no distinctive smell except perhaps of age. The left end of each envelope has been neatly trimmed off. The addresses are written in a clear hand, at once effortless and assertive.

I am apprehensive about what I might find here in these pages and wish to read them undisturbed. I leave the table to give Vincent a rawhide knot to occupy him, to lower the blinds, and to slide the door chain into its slot. Then I sit again and order the five letters by date.

Here are the few pages that remain, the first one written about forty years ago, of my mother's writing:

JANUARY 1964

Dear Mr. Vinterburg,

I hope you don't find me too forward writing to you like this. My name is Jude Blessure. We've met a few times. You know my husband Esau, of course. He counts you among his closest friends.

You may have heard that our fifth child was born recently, and that I was in hospital with toxemia in the months leading up to the birth. Both the baby (a girl, Clara) and I are well now. You may also know that Stenson was hit with a Scarlet Fever epidemic while I was bedridden, and that our daughter Verity came out of that illness with some permanent damage. Esau mentioned that you and your brother Gabriel visited for supper one night while I was in hospital. He was thrilled to see you and still speaks warmly of that visit.

I'm reluctant to intrude upon your friendship with Esau, but I have nowhere else to turn. I'm writing now to inquire if Esau mentioned anything to you that evening or in letters since about his plans for Verity, our four-year-old. Not long after your visit, and before I came home with the new baby, Esau took Verity to a sanatorium or asylum or some such institution for people with psychiatric disorders and brain damage and left her there. It all happened quickly and without my participation or knowledge. Indeed, I've not yet been persuaded that Verity's damage is as extensive as Esau says. More incomprehensible yet, Esau signed papers to place her under Guardianship of the Province, effectively disowning her.

Would you kindly write to me and say if Esau mentioned anything to you about his plans for Verity? If so, could you say where he planned to take her? I'm desperate to locate her and reverse the damned process, but Esau says nothing except that he "did the kindest thing a husband could do." The physician who signed off on the Guardianship transfer is devoted to procedure (and is deeply patronizing to me). He insists he's "bound to confidentiality" and I, her mother, am "no longer her Keeper." Do you remember old Dr. Neb King? He's been the Stenson family doctor since before Esau was born and was probably a fine physician in his day, but he's caught in the past now with feet of clay that do not move forward.

Disowning a child seems so unlike the gentle, playful Esau I know. His mother and sister Matilda are similarly astonished, and I'm sorry to say that Mattie believes the fault is hers. (I confess I don't follow her reasoning.) Esau is in no small amount of anguish — not about his actions, but about the ways in which they've been received. It's as if he feels entitled to an altogether different response. His mother says he had a rough spell as a teenager, and yes, of course, there has always been an edge to him, but I have never seen him in such a bad way. I wonder if this is what a nervous breakdown looks like, and yet Mattie and Esau both insist I ought not to summon the doctor. It's so perplexing to me that I wonder if his decision about Verity was made under influence, though I've never known him to drink heavily.

I realize that I may be asking you to betray a very old friend. It is a great deal to ask. Unfortunately, you are the last person who might know. If need be, I will visit each asylum and sanatorium and institution in the province to bring her home but, if I had some idea of where to begin looking, this ordeal might be over sooner rather than later.

I'd prefer Esau didn't hear about this correspondence, at least for a while. If you can bring yourself to reply, would you kindly post your note to my mother's house? The address is on the reverse. Please do, of course, continue to write Esau at the usual address. Your letters cheer him up so.

Thank you very much for reading this, Mr. Vinterburg. I shall hope for a reply. Please give my warm regards to your brother Gabriel.

Sincerely,
Mrs. Jude Blessure

Dear Michael,

Thank you so much for your recent letters. I can hardly express my gratitude. Yes, I'm still hunting for Verity — that's why I haven't written since July — but not a day goes by that I don't re-read at least one of your letters.

Your insights into "The System," as you call it, are invaluable and have shaped my investigation. Congratulations on your hard-fought battle for funding to care for Gabriel yourself. You must often wish to have a more conventional conversation with him and learn what <u>he</u> thinks of "The System."

Thank you also for your insight into Esau's youth. I think you saw the real Esau, full of promise and verve, back when the two of you went overseas. While reading your <u>Maclean's</u> article on the history of phosphorus weapons, I was again grateful you two didn't see battle. Esau has never been good with stress, as you remarked yourself. He's still not well, I'm afraid. Now that I'm working full-time again (and more, to pay off debt accumulated when I was sick), he spends most days sitting and looking out the window or at the pictures on the mantle. He seems not to see the children. I cannot abide to watch him pass an entire day doing nothing and have made cooking supper his responsibility. He goes about it mechanically but he gets it done.

Your letters made me realize how unusual Esau's father was. I knew, of course, that it was considered indecent in those days not to hide retarded children away. Esau's mother had a lucid spell last week and I asked her then about her experiences — if she was under pressure to euthanize Mattie, if the "it's-the-mother's-fault" phrase was bandied about, if she agreed with her husband's approach to educating Mattie. She looked at me with such a complicated face, Michael, and said she didn't believe she'd ever be able to talk about it, and could we just peel the blasted potatoes please. And then she called me Gertie (her sister's name) and that was the end of the lucidity. How very interesting that war vets changed the ways handicapped people were received — but I wonder how many of those changes would have reached long-suffering mothers like Ellie Blessure or Mrs. Vinterburg in rural towns. You have whetted my appetite with your knowledge and I plan to research further.

About Verity. Esau has still said nothing of use and as yet I know no more about her whereabouts. I weaned the baby early so I could spend weekends on the train searching, and have covered a good deal of terrain these past months. Last weekend, I was in Huntsville, the week before that in Orillia.

You know, while I was hospitalized, I made gifts for the kids. I missed them. For Verity, I made a silly picture book, rough crayon-and-ink sketches, about a bear cub caught in a fox trap who must determine how to open the trap. (Verity is always opening locks, toys, even the kitchen radio once. It's what she's most often scolded for.) I found the book the other day in Esau's office, still in the wrapping. He never gave it to her! It's so unlike him. He loved giving the kids presents and reading to them. He taught her to read, in fact, beginning a few weeks before her fourth birthday.

Well, anyone reading this can tell that I miss Verity terribly. I worry about the little things. Chapped lips, for instance. Are her caretakers applying petroleum jelly? Already before she began walking, I greased her lips or she'd lick them raw.

I shall continue my search and keep you informed of what I learn. Please give my best to Gabriel.

Warmly,

Jude

P.S. I can't think why Esau hasn't written you. You are the one person outside all this grief, I should think. He stares at that photo of the two of you for an hour a day. I'll remind him again.

JANUARY 1965

My Dearest Michael,

A Happy New Year to you and Gabriel! We had a busy
Christmas season here in Stenson and I'm glad it's over.
I can now get back to searching for Verity.

I have visited nearly every institution in the Province of
Ontario and am coming to terms with the possibility
that I might not find her this way. I told you already that
Esau eventually confessed taking Verity to Elora. When
I queried there (at what's left of the place) the staff said
she was transferred away shortly after arrival, and of
course they can't disclose where; I'm no further ahead.
The investigator I hired — surreptitious, yes, but I must
leave no stone unturned — discovered nothing new.
Perhaps I'll begin again and volunteer at each Ontario
institution for a few weeks. I'd be certain to see more
than I can in a one-day visit. Or perhaps I'll go about it
by learning why conditions are what they are generally,
and what must be done to change them. With that
knowledge, I might begin lobbying and public lectures
and all the awareness-raising things the civil rights
people do and affect Verity's life indirectly. I've yet to
decide. Our neighbours are wonderfully encouraging,
as are my parents, and of course you and Gabe make all
the difference in the world.

Your insights continue to be helpful. There's so much I don't understand; the entire System seems opaque. How did these furtive, remote machinations amass such clout? How would we go about cutting them off at the neck? Whose heads must roll? There are, as you say, bits of good news: did you see the Female Refuges Act was finally repealed? I've read the Mercer people are disputing the Grand Jury reports and are downplaying rumours of torture at their Reformatory. To be expected, I suppose. But I'm optimistic that place will be shut down. With the end of the Act, I needn't worry that Verity will end up at Mercer because some guardian finds her "incorrigible," and that's a relief.

(Instead I worry about what kind of institutional culture now shapes her life. Is she in a gardening-as-treatment place? A labour-as-treatment place? An education-as-treatment place? I hope to God and Jupiter and Allah alike that she's not in an asylum that locks people in bare concrete cells with naked drains in the floor for urine and windows that open not more than five inches. The institutions are all so different, and I have no way to know.)

In some ways, Esau seems on the mend. He visits his mother and Mattie more often. With them he is as gentle as ever. He keeps his mother's house in good repair and reads aloud to Mattie every few days. And he gets up from his chair and plays games with the kids.

That's something, at least. But he is <u>harder</u> than he was before. I hear it in the tone, when he suddenly snaps at me about nothing, or whispers quietly "It's a matter of time." Time until what, I wonder, but don't ask. And then the hardness breaks and he begins to weep. Eddie, our oldest, is most able to comfort him; Esau seems not to want me to see. I wonder sometimes if he wouldn't have been more content to continue his life with you sans wife and children.

There are also moments, ever so fleeting, when he's as charming and silly as before. Last week, he had Mattie in our backyard and was coaxing her into a headstand in the snow against the fence. She was self-conscious of her skirt falling up so Esau dropped his trousers and had her remove her skirt — they were both in their underthings — and they tried again. Mattie is not flexible; it was an ordeal. But they managed it in the end: toques, coats, knickers, and middle-aged gooseflesh legs against the fence. I stood at the window and nearly wept for laughing. I've been finding notes he wrote in my absence squirrelled away in the strangest places. Lists, mostly, and budgets with "Expenses > Income = Unacceptable" written in bold letters across. I find them in cookbooks, sewing kits, canning jars. When I found this apron sketch (enclosed), I laughed out loud. I know he heard me, for he joked under his breath about his career in fashion — dashed!, but I pretended not to hear and didn't meet his eye. I love him still and can see he is in great pain, but I cannot move towards him. My distance makes his life more difficult, I know, and I wish it weren't so. But I'm repulsed by him now. Time heals all wounds, they say. We shall see.

Lovely to hear from you again, Michael. My father said to tell you he enjoyed your book. Have a wonderful week and give Gabriel a peck on the cheek from me.

Love
Jude

FEBRUARY 1968

Hello again dearest Michael,

You are one to keep up with the news. I'm sure you've heard about the women from institutions showing up at Alberta hospitals asking to have their fertility restored. Eugenics? In Canada? "Protecting" the rest of us from "the offal of humanity," Judge Emily Murphy said. I once admired her. Again, I'm astonished at the opacity of the System, that so many people kept so colossal a secret for so long.

Now to what you asked me to research at the university. You were right, it <u>was</u> Martin Luther who said children born disabled — he seemed to mean mentally retarded — had no souls. But he advocated <u>drowning</u> and not burning them. (It was in the sixteenth-century witch hunts that they were burned. Do you need a reference for that?) If you couldn't bring yourself to drown a disabled child, Luther said, you ought to pray daily that God would kill it — and guaranteed God would do so within a year. Along similar lines (to my mind), I read that Luther ate a spoonful of his own feces daily, expressing wonder that God would generously provide such beneficial remedies. Can you imagine his breath?? The librarian said they were expecting Xerox machines shortly. Then I can Xerox articles and drop them in the post and you won't have to rely on my paraphrases or your small town library. How is the work coming?

As you know, I've been taking on extra projects to pay down debt accumulated when I was pregnant with Clara. It took longer than expected (mine has been the only income in recent years), and I can't recall the last time I slept seven hours, but it's now finished. The debt is paid, and we're back to the normal weekly expenses of any family. And that means I can devote more time to lobbying. I found a wonderful group of people with similar concerns and we're getting organized. Next time you're in the area, I'll introduce you.

I'm writing you on assignment, in fact. I've told them about you and Gabe, and they've instructed me to ask: what would you say are your greatest needs these days? For what should we lobby that would make the greatest difference in your lives? We're trying to gather information about the System (I'm back on the road again, visiting facilities, collecting histories, looking for Verity) to determine where change most needs to happen and how best to support the population. Some things are obvious: more regulations around electro-shock, an end to those outrageous lobotomies (did you hear Freeman lobotomized a four-year-old?), standards against which all facilities must be measured. Some things are more subtle: how best to reduce stigma? How to address the fact that these people must depend on the very caretakers who limit their freedom? How to see that someone whose condition makes them occasionally violent still gets proper care? And normalization — is it the way to go? Usually I think yes, but sometimes, late at night, hearing Esau shuffle in his bedroom upstairs, I wonder if Verity isn't better off not living under the same roof as a father who so readily abandoned her. I worry the rhetoric — segregation, normalization, integration, etc. — eclipses the individuals themselves.

It's wonderful to be doing social change work again. I do it by day when I'm fresh, and do my work for hire by evening. Eddie and Samantha, our two oldest, do most of the after-school childcare. I don't know what I'd do without them. I did ask Esau to "watch the kids" but he took me literally and sat and watched them — without taking care of them or giving them lunch or preventing them from hurting themselves. It was vexing, but I don't know if he meant it as reproof or if he wasn't up to the task. Another day, Sam surprised him with a cup of coffee and added sugar. (He takes it black.) She has a sweet tooth and meant it as kindness. He shouted at her for wasting food he doesn't have money to buy, and stomped to the kitchen to pour it down the drain.

And so the children are wary around him. They say he hasn't hurt them, but when he's there they behave as if they're waiting for something unpleasant. He blames me for their demeanour, and says they're "suffering" from my "obsession" with Verity, "an albatross 'round all our necks." "You needn't worry," I said. "They still get much more from me than Verity does." I probably shouldn't have said it, it was sharp. I've yet to understand why Esau appears freshly astounded every day I continue the search, why he believes I'd be happier if only I "stayed in my place" (at home, bovinely serene, not thinking of Verity). It is impossible to consider a lifetime of days without her. And I've never been content to be a homemaker; why would I be now?

Esau continues both to improve and to grow more brittle, if that's possible. He's working again, three days a week, in an office doing clerical work. He was let go from the last job for insolence and insubordination (again) but he seems better able to manage the ways life isn't what he thinks it ought to be if he works just part-time. It helps with his spirits to get out of the house and earn a bit of money but I doubt he'll ever survey or quarry again. I know he hasn't written you but you are on his mind. He took three photos down from the mantle — one of me, one of Verity, and one of you — and has been tracing them, over and over, in remarkable detail, as if trying to see who we are by tracing our features. In most respects he's yet another child to care for, but I'm happy for any improvement. It'll be best, I think, that we live under the same roof until the children are older and until he is solidly on his feet and able to manage his affairs again, but some days I don't know how long I'll be able to do what's "best."

It was lovely to meet your beau Raymond. You two look happy together, and Gabriel seems utterly comfortable around him. Raymond looks a bit like Esau did, doesn't he? In the eyes, mostly. And that playful, teasing way.

Give my love to both of them,

Love,
Jude

My Dearest Michael,

Well, the house is sold, the boxes packed and divided amongst kids and grandkids, and Esau looked after. I have purchased an old blue Volkswagen Beetle, I've stuffed a bag with essentials, and I'm hitting the road. I've no idea where I'm going.

I've said this day would come. I've been feeling it for some time. I have done what I can. It's time to walk away from this life and begin another. Esau has held the same job at that hardware store in Toronto for a few years now, and has been living in his brightly lit bachelor suite, paying his rent diligently and without incident. He is as well as can be expected — and your picture still sits on his mantel. The children are grown and on their own with no real need of me either (and some resentment for my absence through the years). I have put thirty years of my life into helping Verity without knowing where she is or whether she's alive. And I believe I have, along with many others, brought about major improvements in the System.

There was a nurse in Orillia years ago. When programs at his institution were cut, he bought tea and flour and sugar and came on his days off to bake with his clients and drink tea and play games. The history is full of crazy therapies to cure people not looking to be cured, but for every crank it seems there are ten decent diligent caregivers who are overshadowed by those few who medicalize and control and confine.

What makes my heart to break: when I ask at a home or institution about people who lived there before, those who moved away or died recently, the people can't recall and usually someone has to check a record book. The memory of them disappears so quickly, Michael. They live in the same place for decades, but appear to make little impact in the very rooms in which they lived. I would yet like to change that. I don't want Verity to be forgotten. But I wouldn't know where to begin. I'm not altogether certain it's something an external activist ought to change. Perhaps the residents themselves have to change that one. And maybe they do change it each time they act out or resist another stupid rule.

I've been thinking about perception. The public wants people with disabilities to be "glad" (wretched Pollyanna) and their families to be jolly, to say "look how much better off we are for our brother's disability." Sometimes they can be "glad," but sometimes they can't. Sometimes it's extremely difficult to live with a disabled person. And some people, with or without disabilities, are permanently miserable. We must make space for these things to be said, we must.

Well, someone must. I am spent. The path is now there
and the door open for Verity if she wants to get out.
If she's actually too disabled to leave the System, then
I hope I've made her life better. Charles Dickens never
recovered from being abandoned, I've read, and his life
and writings revolved around that grief. It's been difficult
to accept that, if Verity goes the way of Dickens, I'll not
be able to prevent it.

As for what happened to her, I still don't know. In
recent years, I've considered that she might have
been transferred out of province, though that would
be unlikely, or that she died in one of the rougher
institutions, more likely, or that the Province changed
her name as soon as it acquired Guardianship, most
likely of all.

I begrudge Esau less now. He couldn't do what I
thought he should be able to do, he wasn't who
I thought he was. He believes her brain damage
was adequate reason for what he did and I cannot
comprehend how any handicap could be adequate
reason. We both felt entitled to what we couldn't
have, and part of the blindness was mine. Esau, I am
certain now, will never fully recover. I wish for him a
peaceful life, free from the little un-met expectations
that make him snap. I hope he eventually contacts
you. He said he might. His times with you were
probably the happiest of his life.

I expect I'll be in touch once my next life has been determined, but if I'm not, know this: you and Raymond (and Gabriel, when he was still with us) are wonderful men who have made my life so much better than it would have been. You have been my anchor, you old fruit, my shelter in the time of storm. I will love you always.

Kiss Raymond for me,
Jude

Vincent and I read these five letters many times. I hold them close. I want to inhale the air of a world where a small deaf girl matters so much. I sleep with them under my pillow.

The next morning, I recall that my therapist wrote Mr. Vinterburg with the original request for these letters.

Surely he will ask about them at our next appointment.

I adamantly do not want to discuss the letters (nor how I feel about them) with him and his vertical interpreter, however well-intentioned they may be. It would be unbearably intimate.

But I also want to live with Arvo, a possibility over which the therapist holds some sway.

I really haven't a choice.

I sit unbended on the therapist's sofa and concentrate on being rational, guarded, understated. I am old hand at this and use techniques from the Facility. Inside my left shoe, where they cannot see, I rub my biggest toe with my second toe. And any time I am not signing or reading signing, I focus on the seam at the armrest edge. Over the long hour, I come to know all of it. The valleys in the topography where stitches draw in fabric, the regular twist in dark thread that binds the seam, the taut swoop where the seam tension tightens, perhaps when the sewer glanced away at the pretty girl sewing two rows over. It is a beautiful seam full of texture and surprise. If necessary, it could provide calmness and distraction for hours more.

The therapist asks if the letters change anything for me.

"Yes," I say, placidly. "They provide concrete proof that my mother Jude loved and looked for me. I had hoped it — and now I know. In that knowledge lies solace. They also allow for Esau to be both in a difficult spot and responsible for a bad decision, to show Mattie unfailing kindness and also to abandon me. He was more complex than I imagined."

These are the answers he wants to hear — and there is truth in them. His facial muscles relax when I say them and his moustache evens out. I notice another swoop in the seam a few inches down. The pretty seamstress probably winked back at the sewer causing him to blush before concentrating again.

When the therapist says the letters moved him deeply, with their unequivocal longing and concern for Verity sometimes even at the expense of the other children, I nod and smile. When he shows me again the Elora intake form with which Esau severed me from his life, I force myself to look at it anew, as if it were a neutral object.

"You know," I say, "I already reconsidered this form and consequently crossed out my former sentimentalized version of my last day with Esau because this record contradicted it. I am past simplistic representations. I even complicated my understanding of Harriet to acknowledge that part of me admires her."

"Yes," he says, "I remember. But I want now to know if your mother's great love allows you to look at this document and feel valued nevertheless."

"Oh," I say. "Yes it does."

And I return to imagining the ardour that left its exquisite scar on the sofa seam. I am, for this entire session, of two minds.

That evening at home, I tuck the letters safely away. I confirm from the kitchen window that the car of the woman living below me is gone.

And then I turn from the window and —

I rupture.

I smash things.

I stomp on the coffee table until the legs snap under the weight.

I bash a stool against the edge of the counter until it splinters, and then I pick up the pieces and, over my knees, break them further down.

I break every glass cup, every porcelain plate, on the floor.

I attack the sofa with the sharp objects that litter the floor.

I rake a cushion over the broken glass until it is well embedded, I shove into it a broken stool leg, and then I lunge and slam that barbed cushion against the wall many times. Eventually the cushion explodes but not before the drywall is satisfactorily shredded.

I break lamps, I rip books, I tear clothes, I shatter the shower door, and so forth.

I have never been so angry in my life. I am made of rage.

At the end of it, I hover over the box of Esau notes and files. I light a match and want to drop it, but when my finger begins to burn, I blow it out. I do this again and again until the matchbook is used up and spent matches litter the floor.

And then I collapse against the wall. Vincent slinks out from under the bed where he has been hiding, climbs into my lap, and begins to lick the cuts on my hands and the tears from my face.

We sit there for a while, Vincent and I, and take care of one another. We look at the Sibelius on the wall with its many faces emerging from chaos (I did not destroy it, it seemed devastated enough) and we contemplate agony paintings through the centuries, from Bellini to Gorky, and wonder aloud if their subjects ever received five such letters.

Then I brew a cup of English Breakfast tea in a Corelle mug that refused to break, and I reach for the broom.

The therapist's face begs apology before he says a word.

"Imran paid me a visit this week. He showed up without warning. I tried to stop him. I said that visiting me without your knowledge was inappropriate unless he were seeking therapy himself. He was distressed, however, and continued to speak while I ushered him out."

I am powerless to conceal my surprise.

"Yes, such betrayal of confidence does rather take the breath away." He shakes his head. "Let me continue. He said your flat was tidy as ever, though tattered and missing many things, and the alley dumpster stuffed with objects that appeared once to have been in your apartment. I said destroying insignificant objects could be a healthy response to the letters from your mother, if indeed it was a response, and certainly not an event that should affect custody. I said the fact that you hurt neither yourself nor the dog speaks well of your coping skills. I said it might be a turning point. I believe I advised him to 'chill.'"

The vertical interpreter looks eager, revelling.

"I will not say you should have told me how you really felt. What happens in this room is to be guided by your needs, Athena. Even when I ask questions, their purpose is to understand your needs more fully. In the interest of transparency, though, I will tell you that Imran mentioned a drawing in the shower — and uh feces on top of it obscuring everything but the name 'Esau Blessure.'"

I think about what the expression on Imran's face must have been, and I begin to laugh.

"It was a drawing of a silly face," I finally say. "It was — child-ish. And satisfying. And yes, I imagine Imran found it startling. He generally finds feces startling, including Vincent's. Had he lived in a Facility, feces might startle him less. Perhaps if Mr. Freud spent time in a Facility, he might rethink his Anal Phase conjectures. Please do not worry — I flushed the feces at the end of the day and Cloroxed the shower thoroughly."

"Oh I'm not worried," he says. "Not in the least. I wanted you to know that I know about it; that's all. Now, what would you like to discuss today?"

SEPTEMBER 2004

The hearing is held in a conference room adjacent to the judge's chambers. I am ushered to the seat at one end of the table, and the presiding judge sits at the other. Imran, who will interpret, sits to one side of the judge and back from the table so as to sign unobstructed, and to the other side are four panel members who will hear the information and make the decision. The remaining chairs are filled by my therapist, Cheery Psychometrist, the IAL administrator who is Imran's boss, and Arvo's Group Home key-worker who is his current guardian. We have glasses in front of us, and several jugs of ice water sweat on the table (with no cloth underneath to prevent staining).

Arvo is not there; his agoraphobia prevented him leaving the house today. In his absence, his photograph, which exagger-ates his generous ears, rests on an easel by the side blackboard. Normally it would comfort me. Today it reminds me what is at stake.

"Look at *me*, Athena," Imran signs, noticing my apprehension.

I calm immediately. "Your hair is freshly trimmed," I sign, "and your green shirt is new."

"I wanted to look nice today," he says.

The judge begins by stating that we have gathered to determine what kind of custody best suits Mr. Arvo Herzog, and that his duty is to chair the proceedings. The final decision will be made by the panel, who are employees in relevant departments of the Provincial Government, and he will vote only if there is a tie. This is not the usual configuration of a custody hearing, he says, but it was determined by the Department of Justice to address the fact that both Arvo and I are under Provincial Guardianship. He quickly outlines who will give information and in what order, and says every custody hearing sets its own pace, but we should expect to hear information for at least two days. It is the duty of the panel to ask questions, but anyone in attendance should interrupt if something is unclear; in something as important as a custody hearing, he says, there can be no room for misunderstanding.

Someone presses the button on the recorder in the centre of the table and we begin. Arvo's Group Home keyworker speaks first. She tells as much of his history before the Group Home as she knows (Arvo's Facility file is very short) and says he has no known family nor recorded date of birth but she knows he was born sometime in 1956 and was not noticeably agoraphobic as a young child in Holdstock. There is no record of when the agoraphobia first manifested nor of whether he has ever been diagnosed with autism or any such condition. She says she understands the principle behind this hearing and remembers and appreciates my assistance years ago in coaxing Arvo from the Facility, but believes "his many special needs" demand several caretakers. She describes his progress since exiting the Facility, his typical day, his eating and sleeping and toileting habits, his preoccupation with wheels and balls, and what kind of daily caretaking he needs. She says he is not epileptic and takes no medications other than a multivitamin, and she speaks at great length, with dozens of examples, about his skin conditions and agoraphobia, and about noises he makes. She talks all morning. When she is finished, she asks if anyone has questions. No one does. She closes her file then, picks up a pen, and begins to doodle.

We break for lunch, and then it is Imran's turn to speak. He quickly summarizes my recorded history in the Facility and Group Home.

The man in a suit and tie asks how I originally came to be institutionalized.

Imran says the record is limited, but it appears I was one of the children misdiagnosed following a high fever during a time when medical establishments encouraged institutionalization.

For a few seconds, the room is still. The people on the panel look uneasy.

Imran begins to describe my life now in IAL when the ponytail man with the tie-dyed shirt interrupts. He wants Imran to talk about what I was like when we first met, at the end of my Group Home days.

Imran takes a deep breath. He describes how quickly I learned to sign and to write, how motivated I was to communicate — and the man interrupts again, wants to know about the first days, in particular about what I could not do.

"So that we can see how far she's come," the lady in denim from a Provincial Government Group Home clarifies, giving Tie-Dyed Man a "for shame" look.

Imran's signing becomes sharper, crisper. He says I had no reflex to open doors nor to flip on lights nor to lift my feet high when walking on uneven ground. He says I appeared unable to comprehend requests with more than three steps.

The therapist raises his hand. The panel ought not to consider this incompetence, he says, but the natural result of being constantly watched and medicated for any pro-active thing I might have done. He says he was surprised I was in this phase such a short time.

"Yes," says Tie-Dyed Man, "but it is Imran's turn to speak."

"Oh please," Denim Lady says. "It's important information. Who cares whose turn it is? I want to understand this brave young woman and Mr.," she looks at her file, "Mr. Arvo."

"I invited relevant interruptions," the judge reminds.

Tie-Dyed Man shakes his head and motions Imran to continue.

Imran describes the first failed work placements they found for me, stuffing envelopes and screwing nuts onto bolts, the years of accelerated schooling, and says I now spend my days researching and writing.

Tie-Dyed Man asks if I had troubles with schooling, and Imran (who was once a teacher) says quadratic equations gave me difficulty at first, but I eventually mastered them.

Tie-Dyed Man and the woman in houndstooth from the Education Department look at one another warily.

"I'm sorry," Imran says — he is flustered and fumbling but presses on — "but if Ms. Blessure's capacity to be a guardian is to rest on her ability to complete a quadratic equation, then others here with custody of another citizen should demonstrate *their* facility with quadratic equations."

He stands quickly and goes to the blackboard at the side of the room and draws up a quadratic equation. His hands are shaking.

"This is a difficult situation," the Tie-Dyed Man from the Resource Department says. "I don't mean to be demeaning and I certainly don't want to belittle how far Ms. Blessure has come. But my question is not about an equation, it's about what it represents. Difficulty with a quadratic equation at the high school level might suggest she doesn't have the intellectual ability to handle Mr. Herzog 's med routine."

"Mr. Herzog doesn't have a med routine," Denim Lady says.

"But he might have one someday."

Denim Lady rolls her eyes.

"Surely, if so much rests on an equation, someone here can indulge me," says Imran, pointing at the equation. "No? Ms. Cordon?" The keyworker shakes her head, eyes not lifting from the pad on which she doodles.

Then, "Athena?"

I sign the solution from my seat, and Imran writes what I sign.

"Can we enter that into the record?" Imran asks. "That Athena is more adept at quadratic equations than anyone on the panel or than Mr. Herzog 's current guardian?"

The judge nods.

"Can we also enter into the record," Denim Lady says, "that all panel members showed up today clean and well-fed despite our glaring troubles with quadratic equations?"

Tie-Dyed Man shakes his head and Denim Lady smirks.

"Please," says the judge, "please. We all want what's best for Mr. Herzog. This is not a competition."

Imran sits down.

Oh Imran, I want to say, Look at you with a spine. I sign instead "I am proud of you. You were naughty and talked back to that man."

Cheery Psychometrist, who speaks Sign and can follow our conversation, bows her head to hide her smile.

"You're a bad influence," he signs, and continues to answer questions posed to him.

Cheery Psychometrist begins her testimony by requesting that we not speak of intelligence "since both Ms. Blessure and Mr. Herzog and indeed everyone here might have intelligences we cannot measure. What we ought to do," she says, "is consider which environment best suits our Mr. Herzog." She is official and businesslike now, smile and bustle gone.

The panel people nod agreement.

She hands out lists of numbers and explains each test Arvo and I have taken, the criticisms levied at the tests themselves, and our various scores. Everyone there studies the scores carefully (except for the keyworker who doodles on her notepad). She notes that Arvo is extraordinarily dexterous and describes his ability to run marbles along his limbs without dropping them, and she says my aptitudes in two areas, language and mechanics, tested unusually high.

"Doctor," Houndstooth Woman asks, ignoring Cheery Psychometrist, "why would Ms. Blessure's language scores be high? She's deaf. Is this an error?"

"Not at all," my therapist says. "She could read before entering the Facility, read throughout her incarceration, and developed an entire language with Mr. Herzog. The part of her brain that uses language continued to be stimulated throughout her Facility years."

"But the medication?"

"It would have slowed her reading speed and interfered with retention, that's all."

Imran raises his hand to say that I picked up Sign "at an astonishing rate." The panel members write it down but Tie-Dyed Man says, "This is a custody hearing. That she exceeds expectations isn't enough."

Denim Lady rolls her eyes again. The tension between them is palpable now, and the judge flashes both of them an exasperated expression. Imran signs to me his disapproval of their unprofessional behaviour.

"And her aptitude in mechanics?" Houndstooth Woman asks.

"Also remarkable. In our earliest sessions, Ms. Blessure was just beginning American Sign Language studies and we could not yet communicate easily. I brought in an old Meccano set, and she built contraptions and small functioning machines. When she depressed a lever, for instance, a little doll on the other end of the contraption did backflips. It was most impressive. I could never have done it. The same principle is at work here. She entered the institution with an aptitude in this area, and, surrounded by machines to dissemble and reassemble, continued to develop her facility."

(I have a sudden memory of being in a pale green room and reassembling the power compressor of a Pneumostat.)

Houndstooth Woman — even her hair has a houndstooth bow in it — turns to me directly: "Ms. Blessure, I don't understand. Surely the machines were locked up where patients couldn't get at them."

The others around the table shift uncomfortably in their seats. Cheery Psychometrist's hand covers her mouth: Houndstooth Woman has used the word "patients."

"Yes," I sign, "they were locked in an empty wing. But a mechanical lock is a simple device, easy to open."

Imran signs that I ought to tread carefully, the judge and panel members are bound to appreciate locks.

"Did you use your ability to enter med cabinets?"

"Yes, when they were unattended which was not often. I replaced my medications with placebos if placebos were available."

A stunned silence settles when Imran finishes interpreting. Denim Lady looks uncomfortable, as if she wishes I had said something else.

I think about it and recover quickly: "Do not be alarmed. My medications in the Facility were wrongly prescribed; I am not epileptic but was being administered epilepsy medications against my will though they made me feel unwell. I would never interfere with Arvo's medication, should I receive custody."

"Still," says Tie-Dyed Man. "To think that you under any conditions would play fast and loose with a doctor's orders!"

"Say nothing," Imran signs, "let it go."

I swallow my anger and take his advice.

Cheery Psychometrist moves on to list Arvo's non-medical concerns, a long list, and then to her recommendation.

"There is no question," she says, "that Mr. Herzog is happier and more capable around Ms. Blessure. His scores on aptitude tests increase and his agoraphobia subsides in her presence. There is no question he wants to be with her. He is euphoric when she is there and distraught when she leaves. There is no question concerning her ability to care for him in an ideal situation. The simple fact that he speaks a language with her and no one else makes her the safer guardian. There is no question that his current Group Home environment is unsuitable. While she loves and accepts him as he is, the Group Home imposes on him an agenda that wholly disregards key rights."

(The Group Home keyworker's mouth hardens, but she does not lift her eyes from her doodling.)

"But not all situations are ideal. His agoraphobia is profound. I doubt anyone can anticipate all the circumstances in which it might be a problem. His fixation on wheels and balls makes an ordinary can opener a dangerous implement. Simply put, Mr. Herzog needs more surveillance than *any* single person can offer. My recommendation is that Athena Blessure receive custody of Arvo Herzog on the condition that Independent Assisted Living hours increase. Currently, she receives two one-hour IAL visits weekly. If custody is granted, an IAL worker must be there daily for two hours minimum, and, after a few months, daily for an hour. Provisions must also be made for monthly respite for Ms. Blessure. In the event the panel rules against granting Ms. Blessure custody, then I strongly recommend moving Mr. Herzog to another Group Home, where he can practise his own beliefs and where his rights to privacy and to his own body are respected. Alternately, the panel might instruct Mr. Herzog to stay where he is and order his Group Home to revamp its policies. Certainly, many faith-based facilities have little trouble respecting client rights. Regardless of the outcome here, I strongly recommend overhauling the policies of this Group Home. Ms. Blessure's grave concerns are entirely warranted and must be addressed."

The Group Home keyworker huffs, continues to doodle, the judge thanks Cheery Psychometrist and calls for a coffee break and I let out the breath I have been holding.

The coffee is tepid, bilge, and I leave my cup unfinished, but the carrot-and-pineapple muffin is delicious indeed.

When we reconvene, the judge asks me politely if I would answer a question "of personal nature."

"Of course," I say.

"Before we hear from more assessors, I would like to hear why you *want* custody of Mr. Herzog. Caring for someone with severe agoraphobia and significant intellectual impairment, I'm learning, is an enormous undertaking for a roster of trained workers, and you aim to take it upon yourself, alone."

"I lived with him for thirty years. He is my family, my lover. I miss him."

After Imran speaks what I have signed, the panel looks at him. Denim Lady is the only one who does not look alarmed.

She looks pleased. Tie-Dyed Man asks if I might not know what "lover" means. Imran translates, and then assures the panel that I do know.

"Intercourse? In the institution?"

I nod matter-of-factly. They look at one another blankly.

"Why not?" I sign. "Why would we not?"

"Well, well," Houndstooth Woman says. Denim Lady eyes her with a challenging expression and Cheery Psychometrist and the therapist both look down to hide smiles.

"Who made the first move?" Houndstooth Woman asks.

"I will answer that after you tell me about the last time someone else gave you an orgasm," I sign.

Cheery Psychometrist covers her mouth, and Imran signs back his refusal to interpret my reply. Instead he says "That's an extremely personal question. Can you explain why she should answer it?"

"It's a matter of consent," Tie-Dyed Man says. Houndstooth Woman nods.

"Oh, I see," I say with my voice. "Do not worry. I consent."

There is uncomfortable laughter all around and the keyworker, who is still doodling, looks triumphant.

Tie-Dyed Man says, more gently this time, "The question is whether Mr. Herzog consents, and, for that matter, whether he has the capacity to consent."

"Brace yourself, Imran," I sign.

And then I tell them. I tell them that Arvo pursues it, I tell them how he pursues it, and I show them a blue mark on my collarbone from my most recent visit to Arvo, planted quickly when the keyworker looked away. "You know," I sign, "Arvo was the one who hunted the good places in the Facility. On the wards that emptied in the daytime, in the locked Doctor's office when he was on rounds, in an abandoned wing. Arvo enjoys — enjoyed — copulation very much and wanted me to enjoy it too. We learned what we liked and practised as often as we were able. *Cosmopolitan* magazine recommends this as an excellent approach."

Imran looks terribly uncomfortable translating this. I apologize to him.

They look at me, the row of them, Denim Lady the only one smiling.

A moment passes.

"It's difficult not to consider this pedophilic," Tie-Dyed Man says awkwardly. "This man has the brain of a four-year-old."

Denim Lady looks at him incredulously. "His brain is three years *older* than hers."

"If I may," the therapist interrupts.

The judge nods to him with visible relief.

"A sex life, some kind of sexual stimulation, is important. It's not something often spoken of outside the field, and consequently some of the panel may find this information uncomfortable. But I would be concerned if the people living in an institution like this for decades hadn't found a way, either through interaction or self-stimulation, to pursue sexual satisfaction."

Now the panel looks at him. Denim Lady is smirking again and Suit-and-Tie man has taken on a shade of green.

The judge breathes deeply, thanks us for our candour, and says it might be best if we continue tomorrow. "Certainly we all have much to consider."

He asks then to speak with Denim Lady and Tie-Dyed Man in his chambers.

Imran stands close to the closed door and signs what he hears. The judge chides them for their adversarial behaviour. Denim Lady then faults Tie-Dyed Man for "disregarding human rights" and he asks "what point can there be to defending rights if their implementation can never be managed?" The judge says he wants to hear their concerns in the hearing but needs the expression of them to be measured and respectful. A custody hearing is to be taken seriously, he says, "even in a case like this," or to risk being found in contempt.

Imran's satisfaction at the judge's words is visible on his brow.

That evening, I practise before a mirror, trying to guess what they might ask, so that I do not again say anything that might surprise the panel. *We will visit the library on Tuesdays. The Canada Food Guide will determine our meals. Arvo will continue to see the physician he sees now and eventually transition to a physician closer by.* I practise the same responses many times, like Gracie at the Facility chanting self-protective rhythms.

Perhaps this is how religion works: repetition becomes belief.

In the night, when I cannot sleep, I dismantle and reassemble my microwave. And then I sleep soundly.

The second day of the hearing begins with the therapist's testimony.

The therapist introduces himself and lists his credentials. And then he reviews, without interruption, my progress from when we first met to last week. He states repeatedly that I have impressed him. It takes about an hour. The keyworker, through it all, doodles on her pad.

"What about Pygmalion effect," Houndstooth Woman asks. "Haven't her experiences made her retarded?"

"Please," says the judge as the room stiffens, "let's refrain from inflammatory language."

"Fine," says Houndstooth Woman. "Ms. Blessure has been treated for decades as if she were intellectually compromised. Hasn't that been self-fulfilling? Hasn't she become intellectually disabled? She looks intellectually disabled."

"This," I sign to Imran, "from a woman with a houndstooth bow in her hair."

Cheery Psychometrist coughs into her tissue.

"Good for you," Imran signs, "for not letting her upset you."

"Certainly we see some of that," the therapist says. "In her gait, for instance, and in the ways she's schedule-dependent and put out by, say, the lateness of a bus. Her thinking is linear and her life routinized. From what I gather, her meals and grocery purchases don't vary from week to week. She's frequently taken off guard by things others might find commonplace."

I am surprised to hear this. I did not realize grocery choices nor regard for schedule were unusual; I do not think of myself as unusually predictable.

"But it's important to understand that while some people never recover from captivity — Pygmalion overwhelms them — others recover beautifully. Certainly, Athena has recovered better than most in that situation. It relates to what I spoke of yesterd —"

"Excuse me," says Tie-Dyed Man who is noticeably subdued today, "Captivity? And yesterday you mentioned incarceration. We've heard she was cared for in an expensive medical Facility. Maybe it wasn't ideal for her, but — captivity?"

"I've been treating her in our sessions for a type of post-traumatic stress that we see in people who have been kidnapped or otherwise held captive. But I can call it 'Custody In A Medical Facility,' if you prefer."

The judge nods, and the therapist continues. "Ms. Blessure kept her mind active throughout her custody in the medical Facility. Reading, setting her brain to increasingly complex machines, that sort of thing. Additionally, she developed this bond with Mr. Herzog. Research shows those with personal bonds are much more likely to recover from uh involuntary custody."

"Has she been electro-shocked?" Houndstooth Woman asks.

"Holdstock records don't mention it, but as records go they're not altogether reliable. Why do you ask?"

"Electro-shock damages people. It would make this request of hers more unreasonable."

"In fact," he states, "judiciously used ECT brings significant relief to some conditions. The uh mythology around it is unfortunate. But to your point. I don't find Ms. Blessure's request unreasonable. A little premature perhaps, but it's not unusual for people to live with those they consider family. Stability is a constant balanced movement between dependence and independence in different situations and at different times. She has achieved this balance, to my mind. She gets a good deal of assistance — she sees me weekly, she sees her IAL worker twice weekly," (Imran nods), "she lives on monthly government subsistence — and I agree with the psychometrist that the level of support, both financial and human, would have to increase substantially if she were to gain custody. But she has achieved stability."

The judge says it is time for coffee. I am the first up and run to get the single carrot-pineapple muffin before anyone else claims it. I ignore the coffee altogether — and notice, as I reach for a juice box, that the panel members are watching me closely.

There are more questions for the therapist after the break.

And then comes a wearisome conversation about funds. It is the least interesting part of the hearing thus far. I almost wish for the distractions of yesterday's adversaries to animate the long session. At one point, my eyes follow a fly around the room. Arvo swats flies with speed and precision but I am slow and clumsy and am forever missing them by a moment and they fly away to breed and multiply.

"Athena," Imran signs, "the financial discussion is important. The panel may be noticing you're not paying attention."

I sit up and focus again as the judge instructs the IAL administrator to assess the probable cost of increased support to me if I am assigned custody, to determine whether IAL would have the capacity to provide it, and to deliver that information by day's end. The IAL administrator agrees and leaves — he appears to have been expecting the request — and the rest of us have lunch.

The remainder of the day is taken with "Special Concerns." Suit-and-Tie Man says he does not sign, but has noticed Imran and I conversing beyond simple translation of the proceedings.

"Yes," I sign. "Sometimes he clarifies things for me, and sometimes we comment on things, like friends do. I hope you do not find it impolite."

"Not at all," he says. "I wonder, though, if you recognize that Imran is not your friend. He is your IAL worker. He is paid to do this."

"I understand," I say. "Nevertheless I enjoy his company and am under the impression he enjoys mine."

Suit-and-Tie Man nods, Imran signs he does enjoy my company, and Cheery Psychometrist's hand goes up.

"I also have a concern about friends. When I last visited your apartment, Ms. Blessure, a Mr. Saarsgard stopped by and asked you to fix something. An oven, I believe. I couldn't help but notice his T-shirt. It was unusually provocative."

"I do not remember what he wore that day. Mr. Saarsgard usually wears shirts from his store. I do not advise him on his clothing."

"No, of course not. I was wondering what your relationship with him is."

"He is my neighbour. He owns an XXX store and when things break down in his stores or in his condominium, I repair them. Our relationship is neighbourly."

"Are you lovers? I wonder because the shirt was so suggestive."

I laugh — I cannot help myself — and sign: "Mr. Saarsgard is a kind and awkward man, and he is less interested in copulation than the most highly medicated people I have known. He attributes his financial success to his ability to make dispassionate decisions that are unswayed by personal taste in an industry otherwise dominated by passions."

The Group Home keyworker raises her hand swiftly. For the first time since finishing her testimony, she is looking at the rest of us in the room, but only momentarily, as if now unsure of what is required of her in this context. The judge nods, her hand lowers, and she stands up!

"As Mr. Herzog 's advocate, I think it's my job to point out that Ms. Blessure's friendship with a sex store owner is inappropriate for Arvo! If the panel assigns Arvo to live with her, well, it will be knowingly placing him in, well, in an oppressive environment! It will be jeopardizing his safety and, well, his right to be free of sexual harassment!" She says the same thing in many different ways, each time with more conviction, and finally concludes by addressing me directly: "I'm sorry those bad things happened to you, Athena, you didn't deserve them, but custody of Arvo is not the solution."

I do not understand how custody could resolve "those bad things," but I say nothing. Denim Lady looks angrier by the minute but also says nothing. Yesterday's scolding has been effective.

The therapist signals the judge, and the judge asks him to speak.

"Judge," he says, "I feel we may be losing our way. Is it in the purview of this panel to select Mr. Herzog 's neighbours? If so, will we be considering his current neighbourhood? Hostility towards Group Homes in his Arlington suburb is well documented."

The keyworker snorts, but sits down.

"I'm sorry," says Cheery Psychometrist. "I didn't intend to raise anyone's ire. I was concerned with how Mr. Herzog might feel if he saw Ms. Blessure in a sexual relationship with someone else. I wish I had worded it differently."

"I wish you had worded it differently too," I sign to her, "but there is nothing we can do about it now."

Imran raises his hand and describes my anxiety attack at Andrzej's seniors' home in Ontario, and asks the therapist if more attacks should be anticipated.

I did not expect to hear this here, and certainly not from Imran. My face is immobile and hides my shock. I congratulate myself on not showing him my new tattoo.

"If you were to remand her again to uh involuntary custody in a medical Facility," the therapist says, "then yes, we should expect more panic attacks. But I'm fairly confident she will not need any such Facility until she is elderly, if ever."

"But what if she has to take Mr. Herzog to a hospital?" Hound-stooth Woman asks.

"That, I expect, is the sort of thing the psychometrist meant when she spoke of situations that are not ideal and can't be anticipated."

"Ms. Blessure," Tie-Dyed Man says, "I don't mean to be insensitive but — why don't you have a job?"

"I have a job. I am researching and writing a book. It takes many hours of every day and a good deal of skill."

"Why don't you have a *paying* job? We've heard you were unwilling to stuff envelopes and screw nuts onto bolts, jobs that so many others in your position would be grateful for. We've heard about your competence, about how far you've come, but as far as I can see here, you've made no attempt to pay your own way like the rest of us have to do."

"I do not need further employment. I receive cheques from the Provincial Government."

"The Provincial Government has paid for your life since you were four. How long must hardworking taxpayers go on paying for you?"

"My subsistence cheques are compensation for decades lost."

His face sharpens, he is about to say something scathing, when Suit-and-Tie man interrupts.

"I understand why you would see it like that, Ms. Blessure, and you may be correct that compensation is in order. But the system doesn't work that way. We in Government send you subsistence cheques because you're unable to pay your own way. You receive the cheques because you are disabled and under the Province's guardianship. If you'd like your cheque to be called "compensation" instead of "disability assistance," you will have to sue the Provincial Government, and for that you will have to hire a lawyer."

Tie-Dyed man nods vigorously.

The therapist raises his hand. "This confusion is partly my fault," he says. "I haven't encouraged Athena to find paying work because of the considerable emotional progress she has made in her book project which I thought more important at the time."

"What kind of book?" Houndstooth Woman asks.

"She's researching her past and the people who looked after her. If I had anticipated her custody request," he continues, "I would have encouraged a job search long ago so that she could support another person. If the panel recommends custody, I'll work with Athena and IAL to find suitable paying work. She'll likely need a transition period of about a year to learn a new income system."

"You think she can hold a job that pays enough to support two people?" Houndstooth Woman asks.

"Yes I do. Of course, if employment took her out of the apartment, there would be the matter of finding someone to watch Mr. Herzog while she is at work."

I see, at this moment, that there exist many more strata of bureaucracy than I have known, than I could have known. An exhaustion presses down on me then, and fills the spaces between my cells.

I am suddenly relieved this process has almost reached its end.

The IAL administrator returns with a sheet of numbers which he gives to the panel, they look them over and the judge announces the testimonies complete. Tomorrow the panel will convene *in camera* to discuss the case. A decision might be available as early as tomorrow afternoon.

That night, after my shower, which is longer than usual, I wipe the steam from the mirror and stand there, looking.

I am not practising anything. I am regarding. Beholding. It has been a day of considerable learning. I feel quite a different person than I was yesterday.

(If I am a different person than I was, or than I thought I was, what exactly does that mean?)

I stand before the mirror until long after the steam has gone and the bathroom become cool again.

We resume our seats at the table just after noon. The judge thanks everyone for their time and effort, and says it has been "a real privilege" to meet me.

"Ms. Blessure," he continues. "While your institutionalization is not at issue here, and the rights of potential custodians do not figure into a final decision, I would like to express that the panel, myself included, is deeply unsettled by your experiences of decades past under Provincial Guardianship. That a person not developmentally disabled be carelessly diagnosed and institutionalized like someone who is, and for so very long, is a serious matter indeed, an historical burden that can never be lifted. It's fair warning to medical personnel to be vigilant and not to allow history to repeat its previous horrors. I am impressed with your remarkable progress thus far and stand in profound admiration of your tenacity and grace through this trying process.

"Now to the matter at hand. This panel was convened to consider Arvo Herzog's needs and available housing and custodial environments, and to choose the best match for him."

He opens a folder then, and says the decision has two parts: first, the panel voted three to one that Arvo remain in custody of the Group Home, but I am to have unlimited and unsupervised visiting rights. And second, they voted unanimously to convene an investigation into the policies of Arvo's Group Home with the intent of overhauling any that compromise client rights, including rights to privacy and freedom of religion. He asks the Group Home keyworker to remain behind so the process can be set in motion and he asks if there are questions.

I am not altogether surprised by this outcome. Nevertheless, the disappointment is so profound that my muscles slacken and my arms fall uselessly at my sides.

I am still under observation, however, and must behave in a controlled fashion. After a moment, I force my useless hands to sign.

I ask which panel member voted in my favour. (I expect Denim Lady.) The judge says voting is confidential — but Houndstooth Woman interrupts. "Oh, it's alright. I don't mind everyone knowing. You convinced me. I voted for you."

I contain my surprise enough to thank her politely (while the other panel members look away).

And then I ask if I can sign something now, today, immediately, to be released from Provincial Guardianship.

The panel members and judge look at one another. Denim Lady appears especially surprised. Even Imran stalls momentarily in his signing.

"Do you understand what dissolving guardianship would mean?" Suit-and-Tie Man says. "It would in no way change the outcome of this hearing. It would mean you wouldn't receive subsistence cheques. It would mean you couldn't see Imran or your therapist unless you found a way to pay them. It would mean —"

"I understand. I would like to sign."

No one seems to know protocol. The judge thinks another hearing would be necessary to release me and Tie-Dyed Man shakes his head resentfully. Suit-and-Tie Man wonders if there is an application in the Foster Care files that could be re-purposed. In the end, I am instructed to visit Suit-and-Tie Man at Residential and Support Services next week. He will have an answer for me then.

The judge thanks us again and dismisses us. I must hold composure just a while longer.

In the hallway outside the Chambers, Cheery Psychometrist approaches me. Pieces of her hair are wet from chewing.

"Oh Honey," she signs, "you were fabulous in there. You never stood a chance, but you sure showed them what you're made of! I'm so proud." She hugs me then, tightly.

When she releases me I ask, "What do you mean I never stood a chance?"

"The liability alone and — Oh Honey, you never stood a chance."

Pause.

The unbearable weight of what she has said.

Finally I sign. "I do not understand. Why all this painful scrutiny then? Why put Arvo and me through all those tests and assessments? Why make all of us in that room endure that arduous, costly, unbearably intimate rehearsal if I never stood a chance?

Why not rather *tell me* I stood no chance?"

"Everyone has the right to due process."

The Facility still, but in words.

I realize then: I have been misled by many people, even Imran. But I should have been surprised at nothing aside from my own willingness to believe.

The thought stops me in my tracks. My desire to be an ordinary citizen generated the conviction that it was feasible. My longing was so great that, without conscious effort or knowledge, I crafted this faith. Surely this is the answer to my question: belief is constructed by yearning.

The IAL administrator touches my arm. He asks Cheery Psychometrist to interpret.

"Ms. Blessure, I would like to offer you employment. We need someone with your skills."

"My skills?"

"We have a family of intellectually impaired siblings with their own language and none of our staff can communicate with them. And we have a number of clients transitioning out of Group Homes and they're not doing well. Your insight would be invaluable. You impressed me in there. I thought of a dozen ways we could use you."

"What an opportunity!" Cheery Psychometrist adds. "You could change the system from within!"

"Thank you for thinking of me," I say. "I cannot answer now. It has been an overwhelming day."

"Fine fine. Have Imran bring you by my office next week. You might like to know that full-time consultancy pays considerably more than any subsistence cheque."

Imran has misunderstood. He enters the cab wearing a sharp charcoal suit and tie. He looks smashing.

"Athena," he says, looking me over, "the ballet is a dress-up affair."

I am wearing clothes that allow movement, a print cotton blouse and jeans. The jeans have an elastic waist, which I know is not fashionable, but I have cut tidy holes in the knees and thighs to compensate and have affixed safety pins along the bodice for added fashion. (I have been reading in a library book about clothing codes: garments with holes and safety pins are characteristic of Punk fashion.) I am also wearing my comfortable sneakers with Velcro closures.

"Yes it is, but I am taking you to a night club where *we* can dance. Dancing is a celebratory ritual and I am celebrating the end of the hearing. I am not taking you to watch dancing."

His discomfort is instant and profound. His chest lifts with sudden tension but he says nothing.

"Speaking of clothing," I say, as the car pulls away, "What did the panelist in the hearing mean when she said I looked intellectually disabled? I was wearing my lined woolen jacket and skirt."

"It's a well-made, beautifully tailored suit, Athena," Imran says. "I thought you looked wonderful. I expect she was referring to the thick socks and loafers you were wearing with it."

"Ah. She might have worn nylon stockings and high heels, I suppose, and tolerated cold feet. I am not yet steady enough for heels."

"Heels are foolish," Imran says. "I never wear them myself." And we both smile.

The club music is fantastically loud. I feel what I cannot hear. Imran leads me to a table at the back where he says the volume is "less abusive to the ossicles." We quietly drink — he has a hot toddy and I try a raspberry vodka cooler — and we sign a pleasant conversation.

"Enough of this hiding, Imran," I finally say. "We are here to dance." I pull him to his feet and towards the dance floor. He stops as we walk by the bar, downs a shot of something, and reluctantly follows me onto the floor. Lights flash everywhere. They would cause seizures in some of my long-ago friends. They are spectacular.

At best, a dancing Imran looks like a rod with legs protruding. A vertical, hopping, walking-stick insect. And me, I flail. I flail in time to a marvellous beat so loud I can enjoy it. On a floor of medicated youth whose bodies glide easily, whose long bones appear fluid and elastic, we look old and strange. Imran and I, we are definitely not "cool."

We catch their attention immediately and they circle us. Imran signs they have called us Grandma and Grandpa. They smile warmly, and they mimic our awkward movements until many of them are dancing like us. Some of these youth wear so much makeup that no skin shows. Some have piercings and tattoos that are hard to look away from and, as I expected, many wear industrial-looking frayed clothes — large pieces of fabric missing — held together with enormous safety pins and silver bars. Nearly all of them have noteworthy hair that has been sculpted into atypical shapes or painted in saturated hues. And many of them wear gloves from which the fingers have been severed. They are appealing people.

A medicated young woman takes my hands and presses her lithe body against mine and rests her forehead against mine. She raises my arms up and around, like the top of a slow jumping jack, and we move lethargically, intimately, so that I cannot flail. After a while she places my hands on her waist and pulls a blue pencil from the waistband of her ripped stockings. She draws on my face as we move. Imran is being passed from young dancer to young dancer and appears resigned to discomfort. A young man brings him a shot of something, and he sucks it back quickly, and then the blue pencil girl is dancing with him and drawing on his neck since his face is too far away and I am dancing with two young men and we are all flailing and then I realize that the margins have disappeared and we are all the same and Imran and I are part of this wonderful group.

"I am horribly embarrassed," Imran signs, hopping.

"Why? We are welcome here. These young people appreciate us."

"They are stoned, Athena, they appreciate anything. It's undignified. Inappropriate for people of our age. We don't fit here."

"Imran, I do not fit anywhere. But there is a white-faced young man over there wearing a suit like you."

"No, it's a costume. He's dressed as Charlie Chaplin. I'll tell you about Chaplin later."

"Imran, you helped me to adjust to a foreign place, a foreign language," I sign. "You are warm and loving and accepting. Why not allow these warm and loving people to accept you and introduce you to a new place and language?"

He thinks for a moment, continuing to hop.

"Your transition was not easy either, Athena. I have overseen many transitions, and each one has been difficult."

He is painfully uncomfortable. But he stays. He stays on the dance floor with me, hopping, he does not try to coax me to leave before I want to, he does not criticize the people around us who are noticeably medicated of their own volition, he does not complain about damage to his ears.

He is a gift. He is entrenched in the system, a gear in its works, but he is a gift.

Later, at my place, we are already a little drunk, and we open a bottle of wine. To complement it, I set out a fine ciabatta, oil in which to dunk it, and a small bowl of olives, the last meal. Vincent eyes us once from his cushion and goes back to sleep.

"You are a gift, Imran. You are richness itself. Next to Arvo, you are the person in my life I treasure most."

He stands then and folds me into his long arms and we lean against one another, wineglasses in hand, and move a little as if we were still on the dance floor. He reaches over with one arm and dims the light, then empties his wineglass and refills both our glasses, the other arm still holding me. His body against mine is relaxed and engaged, open and intimate all at once, with none of the dance floor discomfort. This too is a gift, a great risk for him. Drinking in my presence, hugging me too long and too closely, these could cost him his job.

We finally ease onto the couch and lean against one another.

"I wish for your sake it had gone differently today at the hearing," he says.

"It did not. I have since learned I did not have a chance."

"No, you didn't. But I still wish you had gotten the outcome you wanted."

"Thank you, Imran. That girl drew an armadillo here on your neck, you know."

"Yes, she told me his name is Ted. Theodore the blue arma-dillo. I'm supposed to look after him."

We both drift off a little there, curled into one another, and move only when one of us wants more wine. Much later, the sky a paler shade of grey, Imran gets to his feet and cold air rushes between our bodies.

"It has been a most stimulating evening," he signs, "and now it is time to go." He calls a cab and collects his things.

"Thank you Imran."

"For what?"

"For being a good sport this evening. For everything."

"You're welcome."

"Imran, are you my friend or my worker?"

He stops moving, looks at me with abrupt intensity, comes close, and takes my chin in his hand.

"Athena," he says with his voice while also spelling it out with his free hand, "above all I am your friend. But I need my job. Ted and I, we need my job."

He hugs me one last luxurious time, kisses the top of my head, says he'll see me on Tuesday, and then he is gone.

The moonlight glints on broken glass in the petunias where someone threw a bottle at the old brick house. I peek through the window to confirm the night staff is asleep in the front room and I make my way around to the back. Arvo's room is on the second floor overlooking the ravine and has the only window on the back wall. I wait for my eyes to adjust to the dark, I check my wristwatch, and I begin to plan my climb.

I have set myself an impossible task. As adventurers do.

The wall is more immense than I remember. It is perhaps more immense than anything I have ever seen. I drag and heave the heavy picnic table until the long end touches the wall, and set upon it a short ladder I find behind the garage. The ladder, with rubber gripping affixed to the underside of the feet, slips nevertheless on the smooth tabletop. I return to the garage and lug over two cement blocks I find behind it. They are surprisingly weighty and the sharp edges lacerate my hands. I cannot simply lift them onto the picnic table; I must haul over a plank and use it as both ramp and lever to push each block first to the bench part of the table and then to the top. It is exhausting work. The ladder feels sturdier with the blocks behind it, though I consider Physics and worry the blocks will slide once my weight is higher on the ladder.

Arvo pokes his head out of the window above and immediately bumps it on the raised window in delight.

"You must stay quiet," I sign to him in our language. "They cannot know I am here." He nods, rubs the bump on his head and claps, and signs to me that he's clapping silently.

I tug at the long pipe running down the house: I will be able to use it to steady myself, but it is not robust enough to hold my weight. (Frankly, if it were, I still could not climb it for I am far too inflexible to shimmy.) I similarly test the trellis that holds up the ivy and it too fails the test. I head down into the ravine then and search for something suitable, returning shortly with a thin, strong, springy evergreen tree trunk that someone has cut down and stripped of branches, and with a fresh assortment of cuts and scrapes from aggressive vegetation I could not see in the dark. Arvo balls his fist into a cheering sign when he sees the tree and says he has removed his pajama pants to be ready for me.

After kneeling to dig a post-hole in the ground close to the house, inside of the table leg, I wedge the sawed-off tree bottom into the fresh pocket in such a way that both bench and tabletop support it. The tree top I send up to Arvo and ask him to secure it enough that I can use it to steady myself. He pulls it into his window — several feet of springy trunk poke into his room — and winds it around a stout iron window-side hook on his wall, fastens it tightly with leather shoelaces, and makes another cheering sign.

"We have the beginnings of a good ball-maze," he signs. "Our first two-storey design."

I test the ladder and it seems sturdy enough. I tell Arvo that the picnic table and ladder should get me about two-thirds of the way, but I don't think I'll reach the window.

He disappears for a minute, and returns. His pajama top is gone now too, and his two sheets are bound together, along with a few others. One end is fastened around his naked waist and the other he tosses out the window. They reach about half way down the house.

He signs that I should climb as high as I can on the ladder, and use the sheets and the tree to pull myself the rest of the way. He claps then and sends a marble down the sheet. It drops on my head, painfully, and I look up at him.

"Sorry," he signs. "I had to celebrate with something that rolls."

He looks so silly there, unclothed, sheets knotted around his waist, hands clapping, grinning head with generous ears poking out in the dark, I have to stop and laugh a little before I return to the task.

I am a middle-aged woman whose muscles have never been worked. I am neither supple nor graceful nor strong, I do not have Arvo's dexterity, everything about me is sluggish.

Arvo knows this.

"I think you will probably fall a few times," he says. "Can you cover the hard edges with something soft?"

Behind a neighbour's garage, I find a stack of discarded thick sofa cushions that smell of mould. I carry them over, and set them strategically around the ladder and picnic table to break my inevitable falls. I fetch three sleeping bags forgotten on a clothesline, damp with dew, and drape them over the cushions to muffle sound (though Arvo insists the house walls are too thick for anyone inside to hear). I wind the Group Home garden hose around it all in hopes that it will secure the pieces.

I consider José and Andrzej, Father Matthew and Gabriel. Esau and Michael. Jude. Even Georgia, the last ruffian. Unsanctioned liaisons, risk, my heritage. I begin to climb.

I fall almost immediately. I further scrape my hands, bruise my shin on a cement block, and jar both my chin and knee on ladder rungs. As anticipated, my weight caused the ladder to push the cement blocks away from the house. One of the blocks has fallen to the ground.

When I look up, Arvo's hands are over his mouth, and he cheers upon seeing I am not seriously wounded. I use the plank to return the wayward cement block to its proper position on the table supporting the ladder. Then I unwind the garden hose and re-wind it, again to secure the cushions and sleeping bags, but also to run lengths of it behind the cement blocks, preventing their further travel across the tabletop. I walk around to the front of the house to check on the night staff (still asleep), return, and begin again my ascent.

This time, on the first rung, I reach out to the pipe with one hand and to the tree with the other, trying to shift as much of my weight to my hands as possible so that the ladder is less likely to slide.

I fall again, further injuring the same knee, the same shin, not to mention my buttocks and shoulder, and my forearm appears never to have had skin at all. Somehow I have bashed my elbow and the ulnar nerve threatens to explode.

This is the stupidest thing I have ever done. The romance of balcony scenes is overrated. Romeo is an idiot.

But the ladder did not shift. I might never prevail with limbs and digits intact, but I have solved the Physics problem.

Once more I fall before achieving the top rung. Once there, I do not linger, I grab the sheet with both hands, wind it quickly around them for better grip, and I lunge. I hang from Arvo's window by a sheet — and find I have no remaining upper-body strength with which to climb it.

Arvo has considered this, however. He backs away from the window, dragging my dead weight slowly up the side of the house. I want to curse the rough brick that shreds my skin, but I know it prevents those inside from hearing us. Arvo anchors the sheet around his heavy bedpost that is bolted to the floor. He comes back to the window to help me up the last few inches, and must grab my belt and heave me over the windowsill, first hands and then face, and then the rest of me. The sill's outer edge compresses my breasts painfully, and when I finally thud onto the pillows he has thoughtfully placed under the window, I curl into a fetal position and cup them protectively. He coils around me and rocks us both slowly. I see, from his clock radio, that my journey up the side of the house has taken about two hours.

I am sweaty and bleeding and filthy now and smell of cushion mould. I want to clean up, but they will hear Arvo's shower.

"You can have a bath," he says. "I have baths in the night all the time here. They help me forget."

He tidies his room and replaces the sheets, stows me behind the washroom door, and runs a bath. The night staff pokes her head in when she hears the water (Arvo says it bangs the house pipes), sees naked Arvo with his beach ball and the bathroom light on and a thumbs up sign, and goes back downstairs.

We climb into the bath together then, Arvo and me and the beach ball, and he cleans my wounds. Afterwards, we spend the night quietly, intensely copulating. The relief at finally doing this again is beyond anything I can describe.

In the still moments, I tell him about the hearing, about Houndstooth Woman who surprised me, about Imran who surprised me, about the therapist who surprised me, about Cheery Psychometrist who surprised me, about Tie-Dyed Man whose vexation I came in the end to understand. He cries then, when he comprehends what comes next, and we make love again and again and again.

I have missed this so much more than I have allowed myself to believe.

In the morning, an hour before the day shift arrives, we tie together all his sheets and add a blanket for more length. Arvo lowers me slowly, safely, to the ground and wheels in the bedding.

I return the ladder and sleeping bags to their original homes, but leave the cushions and cement blocks on the table.

I spend the day in Arlington, making preparations. In the evening, I nap under a tree in the ravine as I wait for the night shift to settle in.

When the time comes, I retrieve the ladder and sleeping bags, and with Arvo's help I climb up again. I fall just twice.

Arvo tells me, the moment I am inside, that if they spoke our language he would have given me away a thousand times today, he has never been good at secrets.

Again we spend the night pleasuring each other in dozens of ways until we are both raw from it.

In the grey morning light, I tell him I am leaving.

"I know," he says, "I know. I want so much to be with you, but I cannot do what you do and I don't want to be the reason you stay. You must go. They are mostly kind to me here and I will be okay. I will miss you. I will miss signing with someone who understands. But I will think of you, of what you're doing out there, and I will be okay."

We hold one another ferociously, as long as we dare, until it is dangerous for me to stay another minute.

"Will I see you again?" he asks.

"I do not know," I say. "I want to but I do not know. It would be much likelier if you were to get a first-floor bedroom."

He agrees to work on it.

We say our goodbyes then, weeping, trying not to wail. It is the saddest, hardest minute of my life and that is saying something.

And then I go down that stupid fucking wall, and I leave the love of my life behind.

Epilogue

Dear Imran,

You will be the one to find this and I am sorry for that.

You have been a good friend to me. You have gone far
beyond your paid duty. I want you to know that I am aware
of it, and that I appreciate it. You made my life possible.
I will miss you and will think of you every day.

But I must strike out on my own. In the absence of facts,
I constructed a belief that I was more autonomous than
the custody process revealed me to be. For all its good
intentions, the Provincial Government will never release
me from guardianship, I am certain. I must release myself
and avoid their gaze as long as I can. Please show them
this letter so that they know you had nothing to do with
my decision. If we ever meet again (do not count on it),
I hope we will be equals.

About the maid in your scrapbook, the one who severed a
General's head. I have been thinking of her. I think she did
it for a bottle of wine, a bowl of olives, a loaf of good bread,
and for autonomy to live out her days in a place that was
really hers. Everyday simple pleasures that delight the mind
and keep the body warm. She had, of course, the added
satisfaction of knowing that she — so insignificant as to go
unnoticed in a General's tent — had altered her world.

Might I impose upon you one last time? Would you please
deliver this box and manuscript to my therapist? Thank you.

Vincent sends his love.

Take care of yourself (and Ted),
Athena

Dear Therapist,

I have asked Imran to deliver to you the manuscript and files. Do with them as you will. I considered burning the lot, but in the end I do not want to spend another minute on this project, not even to burn it. I do not care about a legacy, I am not in pursuit of an ideal, I do not want to "change the system from within."

What I want is to live my own life — and for that, I must climb out from under the old regime, away into the wondrous unknown. Ten years ago I would have been unable, but now, I have recently discovered, I am altogether capable.

A friend of mine helped me find work and lodging in another city. We sat and did Accounting. I will have enough to eat well and pay bills with a few extras. I have purchased my friend's motorcycle (with sidecar for Vincent) and will pay in instalments. I shall speak no more of my plans here and my friend will not tell you.

You will want to know how I feel: I feel sad to leave Arvo. That is an understatement.

And I feel thrilled at what lies ahead. After repaying my motorcycle debt, who knows? Perhaps travel across rivers and cliffs, countrysides and towns, perhaps only settling and working in a shop or library, I have not yet decided. Opportunity everywhere, if only I take it. This thrill, I believe, is euphoria.

You asked once if I wanted to find my mother. If I run into her, I may be open to a relationship, but I am done with looking back on my once-rationed life. I want to look forward. A great expanse awaits!

I am deeply grateful for your help with this project, and for everything you have done for me. I have been too harsh with you, I now see, and have laid suspicion on you too often. Perhaps, though, you could hire a different interpreter.

Sincerely,
Athena

Postscript: Ten years ago, I abandoned the name Verity and chose the name Athena because I liked the sound of it. Now I leave it behind too, so that I will not be easily found, and have signed it for the last time.

ACKNOWLEDGEMENTS

I (Athena) is, from beginning to end, a work of fiction. However, in my attempts to craft an authentic sense of time and place, I have drawn on a wide variety of historical records, conversations, documents, and other sources.

For about ten or twelve years in the 80s and 90s, I worked intermittently in various capacities in group homes, day programs, institutions, medical units, and other support services, both in Ontario and Alberta. While none of the people I met there appear in this book in any way, interactions with the clientele (most of whom lived with disability) and with my fellow staff affected my thinking significantly and I am grateful to them. I am also grateful for the professional development training I received through these organizations, some of which is alluded to in this novel.

Several books were helpful: E.J. Miller and Geraldine V. Gwynne's *A Life Apart: A Pilot Study of Residential Institutions for the Physically Handicapped and the Young Chronic Sick* (1972); René R. Gadacz's *Re-Thinking Dis-Ability: New Structures, New Relationships* (1994); Anne Crichton and Lyn Jongbloed's *Disability and Social Policy in Canada* (1998); Molly McGarry and Fred

Wasserman's *Becoming Visible: An Illustrated History of Lesbian and Gay Life in Twentieth-Century America* (1998), especially the X-rays and medical notes surrounding "P.M."; Romel Mackelprang and Richard Salsgiver's book, *Disability: A Diversity Model Approach in Human Service Practice* (1999); Jan Nisbet and David Hagner's 2000 collection, *Part of the Community: Strategies for Including Everyone*; Deborah Stienstra and Aileen Wight-Felske's *Making Equality: History of Advocacy and Persons with Disabilities in Canada* (2003); and Robert McRuer's *Crip Theory: Cultural Signs of Queerness and Disability* (2006). I drew also on *The Merck Manual of Diagnosis and Therapy: Eleventh Edition* (1966); on the *American Psychiatric Association's Diagnostic and Statistical Manual of Mental Disorders,* especially Editions One (1952), Two (1968), and Four (1994); on Anthony Radcliffe's *The Pharmer's Almanac: The Layman's Guide to Psychoactive Drugs* (1985); and on the 1897 Ontario Female Refuges Act in *The Revised Statutes Of Ontario, 1897: Being A Consolidation Of The Revised Statutes Of Ontario 1887, With The Subsequent Public General Acts Of The Legislature Of Ontario: Volume II: Chapter 310: An Act to Establish an Industrial Refuge for Girls*. A key text throughout the writing process was Judith Herman's *Trauma and Recovery: The Aftermath of Violence — from Domestic Abuse to Political Terror* (1997).

Especially incisive articles include Djuna Barnes's "How it Feels to be Forcibly Fed" (1914); Heather Pringle's "Alberta Barren" (1997); Lorraine Wilgosh, Dick Sobsey, and Kate Scorgie's "Cultural Constructions of Families of Children with Disabilities" (2004), Charlotte Wolters's excellent 2006 paper, written for one of my undergrad classes and (to the best of my knowledge) unpublished, "Controlling the Female: The Use of Ontario's Female Refuges Act as a means of Regulating Female Sexuality and Social Behaviour"; Heidi Janz and Sally Hayward's "The Latimer Case and The Media:

If the Right has it Right, What's Wrong with the Left?" (1998); Mike Kendrick's "Why Group Homes are no Longer Optimal" (2017) and other articles; Julia Murphy's "Behind Closed Doors" (2019); and various writings by Temple Grandin.

For many years, at our home, we had a subscription to *Discover Magazine*. Dozens of articles (ripped out and stuffed into an ever-thickening file) influenced my thinking, including "The Sum of All Fears: The Biology of Panic" by Jocelyne Selim; "A Psychiatric Centre is Home to a Stirring Collection of Patients' Art" by Susan Kruglinski; "Seeing the Unseen" by E.L. Doctorow; "What Maketh a Man?" by Stephen Ornes; "That Fine Madness" by Jo Ann C. Gutin; "Fire in the Brain," by Kathy A. Svitil; "The Inner Savant" by Douglas S. Fox, "Stop the Madness" by Charles Schmidt, "Pollock's Fractals" by Jennifer Ouellette; "The Natural Art" by Richard Conniff; "Boy, Interrupted" by Liza Lentini; "Vitamin Cure" by Susan Freinkel; and several articles by Carl Zimmer and by Steven Johnson. Also useful was "The White Gold of Northern Ontario: China Clay in Northern Ontario" (1967), which I found on Ontario Ministry of Northern Development and Mines website. The foregoing list of texts is not nearly exhaustive.

I am grateful to reference librarians and archivists at University of Alberta Libraries, at Paul D. Fleck Library and Archives, at Whyte Museum of the Canadian Rockies Archives, at Edmonton Archives, and at Loyal Edmonton Regiment Military Museum at the Prince of Wales Armouries. They guided me through mounds of historical data and provided good conversation besides.

For funding, I am forever grateful to Edmonton Arts Council, Alberta Foundation for the Arts, Canada Council for the Arts, and to Gertrude and Ernest E. Poole. I am also grateful to Banff Centre Leighton Studios, where I did two residencies, and to Banff Centre generally for the support they have provided me (and thousands of other artists) over the years. Readers familiar with Banff Centre will recognize architectural similiarities between some Banff Centre buildings and the Holdstock Facility. Thanks to Jim Olver for the extensive behind-the-scenes tour.

So many people helped. Rob Gray told me that this was a novel, not a story. Pauline Holdstock mentored me through the early stages. Alix Kemp inspired Uly's tattoos, and Vern Thiessen coined "sinking in paper." Key passages in the novel were checked for accuracy by psychologist Dr Lynn Cook, Sarasota, by exploration geologist Jim Olver, Banff, and by Dr Nermeen Youssef, Edmonton pharmacologist. My parents Abe and Nettye Dyck of Campden, Ontario, remembered and willingly shared so many precise, rich details from the 1930s and influenced young Esau's world a great deal. Pauline Holdstock and Fred Stenson, friends and mentors both, gamely allowed me to use their surnames for fictional towns. Dr. Veronique Pouliot, Banff, talked me through how a psychologist might approach a client like Athena. Endless thanks to draft readers Manikarnika Kanjilal (who also copyedited), Daphne Read, Catherine Gutwin, Grace Hildebrand, Jack Hodgins, Darrin Hagen, and Cassie Rodgers. Cassie enlisted three further readers, Bianca, Sam, and Diane, and I am grateful for their input. Linda Callaghan, Susie Moloney, and Jacqueline Baker helped me navigate the business end of things. Thanks to the canine people Oscar, Roxy, Dervish, Zhabka, Haman, Charlie, Max, Cleo, Scully, Colby, Thumper, Buddy, Shadow, Ripley, Norman, Paxil, Daisy, and Sylvie, among others, who influenced the character of Vincent. For safe writing spaces, I'm grateful to Cyndi Henderson, Randy Rae, Gary Lewis, Eugene Nyamunga, Bill and Lynn Cook, and the James Bay Cree. My university students have pushed my thinking and my craft over the years, and I am grateful. And to Doug Barbour, gone now and deeply missed, longtime mentor/supervisor, friend, so much gratitude. I am lucky to have known you. A hundred thousand thanks to

Paul Hjartarson, trusted editor and friend, whose generous and carefully considered suggestions made this book much richer than it was, and whose editorial meetings were always something to look forward to. Many thanks also to Matt and Meredith and Natalie (a stunning cover!) and the folks at NeWest Press who made it all happen. Above all, my partner David, who supported relentlessly, who willingly listened to this manuscript being read aloud to him I don't even know how many times. You are still the most astute reader of all.

Whoever I have missed naming here, forgive me and know that I'm grateful.

Ruth DyckFehderau is an award-winning writer of literary fiction and nonfiction. Her work has been translated into five languages. *The Sweet Bloods of Eeyou Istchee: Stories of Diabetes and the James Bay Cree* (2017), written with James Bay Cree storytellers, is now in second edition (publ Cree BHSS James Bay, distrib WLUP), and *E nâtamukw miyeyimuwin: Residential School Recovery Stories of the James Bay Cree, Volume One,* also written with James Bay Cree storytellers, is forthcoming in March 2023. Ruth teaches English Lit and Creative Writing at University of Alberta and she lives in Edmonton with her partner. She is hearing-impaired. www.ruthdyckfehderau.com